WILD WICKED SCOT

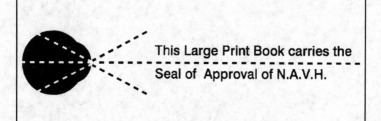

This Large Print Book carries the
Seal of Approval of N.A.V.H.

WILD WICKED SCOT

JULIA LONDON

THORNDIKE PRESS

A part of Gale, Cengage Learning

GALE
CENGAGE Learning·

Farmington Hills, Mich • San Francisco • New York • Waterville, Maine
Meriden, Conn • Mason, Ohio • Chicago

LIBRARY OF CONGRESS CATALOGING-IN-PUBLICATION DATA

Names: London, Julia, author.
Title: Wild wicked Scot / Julia London.
Description: Large print edition. | Waterville, Maine : Thorndike Press, 2017. | Series: The Highland grooms | Series: Thorndike Press large print romance
Identifiers: LCCN 2016056289| ISBN 9781410496584 (hardback) | ISBN 1410496589 (hardcover)
Subjects: LCSH: Large type books. | BISAC: FICTION / Romance / Regency. | GSAFD: Love stories.
Classification: LCC PS3562.O48745 W55 2017 | DDC 813/.54—dc23
LC record available at https://lccn.loc.gov/2016056289

Published in 2017 by arrangement with Harlequin Books S.A.

Printed in the United States of America
1 2 3 4 5 6 7 21 20 19 18 17

For Karen, Rachelle, and Teri,
who accompanied me on that
amazing writing retreat in Scotland.
See? I told you I was working.

PROLOGUE

Norwood Park, England
1706

When Miss Lynetta Beauly challenged Miss Margot Armstrong to name what she liked most about the young gentlemen who buzzed about them as bees to honey — taking for granted, of course, a fortune and suitable connections — Miss Armstrong could not name a single thing with any confidence.

Because she liked *everything* about them. She liked the tall ones, the short ones, the broad ones, the slender ones. She liked them in powdered wigs and with their hair in natural queues. She liked them on horseback and in carriages and strolling about the massive gardens at Norwood Park, where she happened to reside with her father and two brothers. She liked the way they looked at her and smiled at her, and how they laughed with their heads tilted

7

back at all the amusing things she said. Which, apparently, she did with some frequency, as one or five of them seemed always to laugh and say, "How clever you are, Miss Armstrong!"

Margot liked young gentlemen so much that, on the occasion of Lynetta's sixteenth birthday, she convinced her father to allow her to host a ball in her dear friend's honor at Norwood Park.

"Lynetta Beauly?" her father had asked with a sigh of tedium, his gaze on a letter bearing news from London. "She is not yet out."

"But she will be presented this Season," Margot had hopefully reminded him.

"Why do her parents not provide her with a gathering?" her father had asked as he stuck the point of an ink quill beneath his wig to scratch an itch.

"Pappa, you know they haven't the means."

"*You* haven't the means, either, Margot. *I* am the only person at Norwood Park who has the means to provide this young woman, for whom I have no particular regard, with a ball." He'd shaken his head at the absurdity of it. "Why are you so keen for it?"

Margot had, apparently, blushed. Lynetta said that was one of her true faults — it was impossible to hide what Margot was thinking because her fair skin changed from cream to pink to red with only the slightest provocation.

"I *see,*" her father had said sagely, and had leaned back in his chair, resting his hands on his belly. "Some young gentleman has caught your eye. Is that it?"

Well . . . she would not belabor the point, but *all* of them had caught her eye. She'd fussed with a curl at her collarbone. "I wouldn't go so far as to say *that,*" she'd muttered as she'd studied the pattern of brocade on a chair in her father's study. "No one in particular, really."

Her father had smirked. "Very well. Amuse yourself. Give this ball," he'd said, and had waved her away.

A few weeks later, everyone within a fifty-mile radius of Norwood Park descended on the area, as it was well known in northern England that a Norwood Park ball was unparalleled in luxury and company with the exception of London's Mayfair district.

Beneath five gilded wood and crystal chandeliers blazing with the light of dozens of beeswax candles, young ladies dressed in a dizzying array of colors spun around the ballroom floor to the lively tunes provided by the six musicians brought up from London. Their hair, masterpieces of wire and netting, was piled high and artfully in gravity-defying styles. Their dance partners, all handsome young men of privilege, were dressed in brocades and silks, their coats and waistcoats intricately embroidered. Their wigs were freshly powdered, and their shoes shined to such a sheen that they reflected the candlelight from above.

They drank embargoed French champagne, dined on caviar and slipped in behind potted ferns to steal a kiss.

Margot had donned a gown made especially for the occasion — a pale green silk mantua that Lynetta said complemented her green eyes and auburn hair. To her tower of hair, she'd added little songbirds carefully crafted from paper. She wore her late mother's glittering diamond-and-pearl necklace at her throat.

Margot had commissioned a cake in honor of Lynetta's birthday, a three-foot-tall edible structure that resembled Norwood Park, placed in the middle of the dining room to be admired by all. The iced parapets were topped with dancing marzipan figures. In one corner were the tiny figures of two girls, one with auburn hair, one with blond hair, that were meant to be

Margot and Lynetta.

There were so many people in attendance that there was scarcely room for everyone to dance at once. Margot in particular had done very little dancing that night. Nevertheless, she'd kept her eye on Mr. William Fitzgerald in hopes that she might change her luck.

Oh, but Mr. Fitzgerald was quite dashing in his silver brocade and curled wig. Margot had admired him from afar for a full fortnight now and had rather thought, given his attentions to her, that the interest was mutual. But tonight, he'd stood up with every unmarried woman except her.

"You mustn't take it to heart," Lynetta had advised, her face still flushed from the exertion of having danced three sets. "It's clearly one of two reasons — either he is saving the best dance of the night for you, or he can't bear to ask because you're such a terrible dancer."

Margot gave her friend a withering look. "Thank you, Lynetta, for I cannot be reminded often enough of my wretched dancing." According to Lynetta, that was Margot's second most obvious fault — she had no natural tendency toward rhythm.

"Well?" Lynetta said with a shrug. "I mean only to offer an explanation for why he's

11

not shown you any true regard this evening."

"Please, darling, you mustn't exert yourself to help me understand his utter lack of interest in me."

"Better it's because of your dancing than something perhaps even worse," Lynetta cheerfully pointed out.

"And what might that be?" Margot demanded, slightly affronted.

"I mean only that I'd rather be faulted for my dancing than for my inability to make engaging conversation," Lynetta said sweetly. "You have *always* made engaging conversation."

Margot was set to discuss that, but at that very moment, a wave of awareness rippled through the crowd. Both Margot and Lynetta glanced around them. Margot saw nothing obvious. "What is it?"

"I can't see a thing," Lynetta said as she and Margot craned their necks in the direction of the door.

"Someone's come," said a gentleman nearby. "Someone unexpected, from what I gather."

Margot and Lynetta gasped at precisely the same moment, their eyes widening as they gaped at one another. There was only one person of import who was not in attendance tonight — the highly desirable

Montclare, who had sent his deepest regrets that he could not attend, as he had been called away to London. Lord Montclare had all the requisite attributes that made him a desirable match: he had a fortune of ten thousand pounds a year; he would one day assume the title of Viscount Waverly; he had thick-lashed doe eyes and a winsome smile; and he was utterly without conceit. Rumor had it that Montclare had set his sights on a London heiress . . . but that did not keep Margot and Lynetta from hoping.

The girls, quite in tune with one another's thinking, fled the ballroom for the balcony above the foyer to have a look at the unexpected guest, arriving so hastily that their gloves slid on the polished stone railing as they leaned over it.

It was not Montclare. "Oh, bother," Lynetta muttered.

It was not even one of the many men who often came up to Norwood Park from London to conduct business with Margot's father and brothers. Frankly, the men who had walked through the front doors and onto the marble tile of the foyer were unlike any men Margot had ever seen.

"Goodness," Lynetta murmured beside her.

Goodness, indeed. There were five altogether, all of them tall and broad-shouldered and quite muscular, their natural hair tied in long queues. Except for the man in front of them all — his dark hair was a wild tangle of curls around his head, as if he hadn't bothered at all to dress it. Their coats, splattered with mud, were long and split up the back for riding. Their breeches and waistcoats were not silk or brocade, but rough wool. They wore boots that were scuffed and worn at the heels.

"Who *are* they?" Lynetta whispered. "Are they Gypsies?"

"Highwaymen," Margot murmured, and Lynetta giggled a bit too loudly.

At the sound of Lynetta's laugh, the man in front instantly lifted his head, almost like a beast sniffing the wind. His eyes locked on Margot. Her breath caught; even from this distance she could see that his gaze was ice blue and piercing. He held her gaze as he methodically removed his riding gloves. She thought she ought to look away, but she couldn't. A shiver slipped down her spine; she had the terrible thought that those eyes could see right into her soul.

Someone spoke, and the five men began to move forward. But just before the man in front disappeared under the balcony and from view completely, he looked up at

Margot once more, his gaze frighteningly intelligent and potent.

Another shiver ran down her spine.

Once they were gone, Margot and Lynetta returned to the ballroom, jointly disappointed that the arrival of strangers had not brought Montclare into their midst, and quickly fixed their attentions elsewhere.

Lynetta danced, while Margot stood about, trying not to appear anxious. Was her dancing really as horrible as that? Apparently so — no one had asked her to stand up.

After what seemed like hours of waiting about, a bell was rung and the cake was served. A footman handed Margot a flute of champagne. She liked how it tickled her nose and sipped liberally as she and Lynetta stood together, waiting for Quint, the Norwood Park butler, to bring them a piece of the cake.

"Oh *my!*" Lynetta whispered frantically, nudging Margot with her shoulder.

"What?"

"It's *Fitzgerald.*"

"*Where?*" Margot whispered just as frantically and dabbed at her upper lip to blot away any champagne.

"He's coming this way!"

"Is he looking at me? Is it me he approaches?" Margot begged, but before Lynetta could answer, Mr. Fitzgerald had reached her side.

"Miss Armstrong," he said, and bowed over his extended leg, his arm swirling out to the side. She'd noted lately that several young men just up from London bowed in that fashion. "Miss Beauly, may I offer felicitations on the occasion of your birthday?"

"Thank you," Lynetta said. "Umm . . . I do beg your pardon, but I mean to, ah . . . I think I shall have some cake." She awkwardly stepped away, leaving Margot and Fitzgerald standing together.

"Ah . . ." Good God, Margot's heart was fluttering. "How do you find the ball?"

"Magnificent," he said. "You are to be commended."

"Not at all." She could feel an absurd grin forming at the compliment. "Lynetta has helped me, of course."

"Of course." Mr. Fitzgerald shifted to stand beside her, and through the tight sleeve of her gown, Margot could feel her skin sizzling where his arm brushed hers. "Miss Armstrong, would you do me the honor of standing up with me for the next dance?"

Margot ignored the swell of panic that she

might very well break one of his toes. "I would be *delighted* —"

"Miss Armstrong."

"Pardon? What?" she asked dreamily as someone touched her elbow.

Mr. Fitzgerald smiled. "Your butler," he said, nodding at someone over her shoulder.

Margot forced her gaze away from Mr. Fitzgerald and around to Quint. "Yes?" she asked impatiently.

"Your father asks that you join him in the family dining room."

Margot blinked. Of all the rotten timing! *"Now?"* she asked, endeavoring to sound angelic but hissing a bit.

"Shall I hold your champagne until you return?" Mr. Fitzgerald asked.

Margot hoped she didn't look as ridiculously pleased as she felt. But still, she didn't trust any number of the young women who were presently circulating about them like sharks. "Umm . . ." She looked pleadingly at Quint. "Perhaps Pappa might wait?"

But as usual, Quint returned her look impassively. "He asks that you attend him at once."

"Do go on," said Mr. Fitzgerald with a warm smile. "We shall have that dance when you return." He took the flute from her hand and politely bowed his head.

17

"You are too kind, Mr. Fitzgerald. I shan't be but a moment." Margot whirled about, and with a glare for poor old Quint, she picked up her skirts and sailed out.

When she entered the family dining room, the smell of horse and men assaulted her, and Margot had to swallow her aversion to it. She was surprised to see her father seated with the rough-looking men who had arrived at Norwood Park earlier. Her brother Bryce was there, too, watching the five men as one might observe animals in the wild. Four of the men were devouring their food, sounding a bit like a pack of animals who had not eaten in quite a long time.

"Ah, there she is, my daughter, Margot," her father said, standing and holding out his hand to her.

She reluctantly walked forward and took it, curtsying to him. Up close, she noticed the man with the ice-blue eyes bore the dirt and grime of what she guessed was several days on the road. He wore a dark, unkempt beard, and she wondered idly if perhaps he'd lost his razor. His gaze presumptuously raked over her, from the top of her coiffed hair — the paper birds seemed to interest him — to her face and bodice and down the length of her body.

How *rude.* Margot narrowed her eyes on

18

him, but her glower seemed to please him. His blue eyes sparked as he came slowly to his feet, towering almost a foot above her.

"Margot, may I introduce Chieftain Arran Mackenzie. Mackenzie, my only daughter, Miss Margot Armstrong."

One corner of his mouth turned up. Did he not know that to stare so intently was impolite? Margot dipped another perfect curtsy and extended her hand. "How do you do, sir?"

"Verra well, Miss Armstrong."

His voice had a deep, lilting brogue that was quite unexpected and tingled at the base of her skull.

"And how do you do?" he asked, taking her hand in his. It was huge, and his thumb felt calloused as he stroked it across her knuckles. Margot thought of Mr. Fitzgerald — with his long, slender and manicured fingers. Mr. Fitzgerald had the hands of an artist. This man had bear paws.

"I am well, thank you," she said, and lightly pulled her hand away. She looked expectantly at her father. He seemed in no hurry to dismiss her now that he'd introduced her to these men. How long was she to remain here? She thought of Mr. Fitzgerald standing in the ballroom just now, with two flutes of French champagne in his hands. She could imagine any number of young ladies who were closing in around him, ready to cart him off like so many buzzards.

"Mackenzie is to receive a barony," her father said. "He shall be Lord Mackenzie of Balhaire."

Why on earth should she care about that? But Margot was ever the dutiful daughter and smiled at the man's throat. "You must be pleased."

The man tilted his head to one side to catch her eye before he responded. "Aye, that I am," he said, and his gaze moved boldly to her mouth. "I verra much doubt you will understand just how pleased I am, Miss Armstrong."

A strong shiver ran down Margot's spine. Why did he look at her like that? He was so brazen, so unguarded! And her father, standing just there!

"Thank you, Margot," her father said from somewhere near her — she wasn't really sure where he was, as she couldn't seem to tear her eyes away from this beast of a man just yet. "You may return to your friends."

What was this? She felt like the prize county sheep, paraded in for viewing. *Look at the fine wool on this one.* It vexed her — there were times her father seemed to forget

20

that she was not a bauble to be held up for admiration.

She stared steadily into those icy blue eyes and said, "It is a pleasure to have made your acquaintance." It was not a pleasure at all — it was a nuisance — and she hoped the man could see it in her gaze. Well, if he couldn't see it, his companions certainly could. They'd all stopped eating and were staring at her almost as if they'd never seen a woman before. Which, judging by their clothing and wretched table manners, was almost believable.

"Thank you, Miss Armstrong," he said, that voice so deeply lilting that it felt like a feather stroking down her spine. "But the pleasure has been completely mine, aye?" He smiled.

Those words and that smile made Margot feel strangely warm and fluid. She hurried out, eager to be as far from those men as she could.

By the time she reached the ballroom, however, his name was forgotten, because Mr. Fitzgerald was dancing with Miss Remstock. Margot's champagne was nowhere to be seen, and every other thought she had flew out of her head.

The next afternoon, her father informed her that he'd agreed to give her hand in

21

marriage to that beast Mackenzie and then turned a deaf ear to her cries.

CHAPTER ONE

The Scottish Highlands
1710

Under a full Scottish moon on a balmy summer night, the air was so still that one could hear the distant sea as plainly as if one were standing in the cove below Castle Balhaire. The windows of the old castle keep were open to the cool night, and a breeze wafted through, carrying away with it the lingering smoke from the rush torches that lit the great hall.

The interior of the medieval castle had been transformed into a sumptuous space befitting a king — or at least a Scottish clan chieftain with a healthy sea trade. The clan chieftain, the Baron of Balhaire, Arran Mackenzie, was sprawled on the new furnishings of the great hall along with his men, with a fresh batch of ale and a small herd of lassies to occupy them.

At the top of the Balhaire watchtower,

three guards passed the time tossing coins onto a cloak with each roll of the die. Seamus Bivens had already divested his old friend Donald Thane of two *sgillin* with his last roll. Two *sgillin* was not a fortune to a guard of Balhaire, thanks to Mackenzie's generosity to those loyal to him, but nevertheless, when Seamus took two more *sgillin,* Donald felt the loss of his purse and his pride quite keenly. Heated words were exchanged, and the two men clambered to their feet, reaching for their respective muskets propped against the wall. Sweeney Mackenzie, the commander, was content to let the two men battle it out, but a noise reached him, and he leaped to his feet and stepped between them, holding them apart with his hands braced against their chests. *"Uist!"* he hissed to silence them. "Do ye no' hear it?"

The two men paused and craned their necks, listening. The sound of an approaching carriage bounced between the ghostly shadows of the hills. "Who the devil?" Seamus muttered, and forgetting his anger with Donald, grabbed up the spyglass and leaned over the wall to have a look.

"Well?" Donald demanded, crowding in behind him. "Who is it, then? A Gordon, aye?"

Seamus shook his head. "No' a Gordon."

"A Munro, then," said Sweeney. "I've heard they've been eyeing Mackenzie lands." These were relatively peaceful times at Balhaire, but one should never have been surprised by a change in clan alliances.

"No' a Munro," Seamus said.

They could see the coach now, pulled by a team of four, accompanied by two riders in back and two guards alongside the coachman. The postilion held a lantern aloft on a pole to light their way, in addition to the light cast from the carriage lamps.

"Who in bloody hell comes at half past midnight?" Donald demanded.

Seamus suddenly gasped. He pulled the spyglass away from his eye and squinted at the coach, then just as quickly put it back to his eye and leaned forward. *"No,"* he said, his voice full of disbelief.

His two companions exchanged a look. *"Who?"* Donald demanded. "No' *Buchanan,"* he said, his voice almost a whisper, referring to the Mackenzies' most persistent enemy through the years.

"Worse," Seamus said gravely, and slowly lowered the spyglass, his eyes gone round with horror.

"By God, say who it is before I bloody well beat it from you," Sweeney swore,

25

clearly unnerved.

" 'Tis . . . 'tis the *Lady Mackenzie,*" Seamus said, his voice barely above a whisper.

His two companions gasped. And then Sweeney whirled about, grabbed up his gun and hurried off to warn Mackenzie that his wife had returned to Balhaire.

Unfortunately, coming down from the tallest part of Balhaire was no easy feat, and by the time Sweeney had made his way into the bailey, the coach had come through the gates. The coach door swung open, and a step was put down. He saw a small but well-shod foot appear on that step, and he broke into a run.

Arran Mackenzie adored the pleasant sensation of a woman's soft bum on his lap, and the sweet scent of her hair in his nostrils, especially with the golden warmth of good ale lovingly wrapping its liquid arms around him. He'd sampled freely of the batch his cousin and first lieutenant had brewed. Jock Mackenzie fancied himself something of a master brewer.

Arran was slouched in his chair, his fingers slowly tracing a line up the woman's back, lazily trying to recall her name. *What is it, then — Aileen? Irene?*

"Milord! *Mackenzie!*" someone shouted.

Arran bent his head to see around the blond curls of the woman in his lap. Sweeney Mackenzie, one of his best guards, was shouting at him from the rear of the hall. The poor man was clutching his chest as if his heart was failing him, and he looked quite frantic as he cast his gaze around the crowded room. "Wh-wh-where is he?" he demanded of a drunk beside him. "Wh-wh-where is Mackenzie?"

Sweeney was a fierce warrior and a dedicated commander. But when he was agitated, he had a tendency to stutter like he had when they were children. Generally there was little that could agitate the old salt, and that something had made Arran take notice. "Here, Sweeney," he said, and pushed the girl off his lap. He sat up, gestured his man forward. "What has rattled you, then?"

Sweeney hurried forward. "She's b-b-b-back," he breathlessly managed to get out.

Arran frowned, confused. "Pardon?"

"The L-L-L . . ." Sweeney's lips and tongue seemed to stick together. He swallowed and tried to expel the word.

"Take a breath, lad," Arran said, coming to his feet. "Steady now. Who has come?"

"L-L-L-Lady M-M-Mackenzie," he managed.

27

That name seemed to drift up between Arran and Sweeney. Did Arran imagine it, or did everything in the hall suddenly go still? There was surely some mistake — he exchanged a look with Jock, who looked as mystified as Arran.

He turned to Sweeney again and said calmly, "Another breath, man. You're mistaken —"

"He is not mistaken."

Arran's head snapped up at the sound of that familiar, crisply English, feminine voice. He squinted to the back of the hall, but the torches were smoking and cast shadows. He couldn't make out anyone in particular — but the collective gasp of alarm that rose up from the two dozen or so souls gathered verified it for him: his wench of a wife had returned to Balhaire. After an absence of more than three years, she had inexplicably returned.

This undoubtedly would be viewed as a great occasion by half of his clan, a calamity by the other half. Arran himself could think of only three possible reasons his wife might be standing here now: one, her father had died and she had no place to go but to her lawful husband. Two, she'd run out of Arran's money. Or three . . . she wanted to divorce him.

He dismissed the death of her father as a reason. If the man had died, he would have heard about it — he had a man in England to keep a close eye on his faithless wife.

The crowd parted as the auburn-haired beauty glided into the hall like a sleek galleon, two Englishmen dressed in fine woolen coats and powdered wigs trailing behind her.

She could not possibly have run out of money. He was quite generous with her. To a fault, Jock said. Perhaps that was true, but Arran would not have it said that he did not provide for his wife.

His wife's grand entrance was suddenly halted by one of Arran's old hunting dogs whose sight had nearly gone. Roy chose that moment to amble across the cleared path and plop himself down, his head between his paws on the cool stone floor, oblivious to the activity of humans around him. He sighed loudly, preparing to take his nap.

His wife daintily lifted her cloak and stepped over the beast. Her two escorts walked around the dog.

As she continued toward him, Arran had to consider that the third possibility was perhaps the most plausible. She had come to ask for a divorce, an annulment — whatever might give her freedom from him.

And yet it seemed implausible she would have come all this way to ask it of him. Would she not have sent an agent? Or perhaps, he reasoned, as she made her way to the dais, she meant to humiliate him once more.

Margot Armstrong Mackenzie stood with her hands clasped before her and a faltering smile for the stunned, speechless souls around her. Her two escorts took up positions directly behind her, their gazes warily assessing the hall, their hands on the hilts of their small swords. Did they think they'd be forced to fight their way out? It was a possibility, for some of Arran's people wore expressions of anticipation — far be it from any Scotsman to back away from anything that even remotely hinted at the potential for a brawl.

Not a death, then. Not a lack of funds. He had not ruled out divorce, but no matter what the reason, Arran was suddenly furious. How dare she return!

He leaped off the dais and strolled forward. "Has snow fallen on hell?" he asked calmly as he advanced on her.

She glanced around the hall. "I see no trace of snow," she said as she removed her gloves.

"Did you come by sea? Or by broom?"

Someone on the dais chuckled. "By sea and by coach," she said pleasantly, ignoring his barb. She cocked her head to one side and looked him over. "You look very well, my lord husband."

Arran said nothing. He didn't know what to say to her after three years and feared anything he did would unleash a torrent of emotion he was not willing to share with the world.

In his silence, Margot's gaze wandered to her surroundings, to the rush torches, the iron chandeliers, the dogs wandering about the great hall. It was quite different from Norwood Park. She'd never cared for this massive great room, the heart of Balhaire for centuries now. She'd always wanted something finer; a fancy room, a London or Paris ballroom. But to Arran, this room was highly functional. There were two long tables where his clan sat, with massive hearths on either end of the hall to heat it. A few rugs on the floor muted the sound of boots on stone, and he'd always rather liked the flickering light of the torches.

"It's still charmingly quaint," she said, reading his thoughts. "Everything exactly the same."

"No' everything," he reminded her. "I was no' expecting you."

"I know," she said, wincing a bit. "And for that, I do apologize."

He waited for more. An explanation. A begging of his forgiveness. But that was all she would say, apparently, as she was looking around him now, to the dais. "Oh, how *lovely,*" she said. "You have indeed added something new."

He squinted over his shoulder. The dais was the only thing left of the original great hall besides the floors and the walls. It was a raised platform where the chieftain and his advisers had taken their meals over the years. The use of it was not so formal now, but still, Arran liked it — it gave him a view of the entire hall.

It took him a moment to realize she was admiring the carved table and upholstered chairs he'd acquired on a recent trade voyage, as well as the two silver candelabras that graced the head table. He'd taken those in payment from a man who was down on his luck and had needed some horses for a desperate run from authorities.

"It's French, isn't it?" she asked. "It looks very French."

Was what French? And what did it matter at this moment, given the great occasion that was unfurling before them? Mr. and Mrs. Mackenzie of Balhaire were standing in the same room, and no knives had been drawn! Call the heralds! Trumpet the news! What the devil was his wife doing here after three years of silence, nattering on about his dining table? Why was she here without warning, without a word, particularly having left him in the manner she had?

Her audacity made him feel unstably angry; his heart was pounding uncomfortably in his chest. "I was no' expecting you, and I'd like to know what has brought you to Balhaire, madam."

"Aye!" someone said at the back of the hall.

"Goodness, I do beg your pardon." She instantly sank into a very deep curtsy. "I was so taken by familiar surroundings that I failed to announce that I've come home." She smiled beatifically and held out her hand for him to help her up.

"Home?" He snorted at the absurdity.

"Yes. Home. You are my husband. Therefore, this is my home." She wiggled her fingers at him as if he'd forgotten her hand was extended to him.

Oh, he was aware of that hand, and more important, that smile, because it burned in Arran's chest. It ended in a pair of dimples, and her luminescent green eyes sparkled with the low light of the hall. He could see the wisps of her auburn hair peeking out beneath the hood of her cloak, dark curls against her smooth, pale skin.

She kept smiling, kept her hand outstretched. "Will you not come and greet me?"

Arran hesitated. He was still dressed in his muddied riding clothes, his coat had gone missing from his body, his collar was open to his bare chest, and his long hair was tamed by only his fingers and harnessed in a rough queue down his back. Nor had he shaved in several days, and he no doubt reeked a bit. But he reached for her hand and took it in his.

Such fine, delicate bones. He closed his calloused fingers around her fingers and yanked her to her feet with enough force that she was forced to hop forward. Now she stood so close that she had to tilt her head back on that swan-like neck to look him in the eye.

He glared at her, trying to understand.

She arched a single dark brow. "Welcome me home, my lord," she said, and then, with a smile that flashed as wicked as the *diabhal* himself, she surprised him — shocked him, really — by rising up on her toes, wrapping an arm around his neck and tugging his head down to hers to kiss him.

Bloody hell, Margot *kissed* him. That was

34

as surprising as her sudden appearance. And it was not a chaste kiss, either, which was the only sort of kiss he'd known from his young bride, timid and prudish, who'd left him three years ago. This was a full-bodied kiss, one that bore the markings of maturity, with succulent lips, a playful little tongue and teeth that grazed his bottom lip. And when she'd finished kissing him, she slipped back down to her toes and smiled at him, her green eyes shining with the light of the torches that lit the hall.

It was effective. A wee bit of Arran's anger began to turn to desire as he took her in. She looked the same — perhaps a bit more robust — but this wasn't the bride who had fled Balhaire in tears. Arran roughly pushed the hood of her cloak from her head. Her hair was rich auburn, and he touched the curling wisps around her face. He ignored the feathered arch of her brow as he unfastened the clasp of her cloak. It swung open, revealing the tight fit of her traveling gown, the creamy swell of her breasts above the gold brocade of her stomacher. He noticed something else, too — the emerald necklace he'd given her on the occasion of their wedding glimmered in the hollow of her throat. She looked ravishing. Seductive. She was a fine meal for a man to savor one bite at a time.

But she was grossly mistaken if she thought he would be dining at her table.

"It would seem my purse has found you often enough," he said, admiring the quality of her silk gown. "And you look to be in excellent health."

"Thank you," she said politely, and lifted her chin slightly. "And you look . . ." She paused as she took another look at his disheveled self. "The same." One corner of her mouth tipped up in a wry smile.

Her scent made him heady, and a flash of memories flooded his brain. Of her naked in his bed. Of her long legs wrapped around his, of her perfumed hair, of her young, plump breasts in his hands.

She was aware of his thoughts, too; he could see it spark in her eyes. She turned slightly away from him and said, "May I introduce Mr. Pepper and Mr. Worthing? They've been kind enough to see me safely here."

There was some rumbling in the crowd — in spite of the recent union of Scotland and England, there was no love for the English among his clan, particularly not after the disaster that was his marriage.

Arran scarcely spared the English fops a

36

glance. "Had I known that you meant to return to Balhaire, I'd have sent my best men for you, aye? How curious you didna send word."

"That would have been very kind," she said vaguely. "Might we trouble you for supper? I'm famished, as I am sure these good men are. I'd forgotten how few inns there are in the Highlands."

Arran was slightly inebriated and a wee bit shocked . . . but not so much that he would allow his wife to swan into his castle after three bloody years and pretend all was well and ask to be served without any explanation at all. He meant to demand an answer from her, but he was uncomfortably aware that every Mackenzie ear was trained on them. "Music!" he bellowed.

Someone picked up a flute and began to play, and Arran caught Margot's wrist and pulled her closer. He spoke low so others couldn't hear what he said. "You come to Balhaire, unannounced, after leaving like you did, and you are so insolent as to ask for supper?"

Her eyes narrowed slightly, just as they had the first night he'd ever laid eyes on her. "Will you refuse to feed the men who have seen your wife safely returned to you?"

"Are you *returned* to me?" he scoffed.

"As I recall, you were forever impressing on me that the Scots are well-known for their hospitality."

"Donna think to tell me what I ought to do, madam. Answer me — why are you here?"

"Oh, Arran," she said, and smiled suddenly. "Isn't it obvious? Because I've *missed* you. Because I've come to my senses. Because I want to try our marriage again, of course. Why else would I have taken such a hard road to reach you?"

He watched her lush mouth move, heard the words she said and shook his head. "Why else? I have my suspicions, aye?" he said to her mouth. "Murder. Bedlam. To slit my throat in the night, then."

"Oh *no!*" she said gravely. "That would be too foul, all that blood. You can't really believe it's impossible that I would have a change of heart," she said. "After all, you're not unlikable in your own way."

She was teasing him now? His fury surged.

"Frankly, I would have come earlier had I been given *any* indication that you wanted me to," she added matter-of-factly.

Arran couldn't help a bark of incredulous laughter. "Have you gone mad, then, woman? I've heard no' a bloody word from you in all the time you've been gone."

"I haven't had a word from *you,* either."

This was outrageous. Arran couldn't begin to guess what game she was playing, but she would not win. He slid his arm around her back and yanked her into his body, holding her firmly. He pressed his palm against the side of her head, his thumb brushing her cheek. "Will you no' admit the truth, then?"

"Will you not believe me?" she asked sweetly.

He could see that wicked little sparkle in eyes the shade of ripe pears, that glimmer of deceit. "No' a bloody word."

She smiled and lifted her chin. He realized suddenly that she wasn't afraid of him now. She'd always been a wee bit fearful of him, but he saw no trace of that in her now.

"You're awfully distrusting," she said. "Haven't I always been perfectly frank with you? Why ever should I be any different now? I'm your wife yet, Mackenzie. If you won't believe me, I suppose I'll just have to convince you, won't I?"

Arran's blood began to rush in his veins. He gazed into her face, at the slender nose, the dark brows. "You have surprised me," he admitted as his gaze moved down to her enticing décolletage. "That's what your wretched little heart wanted, aye? But be warned, *wife,* I am no fool. The last time I saw you, you were fleeing. I willna believe you've suddenly found room in there for me," he said, and tapped the swell of her breast over her heart very deliberately.

She continued to smile as if she were unfazed by him, but he could see the faint blush creeping into her cheeks. "I should be *delighted* to prove you wrong. But please do allow me to dine, will you? It is obvious that I will need *all* my strength."

Arran's pulse raced harder now with a combustible mix of fury and desire. "I wonder where the fragile little primrose who left me has gone."

"She grew into a rosebush." She patted his chest. "Some food, if you would be so kind, for Mr. Pepper and Mr. Worthing."

"Fergus!" he said sharply, his gaze still on Margot's face. "Bring the Lady Mackenzie and her men some bread and something to eat, aye? Make haste, lad."

He curled his fingers around her elbow, digging into the fabric, and pulled her along. She said not a word about his dirtied hand on her clothing as she would have before, but came along obediently. Almost as if she expected to be handled in this manner. As if she was prepared for it.

Arran was aware of a flutter of activity and

whispered voices around him as people strained to get a glimpse of the mysterious Lady Mackenzie and the two bulldogs who followed closely behind.

"It wasna necessary to come with an armed guard," Arran snapped as he led her to the dais, glancing over his shoulder at the two Englishmen. "You frightened Sweeney near unto death."

"My father insisted. One never knows when one will encounter highwaymen." She glanced at him sidelong.

He'd always thought her uncommonly beautiful, and somehow, she seemed even more so now. But he did not have the same longing in him he'd once felt for her — he felt only disdain. There was a time her smile would have swayed him to accept her bad behavior. Now he felt numb to it. He should deny her food, toss her into rooms and have her held there for leaving him as she had.

It was not yet out of the question.

Margot removed her cloak and sat gingerly in the seat Arran held out for her on the dais, perching on the edge of it. Her fastidious nature was still lurking beneath that cool exterior.

"Your men, they can sit there," he said, pointing to a table down below.

Her guards hesitated, but Margot gave

them a slight nod to indicate that they should obey.

Arran resisted the urge to remind her she was not queen here, especially not now, but he took his seat beside her and kept his mouth shut. For the moment.

"You've been keeping company, I see," she said congenially as her gaze settled on the lass who had been sitting on his lap and was now off the dais, pouting.

"I've kept the company of my clan, aye."

"Male and female alike?"

He put his hand on her wrist once more, squeezing lightly. "What did you think, Margot, that I'd live like a monk? That once you left me I'd take my vows and prostrate myself before your shrine during vespers?"

She smiled as she pulled her arm from his grip. "I've no doubt you were prostrate at *someone's* shrine." She glanced away and curled a ringlet around her finger.

"And I suppose you've been a chaste little princess," he snorted.

"Well," she said airily, "I can't say I've been *completely* chaste. But who among us has?" She turned her head and looked him directly in the eye, a cool smile on her lips, the color in her cheeks high.

What game was this now? She would flirt with him, hint at bad behavior? It made no sense, and it stank of trickery. Who *was* this woman? The woman who had left him would have been appalled by the mere suggestion that her chastity was not practically virginal. But this woman was toying with him, making suggestions and smiling in a way that could make a man's knees give way.

He turned away from that smile to signal the serving boy to pour wine and noticed that half of his men were still gaping at her. "All right, all right," he said irritably, gesturing for them to do something other than stare. "Can you no' play something a bit livelier, Geordie?" he demanded of his musician.

Geordie put down his flute, picked up his fiddle and began to play again.

As Margot lifted the cup to her lips, he said, "Now that you've had your grand entrance, I'll know what has brought you to Balhaire. Has someone died, then? Has your da lost his fortune? Are you hiding from the queen?"

She laughed. "My family is in good health, thank you. Our fortune is quite intact, and the queen is generally not aware of me at all."

He sprawled back in his chair, studying her.

She smiled pertly. "You seem skeptical. I

43

had forgotten what a suspicious nature you have, but I did always quite like that about you, I must say."

"Should I not be suspicious of you? When you appear as you have without a bloody word?"

"Can you tell me a better way to return to you?" she asked. "If I'd sent word, you would have denied me. Is that not so? I thought that perhaps if you *saw* me before you heard my name . . ." She shrugged.

"You thought what?"

"I thought that maybe you would realize you'd missed me, too." She smiled softly. Hopefully.

There it was, that stir of blood in him again, accompanied by another rash of images of his wife's long legs on either side of him, her silky hair pooling on his chest. He swallowed that image down. The truth was that he couldn't bear the sight of her. "I donna miss you, Margot. I loathe you."

Her cheeks turned crimson, and she glanced down at her lap.

"Aye, and how long has it been, precisely, since you began to miss me, then, *leannan*? Did I no' send enough money?"

"You've been entirely too generous, my lord."

"Aye, that I have," he said with an adamant nod.

"As to when I began to miss you so ardently?" She pretended to ponder that as she fidgeted with the necklace at her throat. "I can't say precisely when. But it's a notion that's taken root and continues to grow."

"Like a bloody cancer," he scoffed.

"Something like that. I always thought you'd come to assure yourself of my welfare instead of sending Dermid as you did."

"You thought I'd come all the way to England, chasing after you like a fox after a hen?"

"*Chase* is a strong word. I rather prefer *visit*."

"I didna receive an invitation to *visit*, aye?"

"You never needed an invitation! You're my husband! You might have come to me whenever you liked. Didn't you always before?" she asked with a salacious look. "Didn't you miss me, Arran? Perhaps only a little?"

"I've missed you in my bed," he said, holding her gaze. "It's been a damn long time."

Color crept into Margot's cheeks again, but she steadily held his gaze. "Has it really been so long?"

His gaze drifted to her mouth. An eternity.

He sat up, leaning in. "A verra long time, lass. It's been three years, three months and a handful of days."

Margot's smile faded. Her lips parted slightly and her lashes fluttered as she looked at him with surprise.

"Aye, *leannan,* I know how long I've been free of the burden of you. Does that surprise *you*?"

Something in her eyes dimmed. "A little," she admitted softly.

Arran smiled wolfishly. His pulse was thrumming now, beating the familiar rhythm of want. He pushed hair from her temple and said, "Pity that I donna care to re-acquaint."

There it was again, a flicker of some emotion in her eyes. Had he struck a blow? He didn't care if he had — it would never equal the blow she'd struck him.

CHAPTER TWO

Balhaire, the Scottish Highlands
1706

Battered and bruised, tossed about the inside of a chaise for days upon days now, making an arduous journey north, Margot was utterly exhausted. But at last they had arrived at the place she was to call home.

She could not have been more despondent.

Balhaire was a dark, bleak castle that rose up out of the ground and was shrouded in mist, just like the hills around it. It was a tremendous structure erected in some long-ago time, anchored by two towers and surrounded by a castle wall. Outside the wall there was a small village of humble thatch-roofed cottages with smoke curling up from the chimneys to a leaden sky.

As the chaise slowed, Margot could hear dogs barking, children shouting. She heard the driver cursing a cow that would not move from the road. The coach slowed to a stop, then jerked forward again.

She moved across to see out the other coach window and saw people coming out of their cottages, lining the road, calling up to Mackenzie, who rode somewhere in front of the chaise. She heard his response, too — one word or two, all in a language she did not know.

Margot shrank back from the window. This place frightened her.

She was still in shock that she was here at all. She'd never once thought it was even remotely possible that she would be forced into a marriage against her will, but that was precisely what had happened to her. She'd begged her father, pleaded with him, but he'd been doggedly determined. He'd been adamant that this marriage was her duty to her family and to England, and that the union between her and Mackenzie would safeguard the Armstrong fortune for generations to come. "You're the only daughter I have, Margot," he'd said. "You have a duty to do as I deem best, and you *will* obey me in this."

Margot had fought back, but her father had threatened her. He swore he would never provide a dowry for any other suitor. He wouldn't allow her to see Lynetta, knowing full well that the two girls would conspire. She would have no society; she would be locked away at Norwood Park and turned into a spinster with no hope of happiness.

At only seventeen years old, Margot hadn't known what to do or how to escape her father's tyranny. In the end, her father had bartered against her confusion and uncertainty and fear and had worn her down.

A fortnight before her eighteenth birthday, Mackenzie was granted a barony. That night, he arrived at Norwood Park to dine with Margot and her family. She scarcely looked at him. At least he wore proper clothes and had shaved his dreadful beard. But when he attempted to make conversation, she responded as blandly as she could in a desperate hope he would find her tedious and vapid and would want to cry off.

Apparently he was quite at ease with the picture she presented. Two days after her eighteenth birthday, Margot took her marriage vows in the Norwood Park chapel before her father and two brothers. Mackenzie had a giant of a man stand up with him.

On her wedding night, her new husband had bedded her quickly, as if the task displeased him, and then had disappeared. Two days later, they departed for Scotland. On the first day of the journey, Margot cried until she made herself ill. When there were no more tears to cry, she felt numb. Her husband asked her more than once if there was anything he could do to help ease her, and she shook her head and looked away from him.

By the time they reached the Highlands of Scotland, having traveled for days without seeing any sort of civilization, Margot was afraid.

Now the chaise rolled through the village where people lined the roads, trying to get a glimpse of her before the chaise disappeared behind the thick walls that surrounded the enormous castle.

The castle was even more imposing up close. Margot had to crane her neck to see the tops of the towers as the conveyance slowed and rolled to a stop. She sat up, her fingers curling tightly around the edges of the cushions on the bench.

The door suddenly swung open. Someone put a step there. Margot quickly tried to repair her hair — she must have looked a fright, especially since she'd had to come all this way without her ladies' maid. Nell Grady was traveling behind with Margot's many trunks.

The dark head of her husband appeared in the door. "Come," he said simply, and held out his gloved hand to her.

It was only her desire to be out of that miserable coach that propelled Margot to step out of the chaise. She faltered only slightly, her legs feeling quite stiff after such a long journey. But she managed to right herself and paused to look around her.

"Welcome to Balhaire," Mackenzie said.

Welcome to *this*? Margot was so overwhelmed by the sight of the bailey, she couldn't speak. It was teeming with animals and people. Chickens hurried out of the way of horses, and dogs sniffed around the boots of the men who had come down from their mounts. She scarcely had time to take it all in before the main doors opened and a woman swept out with a shout. She was tall and slender and had a long braid of dark red hair. The woman didn't look at Margot — she was speaking in the language of the Highlands to Mackenzie.

Whatever he said in return caused the woman to jerk a disdainful gaze to Margot.

"Miss Griselda Mackenzie. My cousin," Arran said, sighing.

Margot curtsied. Griselda's brows rose to almost the top of her head, and she folded her arms across her chest, her long fingers drumming on her arm as she studied Margot. "A pleasure to make your acquaintance," Margot said.

The woman pressed her lips together.

"I hope we might be friends," Margot added as an afterthought.

It was clearly the wrong thing to say; the woman said something quickly and quite vehemently to Mackenzie, then twirled about and went inside.

Margot blinked at her departing back. "I don't . . . Did she understand me? Does she speak English?"

"Aye," Mackenzie said, his countenance stormy. "She speaks English quite well."

That was the moment Margot was certain her situation could not possibly get any worse.

But then Mackenzie led her inside that looming castle.

It was dark and close, the corridors lit by candles stuck in old wall sconces. It smelled musty, as if it had never been aired. Moreover, Margot heard a moaning sound that made her blood run cold. It sounded as if someone was dying — until she realized it was the wind whistling down the ancient flues, creating drafts at every doorway.

She wearily followed Arran about those

winding, dark corridors for what seemed several minutes before they emerged into what he proudly announced was the old great hall. There were several people milling about, making merry, all of them dressed in what looked like various layers of wool clothing, not a hint of silk or satin among them. None of them had donned wigs or dressed their hair. Worse, there were dogs. Not the small parlor dogs that Margot was accustomed to seeing in a house, the sort that might nestle in a lady's lap — but big dogs. Big hunting dogs that wandered around the great hall as if they were quite at home here. Two of them even ventured forward to sniff at her clothing as Arran led her toward a raised platform on which sat a long wooden table.

He made his way to a pair of upholstered seats in the very middle of the table, facing the hall. He sat.

Margot stood uncertainly, wondering if a butler or footman would seat her. Arran glanced up at her, then looked meaningfully at the seat beside him.

She sat.

"Are you hungry?" he asked when she had seated herself on the very edge of the chair covered in a dingy fabric.

"A little."

He lifted his hand, signaled to someone — there were so many people milling about, it was impossible to know — and a boy soon appeared and set two tankards of ale before them, his eyes as big as moons when he looked at Margot. She pitied him — he'd probably never seen a woman with hair properly powdered. And she, in turn, was staring wide-eyed at the tankard he'd set before her. "Will we not have wine?" she asked of no one in particular.

"Ale," Arran said, and lifted his tankard and drank thirstily, as if he was sitting in a tavern with a group of men instead of at a table with his wife. She stared at him, appalled by his manners and the fact that she would be expected to drink like a sailor, but was interrupted by a woman who approached the table. She had graying hair and a swath of plaid that she wore draped over one shoulder. She held the end of it bunched in her hands.

"You're the new Lady Mackenzie, aye?" she asked, and held up the bunched end of the plaid. *"Fàilte!"* She opened the plaid. Nestled in it was a small chick.

Margot didn't understand if the woman meant to give her the chick or if she was simply mad — but she shrank back against her chair in horrified surprise. Arran said something to the woman, flicking his wrist at her, and the woman frowned, covered the chick and moved away.

"Who *are* these people?" Margot asked testily as a couple approached the dais and Arran waved them away, as well.

"My clan," Arran said. The boy appeared again. He was carrying a bowl in each hand, and tucked under his arm were two spoons. The boy, who was not wearing gloves, placed the bowls before them, and then the spoons.

"They are your clan now, aye?" Arran said. He picked up his spoon and began to eat.

"Pardon?"

He paused to look at her. "These people are your clan now, Lady Mackenzie."

She hadn't really thought of it like that before now. She looked out at the people milling about, laughing and talking with each other, casting curious looks at her. She looked at the thick soup before her, the spoon the boy had carried tucked up against his side under his arm.

"Do you no' care for the soup?" Arran asked.

The soup? She didn't care for this place, these people! "I'm not hungry after all." She folded her hands tightly in her lap. "I should like a bath now."

55

"A bath," he repeated slowly.

Good God, surely they *bathed* here! "Yes. A bath." She looked at him pointedly.

Arran fit another spoonful of soup into his mouth and shrugged. He lifted his hand once more, and this time, an older man with a pate of thinning ginger hair appeared at his side. Arran consulted with the man about her bath . . . at length. It seemed a long stretch of minutes passed before the man walked away and Arran turned back to his meal. He took three quick bites in succession, wiped his mouth with the napkin and stood, his chair scraping loudly behind him. With a sigh, he held out his hand to her, palm up. "Aye, then. A bath for milady. I'll bring you round to our chambers."

"What do you mean, our chambers?"

"The master's chambers," he clarified.

She was beginning to feel ill. "I don't understand. You haven't private rooms for me?" she asked disbelievingly.

Arran looked so baffled that Margot's belly began to roil. She could not — *would not* — share a room with this man. It was unheard of! It was egregious, a complete lack of decorum! She couldn't imagine it, all that leather and wool and —

She swallowed, and her fingers curled into fists. "A great house generally has rooms for the master and the mistress," she said as calmly as she could, hoping that he might set this entire wretched ordeal to rights if he only understood how things were done properly.

But he showed no sign of understanding anything. He said, "I'll show you to the master's chambers for your bath, madam. We will discuss whatever it is you think a lady must have on morrow, aye? But tonight, I am too weary for it."

Margot had no choice but to follow him out of the great hall. She averted her gaze each time he paused to speak to someone in his clan — she didn't know what to say, to be quite honest, particularly when she was not properly introduced — and she did not look up until she was pressed by him.

Arran's expression grew darker as he led into the twisting corridors, returning to what she assumed was the foyer, then up a staircase that was twice the width of any she'd seen in even the finest of homes. They walked down another dark corridor, this one lit even more poorly, as only every other wall sconce held a candle.

At the end of the hall was a pair of thick wooden doors. Arran slid the latch and pushed it open, then turned back to Margot.

She stepped hesitantly across the threshold

into a masculine room. The furnishings were trimmed in leather. Thick woolen draperies had been pulled across three separate windows. And oddly, a quiver of arrows was propped against a very large chest of drawers.

But there was a bath before a roaring fire, and two young men were busy pouring hot water into it. Margot stood patiently to one side as they continued to tromp in and out of the room, each of them with two buckets, until Arran deemed the small tub sufficiently full. One of them laid a towel and a cake of soap on a stool, and then they went out.

Arran closed the door behind them. His gaze flicked over her. "There you are, then. A bath. I'll leave you to it." He walked out of the room through what appeared to be a dressing room. She heard another door open, heard it close.

Margot remained standing in the same spot a long moment after he'd gone. He hadn't even offered her the assistance of a maid. Well, no matter — there was a hot bath waiting for her and she was going to avail herself. She managed to discard her clothing and then sank into the tub, closed her eyes and, for a few moments, allowed herself to pretend she was back at Norwood

Park, in a proper bathing room, with towels and perfumed soaps and scented candles.

When she'd finished bathing, she dressed in the nightgown from the small portmanteau someone had thought to bring up from the coach. She didn't know what she was to do now, but she was exhausted, and she crawled into the massive four-poster bed and pulled the covers up to her chin. The wind was howling again, bringing the scent of the sea with it. A storm was brewing off the coast.

Margot had no idea what time it was when Arran at last came into the room, but the fire had turned to embers and the wind seemed even harsher. She could hear him moving about the room, the clank of a belt being undone, the slide of fabric over skin. The bed sank with his weight as he put himself in it. She flinched when his hand slid across her abdomen. "Relax, *leannan*," he murmured.

She had no idea what that meant, *leannan*, but she tried her best to relax. Arran moved his hand down her leg and slipped in beneath her nightgown, his fingers trailing up her thigh. His touch was so soft, so feathery, that it almost tickled her. Margot was shivering again. But not from cold. From anticipation.

Arran propped himself up beside her, then picked up her hand and placed it on his shoulder. "Be at ease, *leannan*," he said. "I donna mean to hurt you — I mean to please you." He kissed her neck, and Margot shivered again. As he continued to move his mouth delicately across her lips and her skin, she found the courage to move her hands over his body, her fingers skating over the hard planes of his muscles, the breadth of his back.

As she moved her hands down to his hips, he groaned softly. She abruptly removed her hands. Arran caught them and put them back. *"Aye,"* he said. "Touch me." He kissed her lips so gently that Margot felt herself begin to float.

He was tender with her, asked if his touch was to her liking, if he hurt her when he entered her. Margot could scarcely mutter her answers — she was too deeply submerged in the sensations of what he was doing to her to think clearly. With his hands and his mouth he aroused her and then coaxed her to float like a feather over the edge of a waterfall of her pleasure.

And then he fell, too.

He lay partially on her, his breath hot on her bare shoulder. After several moments, he moved off her body and lay on his stomach, his face turned from her, his breath heavy. Was he asleep? Was she to sleep now? Margot burrowed down into the bed linens, pulling them up to her neck again.

Arran's breathing grew steadier.

She stared up at the canopy overhead. *Does this please you?* he'd asked her. *Yes,* it had pleased her. She was thinking of it, how tender he was with her, when she was given quite a fright by the sudden pounce of something onto the bed. Margot came up with a shriek and stared right into the eyes of a dog. He was enormous, with one ear that flopped backward and a wiry coat. He wagged his tail excitedly as he sniffed first at Arran, who very lazily tried to swat him away, then at Margot.

"Get off," she said, pushing at the dog. The dog's tail wagged harder.

"He willna bite you," Arran muttered through a yawn.

"I don't care — what's he doing on the bed?" she demanded.

Arran shrugged. "He fancies you, aye?" He yawned again and stuffed the pillow up under his head. Meanwhile, the beast of a dog turned in one or two circles at the foot of the bed, then plopped down with a loud sigh.

She was to sleep with a dog? Arran's tenderness forgotten, tears welled, and Margot lay back down, turning on her side, away from him and the dog, silently cursing her father for having bartered her to this hell.

CHAPTER THREE

The Scottish Highlands
1710

He watched every bite she took. Margot was uncertain if he was counting the minutes until he could take her to his bed, or the minutes until she succumbed to the poison he could very well have instructed be put in her stew.

She was counting the minutes until he demanded her duty to him. The prospect of being in that massive bed again excited and frightened her at once. In the few short months they'd existed in their conjugal state, Arran had introduced her to the intimate pleasures husbands and wives shared. She had enjoyed it . . . but she hadn't realized just how much she had enjoyed it until she'd gone and was without it.

She could honestly say that in the privacy of their marital bed, there had been no discord. It was the other twenty-three hours of the day that had undone her.

Margot had quickly discovered that Arran was a man with many passions — there were no degrees with him. It was all or nothing, all brawn, all daring, all lust. There had not been room for a wife.

And while she did like the brawn in him, his passions and appetites could be too intense. Memories had come flooding back to her the closer she and her party had drawn to Balhaire: his passion for hunting. For sailing the sea. For drinking and gambling and training his men to be the best soldiers in the kingdom. She had never experienced a gaze as intent as his, and she'd never seen a look as blackly angry as his the day she'd left.

The matter of her leaving him for England had not been resolved, and quite honestly, Margot didn't know if it could ever be resolved. She hadn't the slightest idea what he thought or wanted, especially after all this time. She couldn't even say what she wanted . . . but she did not want this, to be a pawn in a dangerous game.

For the moment, her husband remained slouched in his chair, his powerful legs sprawled before him, one hand firmly gripping his cup of ale, the other dangling lazily from the arm of his chair. His intent gaze made fear curl around her spine — he reminded her of the hawks he was so fond of training. She could feel his contempt rolling off him and covering her.

Margot did her best to put some stew in her belly. She was truly famished — but the nerves in her were building, making it difficult to swallow, making the food sit sourly in her belly. She could only guess what was coming, how incomprehensibly convincing she had to be now. She had begged and cajoled her father that this scheme would never work, that Arran would never believe she had missed him and wanted to reunite. How could she want something like that after three years without a word? How could *he*? And besides, the man had an uncanny way of seeing right through her.

But her father had taken her hands in his and said, "My darling girl, a man can be convinced of anything if his wife is as pleasing as she ought to be. Do you take my meaning?"

She took his meaning, all right. Lord Norwood thought he could order her to return to her husband and her husband would overlook his wounded pride and welcome her with open arms. He thought that Margot would politely inquire if it were true that

Arran colluded with the French and the Jacobites and intended to give them entry into Scotland through Balhaire. And that Arran would happily tell her if it were true that he and his highly regarded Highland soldiers would join the French troops and invade England to remove Queen Anne from the throne and put James Stuart on it.

Her father apparently believed this so completely and thought it so important that he clearly felt himself justified in threatening Margot to do what she did not want to do once again. She had tried to convey to her father how irretrievably broken-down was her marriage to Mackenzie, how he must despise her now, how she had despised him. Not that she believed for a moment that he was involved in *treason,* for God's sake, but she was in no position to ascertain the truth.

Her father would hear none of it.

This was ridiculous. If, by some small chance, Arran was involved in something so deplorable and indefensible, he would hide any evidence of it. He'd not amassed power and wealth with loose lips and carelessness. He certainly would not talk freely of it to *her,* especially not when he reviled her so. He would hold her at arm's length no matter what he thought of her. Women existed to be bedded and impregnated. They were not included in important discussions. They were told what to do; they were not allowed to choose.

"It is time to finish your meal," Arran said. "You dawdle now, aye? You and I have much to discuss." He stood up.

Margot looked up as she fit the spoon in her mouth. More than six feet of man towered over her. She chewed slowly as she regarded him. He'd always had a physique honed by his training of soldiers, as big and as strong as an ox. Three years hadn't softened him in the least. Quite the contrary — he looked even leaner and harder now, his hair in need of a cut, his ice-blue eyes as shrewd as ever.

"Be quick about it," he added, and stepped off the dais, to where her father's men sat. He spoke to them, gesturing to two of his men who had instantly come forward. Moments later, Pepper and Worthing stood up, glanced uneasily at Margot, then followed the Scots out of the great hall. Arran went in another direction.

Margot panicked slightly, but then again, Worthing had warned her they'd not be allowed to stay. He was her father's confidant — in fact, it was Worthing and two other gentlemen who had brought from London the rumors and accusations against Arran to her father.

"He'll not want any Englishmen in his hall," Worthing had warned Margot. "You must be prepared to see us depart."

"No," Margot had said. "I'll ask him —"

"He will instantly suspect you if you speak for us, madam. You must play the part of a disobedient wife who means to make amends."

Disobedient wife. Is that what they thought of her? As if she were a child who had disobeyed all the men in her life? As if she'd been expected to stay in an untenable position merely because men had put her there? Frankly, it would have helped tremendously if she knew just how a disobedient wife behaved when she wanted to make amends. Margot did not.

She watched Arran walk through the hall, pausing to speak to one or two people, glancing meaningfully back at her once or twice. His long, dark hair was a tangled queue, and his buckskins, lawn shirt and waistcoat were soiled, his boots scuffed. Who knew what the man had done all day? Margot bowed her head and recalled the sensation of his body in hers, carrying her away to that sensual place.

She missed that, anyway. She hadn't realized how much she would miss it, how empty her life would become. She missed knowing that someone could be gentle with her, careful of her.

Margot felt the sickly warmth of fear as she thought of it. She had wounded him in the worst way one could wound a man, and she had no hope that he would care much for her now — she had seen the harshness in his gaze. She was afraid of him, disgusted by him, attracted to him.

Anxiety swelled in her, and she abruptly stood, suddenly desperate to escape to the privacy of her old rooms.

The moment she came to her feet, however, Jock appeared. "Madam."

"Jock!" she said with a cheerfulness that belied the fright he'd given her. It seemed impossible that anyone could be larger than her husband, but Jock was. His dark ginger hair was streaked with gray and had always given her the impression that he carried the gloomy mists of the Highlands around with him.

"How good to see you. You are well?" she asked as pleasantly as she could force herself.

His brows dipped. He was not fooled by her. "Whatever you require, I am at your service, aye?"

Her wish was too complicated for poor Jock. But in that space of hesitation, Jock rubbed a finger against his cheek, and a movement to her left caught her eye. A rat, in the form of a man, went scurrying in the direction Arran had gone to report her attempt to flee.

She sighed and frowned at Jock. "That wasn't necessary, was it?"

His eyes narrowed with his silent disagreement.

He'd always been a worthy adversary. He'd never trusted the marriage brokered between her and Arran. Margot put her hands to the small of her back. "I mean only to stretch my legs. I've come quite a long way."

Jock merely stood there. Typical.

"And I am in need of a ladies' retiring room." She arched a brow, expecting him to retreat as all men did when confronted by women and their bodily functions. But Jock stood like a mountain before her, his expression unchanged.

"Perhaps my old rooms are available?"

"There are no rooms for you, madam. We didna expect you."

Obviously. "You mustn't trouble yourself, Jock. I'm certain my maid has made them ready by now," she said, and slipped past him.

"Milady —"

"I know my way very well, thank you!" She walked quickly down the side of the hall before he could stop her, smiling blindly at all the unsmiling, distant faces. All she had to do was reach the main entrance to the hall. She knew exactly where she was going. In the four months she'd lived here as Mackenzie's bride, when her husband was out hunting or training soldiers or away on one of his ships, Margot had nothing to occupy her. She'd spent many lonely hours wandering about this sprawling castle. She knew every turn, every stairwell, every room.

But just as she reached the main doors, one of them swung open and Arran entered the hall, the rat directly behind him. She instantly turned and started in the opposite direction. Arran caught up to her in a step, clasped her elbow and jerked her backward. Margot's heart climbed to her throat. She put a hand to her heart and said laughingly, "You frightened me!"

He stood with his legs braced apart, and his brows formed a dark vee above his eyes. "You'd no' be running from your husband so soon, would you, *mo gradh*?" he asked hotly. "Having just this night returned to . . . what was it you said, then . . . to try our marriage again? Because you have missed me so?" His lips curved into a cool smile.

Aware that several pairs of eyes were on them, Margot forced a light laugh, as if this was friendly banter between husband and wife. "I meant only to freshen a bit. Wash the dust of road from my skin, as it were."

His smile turned wolfish. "If you wish to wash, I'll have a bath brought to my chamber, aye? It will be like old times."

"Oh, that is . . ." *Predictable. Infuriatingly manipulative.* "Helpful," she said. "But, ah . . ." She shifted forward, standing close so that she could whisper. She laid her hand lightly on his arm, watched his gaze move to her hand, then to her bosom, and whispered, "I have need of a retiring room."

"Then you shall have one," he said instantly.

Margot smiled in the way she'd learned at the soirees and dinner parties, where she'd mastered the art of making time pass by testing all the silly things men would do for a mere smile. "Thank you for understanding." She patted his arm, then slid her hand off it. She bobbed a bit of a curtsy. "I shan't be long." Unless he considered all night a long time.

She moved to step around him, but Arran caught her arm once more. Not her hand, but her forearm, and his grip was tight. "No' a retiring room as you might expect, having come from Norwood Park, but a closet that will suit. There is one in my chambers, you may recall, aye?"

Oh, she remembered. Margot tried to tug her arm free, but he held tight. "I won't trouble you."

"You already have," he said curtly.

She didn't like the look in his eye. He looked a little as if he intended to carve her up, stuff an apple in her mouth and serve her up on a platter.

"And I thought you bloody well *missed* me," he said, his eyes going dark as he squeezed her arm.

There was a time he might have intimidated her into utter silence with such a predatory look, but Margot had changed. She wasn't the inexperienced debutante anymore, and she knew how to fight back. She tilted her head and gave him an even sultrier smile. "Oh, but I *have*, Arran. I'm afraid you've seen through me — the truth is that the journey has left me quite fatigued." She glanced surreptitiously about — she could see how people near them strained to hear. So she rose up on her toes and whispered, "I want very much to please you, my lord, but I really must rest to be *especially* pleasing."

Arran's gaze turned ferocious. It was full of lust and anger, and Margot's pulse quickened with apprehension. He could kill her and no one here would say a word. No one in England would know for weeks, long after she'd turned to dust. He slid his arm around her waist and anchored her there, holding tight. "I think you misjudge your own strength, milady. Thank the saints that you're a sturdy lass, aye? You'll manage, I've no doubt." He began to pull her through the hall, his grip on her unyielding.

"This is hardly necessary," she said, struggling to keep up with his stride. "Naturally I assumed you'd be concerned for my welfare. But never mind — if you desire that I accompany you, then of course I shall. You need only ask."

Arran stopped. He stepped away from her and bowed low. "My apologies, then," he said. "By all means — I desire that you accompany me to my chambers. *Now.*" He gestured to the path in front of him, his jaw set, his eyes boring through hers. There was the hawk again, ready to swoop down and cart her off to be fed to his clan.

Speaking of which . . . Margot glanced

over her shoulder. Necks were craning. Ears were pointed like dogs' ears to them. All eyes were locked on the laird and his wife. That was the way it had always been at Balhaire — a perpetual audience to her marriage.

Margot sniffed. She nervously fingered a loose curl. She had no choice, really — she'd not have word going back to her father that she had been less than a dutiful wife on her first night at Balhaire. God only knew what he would do with her then.

So she lifted her chin, smiled sweetly and began to walk along the path he'd indicated. Arran was right beside her, his hand possessively on the small of her back, the expanse of it covering her waist. She was reminded of other moments when his hands were on more exposed parts of her body, and her stomach began to turn little somersaults.

"That's a good lass," Arran said into her ear, his voice trickling into her bloodstream. "Obedient and eager, just as a man's wife ought to be."

Margot resisted the overwhelming urge to elbow him in the ribs and then run.

They walked up the wide staircase that curled past paintings of Mackenzies, past historic armor that men liked to display for reasons that completely escaped her, past an array of swords fanned above the arched entrance to the hallway. Arran kept his hand on her as he steered her toward the two oak doors that led into the master's chambers.

Their arrival startled two boys in that long hallway who were replacing candles in the sconces.

"Light the laird's chamber!" Jock bellowed from behind them, startling Margot. She hadn't even known he was there. The two lads scurried ahead, into Arran's private rooms.

When they reached the doors to the master's chambers, Arran glanced over his shoulder and said to Jock, "We are no' to be disturbed by anyone, aye? We've a bit of bad business to conduct." He reached around Margot and gave the door a push, then pushed her through. He just as quickly ushered the young boys out, then closed the door and turned the lock.

He slowly faced her and leaned against the closed doors, his head down, his gaze terrifyingly hard. *Bad business.* What did that mean, exactly? She had never thought him violent. Whatever he meant, she would likely die before he did anything — her heart was beating that wildly.

"The chamber pot and a basin are just in there," he said, nodding to a door at the far end of the room. "Avail yourself."

Margot glanced at the closet door warily and walked away from him and into the closet to collect herself.

When she emerged, he was still standing at the door. He suddenly pushed away from it and strolled to the sideboard. He poured two goblets of wine and held one out, offering it to her. "For my wife, who has, remarkably, returned to me. To my bonny wife, who gave me no' a word of apology, nor hope, nor explanation, who now claims to have *missed* me. Aye, what a day this has become."

His expression was so stormy that Margot felt herself begin to shake as she dried her hands. She had to be as convincing as she'd ever been in her life. "People have a change of heart all the time," she said, and turned around to him. She took the wine he offered, drinking more than was polite in the hopes it would calm her nerves.

Arran didn't drink. His goblet dangled between two fingers as he watched her.

Margot warily lowered her goblet.

His gaze moved casually over her now, lingering on her bosom and her hem. But then he clenched his jaw and turned away, as if he couldn't stand the sight of her. "You're as beautiful as ever, then. *Boid-*

heach," he said low, and tossed back his wine in one long swallow.

Margot wasn't expecting that. Anger, indignation, indifference, yes, and any number of questions about why she'd left and why she'd come back. But not that she was beautiful. The sentiment made her feel ill. She was not beautiful — she was bad business. How could he think otherwise?

"Aye, my bonny wife," he said again, putting aside his goblet. "How often I've thought of her."

Margot's cheeks flooded with shame. Was that true, or was he toying with her now? She wished he would rail at her, demand answers — but not tease her. "Surely you've not wasted your energy thinking of me," she said.

He snorted at that. "And why no'? Because you've wasted no time thinking of me?"

That wasn't true. It was *far* from true. She'd thought of him so often, trying to remember how, exactly, it had all gone wrong. But Margot couldn't pretend with him now — she knew him well enough to know he was teetering on the edge of fury, and beyond that, who knew? She looked him directly in the eye and said, "Actually, Arran, I've thought of you often."

One dark brow arched above the other, as if that amused him. He began moving toward her, around her, behind her. "You've a peculiar way of showing it. Have you thought, then, of what I did to make you so unhappy? I have. But do you know what I wonder even more?"

Margot tried not to show any emotion and tried to stand perfectly still. She shook her head.

"I wonder," he said softly as his palm glided across her shoulder, to the back of her neck and to the other shoulder, "what has made you so miraculously eager to return to me that you'd no' send a messenger." His hands closed around her shoulders, and he leaned down and kissed her neck.

A sudden heat rushed through her.

"No' a bloody word of warning. The only party who might arrive here at Balhaire without sending word is the English army. Tell me, Margot — is there an English army lying in wait in the hills?" he asked, and licked the spot on her neck behind her earlobe.

The sensation of his tongue against her skin glittered in every nerve. She grabbed a fistful of her gown in an attempt to steady herself. "That's ridiculous," she said, her voice unsteady. "Perhaps I misjudged you." She closed her eyes as his lips moved on her skin. "I thought you'd want to reconcile."

"With *you*?" He laughed coldly. "With a woman who has betrayed me? You're no' a stupid lass, Margot. You've no misjudged a bloody thing," he said against her neck, and deftly removed the goblet from her hand and put it aside on a table as he continued his mouth's exploration of her nape. "As much as it amuses me to hear it, I donna believe you've thought of me at all, except perhaps to wonder when your next purse would arrive from Scotland." He slid his hand around to her breast and roughly squeezed it. "Is that no' so?"

Margot's lips parted with the sharp intake of her breath. His rough handling of her was causing the heat in her to rise and bloom in her skin. "That is not so," she said, trying futilely not to sound as breathless as she felt in his arms.

Arran grabbed her waist and twirled her around to face him. "Donna lie to me," he said, and clasped her head in his enormous hands and kissed her. It was a hard kiss, one full of frustration. He kissed her in a way he had never kissed her before, his tongue tangling hotly with hers, his teeth grazing her lips.

Margot tumbled off some interior ledge. She wasn't prepared for this, would have said it impossible — but his rough wooing was invoking a fiery response in her. She panicked and pushed hard against his chest. She had to control this between them. She had to keep her wits about her. "Unhand me," she said roughly.

That did nothing to stop him; in fact, his eyes fired with the challenge. "You're still my wife. That you canna change. Thank your stars I've no' locked you away just yet."

Her heart leaped painfully. That would be the utter end of her, to be sent back here, only to be locked away. Margot tried to walk out of his arms, but Arran pushed her up against the wall. When she freed herself, he grabbed both her hands and lifted them over her head, pinning them to the wall with one hand. He held her there, his gaze greedily scraping over her, studying her, as if reacquainting himself with every inch of her body.

She hated how quickly his stark gaze aroused her. It was so virile, so full of lust. This man was a far cry from the one who had so tenderly initiated her into lovemaking. "You're a beast," she breathed.

"You donna know the half of it," he bit

out, and dipped his head to kiss her. Margot stubbornly turned her head, but Arran was not deterred — he lightly bit the swell of her breast above the bodice of her gown, and she gasped with pleasure. "Is this no' what you want, then?" His breath was hot on her skin. "To show me just how much you missed your poor, dear husband, the damn fool you left behind?"

Her pulse soared with fear, with want. "I would prefer a gentler reunion," she lied.

"Then you might have taken a gentler leave of me," he snapped, and pressed his body against hers.

She could feel all of him — the hard plane of his abdomen and muscular legs, his enormous erection. Margot was losing herself in the sensation of his hands and mouth on her. She closed her eyes and tried to drag air into her lungs, alarmed by how badly she wanted him, however he would have her — in his bed, or on her knees. "Are you such an animal that you would force yourself on me?" she demanded, desperate to stop herself from giving in completely.

"Are you such a witch that you would have me stop?" he breathed into her neck before biting her ear as he pressed his erection against her.

His sensual assault was intoxicating and

exhilarating, an explosion of light and color and scents that were dangerously arousing. "Yes. I want you to *stop,*" she hissed.

Arran abruptly hiked her skirt and slipped his hand between her legs. Margot was wet. He pressed his mouth against her cheek and whispered, *"Liar."*

"You're insufferable," she breathed, turning her head to him now, her mouth only a breath from his. "A wild beast of a man, rutting on his wife because his pride has been wounded."

"Aye, I am wild with anger, that I willna deny. But I know that no matter what else has gone between us, you've always wanted me. At times rather desperately, aye? Just as you do now." He slipped his fingers into her body.

She couldn't suppress a gasp of pure desire. "You have mistaken boredom for want," she said breathlessly, and tried to kiss him, but Arran, still holding her hands above her head, jerked back, just out of her reach, removing his hand from between her legs.

He grinned at her expression of fury. "You're a moment from seeing the back of my hand, so donna sweet-talk me, *leannan.*"

Oh, that word, that *word*! It had always dripped down her spine like warm honey, and he knew it, too, the bloody bounder. She couldn't even say what it meant, precisely, but it was the endearment he had used with her in this very room. "Take your hands from me," she said. "You're filthy and you're half-drunk."

He pressed against her again, roughly cupped her face with his free hand. "My clothes are soiled, but they'll come off soon enough. I'm only pleasantly drunk, no' enough to interfere with my husbandly duty." He silenced her attempt to argue with a kiss. This time, a sweetly tender kiss.

And Margot disintegrated.

Everything in her surrendered. He tasted like ale and spice, smelled musky and powerful. Her blood stirred violently in her as he yanked the pins from her hair, let one long tress fall after the other. He claimed her breast with his hand once more, kneading it through the fabric of her gown, his thumb flicking over her hardened nipple.

Arran let go of her hands and slipped one arm around her waist. Lost in the moment between them, Margot let her hands fall to his shoulders as he kissed her and, lifting her off her feet, twirled her away from the wall and stalked across the room to his bed with her. He tossed her down, rolled her over and yanked at the laces of her gown at her back.

She wanted to feel him inside her once more. It felt to Margot as if their estrangement was shedding away from them and an unholy, improbable passion was rising up in its place. He roughly pulled her dress from her, then her stays, then slipped his arm under her belly and effortlessly flipped her onto her back. He pinned her there with his body as his hands freely roamed her, slipping under the silk of her chemise, rough and warm and searching.

His weight was familiar, but his manner was not one she'd ever known. He was wild with lust, wild with anger, and even though he was touching her, he was grunting as if it pained him. His coarse behavior with her was so arousing that Margot was disappearing into nothing but sensation as his hands and mouth moved over her. Her hands sought his flesh. Her mouth sought his. She forgot why she'd come. She forgot everything but the need to have him inside her.

When he pushed her chemise over her head and put his mouth to her breast, to her abdomen and between her legs, Margot groaned with desire, dragging her fingers over his buttocks and his back as he kicked free of his boots and buckskins. He incited a fire the moment he thrust into her, thick and hard, and carried her away on a cloud of physical pleasure so intense that it clawed at her throat, releasing in a soft growl of delight.

They were moving together, his breath hot in her hair. They were each of them desperate to have that primal release of ecstasy . . .

But then Arran did something Margot did not anticipate in that frenetic coupling — he stroked her face. It was a clumsy stroke at that, as one might try to caress a moving child. But she knew instantly it was a caress of true affection. It startled her; she opened her eyes and looked up at him, wide-eyed.

Arran stopped moving. He gritted his teeth as if he was holding himself back. "Turn your head."

"Pardon?"

"Turn your *head*," he said, and pushed her face away from him, so that she was looking now at the windows. She felt his scorching gaze on her as he began to move in her again.

Margot's heart was racing dangerously hard. She was confused and inflamed, suspended between wild desire and the realization that he did not want to see her face. Something in her womb fluttered. A rush of breath escaped her. Her body simmered with the touch of his hands and the stroke of his body, her heart racing too far ahead of her thoughts. She was losing the game already; she was no match for him. He knew how to make her mewl, cry out, laugh. He could ask her anything now and, with a stroke of his tongue, force the answer from her.

And all he wanted from her was that she turn her head. *Don't look at him,* she commanded herself. *Don't show him your face.*

His arousal pressed hard and long into her, and the prurient sensations unfurling in her body numbed her to her misgivings. She tangled her fingers in his hair, scraped her hands across his shoulders and the muscles in his back, moving with him. She burned everywhere he touched and slid deeper into that fog of pleasure.

When he slipped his hand between them and began to stroke her in time to his body sliding inside her, Margot arched into him. She groped for an anchor, her hand hitting a bedside table. She heard something clatter to the ground as she surged up on that pitch to the release of intolerable pleasure.

Arran growled, thrusting hard into her as his own release came.

For several moments afterward, neither of them moved. Both of them sucked air into their lungs until Arran slowly rolled off her and onto the bed beside her.

Margot was stunned. She swallowed hard, then pushed herself up and gathered the bedclothes around her naked body.

Arran had no such bashfulness. He lay sprawled on his belly, one arm hanging off the bed, his face turned away from her. She admired his physique, made hard and lean by his youthful thirty years and his lust for life. She had long appreciated his good looks and his strength, and had felt that flame of attraction from their first meeting when he appeared at Norwood Park with hair that was too long and muddied boots.

Yes, the spark had always been there. But the marriage had been wrong. Surely, in his heart of hearts, he knew that was true.

Margot leaned over him now. His hair had come undone from its queue. She could see a nick or two in his skin, as well. Fresh scars, undoubtedly earned in training his men for war. That was part of their marriage bargain — he would provide the renowned Highland soldiers for the British army. He would have lands in England, and she would have lands in Scotland, belonging to each of them outright. He was made a baron, too, and she . . . she was made the chattel by which two men had feathered their nests. She was the shiny bauble that had brought Mackenzie to the bargaining table.

How could such a glorious specimen of a man be a traitor? She touched one of the scars.

Arran instantly pushed himself up, coming off the bed. He ignored her and walked to the hearth, squatting down to build a fire. When he finished, he refilled his goblet and drank thirstily. He glanced at her over his shoulder, quite at ease with his nudity. But his hand, she noticed, was gripping the goblet. "Why?" he asked gruffly.

It was curious how two people, separated longer than they'd been together, could still understand one another. Margot knew very well that he was asking why she'd left. "You know why."

"Was I unkind, then?" he asked impatiently. "Did I mistreat you?"

Margot sighed wearily. Her reasons had felt so sharp and urgent at the time, but had dulled with the years. "Not unkind. Indifferent. We were so different, you and I."

He stared down at her for a moment, then looked away. "Aye. We still are."

"You had no use for me, Arran."

"No *use* for you? Was it no' enough that you were mistress of all this?" he asked, gesturing around him.

"In name only," she said. "I had no society, no friends."

"Only because you'd not allow it," he countered. "There are women in my clan who would have befriended you with the slightest bit of encouragement, aye?"

"*That's* not true," she said. "I tried to make Balhaire what I thought it ought to be, but they resisted me at every turn."

"You wanted to do things in an English way."

"What other way could I possibly have done them? I *am* English."

He looked away, to the windows. "My own cousin Griselda was your friend."

"Griselda!" Griselda Mackenzie was quite possibly the most unpleasant person Margot had ever met in her life. "She could scarcely tolerate me! She hated me for being English — you know that is true. Can you not see that *you* had what you wanted from our marriage, but I had nothing? I was miserable, Arran."

"What I wanted," he repeated. "Pray tell me, what the bloody hell did I want?"

Margot snorted and pushed her hair from her face. "The barony. Entry into England. Power, like every man before you and after you and around you now."

Arran merely shrugged. "Aye, it's what every man wants. But did you no' want the same? Did you no' want your own lands and a title, and all the trappings that come with it?"

"*No,*" she said, appalled. "I wanted a good match. A companion. I wanted a husband who wasn't gone all day every day. I wanted someone who cared for finer things, who would take tea with me, perhaps bring me to Edinburgh —"

"This is the Highlands of Scotland, aye? No' a bloody London or Paris salon."

Margot could feel her hackles rising and checked herself. "You're right. But that was the crux of it — I needed a more civilized existence."

"Mind your mouth, woman," he said, looking genuinely offended.

"You came to my chamber fresh from the hunt with blood on your shirt!"

"Aye, and I took it off!" he shouted. "Do you think it was easy to be wed to *you*?"

"Me!"

"Oh, aye, little lamb, *you,*" he said, pointing a finger at her. "You were so timid and disdainful of everything. Haughty! Aye, you were a haughty one," he said, flicking his wrist at her. "Nothing was good enough for milady, was it?"

91

Margot looked away. There was some truth to that, she couldn't deny it. She'd been angry she'd been forced to marry him, so determined to find fault with him and Balhaire. "I was so young, Arran. So inexperienced."

"You were definitely that," he curtly agreed.

She glanced at him sidelong. He was pacing now, dragging his hand through his long, unruly hair. "Why didn't you come after me?" she asked softly.

Arran slowly turned to look at her for a long moment, his jaw clenched. "Because I donna chase after dogs or women. They come to me."

Margot's gut clenched. She could almost feel herself shrink and averted her gaze. "What a lovely sentiment."

"I have my pride, woman." He threw back the coverlet and got back in the bed.

"And I pierced it. So there you have it," she said, drawing her knees up to her chest. "The only thing that ever truly existed between us was in this bed. It was the only place where we could agree."

"The hell we agreed here," he spat. "It is your duty to provide me an heir," he said, bending his arm behind his head to pillow it. "And the last time I looked about, I have none."

"I was to be your broodmare, is that it? Of course — I was bartered like one."

"You came of your own free will!"

"My own free will! I had no choice, and well you know it."

"Did I kidnap you and carry you off? We met twice before the nuptials, Margot. By God, if you'd had a doubt of it, you might have expressed it to me then."

"We met two times!" She laughed at the absurdity of it. "Yes, of course, a sum total of *two* meetings is quite sufficient to determine compatibility for the rest of one's life. Whatever made me think otherwise? I had to have reason to cry off, but I scarcely knew you at all."

"What did you want, then, a bloody courtship?"

"Yes!"

Arran suddenly bolted up and over her, pinning her down with his body, his gaze dark and locked with hers. "If you found me and Balhaire so objectionable, why in hell have you now returned?"

Margot held his gaze just as fiercely. "I told you," she said calmly. "Perhaps I've not given our marriage its due. I should like to try again."

"Donna ever lie to me, Margot Mackenzie, do you hear me now?" he breathed hotly. "You will no' like what will come of it if you do." His eyes moved hungrily down her body. He bent his head and took her breast in his mouth, teasing it a moment before lifting his gaze to hers once more. "*Never* lie to me, aye? Am I clear?"

His blue eyes were two bits of hard ice, and Margot was terrified to feel her face coloring with her deceit. Could he see it? "Yes," she said. She was lying to him now! Fate had made her a despicable liar.

Arran grunted. He kissed her belly, pushed aside the bed linens and moved down between her legs, his tongue and mouth on her sex, and Margot felt herself sinking once more. "Are you lying to me now, *leannan*?"

God help her, he'd seen the deceit in her. She knew it. But his tongue slid over her again, long and slow, and he looked up once more, expecting an answer. The gentle lover she'd first known was gone, and this wolf — this brazen, alluring, dangerous wolf — was in his place. *"No,"* she lied, and closed her eyes, giving herself up to the wolf's attentions once more.

CHAPTER FOUR

Balhaire
1706

Arran couldn't understand her. She had everything she might possibly want, and yet she cried.

Jock, Griselda's brother, said Arran should simply command her to stop crying. Jock's father agreed.

"How am I to do that, then?" Arran asked impatiently. "You canna simply command a woman to cease her tears."

"You take a strap to her, that's how," said Uncle Ivor.

Arran blanched. *"Never,"* he'd said thunderously, "and God help me if you've taken a strap to Aunt Lilleas!"

" 'Course I've no'," Uncle Ivor thundered right back, appalled. "She'd skin me like a hare if I had as much as a fleeting thought of it."

Arran didn't understand his uncle, either.

The three men fell silent, thinking about women.

Uncle Ivor suddenly surged forward and slapped the table. "*Diah,* why'd I no' think of it before? It's her courses!" he said, casting his arms wide as if all the mysteries of the world had just been solved. "Women are like beasties when they have their courses, aye? Put a child in her, Arran. That will put it to rights."

Jock snorted. "Molly Mackenzie sobbed buckets of tears when she was with child. Putting a child in Lady Mackenzie will help nary a thing."

"What do you know of it?" Uncle Ivor challenged his son. "You've no' looked at a lass all summer."

"I've looked!" Jock protested, his ruddy cheeks turning slightly ruddier. "I've been a wee bit occupied, have I no', with the expansion of our trade."

While Uncle Ivor and Jock argued about whether or not Jock had sufficiently perused the unmarried lasses of Balhaire, Arran brooded. The truth — which he would never admit aloud, certainly not to these men — was that he felt quite a failure for not knowing how to make his wife happy. It was a dilemma that he'd not given much thought before Norwood had presented an alliance through marriage to him.

He'd been surprised by the agent who had come on Norwood's behalf, but then again, with the union of Scotland and England upon them, men on both sides of the border were scrambling to take advantage of opportunities. There was no doubt that a match with the heiress Margot Armstrong of Norwood Park was one of great advantage for Arran and his clan.

Even so, Arran had not been convinced of it until he'd laid eyes on her. He would never forget that moment — auburn hair, mossy-green eyes, and little paper birds, of all things, in her hair. Arran had traveled in his time, had seen women and their dressing — but he had not seen a beauty quite like Margot, and that was all he'd really needed. Lamentably, his cock had been so convinced of the efficacy of the match that his head had never imagined it would be such work to make her accept Balhaire as her home.

When it was clear Jock and Uncle Ivor would be no help to him, Arran later appealed to Griselda for help.

She was even less helpful. "Why do you ask me, then?" she'd snapped at him. " 'Twas no' my doing to bring a dainty English buttercup to Balhaire."

Griselda did not care for buttercups, he surmised. "You might befriend her," he pointed out. "You've no' been particularly welcoming, aye?"

Griselda shrugged and picked at a loose thread in her sleeve. "Aye, perhaps no'. But I tried to make amends!" she added quickly. "I invited her to join in my falconry, and she acted as if I'd invited her to run bare through the woods!"

"Please, Zelda," Arran pleaded.

Griselda moaned to the ceiling. "Aye, all right. For you, Arran, I will try again."

True to her word, Griselda came back a day later, sat down beside him in the great hall and said, "Your wife wants society. Bloody English, that's all they think of — *society.*"

Arran had no idea what the English thought about, but no matter — he was confused by it. "Here is our society," he said, gesturing around them to his large extended family.

"*Proper* society, Arran. A celebration, a ball. Where she might display her jewels and whatno'," Griselda said, gesturing to her chest uncertainly. Griselda had never been a fancy lass. Griselda liked to ride and hunt and wager on cards. She'd never thought of balls as far as Arran knew.

Moreover, he was quite certain there had never been a ball at Balhaire. But if that's what would make Margot happy, he was more than happy to oblige her. He decreed that a ball would be held to welcome Lady Mackenzie to Balhaire and the Mackenzie clan, and frankly, the idea was so grand that he wondered why he'd not thought of it before.

Margot seemed rather excited about it. "A ball? For me?" she'd asked him excitedly, her eyes sparkling with delight.

"Aye, for you," he said proudly. They were seated in the morning room, she with some sort of needlepoint, and he lacing spurs to his boots.

"Arran . . . thank you," she said, putting down her work. "That is precisely what I need! A *ball*," she said dreamily. "We might invite your neighbors, won't we? And we'll have marzipan cakes."

"Marzipan," he repeated uncertainly. He wondered if Aunt Lilleas knew how to make them.

"No matter. We can do without the cakes. But we must have champagne and ices, of course."

Arran had no idea where he would get either champagne or ices, and he had almost said so. But Margot leaped to her feet, threw her arms around his neck and kissed his cheek, surprising the life out of him. "*Thank you!*"

He decided then and there he would find champagne and ices.

Great preparations were made for the ball. The rush torches were changed out. Carpets were beaten. The tables where his clan took their meals were pushed back against the wall, and proper musicians were hired from Inverness. The clan was instructed to wear their finest clothing.

Margot surprised Arran again one afternoon by inviting him into the rooms she'd taken at the top of the old tower — as far from the newer master's chambers as she could possibly be. He'd trekked across the breadth of Balhaire to sit in her dressing room to help her select the gown she would wear to the ball.

"What do you think of this?" she asked, holding up a scarlet gown to her.

"Aye, it's bonny," he said. He was far more interested in her skin. It was glowing.

"Do you like it more or less than this one?" she asked, and held up a gown of pale blue silk with tiny seed pearls sewed along the hem and sleeves.

"Bonny, the both of them, aye," he agreed.

Margot's brow creased. She stood studying the wardrobe. She pulled out another gown that, quite honestly, looked like the others. The only difference was that it was a forest green. She looked at Arran, then at the gown. "What do you think?"

He thought she ought to choose a color and be done with it. They were all the same to his undiscerning eye. He shrugged. "Bonny," he said again.

Margot sighed with irritation. "Will you not help me? I haven't the least idea which to wear. Which one suits? And please, for God's sake, don't say *bonny.*"

"What will you have me say, then?" he asked, confused. "All of them are . . . *boidheach.*"

Big green eyes blinked back at him. "I don't know what that means!"

"It means . . . bonny," he said helplessly.

Margot groaned to the ceiling. "Will you please choose one?"

"All right. I choose the red one," he said, pointing to the first one she had discarded across her daybed.

Margot looked at the scarlet one. She frowned. She looked at the forest green one she held. "Not this one?"

"*Ach,* I canna help you," Arran said, and stood up, striding across her dressing room. "Wear what you like, Margot. They're all bloody well bonny!" He strode out the door, frustrated that he'd walked all the way here to be tormented in such a way. He was a laird, for God's sake. He had no business choosing gowns.

But the excitement in and around Balhaire was infectious, all the same. Mackenzies were suddenly taking airs, concerned about ghillie brogues and sporrans and the like. On the night of the ball, Arran dressed in the tradition of plaids and formal coats. He went to Margot's dressing room and entered without knocking. She'd complained of that, too, by the by, and thought he ought to be announced in his own bloody house before he entered. He maintained if he would be made to march halfway across the Highlands to see her, he'd enter as he pleased.

This time, though, he was instantly brought to a halt. His wife, his beautiful wife, was dressed in the dark green silk gown with seed pearls interspersed between red crystals in a display of spirals and curls across the stomacher. Her hair was styled in a towering pile of auburn, with more seed pearls threaded into her hair. She looked regal and beautiful, and he was over-whelmed with a rush of prideful affection that made him feel warm in his coat. "Margot," he said. "*Diah,* but you are bonny, aye? You bring to mind a noble queen."

She beamed with delight at him, and her smile filled him up with pleasurable warmth. "A *queen.* That's very kind of you to say," she said, blushing, and curtsied grandly. "Thank you. What do you think of this?" she asked, and laid her fingers across a strand of pearls that looped twice around her throat, and from which hung a ruby that brushed the swell of her breasts above her stays. "I'm not certain of it. Nell said it was perfect, but I thought it might be too ornate."

"Lass . . . you're a vision. You are perfect." He bowed formally and held out his hand to her. She smiled and put her hand in his. She was happy. Quite happy. Arran thought that perhaps things would turn now, that this was what was needed to make her feel at home here.

He was, at last, giving her what she wanted.

The walked down to the great hall together, Arran assuring her the champagne had come. A hush fell over the great hall when they entered. Arran was proud — his clansmen seemed as taken with Margot and her attire as she was with the changes in this room. He could see them all studying her, could see women glance down at their best gowns and could imagine them finding the garments wanting. Was that not the way it should be? Should not the lady of the house be dressed in the finest? Nevertheless, he was proud of his people, too — they'd all dressed for the occasion. Plaids were cleaned and pressed, and the ladies' gowns a sea of color.

But none of them had styled their hair as Margot had. None of them wore jewels glittering at their throats. None of them had seed pearls embroidered into their stomachers.

Margot's grip of his arm tightened. "They're wearing the plaid," she whispered.

"Aye."

"But . . ." She glanced up at iron candle rings above the hall.

"The candles are beeswax," he bragged.

Her gaze moved to the tartan draperies he'd ordered hung over the windows so her view was not that of the bailey. He'd even had the dogs taken down to the kitchens tonight so they'd not be underfoot for the dancing.

"Come," Arran said. He had to tug her a little, but Margot came with him across the great hall. She smiled at the Mackenzies and politely thanked them for attending. When they reached the dais, Arran seated her in an upholstered chair and motioned Fergus to come forward. "Champagne for milady," he said. "Whisky for me." Then he sat beside her, took her hand in his and asked warmly, "What do you think, then, wife? Here is your society," he said proudly, sweeping his arm to the many souls gathered in the hall.

"My society?"

"Aye. It's what you've wanted, it is no'? Society."

She looked at him as if he were speaking Gaelic. "Yes, but . . . where are your neighbors?"

"My neighbors?" He laughed. "These are my neighbors."

She seemed oddly disappointed by that. But she smiled again when Fergus served her champagne in a crystal flute, and asked excitedly, "When will the dancing begin?"

"Now." He signaled the musicians, and they began with a familiar jig.

Griselda, he noticed, was the first one to stand up with her current suitor.

"Would you like —"

"No, no . . . let them begin. We'll dance the next set, shall we?" She smiled and sipped her champagne.

The floor was quickly full of dancers, and

they began in earnest, kicking up their heels in true Scots fashion, the voices around them rising with the gaiety of the occasion. They'd gone down the line once, and Arran looked to Margot to see her enjoyment.

But Margot didn't look as if she was enjoying it at all. She looked dismayed. "What is wrong?" he asked.

She turned her gaze to him, and he was surprised by the terror in her eyes. "Nell and I practiced all week."

Arran laughed. "You donna need a lot of practice for this," he said, and stood up. "Lady Mackenzie, will you dance with me, then?"

"No," she said immediately. "No, I can't."

"Margot —"

"Please don't ask me again, Arran. I won't dance."

She stood up and hurried off the dais, disappearing into the crowd.

Arran slowly resumed his seat, bewildered. What had just happened?

It was a quarter of an hour before she came back, coming up the dais steps as if she were trudging to her doom. She took her seat and stared straight ahead, her hands curled tightly on the arms.

All around them, Mackenzies were dancing and shouting in their tongue, drinking ale — they did not seem to care for the champagne he'd had brought in from England for a dear price — and calling up to the laird and lady their felicitations on their marriage. Margot said nothing. She did not smile, did not nod, did nothing to acknowledge them.

Arran grew angry with her. He didn't understand her sullen behavior, her refusal to dance when she'd seemed so excited by the prospect. When he could bear it no more, he stood up and walked off the dais, and asked a lass to dance with him.

He didn't know how many sets he spun through, but he drank and laughed and enjoyed himself. He would not sit on the dais with his sullen bride.

When he at last looked to the dais, he was not surprised to see she'd gone.

Fueled by whisky and humiliation, he went in search of her. He found her in her bed. Margot's beautiful dress was lying in a heap on the floor, and the pieces of hair she'd used to arrange her coif were thrown onto her dressing table. He sent the maid scurrying.

"What is the matter with you, then?" he demanded.

She sat up and stared at him. "Is it not obvious?"

"*Obvious?*" he exclaimed hotly. "There is no' a bloody thing obvious about you, Margot. I gave a *ball* for you, and here you are, crying into your pillow like a child!"

"I'm not crying into my pillow. I am plotting my escape!"

"You want to escape?" He threw open the door and gestured to it. "Go. Escape." When she did not move, he slammed the door shut and heard the sound of it reverberating down the stairs.

"You canna imagine the effort it has taken to give you this ball —"

"That wasn't a ball!" she cried, and suddenly swung out of the bed, stalking to her vanity. "That was just another night in your great hall!"

"*Diah*, but you are a petulant child, are you no'? Those people came to celebrate your marriage, and what do you do, then? You sulk and mope and then flee like a rabbit instead of welcoming them as you ought as lady of this house and clan!"

She slammed down the hairbrush she'd just picked up. "I tried to greet them, but they speak in that awful language! Not one of them wore a ball gown or a proper evening coat. It was all plaid! They wouldn't drink the champagne, and dear God, the dancing!" she exclaimed, shaking her hands

108

to the ceiling.

"You wanted dancing!"

"Not *that* sort of dancing! I've never seen anything like it!"

"You hate it all, is that it?"

She gasped and looked at him. "No, that's not — I never said that."

"You didna say it, Margot, but it is in your every move, your every glance, your every look! You are —"

He caught himself. He ran both hands over his head and sighed.

"What? What am I?" she demanded, folding her arms tightly. Defensively.

"Bloody impossible, aye?"

"So are you. And this place."

"Diah, what is *wrong?"* he roared to the rafters. "I canna put it to rights if you willna tell me what it is."

Margot stared at him. She seemed to be debating what she would say. She rubbed her nape and said, "Frankly, I'm a poor dancer and I don't know —"

He snorted.

Her face darkened. "You asked, didn't you?"

"For all that is holy, I donna know how to please you," he said coldly.

"And I don't know how to please *you,"* she snapped.

Her tone undid Arran — he strode forward, caught her by the arm and whirled her around. "Enough of playing the wounded lass, Margot. We are married, we are, and you may as well learn to live with it as fight it, aye? You are a Scot now."

"Never," she said defiantly.

Her eyes were glittering in the low light. Her hair fell wildly about her shoulders. It was funny in a strange way — Arran had always thought himself full of might, capable of anything. But he was a very weak man when it came to Margot. She was wretched and haughty, and yet he could see her youth and the abject vulnerability in her eyes.

He cupped her face with his hand, stroked her cheek. "I'm asking . . . no, I'm *begging* you. Donna make this harder than it is, aye?"

There it was, a single tear sliding from the corner of her eye. "I can't possibly make it any harder than it is," she muttered, and closed her eyes and lifted her face to him.

Arran, confused as he always was by her, kissed her. He drew her to the bed, removed her clothes, covered her body in kisses. And as he sank between her thighs and she drew up her knees and curled her fists in his hair, gasping with pleasure at what his tongue

110

was doing to her, he thought that at least they had this. If nothing else, they had this.

CHAPTER FIVE

Balhaire
1710

If there was one thing Arran held as irrefutable fact, it was that the English and women could never be completely trusted. So when he heard a rustling about sometime in the night, long after the fire had turned to embers, he was not surprised to see Margot standing at his chest of drawers, one of the bed linens wrapped loosely about her.

He admired her for a moment as she rose up on her toes and examined the articles on top of the chest. One long, shapely leg was visible. Waves of auburn hair fell almost to her waist, ending a few inches above the curve of her hip. She touched his things, and her delicate, manicured fingers fluttered over the folded vellum that Jock had brought to Arran, an urgent message from the chieftain of the MacLearys of Mallaig.

He silently rose up on one elbow, watching her as she picked up the vellum between finger and thumb and seemed to debate opening it.

God, but she was beautiful, he thought, as he carefully and soundlessly removed himself from the bed. It had been her eyes that had captured Arran's fancy when he first saw her. Wide, deep-set eyes, the color of them reminding him of the moss that grew on the trees at Balhaire, and her gaze discerning. He'd known right away, before even hearing her speak, that she was a perceptive lass.

He'd also known, by the way those eyes had looked at him, that she'd been a wee bit beguiled by him, too.

He made his way to stand behind her and folded his arms across his chest. "What are you doing there?"

With a gasp, she dropped the vellum and groped around the top of the chest as she whirled around to face him. "I couldn't sleep."

"Could you no'?"

She suddenly thrust a gold chain into his face. "Who is *this* for?"

"For you, *leannan*," he said smoothly, and reached around her, pushing the vellum under a pair of gloves.

"That's absurd."

"Who else?" he asked easily, and pried the necklace from her hand. He'd actually taken it in trade for a pistol.

"Maybe the girl who was sitting in your lap when I arrived," she said curtly, her brows dipping into a vee.

He frowned at her attempt to appear jealous and casually laid his hand across her throat. "Would I have loved you as I did tonight if this gold was for that wee strumpet?" He turned Margot about, pushed her mane of hair out of his way and draped the necklace around her throat. He bent his head to kiss her neck. He was aroused again and pushed his erection into her hips. "It's yours now."

"I don't want it," she said, but made no move to remove it.

Arran reached around her abdomen, grabbed the linen and yanked it free of her body. Margot didn't resist; she leaned back against him, her hands sliding down his thighs. She was different than before. Now she seemed to understand the power she wielded over him.

He took her by the wrist and pulled her back to the bed with him, falling onto it and dragging her along to straddle him.

Margot sighed and dug her fingers into his chest. "You're insatiable," she said, and began to move on him, sliding against his erection.

"Mmm." He'd not argue. He had strong appetites for life. He stroked her cheek with his knuckle.

Margot gave him a cool, sultry smile and turned her head, kissing his hand. That was the sort of smile that could inflame a man's blood. *Pleasant,* Jock had said. What a ridiculous word. Ah, but it hurt him to look at her now, Arran thought, as he lifted her hips and guided her onto him.

She sighed, closed her eyes and let her head fall back as she sank down onto him.

This beauty was a liar and was here for some reason he would have to ferret out. But in his heart, fool that he was, he wished she had come back for him. He wished it was true that she wanted to rekindle their marriage. In spite of their differences, he was a loyal man, a man of his word, and he had come to care for his timid, naive wife, in spite of their rocky beginning.

But she hadn't come back for him. She did not want to rekindle their marriage and likely never would. Worse, it was up to him to discover what she was about.

At present, however, she had begun to move on his cock, her eyes the color of a warm summer sea now. She leaned over him and said, "Do you find me haughty now?"

"*Uist,*" he said, silencing her, and began to move more earnestly inside her. He watched her face this time. She'd seen the naked truth in him the first time they'd come together tonight, and this time, he was looking for something, anything, to inform him. But Arran was soon swept under by the ecstasy of her body, of the pleasure of a woman's touch, of the desire that had been buried for three years. In the midst of it, when her hair formed a curtain around them, in the low light of the hearth, he saw an unexpected glimmer in her eyes.

He saw sorrow. *Sorrow.*

For him? For their marriage? For herself?

Their lovemaking had at last exhausted them both, and he fell asleep, wondering.

Early in the morning, Arran had to extract himself from her limbs — she'd rolled into him, tangling herself around him.

It was not yet dawn, so he washed with the cold water of the basin in an adjoining room and dressed. When he returned to the bedchamber, Margot hadn't moved. She was sound asleep, her face deceivingly angelic. He glanced around the clutter of his chamber. Margot had brought nothing other than her clothes last night. He'd send her maid to dress her.

He walked to his chest, retrieved the vellum from beneath his gloves, tucked it into his waistcoat and then stepped out of the room.

There was a sleeping, slack-jawed lad sprawled just outside his door on a cloak. Jock had put him there, probably fearing Margot intended to cut his laird's throat. Arran couldn't help but smile at that — Jock trusted the English and women even less than he. He nudged the lad with his boot, and the young man came up like a shot, his eyes wide with sleep and fear.

"Milord," he said.

"Go to your bed now. The lady is sleeping."

The lad picked up his cloak and stumbled clumsily down the hall.

Arran walked down the hall to his study. It was a small room, the original purpose lost. He liked that it adjoined his dressing room. He sat himself at a desk stacked with papers and books, shipping ledgers and the household accounts. He'd been hard at work of late, preparing for a voyage that would take him to France to trade wool for cloth and wine, which he would then ferry to Ireland to sell or trade for leather goods.

Fergus appeared at the door of his study, looking bleary-eyed, his thinning hair in complete disarray. "Will you break your fast, laird?"

"Aye," he said. "I'll have it here. Send Jock to me when he comes."

Jock joined him a quarter of an hour later. Unlike Fergus, Jock looked as fresh as a spring daffodil. He arched a thick, dark brow above a smug smile. "And how does the morning find you, laird?" he asked with much jocularity. "I expected you to be abed this morning."

Arran smiled. "And risk a knife at my neck?"

Jock laughed.

"What does the day bring?" Arran asked.

"We've men training for unarmed conflict this morn," Jock said, settling into a chair across from him.

Arran perked up at that. He had learned to fight at his father's knee and now taught young men from his clan. His soldiers were widely regarded as some of the fiercest men in all of Britain. "I could use a good brawl just now," he said, rubbing his eyes. There was nothing quite like throwing a punch or two when he was feeling at sixes and sevens, and he was certainly feeling that way this morning. Disappointment, anger, hope and carnal bliss were all mixing dangerously in him.

Why did women have to be so bloody treacherous?

"Did you question the Englishmen?" he asked.

Jock nodded. "Aye, that I did. But they were no' forthcoming."

"And the maid?"

"A cake-headed lass, that one," Jock said with a flick of his wrist. "What do you make of it all?"

"I donna know," Arran admitted. He sighed, removed the vellum from his pocket and tossed it onto the desk. "I caught her in the night at my chest of drawers with this almost in hand," he said.

"Ah. Having a look about, was she?"

"I can think of only two reasons she's come back. Either her father has put her out of the house . . . or he's sent her here for a reason. A pampered woman does no' undertake such a long journey by her own doing."

"But what reason?" Jock asked. He looked at the letter Arran had tossed onto the desk, but he made no move to take it. He knew what it said — MacLeary had written to warn them about rumblings from England. It was well-known that some of the more influential Jacobite clansmen — Scots who were aligned with the son of the deposed king, James Stuart — were increasingly unhappy with the union and oppressive taxation. Rumors abounded that there were those who were plotting a second time to put James Stuart on the throne. Then again, wild rumors were commonplace since the Acts of Union were signed three years ago. This time was different, however, as Mac-Leary had written that Arran's name had been included as one of the unhappy chieftains. It was the first time he had been mentioned as a Jacobite.

Arran had been surprised by the contents of the letter when he'd first received it. He'd been very careful to walk a thin line between chieftains who wanted Scottish independence and the Scotsmen who saw opportunities in the union with England. Certainly he had taken advantage of the union by increasing his trade with France and Ireland. He'd built a wealth where most clans were suffering. He raised cattle and sheep he sent to Glasgow and Edinburgh markets. He traded wool for silks with France. He trained soldiers who found good wages with the English army. And the glen that surrounded Balhaire had soil rich enough that he could grow enough food to feed his own clan. He was one of the few chieftains who had managed to stem the rising tide of emigration and provide for his people.

He was not a Jacobite, and suddenly to be labeled as one had baffled him. Something was definitely amiss.

A kitchen wench appeared with a tray. She set it before Arran, dipped a curtsy and scurried out.

"I donna know what Norwood is about," Arran said between healthy bites of his breakfast. "But it is no coincidence that my wife should miraculously appear and profess a change of heart so soon after I received that letter, aye?"

"Aye," said Jock. "My guess is that he has sent her. But for what reason?"

Arran shook his head. "I've done my duty by her, have I no'? I've sent her money. I've said no' a single ill word against her or him."

Jock shrugged. "Perhaps it is a coincidence. Perhaps it is only that he believes a wife belongs with her husband and has turned her out."

"No," Arran said. "He'd have turned her out long ago were that the reason. It is something more. And to have my name mentioned with the Jacobites just before she has come . . . it stinks to heaven, it does."

Jock nodded. "What do you intend to do, then?"

Arran dropped his fork and leaned back, looking toward the window. The sun was just coming up on the day, rising up over the hills, casting long purple shadows. As much as he'd enjoyed last night, he didn't trust her. This homecoming was gravely wrong.

There was something else niggling at him, too. The sadness he'd seen in her eyes. Did she regret what she'd done three years ago? Or did she regret that she was about to slide the knife into his back? "By the by, how long has it been since you've had word from Dermid?" he asked, referring to the man he kept in England to keep eyes on his wife.

Jock thought about it. "A month. Perhaps longer."

Arran frowned at that. "It's no' like the lad to have allowed something like this to have happened without sending word."

"It's no' like him," Jock agreed. "What do you intend to do?"

Arran dropped the last bit of bread and put his hand to his abdomen. He was suddenly filled with foreboding. "Send her back to England," he said. "Find four of our best men to accompany her and the fops she rode in with. I'll give her the news myself."

Jock stood to go.

"Did you have a look through her things?"

Arran asked as Jock walked across the room.

"Aye," Jock said with a sigh. He looked back at Arran. "We had to subdue her maid, we did. The lass bloody well *bit* me," he added, holding out his hand to show Arran. He gave a curious shake of his head. Poor Jock would always be confounded by women. "I found nothing but gowns and shoes and the like," Jock continued. "Quite a lot of it, too — I've never understood why a woman needs so many bloody shoes. A lot of bother if you ask me."

Jock quit the study, leaving Arran alone.

He looked to the small window. *Why, Margot? Have you no' harmed me enough?*

The memory of her flight from him had dulled with time, certainly, but there were still moments that the pain still felt raw, an open wound exposed to bitter wind.

He hadn't been surprised by her departure, not really. They had argued several days before, at an impasse once more about the course of their marriage. She couldn't seem to find her bearings at Balhaire. She had expectations that did not fit their clan and, Arran could admit, his clan had expectations of Margot that she'd been too young and inexperienced to meet.

He'd thought long and hard about this over the years, and he realized now what he didn't really understand then — Margot Armstrong had been pampered and served from the day she was born. She knew no other way. But at Balhaire, the clan was family — everyone contributed to the greater good. Arran had expected, had assumed, that she would adopt this way of life. Unfortunately, the very few attempts Margot made had been badly done, from a place of superiority. And his clan . . . *Diah,* but they would give no quarter.

It had been a fractious four months of trial and error, and yet Arran had seen a side to Margot that he'd come to adore.

He heard the door of his study swing open and turned his head; Old Roy had followed his scent and ambled over to Arran to have his head scratched.

Arran smiled down at the dog, suddenly reminded of a cold winter morning he'd coaxed Margot out of her rooms and down to the kennels, where a litter of weaned pups were frolicking in a box of straw. They would be herding dogs, but that morning they were just black-and-white balls of soft cotton, tumbling over each other and onto the straw that had been lain down for them.

He would never forget the look of delight on Margot's face. She'd fallen to her knees, laughing as a pair of them had climbed up onto her lap. Arran, too, went down on a knee beside her, and the two of them had remained in that small space with the pups, laughing together at their ungainly attempts to play and move. They had playfully named the five pups. She'd told him about a small dog she'd had as a child, one that she would dress in clothes the housekeeper made for her and take about the garden in a perambulator.

There were other moments like that — unguarded, easy, companionable moments when Arran had seen the promise of their union. Moments when he'd felt things for his beautiful wife he would not have thought were possible only weeks before. He'd seen another side of Margot, and he had loved her.

Margot clearly had not shared his optimistic vision. Why they'd argued so vehemently that day, he could no longer recall. He'd been gone for a few days, hunting red stags. He'd been tired and hungry, and what he recalled most vividly were the tears streaking her face, another round of tears he despised and was helpless to understand. "I want to go home," she'd said flatly. "I don't want to live here like this."

"Aye, then, go. We'll all be the better for it," he'd snapped, and he'd stormed out of her room, furious with her, with himself.

But he hadn't meant it.

Those were angry words, spoken in a moment of fury. He had let them disappear into thin air with so many other angry words. He'd been careless, thoughtless — because he had believed that as they had sworn to each other and to God that they would stride forward in conjugal fealty, somehow they would forge a path in spite of their many differences.

Jock told him she was leaving a day or two later, and Arran still didn't believe it. He went about his tasks that morning, disbelieving. He told Jock to let her go if that was what she wanted, because he never believed she would.

Diah, what a fool.

He didn't like to think of that day. It still pained him — aye, pain, the sort of pain he'd never in his life experienced. He'd come riding up from the cove with a few of his men and had seen the coach pulling away from Balhaire. He had reined to a halt, had glared at her as she'd passed and as the agony of this reality had settled into his marrow. The burn was deep — he was humiliated before his clan and at the same time made to understand what an ignorant man he was. And the burn was accompanied by the ache of watching someone leave him, someone whom he had, against all odds, come to care for very much.

A fool. There was no other word for him.

Arran would never forget that pain, as it burned in him yet. And he realized, as he scratched Old Roy behind the ears, that the time for reconciliation had come and gone. He'd not be made a fool of again.

CHAPTER SIX

Margot was awakened by a dour-faced woman who announced a bath would be drawn for her, then shoved the draperies aside with such verve that Margot cried out when she was blinded by the sun. "Thank you," she said, turning her face to the pillow. "Would you be so kind as to send my maid?"

The woman muttered something on the way out. Margot waited until she heard the door close before she pushed herself up to sit and brushed back the hair from her eyes. She was exhausted. And deliciously sore. And *confused.*

Last night had not been the homecoming she'd expected. Arran had confounded her. The passion he'd shown her — raw, formidable anger and desire — had moved her. She'd been dangerously inflamed by it, her body wanting the coarseness of it all.

But then there had been that slender moment, that tender caress. It had hardly happened at all — but she had felt it. She had *seen it.* And then he had made her turn her head.

What did it mean? Did he despise her? Was there a part of him that didn't? Or had it been only a moment?

Arran seemed different to her now. Older. Wiser. Much more sure of himself than he'd been before. And whatever he'd meant by that touch, however truthful, it had awakened emotions Margot was not prepared to face. Such as regret. Buckets and buckets of regret for leaving him at all. For not having left sooner. Regret that she'd not known how to defy her father and never enter this marriage, regret that she'd allowed herself to be ruled by her emotions for the short months she'd spent here.

In the time she'd been gone from Balhaire, Margot had never forgotten what her husband aroused in her. But the actual physical sensations, so powerful in the course of the act, had dimmed with time. The animal attraction and unbridled pleasure he'd shown her in this bed last night had staggered her.

Before, with few words between them, she'd always felt cherished and beautiful. But the man who showed her that depth of passion was never the same man who rode out with his men the next morning. The man who whispered his devotion to her in this bed was not the same man who seemed inconvenienced by her beyond this room.

And yet, last night, she'd felt such *longing*. Sweet Jesus, such undiluted yearning filling her veins and heart. For what, exactly, Margot didn't know. But she'd realized, after they'd come together a second time, that something was missing in her, something vital, and the hunger felt fresh.

Margot didn't hate Arran, had never *hated* Arran — but she had hated her situation with such intensity that it had eaten away at her and perhaps had clouded her judgment at times. The transition to Scotland had been difficult, to be sure. Her rage had simmered, then turned wild over the circumstances of her marriage, forced by a father who'd demanded her loyalty at the tender age of seventeen, who had allowed her to be carted off without any real knowledge of the world at all, much less the ruggedness of the Highlands — or marriage, for that matter — and there had left her to fend for herself while her husband carried on with his clan.

It had been all too much for her. That last argument with Arran had been explosive and jarring, both of them shouting. She'd tried to express her unhappiness to Arran, how she felt as if she were a single boat on a vast ocean, floating along with no oars and no hope of rescue.

"God help us," he'd said. "For you're no' the only ship adrift in this marriage, Margot."

She never asked him what he meant by that.

Oh, but there were so many hurtful things said between them. And she'd had no one to go to, no friends in Scotland. It seemed like the harder she tried, the less anyone wanted to befriend her.

Perhaps it hardly mattered, because in the end, she lost patience with the situation entirely.

She left Scotland shortly after that final argument. It hadn't been an escape, really, because as the coach was pulling through the massive gates of Balhaire, Arran and his men had come riding up from the sea. He had reined to a halt to the side of the road to let the coach pass. She would never forget the stony look he gave her as the coach slowly rolled by. He remained on his horse, his fists clenched as tightly as his jaw, watching her go.

He hadn't tried to stop her. She'd imagined him happy to be relieved of her.

When the coach had passed, he spurred his horse through the gates and behind the castle walls, and his men had followed him, and that was the last she saw of him. She had collapsed onto the leather squabs of the coach, heartbroken. She'd been such a foolish girl then, wanting both worlds. She'd wanted desperately to go home, away from that crude castle and society. But she had also wanted him to fight for her.

Ah, what silly, romantic notions lived in the minds of girls who were not yet women.

In England, with time, Margot had managed to detach what feelings she had for Arran Mackenzie and go on about her life. Her father had been unhappy with her, but he'd assured her he understood. *"Of course it is well-known that the Highlands are full of barbarians,"* he'd said without hesitation. She'd thought it odd that he did not seem to see the irony in how he had been quite at ease marrying his daughter off to one. *"You've done your duty, my girl."* Now that he had his agreements and lands in Scotland, made inviolable by her marriage to Mackenzie, he'd seemed satisfied.

He'd left Margot well enough alone, and she had turned her attention to . . . what? Nothing. There was no life to speak of as an estranged wife of some distant Scottish chieftain. She was a novelty — that was all. A married woman with no husband in sight who enjoyed vast liberties that other women did not. Margot had a robust social life, free to come and go as she pleased. She hosted soirees and flirted with gentlemen. She attended balls and suppers and flirted with more gentlemen. She was wanted by those men, pursued and courted by those men. However, that attention never seemed enough.

Their desire for her — and hers for them, no matter how shallow — only added to the unease in her. Margot could see years stretching out before her with a lot of flirting and not much else, because she was married. She had opportunity to be touched, of course — men pursued her for that very reason. But Margot had taken a vow before God to remain faithful. She couldn't dishonor her word so completely and irrevocably. She was clinging to the last shreds of her dignity and her moral compass as it was. She began to feel quite numbed by her predicament, as if she was merely going through each day, waiting for something.

Margot sighed and used both hands to push her hair from her face. Her heart was pounding with the memories of last night. Was it possible that she and her husband, both of them older and wiser now, could actually resume their broken marriage? Was it possible that the rumors about him were true? Could this man, this fiercely independent, hardworking man, honestly plot against the queen — *her* queen? No, Margot couldn't believe it, no matter what her father said.

But then again, what did she know of Arran Mackenzie, really? Especially not now, especially after so much time. She didn't know him. She didn't know much of anything anymore.

Nevertheless, she couldn't bear to think what might happen to him if he were truly committing treason. Part of her wanted to warn him. Another part of her wanted to catch him in the act. Part of her wanted to rewind the clock, to go back to that night of Lynetta's birthday ball, so that she could refuse to meet him at all. Unfortunately, it was far too late for that. She was quite mired in this marriage.

Everything about this so-called reunion had happened so quickly, Margot still wasn't certain how it had come to pass. It had begun when her oldest brother, Bryce, had accosted her one evening when she'd arrived home after dining with friends at the home of Sir Ian Andrews. It had been a lively evening — Lynetta was newly engaged to Mr. Fitzgerald, and Margot had passed the time by shamelessly teasing poor Mr. Partridge, who was smitten with her.

She'd come home feeling jocular and a bit tipsy. Bryce was waiting. He was dressed in riding clothes and was not wearing a wig. He looked as if he'd only just arrived home. His jaw was set implacably, his demeanor grim. "Where have you been?"

"Dining at the home of Sir Andrews. Why?"

"Father needs to speak with you," he said, and clasped her elbow and escorted her into the library.

Her father was seated at the hearth with a book in his hand, a blanket draped over his lap. At his elbow, a glass of port. He smiled kindly when Bryce escorted her into the room. Margot's beloved half brother, Knox, was standing at the window. He was dressed impeccably in a gold coat and dark brown pantaloons. He tried to smile at Margot, too, but he couldn't seem to muster it and looked away.

In that moment, Margot knew something unpleasant was about to occur.

"Ah, Margot, my love," her father said.

"Come." He beckoned her to his side. Margot pulled free of Bryce's grip and went to her father, leaning down to kiss his cheek. "You should be abed, Pappa."

"As should you, darling. It is unbecoming of a married woman to be so late in the company of gentlemen who are not her husband."

He rarely mentioned Arran, and Margot thought it odd that he should mention him now.

"Which is why it now seems a good time for you to return to your husband."

Margot's heart fluttered with sudden anxiety. She glanced at her brothers. "I beg your pardon?"

"You are to Scotland," her father said.

Margot gaped at him. "Why? Because I have dined at the home of Sir Andrews? I can't go back to Scotland, Pappa!"

"Calm yourself," her father said sternly. "You are needed."

"*Needed!* How could I possibly —"

"Your *husband* is a traitor." He said it suddenly and acidly, as if she'd brought him a diseased piece of meat, in spite of his having brought Arran to her.

"What? That's not possible. There has obviously been some mistake —"

"The mistake is that you fled your marriage bed like a child and came crying home," Bryce said angrily.

"Bryce," her father said quietly. He stood up, walked to the sideboard. He poured a glass of port and held it out to Margot.

She shook her head, but he still held it out. "Drink it. Calm yourself."

Margot refused to take it. She would not *calm* herself. "Who has said it?" she asked. "Who has made you believe such a foul thing?"

"I have heard it from a reliable source. Don't look so shocked — I warned you there would be consequences for fleeing your husband."

She blinked at him in disbelief. He'd never warned her of anything! "You told me he was a barbarian," she reminded him.

"I did not make your match lightly," he continued, as if she hadn't spoken. "I staked my reputation on that match, vouching for the honor of all of Scotland for the sake of your children and my heirs."

For her children! He had vouched for it to line his own pockets. Margot looked at her brothers. Bryce was watching, but Knox was staring down at his feet. "What has happened?" she demanded.

"I swore to the queen that a union with Scotland would bring her wealth and power.

That every bloody man in that godforsaken land would be her loyal subject," her father said sharply, pointing north. He sounded like the vicar now, preaching from a pulpit. "I believed it so wholeheartedly that I gave my consent to the marriage of my only daughter to a Scottish chieftain. Do you know that it was *my* word that helped tip the balance to uniting Scotland and England? I made your match to make this nation strong and invincible. I was indispensable to the agreement. Now *your* husband seeks to make me *quite* dispensable!"

But that was not at all how it had gone. Her father was speaking as if Margot were completely ignorant of what had happened before. "You told me the match was meant to increase our holdings and provide for our future heirs. You said it was imperative that I do it for our family, Pappa. You never said anything about England and Scotland."

"There were many advantages to your marriage, which is why I agreed to it. That's why *you* agreed to it, if you've forgotten. It was your duty to this family."

"But I didn't agree to it! You *forced* me. You said, 'A woman's place is to bear sons to whomever her family decrees, and nothing else,' as I recall!"

"That *is* a woman's place! But then you

disobeyed me and came home," he said. "I was too lenient with you. I could hardly blame you, I suppose, knowing how the Scots are. But it has caused quite a lot of trouble for us all, and now you must repair it."

Margot began to feel ill. "*What* trouble?"

"What trouble, what trouble," Bryce mimicked her. "Men who have been made a fool will take their revenge, Margot. The husband you have left is in bed with the French. They are plotting to invade England and put James Stuart on the throne. Do you understand, Margot? They mean to take the throne from Queen Anne and install a *Catholic* with the help of England's mortal enemy."

That made no sense. Why would Arran involve himself in that? "But . . . he trains soldiers for the queen," she said uncertainly. "What proof is there?"

"You're a fool," Bryce snapped.

"Bryce," Knox said. "Be gentle."

Bryce turned away from Margot.

Her father took Margot's hand, much like he'd done the night he had introduced her to Arran, his plan already in place. "There is quite a lot you can't possibly understand, darling," he said, gentle once more. "When you left, you relieved him of any loyalty to

139

our agreement. An Englishman would not go back on his word, but a Scot?" He shrugged. "Now, who do you think will be made to pay for the sins of your husband?"

Margot's head was spinning. "Me?"

"*You?*" Bryce exploded, and then laughed. "Who the bloody hell are you?"

"No, Margot," her father said calmly. "*I* will be held accountable. I am the one who brought that bastard into England and into this family, and if he is a traitor, the queen and her men will look to me, as well. We will lose everything. We will be accused of conspiring with the rebels and the French and —" he squeezed her hand so tightly that it hurt "— and I might very well hang."

Margot's breath lodged in her lungs.

Her father was suddenly looming over her. He cupped her face, forcing her to look up at him. His eyes were bloodshot, as if he'd been drinking. "There is only one way to know if he plots against us without drawing attention to ourselves. And that is for you, his precious wife, to go and discover what he's about before anyone else. You must go with all due haste, Margot. You must make him tell you what he is about and then come back to me."

Margot stepped away from her father. She needed to breathe, to *think*. "If it is true, he won't tell me, Pappa. He despises me. I've not had a word from him in three years."

"And whose fault is that?" Bryce said snidely.

"You'd best hope that he tells you," her father said. "You cannot imagine the tragedy that will befall this family if you fail." He caught her arm, made her turn around to face him once more. "You are our only hope. Do you understand?"

"I don't understand any of it!" Margot exclaimed. "I cannot believe that Arran would do such a thing. And even if he has, he won't tell *me,* I assure you —"

Bryce suddenly grabbed her by the shoulder and pulled her around to face him, squeezing hard. "Then you'd best determine how to extract it from him. Spy if you must, lie if you must — we've got everything riding on this. Everything! So you'd best go and please your husband, Margot. Keep your mouth shut, do what you are wed to do, and open your legs and give the man what is his right."

"Bryce! That's enough!" Knox said, and pushed Bryce off Margot as she tried to expel the breath caught in her throat.

Now Margot shuddered at that memory. Her father and Bryce didn't care at all about her feelings in this, no more than when they'd arranged her marriage to Mackenzie. Once again she argued and pleaded, but her father wouldn't even look at her.

Knox was the only one to soothe her. He'd come to her after that wretched arguing had depleted her and filled her with despair. "You know that I will miss you desperately," he said fondly.

Knox Armstrong, her bastard brother, the son of a woman whose identity Knox claimed never to have known. He was the same age as she, both of them twenty-one now, and both of them seven years younger than Bryce. They had grown up in the nursery together, had been as close to one another as twins. When they were thirteen, Knox was sent to apprentice with a duke. He'd come back a grown man with gold hair and dancing blue eyes.

Margot loved Knox above all others.

"You won't miss me. I don't intend to go. Who has said this about Mackenzie, Knox?" she asked him plaintively. "How can it be true?"

Knox shrugged. "I know only as much as you, dear heart. I know only that Father met Sir Richard Worthing, who had been in the company of Thomas Dunn from London. He was quite agitated after speaking with them. That's all I know, really, other than

142

that Sir Worthing will accompany you to Balhaire."

"No. I won't go."

Knox put his arm around her. "Listen to me, love. If there is even an ounce of truth, we must know it, or all will be lost. There is no one else who can do this, is there? Think if I or Bryce were to appear at Balhaire — he'd never give us entry."

Dear God, he was right.

"Look, I have a gift for you." He handed her a box.

Margot opened it; it was lined with silver paper, and beneath the folds of the paper was a pair of goatskin riding gloves. "Knox . . . they're beautiful," she said, pressing them to her face.

"Let Mackenzie know that you've been well-cared-for here." He drew her to him, and as tears came to Margot's eyes, he held her. "It's not as difficult as you think," he assured her.

"You don't know him," she said of her husband. "He's very clever. He will not be happy to see me, Knox."

"You do your beauty a disservice, darling. Men are simple creatures. He might be angry at first, but like all men, he wants to feel as if he is the master of his world and there is a woman to notice and adore him for it. Do that, and he will give you whatever you want."

"He won't tell me about the French," she said plaintively. "He *won't*. I know this man. He will suspect my motives for coming back, and especially if I ask him any questions."

"Then don't ask," Knox said simply.

"There is no one else I may speak to!" she said. "Pappa said I must not tell anyone why I've come back, not even Nell. How am I to discover what he's about if I can't ask him?"

"Observe, love. Look through his things. Listen." He smiled and touched her cheek. "You must trust *your* cunning . . . and your allure. Believe me when I tell you that he will eventually confess all to you. He will give you whatever your heart desires, and you will be home in time for Lynetta's nuptials."

Margot groaned now as she recalled that conversation with Knox. She couldn't imagine Arran confessing anything to her after all that had happened.

She looked to the chest of drawers, to where she'd seen the folded letter last night. She had no idea what she was looking for, really. Would a man of Arran's stature and cunning outline his plans in writing, then leave them on his chest of drawers? That

144

seemed ridiculous. So what, then, was she supposed to find?

Maybe she at least ought to have a look at that letter. Maybe it was from someone in France, someone sending word of when the French would arrive. Could it be so simple?

She wrapped part of the bed linens around her, stood up and looked around the room. In the morning light, she saw the undignified mess of his chambers, something she hadn't noticed last night in those anxious moments after he'd escorted her up. His clothes and boots and a sword or two were scattered about the chairs and floor as if a cyclone had torn through the room. A table near the cold hearth was stacked high with papers and gloves and a pistol.

She glanced down and realized that she'd walked across his buckskins last night, thinking they were carpet. A whisky bottle was on the edge of the rug underneath the buckskins, its contents apparently having spilled out at some point. "Goodness," she said to herself. "Whatever has become of Mrs. Abernathy?"

The room smelled of smoke and intercourse; Margot moved to a window and cranked it open, breathing in the cool morning air. She could see outside the walls here, to the hills beyond, shrouded in the morning mists. The country here had seemed bleak to her when she'd first arrived, but she had come to appreciate its beauty. Balhaire stood a half mile from the sea and what felt like millions of miles from any proper civilization.

Margot turned from the vista and padded across the carpet to the chest of drawers in search of the grimy, folded bit of vellum she'd seen last night. She lifted up the things on top of his bureau, looking for it — but it seemed the vellum was gone.

She absently fingered the gold necklace he'd put around her neck as she thought about it. He'd obviously taken the letter with him this morning. Had he taken it to keep her from reading it? Or had he simply taken it to respond to whoever had written it?

She turned away from the chest and leaned against it. What was she to do now? How did one spy on one's estranged husband?

The door swung open and the dour-faced woman appeared once again. "Your maid is no' to be found, then," she announced, sounding vexed. "I'll help you to dress, then, aye?"

God, please no. But Margot smiled. "Thank you," she said, and mentally prepared herself to face her first full day back at Balhaire as a pariah.

CHAPTER SEVEN

Margot's maid, Nell, was hotter than the bathwater that had been drawn for her.

"How crude it was, milady," she said angrily as she stalked around the old rooms Margot had once occupied, laying out gowns from which Margot would choose. "That man as big as a tree come in here as if he owned this pile of rocks and demanded to be shown your things!"

Jock, she meant. Margot stepped into the bath and sank down into the hot water.

"I says, 'You can't go looking through my lady's things,' and *he* says, 'Stand aside, you wee nymph. I've no bloody time for it.' Beggin' your pardon," she added hastily in apology for her language, and dipped a curtsy.

"It's all right," Margot said. The hot water felt good on her body, particularly those spots that had not been so well used in a very long time. She leaned back and closed her eyes as Nell stomped about, listening to the sweep of her gown on the carpet as she ranted about her encounter with Jock.

"I don't like it here," Nell said, tossing her blond head. "Never did. It's not right that a man can come into a lady's chamber and put his big paws into her things and stir them about like a mutton stew. And with no regard for costly lace and silk! My father always said Scots were hard-hearted and the only redeeming thing about them was the road they built to England."

Margot laughed at that. "They're not as bad as that." She sat up in the bath, water pouring off her shoulders and breasts. "Come and help me wash my hair."

When she'd dressed and Nell had put her wet hair up, Margot ventured out of her rooms. She went down the curving stairs to the main floor. She heard voices in the great hall, Jock's rising above the others. Margot walked in the opposite direction of all those Mackenzies and out the front door.

The mists had lifted and left in their wake a blindingly bright day, and she stood a moment to let her eyes adjust, her gaze landing on Sweeney Mackenzie in the company of three men. At least Sweeney had been kind to her before. She'd never been able to determine exactly where Sweeney fell on the chain of command at Balhaire, but he was always about. She strode forward.

"Good day, Sweeney."

He looked surprised to see her. "G-good day, m-m-milady," he stammered.

She'd always found his stuttering curious, as it seemed to affect him only when he was very anxious. And he did seem quite anxious — he glanced at the young man beside him as he tugged so anxiously at his wig that it began to tilt to the left.

Margot looked at the men. None of them could look her in the eye, and all of them seemed unduly apprehensive. Was it her? Was she so reviled? She shielded the sun from her eyes with her hand so she could better peer at them. "Is everything all right?"

"Ah . . . m-m-madam," Sweeney began.

"Is the laird here?" she asked, pointing to the door.

Sweeney shook his head.

What in blazes was the matter with these men? "Has he gone far?"

"N-no, m-mu'um. He's training the m-m-men." Sweeney seemed pleased to be able to offer up this information, at least.

"Well, then. You can take me to him."

Sweeney's throat bobbed on a deep swallow. "J-J-Jock, he'll t-t-take you, aye? We're to t-t-take your things, that's all."

Her things? "What things, Sweeney?"

Sweeney's face reddened. One of the men behind him jabbed him in the back and muttered something under his breath.

"I think you are mistaken, Mr. Sweeney. Nell is still unpacking my things. You must mean to put my trunk away, is that it?" she asked, her gaze narrowing on the poor man.

Sweeney looked helplessly to the man beside him, but that man was staring at Margot, his expression one of pure dread.

Margot stepped closer. "It would appear there is something I should know," she said coolly.

Sweeney shook his head and studied his feet.

She shifted her gaze to the young man beside him. He was only sixteen or seventeen years old. "You," Margot said.

Sweeney pushed the lad forward, and he bobbed his head and fixed his gaze on Margot's shoulder.

"Perhaps you can tell me what has you all standing about so uneasily?"

He pressed his lips together and shook his head. His gaze slid lower, to her hand, and fixed there.

Margot took a step toward him, dipping down a tiny bit to look in his eyes, but the man would not allow it. "Why did Sweeney say he is to take my things?" she asked, her voice as smooth and as pleasant as she could make it.

The man glanced even farther to the right . . . to the wall. "I donna know, mu'um."

"Oh, but I think you do," she said, stepping even closer. He would have to step back or look at her. He seemed to debate his options and finally looked at her, and when he did, his companions seemed to shuffle away from the poor man, crowding in together, looking at their feet, the sky, each other.

"Tell me what you've heard."

"I donna rightly know, I swear it," the lad said helplessly. "Only that they said you're to leave for home, mu'um."

"But I *am* home," she said.

"To England!" he blurted, and winced, as if he expected the heavens would open up and smite him.

Margot's heart skipped. Arran meant to banish her? She slid her gaze to Sweeney, who could not meet her eye. "Who has said?"

"I d-d-donna rightly kn-know, mu'um," Sweeney said, twisting his cap in his hand.

Oh no. No, no. Sweeney's stammering was all the convincing she needed. She tried not to panic. She couldn't imagine what her father might do if she were sent home within twenty-four hours of arriving at Balhaire. Not to mention that for Arran to send her away so quickly was practically an admission of his guilt, wasn't it? And furthermore, if it was indeed his intent to banish her, did he not have the courage or decency to tell her himself? Margot's pulse quickened with anger, vacillating between utter disbelief and scorn.

Her hands found her waist and she stepped up to Sweeney now, so close that she could see the tiny lines around his eyes. "You'd best hope that no one says a word of taking my things to Nell," she warned him. "She'll have an apoplectic fit, and if she does, you can pray that the least she will do is snatch the hair from your head, sir. Not a word, do you hear me?"

The four men nodded in unison.

"And now, Mr. Sweeney, you can bring me a horse."

"A . . . h-h-h-horse?" Sweeney said with some difficulty.

"Yes, a *horse*. A large animal with four legs and a tail," she said, sketching it in the air with her hand.

None of them moved. None of them so much as breathed. She suddenly grabbed Sweeney by the lapels of his coat and gave him a shake. He was much larger than she, so he barely swayed, but his eyes filled with terror all the same. "By God, Sweeney Mackenzie, you'd best fetch me a horse!" she said angrily. "I may be gone tomorrow, but as of this moment, I am still Lady Mackenzie, and *you* are disobeying me!"

Sweeney gulped.

"Aye, she's right, she's *right,*" one of the young men behind him muttered.

"Uist," said another. "Have ye lost yer mind, lad? Mackenzie gives us the orders."

Margot pushed Sweeney aside as best she could, then stepped around him, glaring up at the man. "Are you quite certain about that? Because if there's even the slightest bit of doubt in you, I'd fetch your lady a *horse.*"

"Aye, m-m-milady," Sweeney said. With a glare for his companions, he stalked off in the direction of the stables, leaving the three of them huddled together like so many sheep.

Margot whirled away from them and marched after Sweeney. She might have seized the moment . . . but Margot guessed these men would probably have a jolly laugh about her in the days to come. They'd tell their children about the time the laird's wife came back from England and he sent her home straightaway. Ballads would be written about this monumental occasion and the story would grow . . . but not before she had a word with the man who didn't have the courage to banish her himself.

CHAPTER EIGHT

There was an art to training men for hand-to-hand fighting. It required a balance between distracting one's opponent and a relentless assault on their defenses. Arran rode slowly around the field, calling out suggestions and warnings, corrections and encouragement as he watched the men go through their paces.

His more experienced men were engaged when he noticed that several of them had stopped fighting and were looking in the direction of Balhaire.

Arran glanced over his shoulder to see what had their attention, half expecting an invading English army. Or a funeral procession. Or a comet. What he did *not* expect to see was his wife riding astride a bay as if running from a fire. Her gown was hiked up around her knees, and her slippers were in the stirrups. Her hair had come partly undone from her coif, and she had no hat.

He recalled that she was not a particularly experienced rider and wondered who had given her this horse.

Arran wheeled his much larger horse around. Son of a devil, what was she doing here? And why the bloody hell had someone not intercepted her?

She reined to an unsteady halt, slipping to one side but somehow managing to keep her saddle. "There you are!" she said with breathless cheerfulness.

"What are you doing here? This is no' a place for a woman." For an English buttercup, he meant, as any woman from the Highlands would be quite at ease with a bit of brawling.

"And why not?" Margot asked, leaning over to stroke the horse's neck. "It's grown men, punching each other. Nothing untoward in that, is there?"

She said it as if she rather enjoyed a good fight, which he knew could not be further from the truth. Arran looked past her to Balhaire. He expected to see Jock riding after her to corral her like a stray ewe. But no one was coming. Where were his men?

"Splendid day for it, too," she continued breezily. "A day *so* splendid that one might expect a man to accompany his wife on a picnic." She arched a brow.

"A picnic," he repeated slowly. He was fairly certain that was the first time in his life he'd ever uttered that word aloud.

"Or . . . or if not a picnic, then perhaps a walk about the gardens. Or an afternoon stroll along the shore. We've so much to discuss, haven't we?"

He had never wasted a single day of his life with picnics or strolling gardens. "I've work to do," he said flatly.

"Of course you do!" she said, her smile slow and easy, which he considered to be a practiced bit of women's sorcery. "You may rest assured I've not forgotten your preference for work."

He tilted his head curiously to one side. "I must be losing my hearing, aye? For when you said *work,* it sounded a wee bit sharp."

"Did it? My apologies," she said with a graceful nod that caused her loose tresses to fall into her face. "But I thought perhaps that as I have only just returned, we might enjoy one another's company today. Don't you want to talk? Haven't you anything you'd like to say?"

A cough behind Arran reminded him that they had an audience. He tried not to squirm in his saddle; he could think of nothing more undignified than squabbling with his wife in front of his men, but he could see from the high color in Margot's cheeks that it was a definite possibility.

"Madam, I —"

"I *thought* we might, mind you, but then I heard the most *distressing* news."

He sighed.

"Would you like to know what I heard? I heard that *you* would like me to return to England."

Arran opened his mouth, but she interrupted him before he could speak by raising a slender finger.

"Actually," she said, "what I heard is that you are *sending* me back to England. That rather makes it sound more like a fait accompli, doesn't it? A banishment of sorts. But as I said to the poor man who finally admitted this awful rumor, it couldn't possibly be true, because if it were, you would tell me yourself. Is that not so?" She smiled fully then, quite prettily, too. Except that her eyes were staring daggers at him.

Arran groaned. He glanced over his shoulder. He had the rapt attention of a dozen men. "All right, carry on, then," he snapped. "Do none of you have wives?" He leaned down to grab the bridle of Margot's horse. He wheeled the beast about, pointing it in the direction of Balhaire. "What do you think you're doing?" he demanded as they pulled away from the group.

"Asking a legitimate question."

"Have you lost your mind, then? Riding down here on a horse you can scarcely control to interrupt the training?"

"I can control it! Perhaps it was a bit rash, but you can imagine how confused I was. I will admit, in the spirit of complete honesty between us, that I was quite hurt you could think to *banish* me away after last night. I know you are displeased with me, Arran —"

"Displeased?" he echoed incredulously.

"But surely even *your* heart is not so hard that it can turn me away after I have humbled myself and we have come together as husband and wife again." She arched a brow, daring him to contradict her.

"You think *my* heart is hard?"

"I only mean that you're not as sentimental as some."

"For God's sake, woman — whatever this is about, whatever you mean to do here, I've no' the time or the patience for it, aye? I canna guess what's brought you back so suddenly after a three-year absence, but it's no' for good or any other reason you claim."

"But it is!" she insisted, pressing a hand to her heart. "I mean only to be a good wife."

"You made that choice three years ago, did you no'?"

"That's not true!" she cried, loud enough for the men to hear. Arran spurred his horse forward, forcing her smaller one to come along, moving them out of earshot of the men.

"All right, of *course* I understand why you might have come to that conclusion," she said, suddenly agreeing with him as she clung to her horse. "I *did* make a wretchedly uninformed choice when I left."

He snorted.

"But on my life, it was a mistake! A horrible, wretched, awful mistake, and I am terribly sorry for it now. I am desperate to make amends! Won't you at least allow me to try? Did last night mean nothing to you?" she asked, reaching for his gloved hand.

God, how he wished she wouldn't touch him. He was weaker when she touched him, and he yanked his hand free. "Bedding a beautiful woman doesna change the fact that I canna believe a word that falls from your lips. There is no reason you'd come back to me now, save some abominable purpose that I donna care to know."

Margot looked stricken. *"Abominable!"* she repeated, making the word sound far more vile than he'd intended. "I'll tell you what is

161

abominable, sir! Banishing me without even bothering to say goodbye — *that* is abominable! Having a change of heart for the good most certainly is *not* abominable."

"You say change of heart. I say duplicity," he said with a flick of his wrist. "Alas, we'll never know which it is, will we, for I donna intend to play along with your charade, Margot. Fare thee well, wife. Give Norwood my compliments." He let go of her horse and moved to slap its rump, sending it back to its oat bag.

But Margot suddenly lunged for him. It startled Arran, and he surged forward, catching her before she fell between the two horses and was crushed. He caught her under the arm and hauled her up, but the horses began to shift and move, and he had to drag her onto his horse to keep her from falling. "*Diah,* what are you thinking?" he demanded roughly. "You might have been trampled!"

Margot made a sound of despair and threw her arms around his neck. "Was last night just a dream? Will you really send me away when I've bared my heart to you?"

He tried to dislodge her arms from his neck. "You bared your body, no' your wretched heart."

"Let me prove it to you," she said quickly,

and turned her head to kiss his cheek. "Please, Arran — I'll prove it to you."

"Prove *what*?" he asked with great exasperation as she kissed the skin of his neck just above his collar, sending a white-hot shock through him.

"That I've come back to repair our broken marriage. To begin again! We can start anew, we can, because I've changed. I swear to you that I have." She kissed his cheek again. And his jaw. And his ear.

"Donna kiss me again," he said sharply. He was already distracted, already losing his ability to focus on the words she was saying, and managed to push her back so that she could not kiss him. "Why should I believe you've changed? On what grounds? For what reason?" He roughly cupped her face. "Why in God's name would I believe a word you utter, then? You made a bloody fool of me, Margot. You rejected my clan. You despised my professions and my occupations. You complained there was no society for you here. But this is where I live. I am the laird here. I do as a laird does, and I always will. That will never change, and neither will you. I donna trust you, aye? I will *never* trust you."

She paled. Her arms slid from his neck. "I know you don't trust me," she admitted dolefully. "How could you? But I'm not the girl I was then. I want to show you I've changed."

He snorted.

"And I want a child."

The moment she said those words aloud, she looked as if she wanted to gulp them back. Arran's gaze narrowed skeptically on her. "You would use that to persuade me?" he asked scornfully. She knew his desire to have a child; she knew it very well. She knew his disappointment each month when her courses came. And he knew her happiness that they had.

"Please don't look at me like that," she said, squeezing her eyes shut for a moment. "I *do* want a child. I want to be a mother. I want to be a wife. I was too young before. I was too naive. But you are my husband, and you need an heir, and I want a child of my own."

She had just said the one thing that could cement her hold on him — she wanted his child. More than anything he wanted children, squads of them, hanging from rafters, filling the old bailey and bouncing on his bed. He would give everything he had to his children. Could she ever understand how difficult it had been for him after she'd left to suppress his own needs so that he'd not bring an illegitimate child into this clan? Could she understand how, if she were to give him a child, he would live every waking moment fearing she would flee once again with that child?

But Arran saw something in her green eyes in that moment. It was the same thing he'd seen last night — the sorrow.

He glared at her, furious with her.

"Please don't banish me," she whispered.

He curled his hand into a fist and held it tight against his thigh. "All right, then," he said, slowly nodding. "Prove to me that you want to be my wife, Margot. No' the wife of some English dandy, mind you, but *my* wife. A woman who is no' afraid of feast or famine, of toil, of trouble. A *Highlander's* wife. And you a Scot. Can you be *that* wife to me?"

"Yes!" she said. But the confidence in her voice belied the look of alarm in her eyes, and for that, he had to endeavor to suppress a wee bitter smile.

CHAPTER NINE

Margot hadn't been at Balhaire even twenty-four hours, and she'd already made a shamble of things. Mostly by lying to Arran after he'd expressly warned her against it.

A *child,* she'd said!

It wasn't a complete lie, because Margot truly wanted children. But that was not why she'd come back, and frankly, she could think of nothing worse than conceiving a child with a traitor to the crown. Unfortunately, her pride had gotten the best of her, and she'd said a desperate thing in a desperate moment.

God, but this was confusing — now she had to *prove* to Arran she wanted to be a good wife? As if she were one of a dozen debutantes vying for his hand?

Oh, but the charade would begin in earnest tomorrow night, apparently. He'd *delighted* in telling her that in honor of her change of heart, there ought to be a gathering with singing and dancing to celebrate her return to the clan's fold. And then he'd sent a lad running up to the castle to inform Fergus of it.

"A splendid idea!" Margot had exclaimed with false cheer, and Arran, damn him, had knowingly smiled with the pleasure of having riled her.

After the disaster of the ball he'd tried to give her, she knew what to expect. Singing in a language only Highlanders understood and dancing chaotic reels with a lot of hopping about and kicking of legs that the Scots seemed to prefer. He meant to intimidate her with this so-called celebration.

But Margot wasn't going to allow that to happen. If her husband wanted her to dance and sing to prove herself to him, then she would oblige him, and in high style, too. She might be the most ungainly dancer, but she would console herself by being the most finely attired one.

Margot and the beast Sweeney had saddled for her thundered into the bailey, and Margot managed to slide off without revealing too terribly much of her leg to the groom who had run out to attend her. She straightened her skirts and her bodice . . . and noticed that her hair had come undone. She was trying to tuck it back into its pins when Jock came striding out of the castle doors. The lad Arran had sent up to inform Fergus of the celebration was close on Jock's heels.

Jock slowed his step when he saw Margot. He clenched his jaw as he passed by.

Margot muttered a few choice words about Arran's ridiculously loyal cousin, gave up on her hair and stalked inside. As if her day could possibly get any worse, Pepper and Worthing were just emerging from the hall when she entered, their wigs freshly powdered and their lace cuffs and neck cloths pristinely white. Frankly, they looked ridiculous in this rugged Highland castle.

"Dear God," Mr. Pepper said, his gaze sliding down Margot and up again. "Have you been assaulted?"

"Assault — *No!*"

"Then what has *happened*?" he asked, holding up his hand as if to keep her at a distance.

"Nothing! I've been riding and I . . . Never mind," she said.

"Madam, if I may," said Worthing. He stepped closer, glanced around and said softly, "He cannot turn you out and send you to England, not without consequence. There are laws governing marriage."

"Laws!" Margot snorted. "What law is it

that prevents a man from banishing a wife who once abandoned him, sir? Don't speak to me of laws — men may do as they please. But you may rest assured he is not turning me out. We've had a slight misunderstanding, that's all, and everything has been set to rights."

Her two keepers exchanged a dubious look.

She suddenly wished these two men were not here to complicate her return. "When did you say you'd be returning to England?"

Worthing frowned. "We did not," he said. "But I shall be more than happy that we take our leave when you have a message for your father. Have you any message for him, Lady Mackenzie?"

"As a matter of fact, you may hasten back to tell his lordship that I've arrived safely at my destination. I'm certain he's on tenterhooks waiting for *that* word." She smiled, dipped a pert curtsy and stepped around her keepers.

When she reached her chambers at the top of a long and winding staircase — rooms *she* had chosen when she'd first married Arran, insisting that it was proper for a lady to have her own set of rooms, and finding those as far from her husband as she possibly could — she found that Nell had finished the unpacking.

Her maid was sitting in a chair, her feet up on an ottoman. She started so badly when Margot threw open the door that she fell haphazardly out of the chair. "I beg your pardon!" she said frantically as she righted herself and her lace cap. "I meant only to rest my back —"

"Be easy, Nell. I don't care," Margot said. "Mackenzie intends to have a soiree of the Scotch variety tomorrow evening. I'll need my best gown. One that is entirely unforgettable." She had no doubt that every eye at Balhaire would be on her, searching for the reason she'd returned.

"Ah," said Nell. She nodded, understanding. "The blue mantua, with the birds embroidered on the stomacher."

"Yes, that's perfect," Margot agreed. The gown had been made for her in London. Tiny birds fluttered about the stomacher in vivid colors. The damask pattern of the silk gown had been sewn with both gold and silver threads so that when Margot moved, it looked as if the skirt was rippling around her.

"Anything else, mu'um?"

Margot looked around her. "Yes," she said thoughtfully. What a silly choice to have taken these rooms! She'd always felt like a

170

bird in a cage up here, at the top of a tower. It was true she had a stunning view of the castle and the lands around it, which she supposed had drawn her to this room in the beginning. She could even see the sea from here. But she couldn't hear a sound — not a voice, not a sheep's bleating, not even a barking dog. She was practically suspended above the world, isolated from all the Mackenzies.

Arran had wanted her to share his chambers. He'd made a set of rooms adjoining his master's chambers available to her for sitting and dressing, but Margot had been too prim, too proper and, God, so naive.

Well. She was no longer that foolish girl.

She looked at Nell and winced apologetically. "We must change rooms."

"Pardon?" Nell asked disbelievingly.

"I have put us away from everyone by taking these rooms. I am too far from my husband. How can I possibly be expected to repair anything when I am, for all intents and purposes, in another house altogether?"

Nell looked as if she might collapse.

"Now, Nell," she said, taking her maid's hand and caressing it. "I know you've done quite a lot of work. But I will tell you in confidence that my husband is displeased with me for having ever left Balhaire, and

171

he means to send me back to England straightaway. I can't allow that to happen." Not yet, anyway.

"Aye, milady," Nell said morosely.

As Nell began to work to repack her things, Margot went in search of Fergus to inform him she would be changing rooms. She found the older man in the great room, overseeing the preparations for the evening meal. He tried to avoid her gaze as she walked in, but Margot knew what he was about and stopped him with a cheerful, "Good afternoon, Fergus."

"Milady."

"I thank you for airing out my old rooms on such short notice. But I've decided that I should like to be closer to my husband. Would you please ready the sitting room and dressing room adjacent to the master's chambers? Nell is packing my things."

Fergus blinked. And then his eyes narrowed on her. "Next to the laird," he said, as if she'd misspoke.

"Yes, that's right," she said calmly. "Next to my husband. Good heavens, you do look alarmed, Fergus. Will it help if I give you my word I'll not murder him in the night?"

Fergus's eyes narrowed more. "No, it doesna help. I canna do so without speaking to the laird himself, aye?"

"Of course you can!" she said cheerfully. "Because I am mistress here. And besides, I've already spoken to him, and he was pleased with my decision."

Fergus's eyes narrowed into little slits. "I donna think —"

"Do as the lady asks," said a deep male voice from behind Margot.

She should have known Jock would be lurking somewhere close by. Wasn't he always? She glanced over her shoulder. "*There* you are," she said. "I had begun to fret you'd gone missing."

"Go, then," Jock said to Fergus.

"That was unexpectedly helpful of you," Margot said as Fergus went on.

"No' at all. It's a wee sight easier to keep an eye on you there than in your tower, aye?"

"So you may think, my friend," Margot said, and walked away from his piercing gaze.

Unfortunately, with no occupation, no task, no role to play, Margot found herself in the bailey once more. She had no idea where she was going, but she lifted her chin and walked through.

No one stopped her. Most hardly noticed her — that, or they were taking great pains to avoid looking at her.

She wasn't as wretched as that, was she? Was it truly so condemnable to have left an impossible husband? She was determined to prove that she was not the witch they clearly thought she was. Just how to do that would require some thought.

She walked down the road, where shops and houses had sprung up over the years, forming a small village around the walls of Balhaire. She had rarely come out here before — these were not the sorts of shops she was accustomed to frequenting. There were no silks and china here. No gloves of the finest leather like she wore now.

But one shop caught her eye as she walked down the road. It had boxes of peonies beneath the window, and a wooden sign that proclaimed Miss Agnes Gowan, Proprietress.

A tiny bell twinkled as she stepped through the low door into the building. Something smelled quite delicious, and there, on the counter, was a tray full of freshly baked muffins that made her mouth water. There was a variety of goods and staples — jars of jam, china plates and cups. Sachets of bath salts and milled soaps. Margot picked up a sachet and held it up to her nose. It smelled of heather and lavender.

The sound of whispers brought her head around. Two women had appeared behind the counter, one of them short and round, with a lace cap over gray curls. Margot recognized her from before — she'd been one of the ladies from the kirk she'd tried to involve in charity.

The other woman, whispering into the shorter one's ear, was younger but had the same bulbous nose. She, too, wore a lace cap and an apron. A daughter, no doubt.

"How do you do?" Margot said pleasantly.

Neither of the women spoke.

"The scents of your sachets and soaps are lovely. I believe the last time I was here, people were still using nettles to clean." She smiled.

Nothing.

Margot cleared her throat. "You remember me, do you not, Mrs. Gowan? We met when I was last at Balhaire. We spoke of collecting alms for the poor." Except that they had never collected any alms. None of the ladies of the kirk seemed to understand that raising money to assist the poor was a worthy cause. *We take care of our orphans here,* they'd said. But Margot had insisted. She'd assumed it was necessary. She had always been involved in charitable endeavors on behalf of Norwood Park and assumed it was

175

expected of her here.

It was Griselda who had finally informed her, quite impatiently, that there was no need to raise alms, as the poor were taken care of within the clan itself. "That's what a clan *is*," she'd said irritably. "We mind our own."

"Aye, I remember," Mrs. Gowan said coolly, her gaze narrowing slightly. She made no effort to greet Margot.

Margot lightly traced the gold leaf on a china plate beside her. "I don't recall such porcelain being available here. Wherever did you get such exquisite china?"

"From France," the daughter said. "The laird give it to us to sell."

Gave it to them to sell? "It's beautiful." She looked around. "You have so many fine things. The ships from France must come often."

Mrs. Gowan shrugged and folded her arms as if she were uncomfortable.

"A ship came last night," her daughter offered helpfully, earning a glare from her mother. The daughter pressed her lips together and looked down.

Was the ship meant to be a secret?

"Well. I'm quite impressed with your wares. I should like some soaps and bath salts to be delivered up to the castle, if you please. You may tell them Lady Mackenzie requested them and have them pay you." Margot smiled with pleasure at her good deed. That ought to satisfy Mrs. Gowan. Surely the woman would be thrilled to have an order for goods from the laird's own wife. Shopkeepers always like to have their wares in the finest houses. In the village near Norwood Park, shopkeepers practically sought her out, so desperate were they to have this candelabra or that chair at Norwood Park.

But Mrs. Gowan did not move as much as a finger.

Margot tugged uncertainly on her earlobe. "A selection of your choosing," she offered helpfully.

"Milady," the younger one said, and dipped a curtsy. She stepped out from behind the counter and began to gather a selection of soaps and sachets.

But Margot kept her gaze on Mrs. Gowan. Why was she casting such a cold glare at her? Perhaps she didn't care for Margot's money, but why be unpleasant to the laird's wife? Didn't she realize Arran would hear of it? She couldn't possibly still be upset about the charity.

As her daughter wrapped the soaps and sachets, Margot said, "I beg your pardon,

Mrs. Gowan, but I've clearly done something to displease you."

"Aye, you have," she readily agreed.

"*Ma*," the girl whispered. Her mother paid her no heed.

"Is it the alms? On my word, I truly meant to help. I didn't know about Highland clans," Margot said, pressing a hand to her heart.

Mrs. Gowan and her daughter exchanged a look. "The what?" the older woman asked, squinting at Margot again.

Margot could feel her face turning red. "If your displeasure with me does not stem from the charity, how can you be so clearly cross with me?" she asked. "I've only just returned to Balhaire."

"Well, that's just it, is it no'?" Mrs. Gowan asked.

"Pardon?" Margot asked, taken aback.

"I donna know how it is where you come from, milady, but here, when you wrong a Mackenzie, you wrong *all* the Mackenzies. And I'm a Mackenzie through and through. My son was schooled alongside the laird, he was."

"Ma, please, no' another word," the girl begged her.

"I'll say what I will," Mrs. Gowan said. "I'm no' afeared of her, I'm no'."

"I'm not afraid of you, either," Margot said. "You may be surprised to know that I rather believe the wrong was done to *me.* And yet it should hardly matter to you, because whoever has been wronged is a private matter between me and my husband."

"I would that you'd never come back, aye?"

Margot and Mrs. Gowan's daughter gasped at the same moment. Margot had never been addressed so bluntly. She opened her mouth to warn the woman she'd best not ever speak to her again in that fashion, but Mrs. Gowan said, "I donna know why you did. I hope to never see the laird so pained again, no."

Margot stilled. Her retort flew out of her head as she stared at the woman. *"Pained?"* she echoed incredulously.

"Aye, pained, that he certainly was," Mrs. Gowan said angrily. "Moping about like a cow lost its calf."

"Ma!" the girl cried.

Margot swallowed down her shock. She glanced around the room, uncertain what to say. Uncertain if she even understood what the woman meant, or if she should even believe something so outlandish. Arran had been angry, very angry. But he'd not

179

been *pained.*

She looked sidelong at Mrs. Gowan again, whose round cheeks had turned slightly pink. "Do you mean to imply that the laird was pained by his marriage to me?" she asked uncertainly.

"No," the woman said, her gaze raking over Margot. "He was pained by your leaving us! Everyone could see it, aye? He'd no' speak of it, but it was mighty plain to me that ye right broke his heart!"

A chill went up Margot's back. "No, I didn't," she said defensively.

"Completely dispirited, he was," she said emphatically. "And I've no use for a woman who can do that to our Mackenzie, no, I donna."

Her daughter spoke sternly in Gaelic to her mother.

Her mother glanced reluctantly at her girl, then at Margot once more. "I've said what I will. I'll have the soaps sent up to you, then," she said, and turned away.

Margot was speechless, reeling from the idea that Arran could have been broken-hearted. She backed up, her hand groping behind her for the door, and stepped out of the shop.

Once outside, she stood with her gaze fixed on the hills beyond Balhaire. She had assumed, given the tension between them, that Arran had been happy to see her go. When her father told her that she must come back to Balhaire, Margot had thought only of how displeased Arran would be to see her again. But *pained*? Was that true? Had she really pained him, or had this woman interpreted his foul mood as hurt? Wouldn't Margot have known if Arran wanted her to stay? Would he not have *asked* her to stay?

She was still standing there trying to sort things out when a group of men came thundering onto the main road on their way to the castle. Several people came out of their houses and shops to have a look. Margot stepped back, flattening herself against the wall of Mrs. Gowan's shop as they rode past.

She closed her eyes against the dust and opened them again as a lone rider reined to a hard stop.

It was Arran. He stared down at her as his horse danced impatiently beneath him. "Margot? What are you doing here?"

"Ah . . ." She glanced at the door of the shop. "Mrs. Gowan has kindly agreed to send up a few things to the castle."

Arran glanced at the shop, then at Margot. "You'll make do without me tonight, aye?"

he said brusquely. "I've business in Loch-alsh."

Business in Lochalsh? What business might he have there? It was a tiny hamlet on the western shore with only a few fisher-men. "You'll be away?" she asked plaintively. "But I thought we might —"

"You donna mean to complain of it, surely," he said, his voice full of warning.

Margot clenched her jaw to keep from do-ing precisely that. "Not at all. I wish you a safe journey," she forced herself to say.

"Aye, exactly as I thought." He spurred his horse on.

Margot watched him go, hating the suspi-cion rising up in her. With a sigh, she began to trudge back up the hill to the castle, wav-ing away the dust the horses had kicked up.

CHAPTER TEN

At the end of the very long day, after dining with Nell in the sitting room adjacent to the master's chambers, Margot retired to Arran's bed.

Fergus was agitated. "The hearth has no' been lit, milady."

"Then perhaps you might light it," Margot said as sweetly as possible.

Fergus lit the hearth . . . but then he sent the dogs in. Quite literally sent them in. That was another thing she and Arran had argued about in the past — he allowed old and retired working dogs into Balhaire to live when they were no longer useful to their masters. At one time there were ten of them wandering about, sniffing corners and following behind people with the hope of earning a table scrap or a head scratch!

Tonight, three dogs ambled in from the master dressing room, pausing to stretch and yawn. Margot had already put herself in bed, feeling miserably alone and a little uneasy. Though she'd never cared for dogs freely roaming the house, tonight she was not altogether cross when their heads popped up over the edge of the bed, their tails swishing on the floor, their gazes hopeful.

"Very well, then." Margot sighed, feigning impatience, and tapped the bed. The three of them leaped as one over her, circled about and finally settled themselves in with their backs pressed up against her.

She remembered the wintry afternoon Arran had brought her down to the kennels to see a litter of puppies, hoping it would cheer her. It had. She remembered how he would cradle them one by one in his hand against his chest, stroking their heads. *This one shall be a fine herder, aye? But this one . . . I suspect he will spend his time digging beneath fences."* It had been a lovely afternoon.

There'd been a few occasions like that with Arran, moments where they had been content with each other. Margot had thought of those moments at Norwood Park from time to time. Sometimes, when ennui consumed her, she'd thought of those moments rather wistfully.

By morning, not only had Margot been nudged to the edge of the bed by her bedmates, but also two more had found their way inside and were laid out on the carpet at the foot of the bed.

The only thing missing from this rather domestic scene was her husband. Was he still in the village of Lochalsh? Surely there was no treason to be done there, so what business could he possibly have? Perhaps he hadn't gone there at all.

No matter where he'd gone or what he'd done, Margot could not let anyone see her apprehension. It was imperative that she appear the repentant wife.

She shooed the dogs out with a command to go and find their breakfast. She called Nell to her and dressed. She went down to the great hall as she ought, greeted as many Mackenzies as would look at her, forced herself to eat something, then quit the great hall as servants began to clear the hall, preparing the room for the celebration to take place that evening.

As to that, Margot had a plan. She donned a cloak and left the castle, walking down the main road, past Mrs. Gowan's shop, then turning a corner onto a well-worn footpath. She hopped over puddles and sidestepped a pair of chickens searching the road, and arrived at her destination: a small square of a house, with two small windows facing the path. She rapped on the door and waited. As she knew he would, a wizened old man opened it and squinted at her.

"Good morning, Mr. Creedy."

He stared at her.

"I'm Lady Mackenzie. We met a few years ago."

"Aye."

Margot cleared her throat and adjusted her cloak. "*Ahem.* I've come to inquire about a bit of tartan plaid."

He looked surprised. Then suspicious.

"There is to be a gathering of sorts tonight . . . that is, the laird has kindly offered to host a gathering to welcome me home . . . and I should very much like to don a bit of plaid."

"Ye want to don a plaid," he repeated incredulously.

Was that so shocking? "I would like to, yes."

"Hmm," he said. "Ye've had a change of heart, is that it?"

Margot could scarcely blame his skepticism — he had come offering her various plaids before. He'd had a cart of them, proud of his work, and she . . . well, she had refused them. She could recall how appalled she'd been that anyone would think she would suddenly don the rough wool, and she had politely . . . or perhaps not so politely . . . refused them. "I suppose I have. I apologize, Mr. Creedy. I should never have been so hasty —"

"*Ach,* never ye mind, milady. It doesna matter what was said before, as long as we come back round to right."

Margot blinked. She felt strangely deceptive, as she wasn't entirely certain she'd come back to the fold. Or had she? Her purpose at Balhaire seemed so suddenly confusing.

Mr. Creedy read guilt into her hesitation. "Donna trouble yourself with regrets," he said. "What sort would you like, then?"

"What sort?"

"An *arisaid,* then? A waistcoat? I've no' enough time for that."

"A what? No, not a waistcoat."

"Aye, come, come," he said, waving her in with a hand bent with age.

She ducked her head and stepped inside his house. It was a single room and it smelled of fish. In one half was a bed. In the other half sat a large loom, as well as various fabrics and yarns hanging from the walls. There was a shelf where several plaids were neatly folded and stacked. He took one from the stack and unfurled it, holding it up to her. It was an enormous cloth, a blanket big enough to cover the master bed.

"I'll show you how it's worn, then, if it suits ye. I'll cut a strip and make a sash of it, aye?"

"Aye," she said without thinking.

He draped it over her shoulder, reached around her and pulled one end to her hip, and then met that end with the other. "Fasten it here with a *luckenbooth,* aye?"

"A brooch? Ah. I see," she said. "Yes, it's perfect, Mr. Creedy. Thank you. Is it possible you might have it ready for this evening?"

"I'll have it done in the hour. I'll send it up with me lad then, shall I?"

"Thank you." Margot smiled and gratefully squeezed the old man's hand.

The day went quickly enough — it seemed there was quite a lot to do, settling into new rooms and reacquainting herself with Balhaire. And still, there was no sign of Arran.

That evening, when Nell came to her to help her dress, she was full of news.

"The laird has come back," she whispered. "He's come with two men, and quite a lot of fish hanging from a line."

Margot twisted about on her seat to see Nell. "He went *fishing*?" she asked incredulously.

"I don't know, mu'um. I only know he's come back with a lot of them."

All right, she wasn't going to allow her hackles to rise. At least, she told herself, he'd come back.

When she'd finished dressing, Margot took a moment to admire herself. She looked like a queen; a crown was the only thing missing from the ensemble. Her hair was an artistic construction of loops and curls, fastened to her head with pearl-tipped pins. Her mantua was as rich as anything the queen might wear, and Margot felt quite regal in it. But tonight, the jewel-encrusted stomacher she'd been so proud of was covered by a swath of plaid, fastened at her hip with a brooch that had belonged to her mother.

Unfortunately, effecting that regal look had taken a bit longer than either Nell or Margot had anticipated, and she arrived at the great hall a little late for dinner. She paused outside the big oak doors to compose herself. There was no footman here to see her in, no servant to whisper to Arran that she'd arrived so that he might escort her in.

She felt jittery. As if she were standing on the edge of the cliff above the cove about to jump to the sea below. She was afraid. Of what, precisely, she wasn't certain, but enough that she had to force herself to take a deep breath. She lifted her chin, and allowing herself not a sliver of hesitation, she pushed through the door, pausing just over the threshold to ensure she was seen.

Oh, but she was seen, all right. Her entrance had the desired effect — everyone paused and all heads in the hall turned toward her. Conversations were dropped and forks were put down. And there, on the dais, sat her husband, his gaze fixed on her. His hair was combed back and bound in a queue, and he was clean-shaven. He looked like the laird of this castle. He looked strong and powerful, and Margot's heart began to skip along with anticipation. She felt warm, felt that strange sensation that he could see past her gown and right inside her.

And yet his expression was inscrutable — if he was impressed with her appearance, she couldn't say.

Honestly, she couldn't say that anyone was particularly impressed with her as much as curious. She'd felt so sure of herself until this moment. Now she was uncomfortably aware of how overdressed she was. No other woman wore a mantua gown. And if she had, Margot could well imagine the stays wouldn't have been as tight as hers. Nell had said it was imperative that her waist appear as tiny as possible. "The gents, they like the tiny waists," she'd said with authority. But as a result of that tiny waist, Margot's breasts were spilling out of her stomacher. Moreover, the long, thick curl that artfully draped her shoulder practically pointed to her exploding bosom.

Well. It was too late to fret about it. Certainly she couldn't stand here all night as if she desired to be admired, so she began to walk through that crowd. The silk and taffeta in her skirts rustling together sounded almost deafening to her. Margot was acutely modest now. She could feel her cheeks warming with her mortification and hoped the blush didn't extend to her breasts and make them appear like a pair of pomegranates. She glanced around, smiling, desperately searching for a friendly face. Her grand entrance, which surely would have been applauded in England, had all the markings of a huge mistake in Scotland.

Arran did not come to her aid. He couldn't be bothered even to come to his feet to greet her.

Margot might have hated him in that moment. He seemed wickedly smug, as if he enjoyed her humiliation. His smugness made her wish to deflect it that much stronger. She began to speak to those around her, as if she had never been gone, as if this were the normal way of things at Balhaire.

"Good evening, Mr. Mackenzie," she said to one elderly gentleman. He did not seem to hear her. "Reverend Gale! How do you do?" she asked, taking the reverend's hand between hers and squeezing it.

"Very well, milady, very well indeed."

"And your daughters? How are they?"

"Sons," he kindly corrected her.

"Yes, of course," she said quickly. Her cheeks were on fire.

"Oh, they're married, my lads," he said proudly. "The eldest will make me a grandda before the year is done."

"Congratulations!" she said gaily, and moved on. "Mrs. McRae, how good to see you well!"

"McRaney, milady," the woman said as she sank into a curtsy. She did not look Margot in the eye. Scots! So stubbornly loyal to one infuriating man!

Margot had made it halfway through the hall before Arran finally deigned to come out of his blasted seat. He stepped out from behind the table. He had dressed for the occasion, too, wearing a plaid that hung to his knees above his stockings and brogues.

He wore the plaid with a waistcoat and coat, and an inky black neck cloth at the collar. One curl of hair fell disobediently across his brow. He did indeed cut a fine figure, yet as much as Margot admired him, a sickly little thought flitted through her brain. Was that not the dress of the Jacobites?

Arran casually strolled down from the dais as if he had nowhere to be. When he reached her, he folded one arm behind his back and bowed over the other one. "Lady Mackenzie," he said. "Welcome."

"Thank you, my lord." She slipped her hand into his and sank into a curtsy.

"How bonny you are tonight," he said, his gaze on the swath of plaid she wore as he lifted her up. "It appears as if you've made amends with Mr. Creedy."

"He was very kind. Do you like it?"

"That I do," he said, taking her in. "Verra much. Will you join me on the dais?" He was awfully formal with her this evening.

Margot allowed him to escort her up to the dais and hand her into a chair next to his.

"Shall I have the lad fetch you an ale?" he asked as he resumed his seat, gesturing to one of the young men who served the main table.

"Wine, if you please."

Arran arched a dubious brow.

"You do have wine, do you not?"

"Aye, we've wine. Of course we've wine," he said impatiently. "But the Mackenzies prefer ale. Perhaps you might like to sample the batch Jock has brewed. He's quite proud."

So she had to prove herself to him even in what she drank, it would seem. Margot kept her countenance pleasant as she drew a calming breath. "I'd like nothing better than to sample Jock's ale! I've no doubt it's astonishingly good and, I hope, free of poison."

Arran smiled. "Alas, I canna promise you that. Jock! Lady Mackenzie has expressed a rather keen desire for your ale."

Jock gave Margot a disbelieving look.

"Please," she said, and put her hand on Arran's. "My husband's praise is hard earned, and he has sung it long and loud for your ale, sir. I simply must try it myself." She said it as brightly and as convincingly as possible. Which wasn't very brightly or convincingly at all.

Jock bowed curtly, straightened curtly and walked away curtly. Margot shifted her gaze to her husband. "Happy?"

"No," he said easily. "But a wee bit mollified," he added, his gaze full of amusement.

194

"Jock is even more distrusting than I."

"That, my lord, was not distrust. *That* was utter disdain. And it's your fault."

"My fault?" He looked astonished.

"Yours! You told Jock I was difficult and made it quite clear you didn't care for me."

"What the devil? I've no' said any such thing."

"I believe your *exact* words were that you'd married a fishwife clad in silk and lace."

Arran laughed. But then his brows sank into a dark frown. "I didna."

"You *did*. Right there," she said, pointing to the massive hearth. "Don't you recall it?" It had been a stormy, snowy night. Margot obviously hadn't been meant to hear, but with the wind howling, Arran and Jock hadn't heard her come into the great hall.

"No, I . . ." Arran paused. Clearly he recalled it now, his complaining to Jock about his impossible English wife. "Hmm," he said, his gaze moving over her face. "I had forgotten it."

She smiled. "I haven't forgotten anything."

"Ach," he said with a flick of his wrist. "A woman's memory is as long as a loch."

"And a man's attention is as short as an inchworm."

"That's no' necessarily so, *leannan*. There

is quite a lot I remember, as well." His gaze moved lower, to her mouth, lingering there. "I remember that your list of complaints was quite long."

She could feel the skin of her chest heating beneath his study of her. She had to look away or be devoured by that penetrating gaze. "Were they complaints? I always rather thought them pleas to help me reconcile to my new surroundings."

"Ah, is that what they were, then?" he mused. His hand found her leg. "My apologies. I thought you meant to list all the ways Balhaire didna suit you."

She slid her hand over his and squeezed it before peeling it free of her thigh. "I meant to list all the ways I needed you," she said truthfully, and looked at him then. His gaze had gone dark and cool. "Perhaps I was inarticulate."

"And a wee bit shrill," he reminded her.

A curl of nausea swam through her. He would never forgive her. The peculiar thing was that for the first time, she wanted his forgiveness. "Perhaps I was," she admitted. "I hope one day you can forgive me for not understanding the best way to capture your attention. At the time, shouting seemed to be the only way that you'd notice me at all."

"Diah," he muttered as Jock approached

with the ale. "Was there anything I did to please you, Margot? Or was it all to your disliking?"

"On the contrary — there was much you did that pleased me very much. Was there anything I did to please you?"

Arran did not answer her as Jock put the ale before them. Just behind him, a boy carried two plates for Arran and Margot. Their discussion — if one could call it that — was put aside for the sake of dining. They ate in silence. Arran was brooding.

Margot was ravenous. She realized how very little she'd eaten since she'd arrived at Balhaire. The haddock was delicious, cooked to perfection in a creamy broth, and surprisingly, the dark ale complemented it nicely. But the ale had the unfortunate effect of filling her belly to the point of bursting. Her stays began to dig into her ribs.

When they'd finished the meal, Arran signaled the musicians to play.

Margot leaned back, one hand lying across her ailing abdomen, stifling a small and undignified belch, when a young man came forward wearing a pair of plaid trews. He had curly hair like Arran's and reminded Margot of a medieval troubadour. She wouldn't have been at all surprised if he'd produced a lyre and begun to play.

He bowed low in a courtly fashion. "Laird Mackenzie, may I have your leave to ask Lady Mackenzie to stand up with me?" he asked in his lilting brogue.

"Oh." Margot sat up, wincing a little at the discomfort of her gown. "No, thank you, sir —"

"You are quick to deny him, aye?" Arran said. "Does a Scotch dance displease you, *wife*?"

"Not at all. But I —"

"Oh, aye, I remember — you're a poor dancer. Is that no' what you said?"

Margot stared at him.

He shrugged. "Aye, I do remember a few things."

Oh, this wretched man! "I only wish that I was more familiar with the Scotch style of dancing," she said apologetically to the young man. "Would you not prefer a more adept partner?"

"Of course no'," Arran answered for him. "For there is no bonnier partner than my wife, is that no' so, lad?"

"It is indeed, laird."

"Go on, then, Margot," he said, gesturing to the hall. "You will always be a poor dancer if you donna at least try, aye?" He smiled wickedly at her.

Heaven help her, but she would have

kicked him then and there if she hadn't been so uncomfortable in her gown. Instead, she turned the full force of her smile she'd learned in English salons on that young man. "I would be *delighted,* sir. Thank you." She stood up.

The young man's face lit; he hurried forward to offer his hand. Margot cast her smile to Arran, whose eyes were shining with delight. "Donna hold back, Gavin. What my wife lacks in skill, she makes up tenfold with jolly enthusiasm."

If looks could kill, Arran would be lying in a pool of blood right now. But Margot laughed gaily. "You might want to consider removing all the knives from the table before I return, my lord."

She heard Arran's full laugh as she allowed the young man to lead her off the dais.

Gavin led Margot to the center of the room with great élan. When they reached the line for dancers, he bowed low, his hand nearly scraping the floor.

"You are very polished, sir," Margot said admiringly. "You bring to mind the French court."

His eyes shone with pleasure. "Thank you. Indeed I have learned from the French," he said proudly.

Interesting, that. She wondered what had taken this young man to France. But before Margot could inquire, the music began, and Gavin linked his arm with hers and twirled her around in a circle, then let go of her. "Let your feet do as they might, milady!" he cried. Someone else grabbed her arm, and as quick as that, she was being hurled about from one waiting arm to the next.

It was apparent to her and, sadly, everyone else that Margot was a horrible Scotch dancer. She had not miraculously acquired any sense of rhythm and couldn't keep up. She kicked the poor gentleman next to her at least twice, and Gavin repeatedly, as she was always one or two beats behind. Her breasts were dangerously close to being freed from the prison of their bodice, and her hair, so artfully put together by Nell, was coming down in big auburn loops.

As the dance continued, she could feel perspiration sliding between her breasts. Her feet, encased in gorgeous and very expensive slippers that were no match for all this hopping about, had begun to cramp. And yet the most extraordinary thing happened. No one looked at her askance. No one seemed appalled by her. They all laughed; they all called out strange words to one another, and some or other person would grab her hand or arm and fling her along with them. It was mad, it was chaotic, it was *merry*. It was the most diverting dance Margot had ever experienced. She felt alive, exhilarated. She felt as if this was the sort of dancing she should have been doing all her life.

When it at last ended, an exuberant Gavin escorted her back to the dais. "Well done, milady!" he said.

She laughed. "I am a *wretched* dancer!" she proclaimed. "But *you,* sir, are an expert at dance. You must have been formally trained."

"Aye, that I was. My mother married a Frenchman when my father died. Monsieur Devanault saw to it that my siblings and I were instructed in what he called courtly arts." His smile was infectious — she could imagine him a few short years from now, wooing debutantes with his handsome face and fine dancing skills.

They had reached the dais, and he tried to hand her up, but Margot held on to his arm.

"Wherever did Monsieur Devanault find dance instructors in Scotland?"

"No' here, mu'um, no. I learned the Scotch reel from my aunt, aye? I took dance instruction in France before the war. Here, then, is your seat."

Margot allowed him to hand her up onto the dais. "Thank you," she said. "Again, my sincere apologies for the many times I kicked you."

He laughed, bowed low once more and disappeared into the crowd.

Arran laughed as she resumed her seat. "Your face is as red as a robin's breast," he said, making a circling motion around his own face.

"It was quite diverting!" she said gaily, still panting slightly.

"I owe you an apology," he said. "You were right, then — you are indeed a horrible dancer."

Margot wanted to grab her husband by the collar, toss him to the ground, leap on him and pummel his face. But as she couldn't do that, she laughed. "I quite liked it! What a wonderful way of dancing you have here in Scotland. I never would have believed a lot of hopping about with no direction in mind could be so engaging. Now you must come and dance with —"

"Oh, I think no'," he said, and suddenly stood. "I've an early day on the morrow."

He was going to leave her here with her hair half down, her cheeks stained red with exertion and her feet aching? *Alone?* Knowing full well that most people in this hall couldn't abide her? And to make matters worse, she noticed that Worthing and Pepper had taken seats on the dais, staring down their angular noses at the dancing. "You're not *leaving* me," she said, disbelieving. "You said this was to be a celebration."

"Aye, that I did. And it is. And I've celebrated." He smiled, slipped two fingers under her chin and lifted her face to him. "And now is the perfect opportunity for you to acquaint yourself with your clan, Margot," he said, and kissed her lightly on the lips. "The plaid is a nice touch, it is. Good night, then." With that, he proceeded down off the dais.

When that rotten, distrustful boar had disappeared into the crowd, Margot slowly turned her head around to her keepers. They were staring at her as if she'd just risen from the crypt. "My husband is *exhausted,*" she said cheerfully. "Have you danced, Mr. Pepper? It's quite exhilarating."

"*No,*" he said, sounding as horrified as he looked.

She shrugged and glanced at the crowd. She felt entirely self-conscious, which, of course, was Arran's intent, that damn rooster. Adding to her humiliation was the knowledge that in England, she would be surrounded by friends now. But here? Everyone who remembered her hated her, and those who didn't recall her in the least were afraid of her. The only person who looked at her with any sort of kindness at all was young Gavin Mackenzie.

Margot tipped up her forgotten tankard of ale and drank to quench her thirst, then set it down with a thud on the table and stood. He thought she ought to acquaint herself, did he? She spotted Reverend Gale across the room. She picked up her skirts and marched across to him.

Reverend Gale was startled by her sudden appearance at his elbow. "Lady Mackenzie," he said, his face full of concern.

"I beg your pardon, Reverend Gale, but will you dance with me?"

"What?"

"Dance," she said again. "I know I am a wretched dancer, and I shall do my best not to kick you. But I should very much like to dance."

"Oh. Ah . . ." He glanced around as if looking for an escape. But finding none, he sighed softly and put aside his tankard of ale. "Aye, milady," he said, and held out his arm to her.

After what seemed like hours, when Margot could no longer feel her feet, she made a point of saying good-night to every Mackenzie in that hall who would allow it. Before, she would have been undone by so many indifferent expressions and uncertain glances, but tonight, she was quite pleased that the number who would address her at all had grown.

She made her way to the master's chambers feeling defiant. She knew what Arran was doing. He was deliberately putting her through her paces. He wanted to punish her for having left him, any fool could see that. She had taken up his challenge. She had talked to whoever would listen, had danced with every man she could catch unawares.

He thought he could humiliate her into leaving, did he? Well, he would not be so fortunate. She was most certainly not the same young woman who had come here so long ago.

Margot entered her sitting room and called for Nell. Her maid appeared from the dressing room and gasped when she saw her. "What *happened*?"

"What happened? I shall tell you what happened. I *danced*," she said, kicking off the offending shoes from her aching feet. She plopped down onto an ottoman, reached for a foot and began to knead it.

"Have you been here all night?" she asked Nell.

"No, mu'um," Nell said as she picked up Margot's discarded shoes. "I went down to the kitchens, and I was having a lovely chat with one of the kitchen maids, but that ox interrupted."

"Jock? What was he doing in the kitchens?" Margot asked curiously.

"I hardly know. He seems to follow me about," Nell said angrily. "Shall I bring your nightgown?"

"No. I mean to wash my hands and then go and speak to my husband," Margot said firmly.

After she'd cleaned herself up, she allowed Nell to repair parts of her hair that had come undone. She dabbed perfume behind her ears and then went into the master's chamber.

The hearth had been lit, but there was no sign of Arran. Now, just where did a man go when the whole of his clan was eating and drinking in his great hall? With whom did he consort? Was this how it was done? One betrayed one's country while everyone was occupied?

She held up a candelabra and glanced around the room — Mrs. Abernathy still had not come to visit this dreadful mess. In addition to the piles of clothing and the assortment of knives scattered about the floor, there were muddied riding boots standing at the foot of the bed, the spurs still on them.

She bent down and picked up a pair of stained buckskins. If she was going to keep near to him, she would not abide this field of debris.

CHAPTER ELEVEN

On the way to his chambers, Arran was intercepted by Sweeney, who informed him that MacLeary and his men were at the gates.

"Now?" Arran asked. He wasn't expecting them.

"Aye, milord. Donald Thane has put them in the barbican with a flagon of whisky."

The old barbican had once been used for defense of the castle, but Arran's father had refurbished the rooms to host travelers for the night. It wasn't unusual that persons who had arrived in Scotland by sea would find their way to Balhaire. "Find Jock and send him to me," Arran said, and reversed course, headed for the barbican.

MacLeary was a large man with a shock of white hair that made him look a wee bit like a snowcapped mountain. He had meaty jowls and hands, and when he greeted Arran, he clapped him so hard on the back that Arran might have gone sprawling had he not been prepared for it. MacLeary had come in the company of two men; the three were passing the flagon of whisky between them.

"Arran Mackenzie, look at ye, lad," MacLeary boomed. "There is no' a bonnier man in all of Scotland, is there? Were I no' married these thirty years, I'd ask for yer hand."

His men laughed heartily.

"I must remember to send round thanks to your wife and pray for her continued good health," Arran drawled. "What brings you to Balhaire, then?"

"We're bound for Coigeach and a meeting there," he said, referring to another MacLeary holding north of Balhaire. "You'll want to attend as well, Mackenzie. I've news for you."

The door opened behind Arran; Jock walked into the room. Arran waited for the men to exchange greetings and Jock to settle onto a bench.

"What news, then?" Arran asked MacLeary.

"Tom Dunn has come round," MacLeary said.

Arran hadn't heard that name in several years. Tom Dunn was a controversial figure in these parts. Some regarded him as a loyal patriot of Scotland and the Highlands. Others considered him a traitor to Scotland. Dunn had been friend to the Mackenzies for as long as Arran could remember, but in recent years, he'd heard some unsettling things about the man.

It had begun after the official union of Scotland and England. Dunn had settled in London to capitalize on the new connections. Or spy for the English, depending on whom one believed. "Lined his pockets with English gold," Arran had heard one man say. There was no proof of it, but since the union, rumors about everyone flowed like a burning river through these hills.

"What of him?" Arran asked.

"I've no' spoken to the man, but I've heard something interesting from Marley Buchanan." MacLeary paused to pour whisky into a glass. "Dunn told Buchanan that your Norwood has been . . . what's the word, then, lads . . . *mi-onorach,*" he said with a swirl of his hand.

There was not an exact translation for the word, but Arran understood MacLeary — he meant Margot's father was involved in something dishonest.

"In what way?"

"They say he's making bedfellows of the

French in the war against England to keep his pockets full, aye? But when suspicion was cast at him, he blamed it on you. Said he had no knowledge of any dealings with the French but had heard that *you* are plotting with them."

Arran was stunned. "I trade with the French openly and honestly. And lawfully by the Acts of Union."

"It's no' your trade he impugns, lad. He insinuates that you mean to bring French troops to Balhaire and, together with your Highland men, support the effort to put James Stuart on the throne."

Arran stared at MacLeary. James Stuart was the surviving son of King James II, who had been displaced from the throne before Arran was born. James Stuart lived in the French courts and practiced Catholicism. His half sister and reigning queen of England, Queen Anne, had been raised as a Protestant. The queen had no surviving children, and her health was not good. It had been decreed by the Acts of Succession that when she died, her successor would likewise be a Protestant. Therefore, her brother, James Stuart, would have no claim to the throne. It would go to the queen's nearest living Protestant relative, George Hanover.

There were many in Scotland, and even a few in England, who believed that the rightful heir to the throne was the queen's half brother and son of King James II. Moreover, there were many who would prefer to see that line of Stuarts restored to the throne sooner rather than later. Those who actively sought that end were known as Jacobites.

It was impossible to believe that Norwood would be involved in such deadly politics. And to be involved to such an extent that he would label Arran a Jacobite sympathizer seemed out of character for him. After all, Norwood was the one who had proposed that Arran marry his only daughter to expand both their holdings. Why would he want to tear apart what he'd worked so hard to put together?

"I'm no' a Jacobite. There's no' a man in the Highlands who believes I am. I donna believe it," Arran said flatly. "Norwood helped design the union. He staked his reputation on it, and he is loyal to the queen. Why would he seek to harm that?"

"*Ach,* the queen," MacLeary said with a beefy wave of his hand. "She's no' right in the head, that one. She sleeps with her maid and wars with the Duchess of Marlborough over jewels or some such nonsense. She's no' meant to lead nations, and word from

London is that she's no' long for this world, aye? Donna close your eyes and ears, man. Men are aligning themselves with whomever they believe will prevail. And ye know as well as I do that ye canna trust a *Sassenach* as long as a day."

Arran didn't disagree with that, but still, it seemed too risky for Norwood. "It doesna make sense," he insisted, holding up a hand. "If I were accused of treason and made to stand trial, that would mean that my lands — his *daughter's* lands — would be forfeited to the crown."

"Or . . . perhaps yer lands would be forfeited and given as reward to whoever exposed the treason," MacLeary suggested. "It's a gamble a man might find worth taking."

"Norwood would stand to gain," Jock agreed.

"No' bloody likely," Arran scoffed.

"I canna say it delicately, lad," said MacLeary. "So I'll speak to the point. Your wife is English. If your holdings were forfeited, they'd most likely revert to her father and brothers, would they no'? By the same token, if Norwood was guilty of treason, his lands would no' go to his sons. You'd have a decent claim to them through your wife. No, he'd no' risk losing what he's got, no' to a Scot, no matter how he might have wanted this union ere now. He could very easily make you a scapegoat in his schemes." He paused to drink more whisky, then fixed his gaze on Arran. "There are some who could be persuaded that perhaps you conspire with Norwood to line *your* pockets."

"Norwood! That's contrary to everything you've just said of me, is it no'? Whom do I conspire with, MacLeary? The Jacobites? Or Norwood? What possible reason would I have to conspire with either? What the bloody hell would I gain?"

MacLeary shrugged. "An argument could be made that you'd gain more lands in England if you were to betray anyone here. If, for example, you were to name anyone who might want to see James Stuart sit the throne." He slowly brought his glass to his lips and watched Arran as he drank.

"By God, MacLeary, you willna come into these walls and accuse the laird," Jock growled.

"I didna accuse him," MacLeary said with a shrug. "I merely repeat words that already have been said."

"If it's reassurance you seek, I will give it to you," Arran said evenly. "I no more conspire with England than I do with Jacobites."

"And *I* believe you," MacLeary said, clapping a hand on Arran's shoulder. "But I think you'd best come to Coigeach on the morrow and say it again. No' everyone is as sure of it as me, aye?"

Arran had been nothing but loyal to the Highlands and to Scotland. He was guilty of nothing more than seizing an opportunity to keep his lands and to save his people from hunger. "You may count on me to join you in Coigeach," he said darkly. "If any man believes I have betrayed him, let him say it to my face."

"It was always a wee bit of a gamble taking an Englishwoman to wife, was it no'?" MacLeary asked slyly, and tipped the glass back against his lips, draining the whisky from it.

Arran wanted to put his fist in MacLeary's face for saying a single word against his wife. But he wasn't sure what the landscape was between them now, especially with this swirl of rumors. "Aye, that it was," he agreed. He moved for the door, his head spinning with questions. "We've a warm bed for you and your men," he forced himself to say. "I'll see you at Coigeach on the morrow." He walked out of the room, leaving Jock to deal with the MacLearys.

He could well imagine what Jock was

thinking just now — that he should never have married Margot Armstrong. That his warnings of the trouble it would cause were coming home to roost. Jock could very well be right, and yet there was something about it that didn't ring true to Arran. No matter what had happened between him and his wife, he couldn't believe Margot was involved in any attempt to make him a scapegoat. She might dislike him, and she might have been sent by Norwood for some purpose. But he didn't believe she wanted to see him hanged.

If she did, she was the finest liar he'd ever met.

And yet, Arran had a gut-wrenching feeling as he walked back through Balhaire and up the staircase to his suite. Oh, the irony of having built a small empire here in part by marrying a woman who would, in the end, see him hanged.

When he reached his chambers, he opened the door and stepped inside. It was dark — he'd not sent the lad up to light the room. He stood a moment at the threshold, allowing his vision to adjust with the moonlight streaming in through the open window so that he might find a candle. He slowly became aware that something was different.

There was nothing on the floor.

The clothes and boots and hats and coats he'd left scattered about the room were gone. And there was a dark shadow draped across the back of a chair. He recognized the shimmering threads that seemed to move in the moonlight. Aye, that was the gown Margot had worn this evening. She'd taken his breath away, arriving in all her glory as she had, that swath of plaid across her breast. There was not a fairer woman in all the Highlands, and he'd been acutely and painfully aware that she was his.

He might have treated her more fairly. But her appearance had reminded him of a night long ago, when two Mackenzie chieftains had come to Balhaire to meet with him. Arran had ordered supper to be served in true Scotch hospitality. He'd informed his unhappy bride of her obligation to play the dutiful wife of a new Scottish baron.

Margot had attended in all her finery. She'd been a bonny vision, a jewel in this rugged, heather-strewn landscape. And then she'd proceeded to express her ennui. *"Is that all you talk about, you Scots — seafaring and sheep?"* she'd asked disdainfully.

"Aye, madam, when one or the other will provide for our people," Brian Mackenzie had said.

Margot had rolled her eyes, propped her

head on her hand and carried on as if she were a sulking child instead of a grown woman and a chieftain's wife, as responsible for the welfare of their clan as he.

She had embarrassed him, and they'd quarreled about it afterward. Arran had accused her of sabotaging his friendships and affiliations. She'd claimed not to have understood the importance of the men who had come to dine, and blamed him for failing to inform her.

That night had ended as many of their nights had — with each of them retreating from the other.

In truth, Arran had expected the same of her tonight. He'd pushed her, had challenged her and had fully expected — even hoped — she would cry off and go scampering back to England and free him of his doubts. But Margot had kept her countenance serene, had done her best to be one of them. She'd danced, for God's sake, something she'd steadfastly refused in the four months they'd lived as husband and wife.

He touched her gown now, felt the smooth texture of the silk, the raised bits of thread so artfully woven into the skirt. If her gown was here, where was she?

He squinted into the darkened room and

spotted the mound of a person beneath the coverlet, three dogs beside her. That was a surprise.

Arran leaned down and quietly removed all but his plaid and his shirt. He padded over to the bed, pulled his shirt free of his plaid, and then, with hands on his hips, he stared down at his wife. The dogs lifted their heads and began to beat their tails against the coverlet. He signaled them down and ushered them out of the room, then returned to the bed.

She lay on her side. A thick braid of her hair spilled behind her like a rope. Her face was buried in a pillow and her limbs, covered by the bed linens, seemed to be folded at strange angles. It was strange finding her here like this — she'd never slept a full night in his bed without being commanded to do it.

He stripped out of his shirt and plaid, leaving them where they fell, and lifted the bedsheet to slide in beside her. He moved to her back, draping his arm across her abdomen. She was wearing a silk chemise that felt like water to his hand, and her hair was fragrant, as if a vine of clematis had curled around his bed. Her small, supple body was invitingly warm, and he was suddenly and unwelcomingly filled with longing. A desire to protect. To keep, to hold.

"Where were you?" she murmured sleepily into her pillow.

"Minding things."

"Do you have a mistress?"

Arran sighed impatiently. "No. I've been unfailingly and uncomfortably and some say foolishly loyal to the marriage vows I made before you and God, aye?"

Margot shifted onto her back and blinked up at him with lids heavy with sleep. She smiled softly and touched a lock of hair on his forehead. "Truly?"

"I would no' say so were it false. There has been no one but you since we wed. Can you say the same?"

She touched the tip of her finger to his lips.

"Before you answer, I will caution you against falsehood," he said, and lightly bit the tip of her finger before pulling her hand down. "Dermid has been near Norwood Park since you left, aye?"

"Oh, indeed he has," she said with a sigh. "Someone is *always* watching me. I will be entirely honest, but you will not like my answer."

Bloody hell. He steeled himself. "Go on, then. Donna trifle with me."

She looked him in the eye. "Shortly after I

returned to Norwood Park, I allowed a gentleman to kiss me."

Arran frowned. He waited. Surely there was more to it. "Who?"

"Does it matter?"

"Aye, it matters," he said, catching her hand and keeping her from touching him again. *"Who?"*

"Sir William Dalton," she said, and pulled her hand free. "I shouldn't think you'd know of him."

Arran didn't know him, but he would commit that name to memory and kill the bloody bounder one day. "Why did you allow it, then?" he demanded. "Do you love him?"

"Love?" She giggled. "No! Not for a moment." She rolled onto her belly beside him and came up on her elbows; the scent of her perfume wafted over him. She smelled like flowers. A bouquet of flowers. "God's truth, I don't know why I did it," she said low. "I'd had a bit of port that evening and I was feeling a bit morose. And vexed."

"What had you vexed?"

"Well, *you,* my darling husband," she said, as if he should have guessed as much. "I was angry that I'd been forced into marriage and suddenly had no hope of another one."

"Thank you," he said, and fell onto his back. He threw one arm over his eyes, not wanting to see her face.

Margot clucked her tongue. "Don't be missish, Mackenzie. You know very well what I mean."

"I donna know what you mean, Margot. I *never* know what you mean."

"Are you really surprised? Our marriage was arranged to expand my father's and your fortunes. It was not made for compatibility. Surely you can see it is not one I would ever have chosen for myself."

"I donna see why no'," he said petulantly.

"Because I'd only met you! One cannot determine compatibility for a lifetime in one or two meetings. And the marriage didn't seem to suit either of us, did it? And there I was, come home from the disaster of it —"

"It wasna a *disaster* —"

"— and Sir Dalton was quite convincing in his esteem for me."

"This is no' easing me," he said gruffly.

"I allowed him to kiss me in a moment of weakness. And then . . ." Her voice trailed off.

Arran removed his arm from his eyes and peered over at her. "And *then*?"

"And then I realized what I was doing. And I further realized that I didn't want to

222

do it. I'd been caught up in a moment, and thank heaven, I remembered myself, for I never would have forgiven myself."

He didn't know if he believed her. "Why no' go on with it, then?" he scoffed. "You clearly held no regard for me."

"Now, that is simply not true," she said patiently, and lightly kissed his shoulder. "I hold a great deal of regard for you. I didn't go on with it for the same reason you didn't. Because I had taken vows before God and made them to you."

"Aye, that you did," he snapped.

For some reason, his irritation made her giggle. Before Arran could say that he did not find it the least bit amusing, she bent down and kissed his nipple, her teeth grazing it and igniting a fire in him. He rolled away from her, onto his side.

Margot stubbornly kissed the point between his shoulder blades. "Were you *never* tempted?" she asked.

"Aye, of course I was tempted," he said, making a feeble attempt to bat her away. "I'm a man. But I was married and I didna act on it."

"Then you're much stronger of character than am I."

He grunted at that. "You'll be astonished, no doubt, that admitting your weakness does no' pacify me in the least. It only makes me more suspicious of you."

She kissed the back of his neck. "I didn't tell you to pacify you. I told you to be completely honest and offer you my *sincerest* apologies."

"Then you'd best start offering, madam — the list is quite long."

"Yes, it is, and I do offer them, Arran," she said, and her hand slid around to his chest. "I offer my apologies for everything."

Everything. What did that mean, really? He looked over his shoulder at her. *Diah,* but the woman could fire his blood, her lips dark rose against her skin made milky by the moonlight. She looked so earnest. So treacherous. So desirable. His head warred with his heart. His heart warred with his cock. What was he doing with her? Why had he not sent her home straightaway?

"I *am* sorry," she said, biting his arm lightly. "Can you not see how I've tried to show you? I danced. I drank ale. I came to you. It's not pretense — it's my sincere effort to please you."

"*Ach,* it shows me nothing," he said with a flick of his wrist. "You might do the same for a new gown."

"Then perhaps this will convince you," she said, and kissed his ribs.

Arran jerked. He was ticklish there. "Donna do that."

Margot moved lower, her hair trailing down his arm as her mouth moved across him. She kissed his abdomen, lingering there.

He wouldn't fight it. He was incapable of fighting it. He was brought to mind of their wedding night, of how beautiful and innocent she'd been. And completely ignorant of what went on between a man and a woman. It was utterly impossible that she should have reached adulthood with no carnal knowledge, but it appeared that was precisely the case. He had not relished taking her virginity the way some men did, but when the task was done, he had loved teaching her what pleased her. And what pleased him. And the many ways they could enjoy each other.

She moved lower, her tongue teasing the tip of his cock. Had he taught her this, as well? How to drive a man to utter madness? "I'm no' a woman," he warned her. "I'll no' be swayed by a bloody kiss. I'll trust you no more by morning's light."

"You most certainly are not a woman," she agreed, and took him into her mouth.

Arran lost his will to argue; his eyes fluttered shut as her lips moved over him, her tongue circling the girth of him. She wasn't an innocent virgin anymore. Just a touch, a kiss, and he found himself unable to deny her a bloody thing. He'd always been tender with her, conscience of her youth and naïveté. But she was different now. She was lustier. Mature. Seasoned in a way that could only come from a marriage bed and time. She stoked something unworldly in him that made him feel as if he could hurl cabers, swim oceans and wrestle bears.

She was quickly driving him to the point of oblivion, and Arran suddenly surged up. He caught her beneath her arms, and in one swift movement, he put her on her back and moved between her legs, pushing them aside with his knees. Margot clawed at her chemise, pulling it up, clear of her pelvis, and Arran pressed the tip of his massive erection against her, moving in tantalizingly slow motions against her wet, warm sex.

Margot grasped his hips, pulling him closer, arching her back so that he could feel her body pulsating against his. She was clearly enjoying herself. She was as willing a partner as a man could ever hope to have, unafraid of Arran or his body, unafraid to take pleasure where she could. She had become the sort of lover that men dreamed of possessing in a moment like this.

He slid into her body, and Margot flung her arms wide with a sigh of pure pleasure. Arran closed his eyes and lost himself in that exquisite sensation, slipping his hand between her legs to caress her as he moved with increasing urgency. She responded by raking her hands down his back and lifting her knees, locking her feet behind his back. She was breathing heavily, as lost as he was in the physical sensations of their lovemaking. Her deepening pleasure made him burn madly to give her more.

When she began to pant, Arran clasped her tightly, lifted his hips and thrust deep into her, over and over again until Margot cried out and her body spasmed around his. His own release followed, the force of it racking his body.

He dropped his forehead to her shoulder, and it was several moments before he could find the strength to lift his head again. When he did, Margot's smile was seductive and sated. "Oh, Arran, you've always pleased me so," she murmured, and kissed his eyes, his temple.

This woman was terrifying. She could snatch his breath with only a smile. She could make him overlook her perfidy, could make him forgive everything just so that he might have her. "Have I pleased you more than Sir Dalton?"

"*Infinitely,*" she assured him.

Arran grunted his satisfaction with that answer. He kissed her again as he eased out of her body and rolled onto his back. Margot sighed happily and nestled against him with her head on his chest, her arm draped across him.

He casually stroked her arm. "You'll tell me the truth now, aye, Margot? Why have you come back?"

She sighed, her breath warm on his skin. "This again?"

"Aye, this again, until I have whatever it is you're hiding."

"Why won't you believe me?"

"Because it seems verra convenient, your sudden appearance like a waif in the night."

"It wasn't convenient at all, really. Very inconvenient, if you must know, what with all the packing, and the journey is really quite long and difficult. And did you see my companions?"

"Aye. English fops, the both of them."

Margot lifted her head and smiled at him. *Diah,* that smile.

"Weren't you even a *tiny* bit happy to see me?" she asked as she traced his initials on his bare chest.

"No," he said. A lie. "And if you willna

tell me the truth, you may go back to your rooms. Shall I put you in your gown?"

"No."

"Do you intend to walk through Balhaire in only this?" he asked, slipping his finger under her chemise.

"I intend to stay here, with you. I'm not keeping separate rooms."

"Aye, you are —"

"You always wanted me with you before. You never liked for me to have separate chambers."

"It's different now," he said, panicking a little at the thought of having her in his bed every night.

"Yes, because *I'm* different now. I want to please you. And besides, you need someone here. This chamber is in utter disarray."

"Mrs. Abernathy's sister is ailing and she's away. I donna trust anyone else to tend my rooms."

"There, you see? All the more reason you need me," she said, and kissed him on the lips.

She was winning this battle. Arran roughly took her face in his hand. "Have you no' heard me? I *donna* need you, Margot. Donna convince yourself that I do," he said coldly.

"Whatever you say," she murmured

sweetly, and pushed his hand from her face, then floated down, nestling against him, in the crook of his arm and shoulder, just like she used to do after they made love.

It felt maddeningly right. *God damn this,* Arran thought. The woman knew very well what she was doing — she was playing him like a bloody fiddle, wooing him to her, countering him at every turn. She might as well run a sword through him. She had rendered him that useless.

And for what — to see him hanged? Not if he could help it.

Unfortunately, judging by his patent inability to dismiss her, he could *not* help it. He was doomed.

A gentle slap to her bottom startled Margot awake; she rose up with a sleepy mewl of alarm to see Arran standing beside the bed, already dressed for the day. The dawn sky was pink, and yet she could hear voices drifting up to them from the bailey below. She pressed her fingertips to her eyes a moment before opening them again.

Arran grinned at her. "How does a woman go to bed looking as bonny as a woman has ever looked, and wake up the very next morning looking like this?" he asked, tousling her hair. "Come, then, it's time to rise.

Summon the lass who attends you." He shrugged into a coat. "I'm to Coigeach for the day."

"You're leaving Balhaire again?" she asked plaintively.

"I'll return by nightfall," he said, and leaned over to kiss her forehead. "Mind you behave. Donna frighten my clan with a lot of wandering about, aye?"

"Oh, I think there is no danger of frightening them," she said with a yawn. "You've always confused their dislike for fear."

"On the contrary, I've known it to be both dislike and fear." He winked, tossed her gown onto the bed and strode out of the chamber.

Margot fell back against the pillows and yawned again. She didn't want to think of anything at the moment. She felt content lying in his bed with a cool morning breeze drifting in through the window. It had been quite nice sleeping with her husband last night. She had liked the warmth of him at her back. She'd liked the feeling of utter safety with his arm anchored firmly around her waist.

She rolled over and buried her face in Arran's pillow, breathing in the musky scent of him. God, what a little cake-headed fool she'd been before. There was something so intimate about sleeping with him. She'd never realized how it adhered two people to each other. She couldn't help but wonder what other things she'd been so desperately wrong about.

Her reasons for being here were becoming muddier and muddier to her. She wanted to know if she had ruined any chance of a marriage with him. But she also wanted to know where it was he was going, what he was doing. Was she feeling these intimate ties to a traitor?

She looked around her. She supposed she had the perfect opportunity now to have a look about, but she had no stomach for it. Last night, when she'd picked up this room, she'd made a halfhearted attempt to look for some clue as to what he was involved in by poking under the bed and into his chest of drawers.

She didn't like it. It felt wrong, dishonest. Especially when she wasn't certain what, exactly, she should be seeking. Especially when she was going to crawl into the man's bed and kiss him.

Maybe she'd ride today, she thought idly. She was not a good rider, but she could manage. She had to do something with Pepper and Worthing watching her all day. She would tell them she was going to pay a call to someone — she'd think of someone, anyway — then slip out, perhaps ride down to the cove to have a look. It would be a relief to go beyond the castle walls. She needed time to think and reassess, away from everyone.

Margot groped over her head for the little bell that would summon Nell from the antechamber.

An hour or so later, Margot emerged dressed for riding. She wandered down to the great hall, where she knew she would find a sideboard laden with breakfast food. Since the laird lived with his entire extended family — and *their* families, et cetera and so forth — it was necessary to lay out a feast most mornings. These large breakfasts had vexed her before, particularly when Arran had told her she was expected to be present. Margot had never been one to enjoy early mornings. She had reasoned that while an early breakfast might be prudent for the many Mackenzies who had many things to accomplish in a day, it was hardly the thing for the lady of the house.

What foolishness.

The hall was still crowded, mostly with women and children. A few looked at her as if they expected her to cock up her toes at any moment, but their numbers were dwindling.

The sideboard was filled with food, as she knew it would be, and she perused the selection.

"*Madainn mhath,* milady."

She turned her head and saw Lennon Mackenzie, the blacksmith at Balhaire. "Good morning," she said.

"Good day for a reel, aye?" he asked. His companions snickered.

Margot smiled, too, and turned around to him, surprising him, judging by the way the man swayed back and away from her. "I beg your pardon, Mr. Mackenzie. Did I kick you last night? My apologies! I have not yet learned the fine art of the reel, but I am *quite* determined."

He looked uncertainly at his companions. "It's all in the skip, it is. You master that wee kick, and you've learned it."

"Will you teach me?" she asked, and popped a berry in her mouth, her eyes fixed on him, amused at how many emotions flitted across the man's face. Lennon Mackenzie and his companions looked shocked. They waited, wide-eyed, for his answer.

"Aye, milady," he said. "Aye, I'll teach you."

"*That's* a promise," she said, and patted

234

him on the shoulder. "Thank you." She turned around and continued her perusal of the sideboard.

She was dithering over the cheeses when she felt someone sidle up to her. She half expected Lennon Mackenzie begging to be relieved of his promise. But it was Mr. Pepper standing beside her, holding a lace handkerchief to his nose, as if he were offended by the smell of breakfast. "Good morrow, Lady Mackenzie," he said, inclining his head.

"Mr. Pepper." She returned her attention to the sideboard. "Have you come to ridicule my dancing, too?"

"I don't consider what they do here to be dancing," he said primly. "I have heard that the laird has left Balhaire."

Well, then, Mr. Pepper didn't miss a thing, did he? "So he has."

"Where has he gone?"

"He did not say," she said, and began to pile cheeses onto her plate.

Mr. Pepper watched her. "You are dressed for riding."

A rather ridiculous observation, seeing as how she clearly already knew she was dressed for riding. "Yes."

"Where do you mean to ride?" he asked casually.

Margot paused and looked at him. "Why?"

"Why indeed," he said impatiently. "I am here to ensure your safety. I would not like to see you ride out alone without even a proper dog to accompany you." He looked meaningfully to his left.

Margot followed his gaze. An old hound with a white muzzle was stretched out on his side near the hearth.

"The laird is quite fond of dogs," she said coolly. And she thought if Mr. Pepper didn't care for them, he ought to find lodging elsewhere. She was suddenly reminded of a young dog here at Balhaire who'd been badly injured by a trap that had been illegally. When the gamekeeper determined the poor dog could not be saved and, furthermore, would suffer in his last hours, she had watched Arran scoop the dog up in his arms and carry him from this very hall with tears on his face.

He'd taken the dog into the woods and mercifully put it out of its misery.

She shivered at the painful recollection of how he'd grieved for the dog.

"I heard the laird departed in the company of several other men. Highland clansmen."

She glanced curiously at him. Mr. Pepper had a handful of berries and was casually eating them. "He did?"

"You don't know?" Mr. Pepper asked irritably. "Here now, you must have at least a groom to accompany you. You cannot be too cautious now —"

"I am at home here, Mr. Pepper. I won't need a dog or groom to accompany me. I mean to call on a friend who might have something to tell me." She arched a brow. "But she won't tell me a thing if I come in the company of anyone."

Mr. Pepper popped another berry in his mouth, shrewdly assessing her.

"But thank you kindly for your concern for my safety." She moved down the sideboard, ending the conversation.

Mr. Pepper didn't press her further, but she noticed that the moment Worthing appeared, Pepper was at his side, whispering in his ear. How long did these two men intend to remain at Balhaire? They really served no purpose other than to make her anxious. She would be much more at ease in her odious task if she didn't feel as if someone was constantly watching her.

When she finished her breakfast and was certain she'd not be accosted by either Mr. Pepper or Sir Worthing, Margot put on her hat and gloves and went out into the bailey in search of Sweeney.

She found him easily enough. "A horse

please, Sweeney," she said after she'd greeted him. "Preferably one a bit smaller than the one you saddled for me earlier this week. One that I might actually ride without fear of being thrown. Oh, and if you please, a proper saddle."

"Proper," Sweeney said, his nerves apparently calmer today.

"Yes. One suitable for a lady to ride."

His eyes narrowed. "I'll have a look around, then," he said, and disappeared into the stables. When he at last reemerged, he was leading a black Fell pony behind him. The horse had a shaggy, thick mane that covered his eyes. He was broad, but much shorter than the one she'd ridden two days ago.

"Oh, this one is lovely," Margot said, stroking the horse's nose.

"Aye, he's a good-tempered mount, and sure-footed, he is. He's good with inexperienced riders, aye?"

"Yes, well. I suppose that would suit me perfectly." She sighed.

Sweeney cupped his hands for her and helped her up onto a sidesaddle so ancient that it was cracked across the seat. It took her several moments to find her balance, but when she felt as if she was sitting as confidently as she could, she said, "Should anyone inquire, I am calling on a friend."

"You are?" Sweeney asked, clearly dubious.

Margot looked pointedly at him.

"Aye, mu'um," Sweeney said with the confidence of a man who knew no one would inquire.

After she made several attempts to get the pony to move, Sweeney resorted to giving the beast a slap on the rump. Margot eventually rode out, the pony trotting out the gates as sure-footedly as Sweeney had promised.

She rode down a wide, flat path that took her through fields of heather before becoming noticeably steeper. The path moved from there into the woods, where patches of primrose and harebells grew, and the air was sweet with the scent of honeysuckle. There wasn't a sound in the air besides birds chirping and the tide coming in to shore, and Margot very much appreciated the solitude. Remarkably for a woman who was estranged from her husband, she never had solitude. Someone was always watching her. Her father, her brothers. The man Arran had sent from Scotland.

The pony seemed to know precisely where she wanted to go and moved down the path with ease. When she reached the beach, she could see a ship anchored quite far out. She could see the figures of men moving about on the deck of that ship and noticed that someone had pulled a rowboat up onto the shore.

A month ago, Margot would have thought nothing of this ship. She would not have been particularly interested if it had just come in or was preparing to sail. But now she wondered if that ship was a key to her husband's guilt or innocence.

She was gazing out at the ship when a movement caught her eye, and she turned to see a man coming out of the woods. When he saw her, he stopped. He rubbed his hands on his dirty trousers and glanced at the ship, then at her.

Apprehension swooned in Margot's belly. "Ah . . . good afternoon," she said uncertainly.

He said nothing; he stared warily.

Perhaps she should have heeded Mr. Pepper and at least brought a dog along with her. "I am Lady Mackenzie."

"Aye, I know who you be, mu'um."

Well, then. At least he knew there would be consequences for murdering her. Or rather, she at least hoped the possibility of dire consequences might cross his mind. Frankly, she wasn't entirely confident of it.

"What . . . what were you doing there, in the woods?" she asked. When all else failed, assume an air of authority and hope for the best.

The man glanced back over his shoulder. Several wooden crates had been stacked in the shadow of the trees, and she immediately assumed guns. If her husband was planning a rebellion, he would need guns. And didn't guns generally arrive in crates?

"Nothing, milady," he said. "We've brung back bolts of cloth and fine china. We've got to get them off the ship."

"But . . . where have you come from?"

"From the Continent, milady." He was nervously twisting the cap around in his hands.

The Continent. Margot felt a little ill. Guns from France! First guns, then men. Didn't that seem logical? "Have you brought any men with you? Any soldiers or officers?"

He looked confused and glanced at the ship. "No."

Another rowboat had been put in the water at the ship, and two men were slowly making their way toward shore with several crates between them. She didn't have much time.

"Who has commanded the ship?" she demanded, as if that would enlighten her in any way.

"Cap'n Mackenzie, mu'um."

That was no help — there could be dozens of Captain Mackenzies around here.

"Aye, Cap'n Mackenzie," he said again.

He began to move toward her, and Margot's heart climbed to her throat. "The laird shall be along at any moment," she said, and even glanced over her shoulder with the insane hope that he might somehow miraculously appear.

"The laird?" the man said. "But he's gone to Coigeach," he said, moving closer.

Margot's short breath turned to sheer panic. She imagined this man tossing down his cap just before he tackled her. She'd fall like a rock, as she'd never be able to hold her balance on this ridiculous sidesaddle. Arran was right — he'd once said she should have a pair of buckskins fashioned and learn to ride astride. If she lived to see another morning, she would do precisely that.

As he moved closer, he shoved one hand in his pocket.

"Dear God," she murmured. She expected him to produce a knife and tried to pull the fool horse around. But the horse wouldn't budge at first, confused as to what Margot wanted. She jerked hard to the right and the horse came around halfway.

"Milady!" the man said, walking faster.

Margot begged the beast with the pull of the reins and her heel to turn around —

"I've something for you, I do," he said. "A gift." He had reached the pony's head and grabbed the bridle, holding the horse in place.

"Let go," Margot said, her voice shaking with fear.

The man pulled his hand free of his pocket and held it out to her. In his palm was a small, exquisitely carved figurine of a woman, dressed in a court dress. One of her legs was extended, and she held the sides of her skirt up in her outstretched hands, bowing over it. But one of her arms had been broken off at the shoulder.

Not a knife. A figurine. She tried to understand what it was, what it meant.

"One of them boxes, it was dropped, aye? The china, it's packed tight in straw, so we lost only a few fine things. But a few come up broken, and Cap'n said to throw it all overboard, he did. But I fancied it. Thought it would make a fine gift, aye?" He held up his hand to Margot. "Her arm's broken, but she's bonny all the same. A gift for the laird's lady. If you'll have it."

"You mean to give it to me?" Margot

243

asked uncertainly.

"Aye, mu'um. Please," he said.

Margot hesitated. She gingerly lifted the figurine from his hand. "Thank you."

"I wasna stealing it," he said. "I donna thieve."

"No, no — I never thought so." Of course she'd thought so, and he knew it.

"I only put it in my pocket to give the laird, aye? But then we heard his wife had come beg—" He blanched at what he'd just said and looked down, ran a hand over his head.

"That she'd come back, I mean to say," he hastily corrected himself. "And I thought it a fitting gift for ye, then. To welcome you to Balhaire once more."

She blushed, bent her head to examine the figurine. "Well, at least I have crawled back for a fine gift, haven't I?"

The poor man looked stricken, and Margot had to laugh. "Thank you, sir. You cannot imagine how I appreciate this." Or how much she appreciated he did not mean to harm her, but to greet her.

The man nodded and stepped back. "No' all of them are happy to see you. I'd be a liar if I said otherwise. But a man needs his wife, aye? Me, I didna know how much I needed the wife 'til she'd gone."

"Gone?"

"Black fever."

"Oh. Oh my. I'm so — My condolences, sir." She didn't know quite what more to say to that. She couldn't imagine how devastating that would be. She and Arran had their differences, but to think of that possibility . . .

Margot swallowed. "Thank you again." She tucked the figurine into her pocket for safekeeping.

This time, she managed to pull the pony around.

She thought about what the man had said as the pony picked its way up the hill to ride along the low cliff above the shore. She had never pondered if Arran needed her or not — she'd thought only how she'd needed him.

Did he need her? How could she ever be useful beyond her dowry to a man like him? She was more burden than helpmate.

She looked out to the sea. From here, she could see the ship more clearly. It was a small ship, the sort designed for speed. She was no expert on sailing vessels, but she was aware that the ships carrying troops were generally larger. This was absurd — she would never find evidence of Arran's treachery by riding around the land, looking for clues. It was absurd.

She turned the pony away from the sea and rode up the glen. Her progress was slow as she didn't know how to persuade the pony to do more than plod along. It hardly mattered — she was entranced with the landscape. She had forgotten how the green Highlands turned gold in a certain light, purple in another light. The air smelled of wet leaves and the musky scent of peat.

Presently she heard voices, and as the pony followed the path out of the forest, she rode past crofters working to cut and bind hay. Such a simple but meaningful existence. These people worked to fuel their lives and raise their children. They didn't worry about social standing or connections.

It was quite easy to see that Balhaire was prospering. It made no sense that Arran would jeopardize all that he'd built here to put James Stuart on the throne. What would he have to gain from it? Nothing! He had everything to *lose.*

A thought suddenly occurred to Margot. She didn't need to find proof that he was involved in treason. She had to find proof that he was not.

And how did one do that?

The same way, she supposed, one found proof of treason.

When Margot returned to Balhaire, she was more confused than ever. She was so lost in her own thoughts that when she handed the reins of the horse to a stable boy and walked into the castle, she cared not a whit who saw her or whether they looked at her or not. She felt quite at a loss for what to do now. She hurried upstairs to the rooms next to Arran's bedchamber and threw open the door — and very nearly startled Nell to death.

"There you are, milady!" Nell said. "I thought you'd never return. What a day I've had! That man has come round again, and he says I'm not to enter the laird's rooms without invitation. I says, 'My lady is sharing those rooms, and I guess I'll enter when she says!' And *he* says —"

"Nell," Margot said, holding up her hand. "I would like to lie down a bit before supper."

"Pardon, milady. Are you unwell?" Nell asked.

"A bit of a headache. It's been rather a long day."

"Shall I fetch —"

"No, nothing. I'll ring for you when I need you." She backed out of the room, pulling the door closed, and retreated to the master bedchamber. She closed the door carefully behind her, then stood in the middle of the room, her hands on her hips.

She meant to have a lie down, but her gaze moved to the large chest of drawers. If a man had secrets to keep, he would keep them close. Margot moved hesitantly to the chest of drawers and, with finger and thumb, lifted the drawer pull and pulled it open. The drawer contained shirts. She grimaced as she put her hand beneath them, groping about, hoping to find something. And indeed, her fingers closed around a metal piece; she quickly withdrew it from beneath the shirts and held it up.

It was a signet ring.

Margot put it back and shut the drawer.

She opened the next drawer and found more articles of clothing. A third drawer contained two hunting knives and a pocket watch. She closed that one and then came down to her knees to open a pair of doors at the bottom of the chest. She pulled on one door — it didn't open. Thinking it was stuck, she gave it a stronger tug. The door came open, and inside, she found nothing but more clothing.

She stood up and looked toward his dressing room. His study. Of course! She'd forgotten that small circular room on the other side of his dressing room.

She glanced behind her and stepped into the dimly lit dressing room. She was aware of Arran's things hanging around her, heavy with his scent. Scuffed boots on the floor. Plaids and coats, buckskins and lawn shirts hung from hooks and in a wardrobe standing open.

Margot's fingers trailed against his things as she moved through to his small, private study that adjoined the dressing room, and slowly, carefully turned the door latch. She held her breath, opened the door a fraction and peeked in. She was almost expecting to see him sitting there, his head bent over a ledger, his quill moving quickly across the columns. But the room was empty and the hearth so cold that the acrid smell of old smoke lingered. The only light came through a pair of windows that looked out to the hills.

Margot stepped in and left the door open so that she might hear if someone entered the master bedchamber. Frankly, it would have been a miracle if she heard anything at all — the sound of her wildly beating heart filled her ears.

Voices in the hallway caused her heart to stop beating altogether for a moment, and she jerked her gaze over her shoulder, holding perfectly still, straining to listen. The

voices passed by — servants, by the sound
of it. She glanced up at the mantel clock —
it was a quarter past five o'clock. Nell would
come in soon to help her dress for dinner.
And God knew what Balhaire servant would
pop in to ready things for the return of Arran.

If she was going to look, she had very little
time. Margot hurried to his desk and quickly
opened two drawers. Nothing. There were
only a few items on his desk — the estate
ledger and some correspondence that had
come from one of the clansmen. She was
feeling anxious now and started to leave the
room, but noticed a small cabinet set apart
from the desk and up against the wall. She
leaned over and pulled on the door. It was
locked. Margot squatted down beside the
door and pulled again, just to be sure. Yes,
the door was locked, and her heart began to
beat mercilessly against her chest.

She stood up and looked wildly about for
something to pry open the door, but seeing
nothing immediately, she remembered the
knives in the bedchamber. She swore under
her breath, raced across the room to his
chest of drawers, retrieved one of the knives
and ran back again. She slid the tip of the
knife in at the lock and tried to jiggle it
open, using both hands to hold the knife

and steadying the cabinet with her knee.

She thought she could feel the doors begin to give when she suddenly heard a ruckus in the corridor.

"Water to bathe, Fergus! I've the dust of the road in my throat and in my ears."

Margot gasped almost soundlessly at the sound of Arran's voice. She hadn't expected him back until much later.

"Aye, now," she heard him reaffirm to a distant voice.

She stared with horror at the knife in her hand. She sprang to her feet and looked around the small study.

But there was no place to hide.

CHAPTER TWELVE

Arran opened the door to his chamber and barely had time to register Margot's presence before he was knocked a step backward by the force of her leaping into his arms. "What the devil?" he asked, catching her.

"I'm so happy you've come back!"

"Did you think I'd deserted you?" He gave her a wry smile as he eased back from her strong hold on his neck.

Margot answered by taking his face between her hands and kissing him fiercely.

His blood began to stir, but then the events of the day nudged back into his consciousness. He pulled her arms free of his neck and set her down a few inches from him. "To what do I owe such an enthusiastic welcome?" he asked wryly. And what was she doing, skulking about his chamber at this time of day? She ought to have been in her sitting room or her dressing room. He was suspicious of her — even more so now, having heard what he had in Coigeach — and moved deeper into the room, looking around.

"I missed you," she said earnestly. "How was your journey?"

"Tedious." That was the most civil thing he could say for what he'd endured today. At a meeting of four Highland chieftains — all of them known Jacobites — Arran had been accused of colluding with the English.

It was as absurd as it was insulting. He'd been married to Margot for more than three years. As he pointed out to those men, if there was any colluding to be done, any betraying of his fellow Highlanders, would he not have done it when he was actually on speaking terms with her? Instead, he'd spent several years without his wife, working to make Balhaire prosperous so that it might sustain the many Mackenzies who lived there. "I've had quite a lot more to occupy me than one man's claim to the throne, aye?"

"Aye," Buchanan said. He was a mountain of a man whose unruly beard was a more fiery-looking ginger than that on his head. "But suppose a man who openly trades with France could earn even more money by keeping the English in his sporran? Would he no' do so?"

"And betray his clan and his country?" Arran asked tightly. "I'm no' a greedy man. I earn what I have — I donna need to betray my land and my people to line my coffers."

"And yet ye canna deny that the sudden appearance of Lady Mackenzie is puzzling?" MacLeary had asked slyly. "Just as we've begun to hear rumors of it from England?"

"What is between me and my wife is none of your affair," Arran said stiffly. "She's come to Balhaire with nothing more than a desire to repair the marriage she abandoned."

The men had snorted at that. Several remarks were made about a woman's place. Arran's blood had boiled, but he'd kept his temper. He was a traditional man in some respects and held certain expectations for any wife of his. But he'd never been one to view a woman as his personal property, and that Margot hadn't met his expectations could not be helped by him. He could no more put thoughts in her head or force her to a course of action than he could these men.

"You can understand our concern, Mackenzie," said Rory Gordon. "Dunn has warned us all that there is talk of forfeiture of our holdings for conspiring with Stuart."

"The crown has no legal grounds for it,"

Arran argued.

Buchanan laughed low. "And when have you known the English to mind legalities when on Scottish soil, aye? I take you at your word, Mackenzie. I've always known you to be an honest man. No matter how peculiar it seems that your bonny English wife has come back to her marriage bed at a time we are all looking round for the English spy."

"I will say it only once more — she's nothing to do with it," Arran had said evenly, his temper threatening to erupt. "Say what you will of me, but I'll call out the next man who says a disparaging word against my wife."

"Mayhap the disparaging word should no' be said against the lady, but her husband," Gordon said quietly.

Arran had stood up, spoiling for a good fight. "Say it now, then, lad, and let us resolve it."

Gordon had shrugged and kept his seat. The men assembled there had remained silent. But they had eyed Arran with suspicion and had merely nodded when he took his leave of them. He'd thundered back to Balhaire, veering off the main road to Kishorn. There, he met with his cousin Griselda and discussed with her what had happened.

Griselda, wise to the ways of the Scots, had frowned when Arran explained Margot's return and MacLeary's late-night call at Balhaire. "Aye, but she's trouble, that one."

He could not argue Griselda's suspicions, nor put down his own. "Nevertheless, will you do as I ask, Zelda?"

"Aye, of course," she'd said, and had seen him off.

What to do about Margot, precisely, had plagued Arran on the return to Balhaire, and now here she was, as bonny as ever.

Arran shrugged out of his coat and dropped it onto a chair. Margot was right behind him, picking it up and dusting it off with her hand. He looked curiously at her.

"I should not like it to appear unkempt." She suddenly smiled. "I rode down to the cove today," she said lightly as she carefully folded his coat.

Arran furtively looked around the room again. What the devil was she hiding? "Why?" he asked as casually as he might.

"To take the air." She leaned back against the chest of drawers, her arms crossed over the folded coat to hold it against her body. He studied her in that casual pose. Margot smiled sweetly.

He glanced at the coat. "Mrs. Abernathy will want to give that a good cleaning."

"Well, then, I will put it away until she returns."

"Very well." He moved to the chest to open one of the drawers for her, but as he reached around her, Margot said, "Actually, it should hang, shouldn't it? To air it out." She suddenly let the folds of the coat drop.

But she'd just folded it.

She wrinkled her nose at his look of confusion and said, "It smells of dirt." She whirled about and walked into his dressing room. He heard her within, hanging the coat. She returned, strolling into the room with her hands at her back.

Arran stood where he was, studying her. "You were never interested in riding or tidying things, aye? What other things have you a sudden desire to do?"

She blinked. "What do you mean?"

"Exactly what I asked."

Pink was slowly settling into her cheeks. "Nothing."

Diah, she was a horrible liar. "Nothing," he repeated dubiously as he walked into his dressing room.

He picked up a fresh coat and returned to the main chamber. His wife was leaning against the chest again, and now she was studying a fingernail. "Your friends are still here," he said.

She looked up, her expression almost hopeful. "My friends?"

"The two fops who saw you here. How long will they be our guests, then? Or do they wait for you?"

The hopefulness bled from her face. "For *me*? No." She shook her head. "Frankly, I don't know why they've remained. I hardly need an escort now that I have been safely delivered to Balhaire. My father is overly cautious."

One corner of Arran's mouth tipped up in a wry smile. "*Is* he? I never thought him so. In fact, he seemed a wee bit incautious to me, making deals with Scots and God knows who else." He looked at her pointedly. "Is that no' so?"

She shrugged. "I really wouldn't know. My father is not in the habit of informing me whom he deals with. Quite the opposite, really. Unless, of course, he insists I marry one of them." She arched a brow.

"Then . . . you donna know anything you want to tell me?" he asked as he sat on the edge of the bed to remove his boots.

Margot suddenly moved and knelt before him. "I don't know what business my father has, if that's what you're asking." She lifted his foot.

"What is this?" he asked as she tugged on his boot to remove it. "Now you are removing my boots?"

"Do you believe I have changed?"

"No," he said flatly. "What I believe is that a kelpie took my wife and now comes to me in her form."

Margot smiled. "I don't know what a kelpie is," she said, and yanked his second boot harder than the first. "But I am sincere." She put his boots aside.

"Mmm," he said. "Well, then, *leannan,* now that you've done your wifely duty, you may retire to your dressing room. I mean to have a bath and dine in my rooms tonight."

"Then I'll join you —"

"I'd rather you no'," he interjected. "I'm bloody well worn from the road."

Her brows dipped slightly. "But I thought —"

"No, Margot. I'm tired, aye? I donna want to listen to a lot of nattering and questions tonight. *Diah,* I had enough of it today."

"Nattering!" she said. "I see." She stood gracefully and walked to the door. He thought she would continue on through the door in a huff now that he'd made his wishes known, but instead, she yanked the bellpull so hard it was a wonder it didn't

259

pull free. She stood, her arms crossed tightly over her trim middle, glaring at him as her fingers drummed against her arm.

"Off with you," he said, and gestured to the door.

The door swung open and a lad entered. He bowed to Arran, then to Margot, who never took her eyes from Arran as she spoke. "Please tell Fergus that after the laird has bathed, he will dine in *private*. Quite alone and at his leisure."

"Aye, mu'um."

"And then please do send my maid to my sitting room."

The lad nodded and darted out.

Arran arched a brow at Margot. "Well, then? I know you heard me plainly, so I canna guess why you still stand there."

"Oh, yes, I heard you, Arran. But I'm not ready to take my leave of you just yet. I'm your wife. I'm the mistress of Balhaire, and I have a say. And moreover, you really must forgive me!"

He shook his head. "For disobeying me?"

"For leaving you!"

An unexpected surge of pain shot through him. He thought of that day, of watching that chaise roll away from Balhaire, and how he'd felt a small part of him harden and die. The assumption that he should forgive her for having left him, or that she could demand it of him, rankled. He slowly rose to his feet and walked to where she stood. He slid his hand to the side of her neck and held her firmly so that she could not look away. "No one commands me, madam," he said low. "Least of all *you.* I donna have to forgive you. I donna have to *keep* you. So mind your fool tongue before I throw you out on your arse, aye?"

Once again, he expected her to flee — in tears, naturally — but Margot merely tilted her head to one side and said, "Is there more? Or is that all you have to say?"

"Woman, donna push me. You'll take your leave now," he growled, and let go of her neck before he did something foolish . . . like kiss her as he was suddenly burning to do. "I am but a wee moment from tossing you," he warned her.

She smiled. But she turned to the door. "I'll see that your bath is made ready," she said, and yanked open the door, then walked through without shutting it behind her or looking back.

Arran watched her go, the confident sway of her hips, her regal bearing. *Damn her.*

Arran emerged from his dressing room sometime later, with letters and bills of lad-ing to attend. But he halted in his bed-chamber, confused to find that a small table had been moved to the windows, which had been opened to a cool evening breeze.

"What is this?" he asked Fergus, who was lighting the candles in a silver candelabra.

"Lady Mackenzie," Fergus said simply, frowning. He poured wine into a crystal goblet.

Arran had forgotten the crystal goblets even existed. He'd brought them from Antwerp a year or so ago and had them put in the stores. Now he groaned at the sight of them. "I said I would dine alone. I donna want a fancy table in my chamber, aye? Does no one heed me?"

Fergus paused in his task and looked up. "The lady . . . insisted," he said, searching for the appropriate word.

"Diah," Arran muttered, and accepted the goblet from Fergus. "All right, then, you've made me king. Now go on about your business and, for the love of Scotland, leave me be, aye?"

Fergus quit the room without another word.

Arran finished his meal as he tried to look over documents that desperately needed his attention. But it was hopeless — he could not rid his mind of the meeting he'd had today, of the accusations against him.

He sighed, pushed his plate away and stood up. He deposited the papers on his chest of drawers, then rang the bellpull. A moment later, a lad came into the room.

"Take it away," he said, gesturing to the table. "And return the table to its place."

"Aye, milord."

Arran paid no attention as the young man picked up the remnants of his meal. He went to his basin and washed his hands and face. He heard the lad go out, but he did not hear the sounds of the table being moved.

He turned around, prepared to resume his work . . . but there, in the open door, stood his wife, her hands behind her back. She was wearing a beautiful gown the color of butter, the underskirt and stomacher sea blue. Jewels glistened in her earlobes and just above the mounds of her breasts. She looked like a lone flower in this old gray castle.

Ah, but he was weak for her, had always been and, *Diah,* likely would always be. An attraction that could very well prove to be the death of him. "What are you doing there?"

She produced a box. "I have a chessboard and chess figures. I thought we might have

263

a game."

Arran couldn't help himself — he let his gaze wander over her full bosom, down her waist, to the tips of her slippers peeking out from beneath her skirts. "Chess," he scoffed. "I've no' played games in an age."

"Splendid. That means I will have the advantage, as I am forever playing games." She smiled wryly at her jest and opened the box.

"I didna say I would," he said, but he made no move to stop her as she began to set up the pieces. When she'd finished, she walked to the sideboard, poured a glass of port and held it out to him.

"What a presumptuous thing you are."

She smiled as if she'd known all along that he would relent, and Arran sighed. He pushed his fingers through his hair, still damp from his bath. He stood before her in shirttails and with bare feet and would have liked nothing better than to crawl into his bed and sleep. He'd spent a day convincing grown men that this woman wasn't treacherous when he himself had doubted it. The task had exhausted him, made him damnably feeble.

He looked at the glass of port she held out and said, "I prefer whisky."

A softly triumphant smile lit her face. She

put aside the port, poured whisky, then moved to where he stood to give it to him.

"I told you I did no' want company this evening," he said low, his gaze on her mouth.

"Did you?" she purred. "I forgot."

Arran clasped his hand around the tot and her hand and pulled her closer. "I'll allow your disobedience this time, Margot. But no' again."

"It won't happen again," she said, her smile like a bright flash of lightning in a stormy sky.

"Donna mistake me for one of the lovesick puppies that follow you about Norwood Park."

Her brows dipped over a deeper smile. "I would *never* mistake you for one of them." She bent her head and touched her lips to the back of his hand. The softness and warmth of her touch tingled in Arran's skin, and he was painfully reminded of her mouth on his body just last night. His groin began to kindle.

Arran stepped away before that kindling turned to fire. He went to the table and sank into a chair, his gaze on the twilight sky. Bloody hell, he was being undone by her once again.

Margot helped herself to the port and very

gracefully took her seat across from him. He remembered that once she'd told him a gentleman ought to seat a lady. The implication being, of course, that he was no gentleman, for he rarely did it. Perhaps he should have endeavored more to be what she wanted. Perhaps then she wouldn't have thought of betraying him. But *had* she betrayed him? He couldn't look at her sitting across from him, smiling happily at having her way, and believe that she had. Aye, but he'd never believed that she would leave him, either.

"There," she said as she adjusted the placement of a rook.

"Are you happy now?" Arran drawled.

"Not entirely. I would be happier had I dined with you." She sipped elegantly.

She was quite young yet, but she seemed so much older than before. More sure of herself. "You have indeed changed, Margot."

"Have I?" Her eyes sparkled with pleasure in the candlelight. "For the better, I should hope."

He wasn't certain of that — but she was definitely more intriguing.

"You have the first move," she said.

Arran lifted himself up and moved a pawn forward. Margot matched his move.

They carried on, the movements quick in the opening of the game. Arran couldn't help but notice how Margot delighted in the challenge. She was quite good at it, even instructing him on how to attack her pawn with his. He could imagine her surrounded by admirers as she challenged one gentleman after the other to a game. Her eyes glittered every time she looked up at him, filled with pleasure and laughter, and Arran could further imagine how those men had been drawn to her. Had he somehow missed this playful side of her before? Would things have perhaps been easier between them if he'd discovered it? So many questions from that time lingered.

Margot was the first to take a pawn. "Aha!" she said, and tapped his ivory piece from the board. "You must pay closer attention, Arran, or I'll have your queen."

"Never doubt it," he said.

"Ooh," she said. "That sounds quite ominous." She looked up, but her smile faded when she saw his expression.

"Aye, you're bonny," he said low. "I can scarcely bring to mind the trembling lass who met me at the altar."

Margot laughed softly. "I *was* trembling, wasn't I? In truth, I could scarcely stand, I was so frightened."

Arran moved a rook into position. "Was I such a beast?"

"A beast!" She laughed lightly. "You were no beast. You were the strongest and most handsome man I'd ever laid eyes on."

He snorted at flattery he considered false.

"I am sincere! You had completely captured my imagination, though," she said, putting up a hand, "I will admit I was terribly innocent. But I had scarcely turned eighteen years. I had not the slightest idea what to do with a man like you. I remember looking up, and there was Christ smiling down at me and I thought I might faint dead away." She smoothly matched his move. "Nor had I any notion of how to be a wife. My mother had long been dead and there was no one to instruct me, no one to tell me about Scotland. Certainly no one to tell me all that went on between husband and wife." She glanced up and smiled saucily.

"Aye, you trembled then, too," Arran reminded her, and her smile broadened.

"As did you, as I recall."

He chuckled. "Perhaps a wee bit."

"And then I came here, to Balhaire. It felt as if I had journeyed to the end of the world! The people spoke a different language, and none of them were happy to see me. It was so overwhelming, really. I felt quite lost."

Arran moved a bishop. "I felt a wee bit lost myself."

"You?" she said, surprised.

"Aye, me. I'd been accustomed to coming and going as I pleased, to dining when I wanted — and alone if I so desired," he said with a pointed look at her.

She gave him a light laugh and shrugged.

"I didna know how to incorporate a wife into this life, and like you, I had no one to instruct me."

"But you seemed so confident!"

"I wasna confident, Margot. I hadna been a husband, and I didna want to harm you or displease you in any way."

"Oh." Her expression softened. "Oh, Arran, you never harmed me. And any displeasure I suffered was my own doing."

"Hmm . . . you have said to the contrary many times."

"Oh dear," she said with a rueful smile. "I'm afraid I've said many things in the last few years that I wish I'd never said."

"Well . . . your displeasure was not entirely of your own doing," he admitted. "I might have made a greater effort."

"Perhaps," she said with an indifferent shrug.

Arran moved a knight and caught her gaze. "What turned so wrong between us, Margot? I canna say what it was that went so terribly wrong."

"I don't know," she said, sounding morose. "I know only that I was naive and I felt abandoned. I had no friends or family here — only you."

"You might have made friends."

She snorted. "I didn't have many opportunities, did I?"

"No," he said truthfully. "And it didna help that you were English. That made your conceit a wee bit worse, aye?"

Margot blinked at his blunt assessment. And then she laughed, the sound of it warm. "I shall never accuse you of being anything less than unfailingly honest, my lord. Do you mean to say that I was condescending?" she asked, pressing a palm to her chest and feigning offense.

"A wee bit, aye," he said, smiling.

"Well, I didn't mean to be," she said, and moved one of her pieces. "I behaved as I thought was appropriate for the lady of a castle." She sank back into her chair. "My God, but I was so violently afraid of saying or doing the wrong thing," she said thoughtfully, and worried the end of a curl. "Yet that's all I seemed to do. You are beloved here, Arran. It felt impossible to live up to that, and I was quite intimidated by it."

"And now?" he asked curiously.

Her smiled turned playful. "No."

God save him, he could not keep a smile from his face. "I didna abandon you," he said amicably.

"You *did,*" she insisted. "You left every day to hunt or to train men, or what have you."

"Aye, all right, perhaps I was a wee bit intimidated by you as well, *leannan.*"

"Of me?" She laughed and gave a shake of her head as if he amused her.

"Aye, of you. You're bloody well bonny, Margot, how many times have I said so? We were both of us naive."

She smiled indulgently. "Lord in heaven, *yes.* I'd never been truly courted. I'd never even had a first love. Can you imagine?"

"Aye, that I can imagine."

"Arran!" she said, laughing. "I was far too young for it. No doubt you've had a first love, and many more since." She reached for her queen.

"I've had a first love," he agreed. "It was you."

Margot's hand froze on her queen. "Don't tease me like that," she said, the light gone from her voice. "Don't say that if it's not true."

Arran slowly reached for her hand. "I would never say it were it no' true." To his thinking, there was nothing truer about them. Even now, he had that strange feeling of being tossed into an abyss of empty longing.

Her gaze searched his face. "When did you love me?" she asked softly. "I never knew it."

Diah, but he'd failed her in so many ways. How could she not know? "From the moment I saw you standing on the balcony at Norwood Park."

Her lips parted with surprise. "Even then?"

"There's no logic to how love arrives."

"And yet you never once said —"

"No, because I was bloody naive, and I foolishly believed that my love would never get away from me. I tried to make you happy, Margot, in all the ways that I knew how. I tried, but I couldna set it all to rights for you. But it was no' from a lack of devotion. It was from a lack of understanding."

"I had no idea," she whispered.

"I know." He hadn't known it himself until after she was gone.

"Do you . . . Do you still feel the same?"

she asked uncertainly.

Arran glanced at the chessboard. She could move her queen to his king now and hold him at checkmate. She could knock him from his throne, could send him sprawling off the board that was his life. He looked up again. "No, I donna feel the same. I donna trust you, *leannan.* Tell me, how can I trust you?"

He desperately wanted her to tell him that he could trust her. Tell him anything, tell him she had nothing to hide. But Margot didn't say that. She sighed and rubbed her forehead as if she had a pain there. "I wouldn't trust me, either," she quietly admitted.

His heart sank, tumbling deeper into that abyss, carried on a storm of uncertainty and mistrust.

She suddenly stood up from the table, leaving her queen within striking distance of his king. "Only *you* can say if you will trust me," she said as she moved around the table to him.

"And only you can say if you mean to leave me again," he said curtly.

She sighed and ran her hand over the top of his head. She lifted her skirts, revealing her long, slender legs, and straddled his lap. Once more, Arran didn't stop her — but he was keenly aware that she was trying to change the course of the conversation, using the only means at her disposal to best him. She wrapped her arms around his neck and said, "I don't want to leave you again." And she began to move on him.

He grabbed her hips in his hands to steady her. "That is no answer. Do you think I donna see what you are about, how you use your body to avoid answering me?"

"But I *have* answered you, as best I can," she said sweetly, and kissed his temple. "Now I am trying to please you as best I can, in a way that you have taught me. Now I think of how it could have been between us had I stayed. I think of the children we might have already brought into this world, and I want to make it up to you. I want to begin fresh." She kissed his cheek. *"I don't want to leave you again,"* she whispered.

"It's too late for this, Margot," he said brusquely, and turned his head.

"It can never be too late — we are married." She looped her arms loosely around his neck and moved seductively on him, arousing him, hardening him. "Think of it — we could sail to France and begin anew . . . just you and me." She kissed his cheek.

"France!" he muttered as she took his face

between her hands and kissed one eye, then the other.

"Wouldn't it be lovely, to go away from Scotland and England, to someplace new? Where no one knows us?" she asked between kisses. "No one to trouble or inconvenience us?"

He wondered who troubled or inconvenienced them now, and this desire, expressed by a wife he scarcely knew now, pricked at his conscience. Arran's head urged him to stop her, to understand what she meant, not to be fooled by pleasures of the flesh. But his flesh — Christ, tonight his flesh was much stronger in its need of her than his heart.

He would deal with her duplicity on the morrow. *Tomorrow, tomorrow.*

"We could sail on one of your ships," she whispered.

There was something quite wrong with her wish to escape, but Arran didn't want to think of it at that moment. He was in the abyss. "You're nattering, woman," he said, and suddenly grabbed her and stood up. He carried her to his bed, deposited her on it and moved over her. He could put his distrust of her on hold for one more night . . . but only one more night.

CHAPTER THIRTEEN

It was wonderful, beautiful, extraordinary. There was something so delicious about the way Arran took command of her body, arousing her with kisses and caresses, his tongue lapping her into oblivion, his cock pressing her to a crisis so utterly shattering that she marveled she could find all the pieces of her and put them back together again. It was carnal bliss, wholesale ecstasy, and it left her feeling warm and adored and very lethargic.

But when the morning light began to filter in through the drapes, the questions about who this man was, about who *she* was now, began to slip back into her thoughts, and the bed felt less warm to her.

She had begun last night wanting only to gain his trust. But then, quite unexpectedly, they'd had perhaps the most honest conversation about their marriage they'd ever had, and a window had opened in Margot. Feelings she'd not expected had come in through that window, and she'd meant it when she'd said it could never be too late for them. She'd wanted to forget the strife between them and rebuild what she had torn down when she'd left. She wanted to believe that there was a path for them, that they could be happy.

And still, a tiny doubt crept into her thoughts. What if her father was right about him? What if he was right and she was wrong?

Margot pretended to be asleep when Arran rose. She lay on her side and listened to the sounds of him dressing and gathering his things. She kept her eyes closed when he leaned over the bed and kissed her shoulder.

"Good morning," he murmured, and quit the room.

When he'd gone, she rolled onto her back and sighed to the canopy above the bed. What he'd said to her last night — that she was his first love — had pirouetted into her dreams, and she had awakened more than once in the night to assure herself that he was still there, that he had spoken those words to her. She thought about how he held her, as if she were his only love. She thought about what Mrs. Gowan had said of his demeanor after she'd left. She thought about all of this, and with a single tear slipping from the corner of her eye, she thought about how he said he didn't feel the same any longer because he could not trust her.

For God's sake, why would he?

He wasn't wrong about her. He had every reason to be suspicious of her. She *had* been condescending when she'd first come to Balhaire; she could see that now with the clarity the past few years had given her. She hadn't shown him much affection, in spite of having felt some for him. She'd been so determined to be wounded and indignant about the injustice her family had done to her that she'd never been able to nurture her feelings for him properly. And God knew she'd been damnably blind to his affection for her.

Her confusion about what to do was only growing. She'd never dreamed that her feelings and desire for him could be rekindled.

She didn't want to know if he conspired with the French. She wanted to prove to her father that it was a lie.

Margot got up, wrapped the coverlet around her and walked into his study. She stared at the cabinet. She could still see the handle of the knife that she'd shoved beneath it when she heard him approach.

She wasn't going to open it. She didn't want to know what he'd locked away . . . unless it was something that would prove his innocence. And what sort of proof would that be?

Tell me, how can I trust you?

There came a soft knock at the bed-chamber door, and Margot hurried in through the dressing room, arriving as the door partially opened. Nell stuck her head in. "Awake, madam?"

"Yes. Come in."

Margot dressed, and as Nell was putting up her hair, she picked up the figurine the man at the cove had given her and turned it over in her hand. It reminded her of how distant she'd once been with the clan here. She put the figurine in her pocket.

When Nell had finished her hair, she went downstairs. But before she had breakfast, there was something she very much wanted to do.

She went out into the bailey, through the gates and down the road until she reached the whitewashed cottage with the peonies in the window boxes.

The little bell sounded as it had the first time Margot had come into Mrs. Gowan's establishment, and as before, Mrs. Gowan appeared from the back room with a cheery

"Madainn mhath!"

The cheeriness left her the moment she saw Margot.

"Good morning," Margot said. "I've come to thank you for sending the soaps."

"Aye," said the woman, folding her arms. Her daughter appeared behind her, but Mrs. Gowan seemed not to notice.

Margot stepped forward. "I brought you something I thought you might put to use."

Mrs. Gowan said nothing.

Margot held out a small bottle shaped like a swan. It was her perfume. "My father gave this to me. It comes from an exclusive perfumery in London. It's a floral scent, and one that the laird particularly likes."

Mrs. Gowan stared at the bottle, then glanced warily at her daughter.

"I thought you might use it in the making of soaps and whatnot."

"For you?" Mrs. Gowan asked.

"Not for me, but for any Mackenzie who might like it." She held out the bottle.

Mrs. Gowan didn't immediately move to take it. But her daughter did, hesitantly coming forward and putting the bottle to her nose. "It's bonny," she said.

"It's my favorite," Margot agreed. She looked at Mrs. Gowan again. "I regret that I did not discover your shop when I was here before, Mrs. Gowan."

The woman's frown seemed to ease a tiny bit.

"I regret so many things, really. That I didn't listen, that I didn't try to understand the ways of the Mackenzies instead of imposing my own ideas. I can't change that, I know, but I should like to start fresh if we might."

Mrs. Gowan didn't speak. Margot didn't care, really — she had said what she needed to say, and she smiled. No matter what happened with her and Arran, no matter what truths she discovered, she meant this sincerely. "Well, there you are. Good morning."

"Morning, mu'um," the daughter said, gazing at Margot with eyes wide with surprise.

Margot left the shop, the little bell tinkling behind her.

When she returned to the bailey, shooing chickens from her path, she happened to see Sir Worthing lurking about the main door. Margot had no idea what to make of her situation at the moment, but no matter what else, she knew she couldn't navigate her way through her marriage with Sir Worthing and Mr. Pepper watching her every move.

She smiled as she approached him. "Good morning, sir."

"Good morning, Lady Mackenzie," he said, bowing low over his leg. "I trust you slept well?"

"Thank you, but I cannot properly express how well I slept, sir," she said gaily. "Sir Worthing, might I have a word?"

"Of course. Shall we go inside?"

"Here will do," she said. She preferred the bailey, where no one would overhear what she would say to him.

"By all means. Is something amiss?"

"Not at all." She clasped her hands tightly before her. She wanted to phrase this perfectly, knowing that every word she said would be repeated to her father. "I think it is time that you and Mr. Pepper take your leave of Balhaire."

"Oh?" His voice was as politely mannered as ever, but his eyes were instantly hard and cold. "May I ask the reason so that I might convey your feelings to your father?"

"I have no message for my father as of yet. It would seem that your presence here at Balhaire is hindering me somewhat in that regard — my husband is quite suspicious."

"Of?"

"Of me," she said. "Of you."

Sir Worthing glanced over her shoulder. So did Margot. There were Mackenzies milling about. He put his handkerchief to his nose and sniffed, then slowly turned his attention back to Margot. His gaze was hard, two pieces of polished obsidian staring down at her. "I shouldn't think you would like to be left alone here, Lady Mackenzie, with no one to protect you. This is rough company."

Rough! Because they did not don lace and wigs and bow so far over the leg that it was a wonder they didn't topple over? The only thing rough about the company here was the way Arran Mackenzie had made love to her last night, his body moving so persistently in hers and lifting her up to new heights. She was loath to leave that sort of roughness behind.

"I will be perfectly fine."

"If I may . . . is it your desire that we take our leave? Or his? Frankly, I think it best if Mr. Pepper and I —"

"You really must go," Margot interrupted. She paused a moment to catch her breath, still fuming from his slight of the Mackenzies.

Sir Worthing looked her over, as a father might when considering a small child's request. And then he patronizingly agreed.

"Very well, madam. If that is truly your desire."

Margot's heart began to race with indignation. She was a grown woman, the lady of Balhaire — did he think he could condescend to her in that way? "Whether it is truly my desire or a moment's desire has no bearing, sir. I am the lady of Balhaire, and I have asked you to leave."

He bowed his head in acquiescence.

"Thank you." She shifted, intending to step around him and walk away, but Sir Worthing suddenly clamped his hand down on her arm to stop her and held it in a tight grip.

"I beg your —"

"We will go, *Lady* Mackenzie. For now," he said coldly. "But I must impress on you how important it is that you send some word to your father, posthaste."

"I *know,*" she said, and tried to remove her arm from his grip.

"Do you?" he asked icily, squeezing harder. "Do you desire to see your father swinging from a gibbet?"

Margot gasped. "*No!* How dare you —"

"If you think this is some sort of parlor game, allow me to be *quite* clear — if you fail to do what you've been sent here to do, the blood of your father will be on *your* hands, and believe me, there will be no harbor safe enough for you. Not here. Not in England. You'll have no place to go, madam, so you'd best do as he has bid you."

He was not only clear, he was also terrifying her. What had her father done that would warrant his hanging? She tried again to jerk her arm free of his grip, but he held tightly. "Do you understand me?"

"*Quite,*" she said sharply. "And do you in turn understand that my father will hear of this?"

A cold smile turned up the corners of his mouth, and he chuckled darkly. "You are a child," he sneered. "I knew the moment you fled your marriage that your mettle was as weak as a dandelion."

Stunned, Margot could only gape at him.

"Take your hand from my wife, lad, or I'll take your hand from you."

A flood of relief swept through Margot at the sound of Arran's deep voice. Sir Worthing let go of her arm, and she stumbled back into Arran's chest. His hand settled possessively on her waist.

"Sir Worthing was just informing me that he and Mr. Pepper will take their leave of Balhaire," she said breathlessly.

Arran glared at Sir Worthing, who now looked ridiculous to Margot in his foppish wig and lace cuffs next to her husband. "Today," she added. "Straightaway. It's quite a long journey to England."

Sir Worthing's jaw clenched, but he inclined his head politely, as if they'd been chatting about the weather. "We'll gather our things after breakfast —"

"Lady Mackenzie said straightaway," Arran said, moving to stand in front of Margot. "You'd best heed her."

Sir Worthing tilted his head back to look at Arran, his expression full of contempt. "Very well, my lord. If that is what the lady desires, then certainly we shall leave at once. God knows I've done all that I might do," he said, and glanced meaningfully at Margot before turning on his heel and walking away.

Jock appeared seemingly from nowhere, trailing after him.

Margot's heart was pounding so hard now that she could scarcely breathe. She didn't realize how tightly she had folded her arms around her until Arran looked down at her, his expression one of concern. "Are you all right? You look ill."

"I'm fine." She pressed her palm to her belly to calm the roiling there.

"What was that about?"

"He did not care to be asked to leave," she said tightly.

286

Arran nodded. But he was looking at her closely. "What did he mean, that he's done all that he might do?"

Margot blinked. "I've really not the slightest idea." Her husband's gaze was boring through her, and Margot had to look away for fear that she would give herself away. "I suppose he meant that he has seen me safely here and there is nothing more for him to do."

"He didna mean that, Margot," Arran said flatly. "What else might he have meant?"

Margot wanted to tell him. She desperately wanted to tell him then and there what was said of him in England and hear him deny it.

But what if he didn't deny it? Worse, what if her answer fractured the fragile truce between them? What if it forced him to do something for fear of the news getting back to her father? What if the truth was the thing that proved to him he could not trust her? *What if, what if . . .* So many doubts. Margot felt strangely dizzy, as if the earth was falling out from beneath her feet.

Arran caught her elbow. His brows dipped. "What is it, *leannan*?" he asked softly. "Whatever it is, you can tell me, aye?"

She was treading on dangerous ground, torn between two men in a loathsome duel of wills. She knew if she said too much, she risked her father and risked herself. On the tiny chance that what was said of Arran was true, she risked her father's life. Was that what Worthing had said? But if she said nothing, she risked destroying this marriage once and for all, and she didn't want that to happen.

She somehow mustered a smile at her husband. "I feel peckish, that's all. Will you join me for breakfast?"

His frown deepened, and something shuttered in his blue eyes, making them look as icy as a winter morning. He knew she was dissembling, any fool could see that she was. But Arran pondered her a moment, as if debating if he was going to press her. At last, he glanced down at his hand and said, "No' today. We need grouse for the hall tonight." He glanced across the bailey, to where Sir Worthing was leaning over Mr. Pepper's shoulder, whispering in his ear. "And I think you'd best come with me."

"Come with you . . . to hunt?" she asked uncertainly. She was a poor rider, a worse shot.

"I will have you at my side today, Margot. There is no more to be said about it. Go, then. Dress properly for hunting. Meet me in the bailey in a half hour." He turned away from her to have a word with Sweeney.

Nell was in quite a state as she helped Margot search through her clothes. "Hunting!" she said, pausing to put her hands on her broad hips. "I beg your pardon, milady, but I've never known you to hunt."

"I have no choice," Margot muttered. She was still feeling on edge from her encounter with Worthing and all the lies and doubts that were swirling around her.

Nell sighed. She fingered the sleeve of one of Margot's gowns when she should have been helping her assemble attire for the hunt.

"What is the matter with you? I need something to wear."

"I shouldn't like to bother you," Nell said, and resumed her task.

Privately, Margot was relieved. She had enough on her mind without Nell's complaints.

"Oh, all right," Nell said, as if Margot had pressed her. "It's that *man.*"

"Jock?" Margot asked, distracted as she held up a wool riding skirt.

"Yes, milady, for there is no one else who comes tromping about the master's chambers without so much as a knock."

"What did he want?" Margot asked as she

searched through a selection of riding coats.

"I wouldn't know." Nell sniffed. "He looked around, quite closely."

Margot's stomach dropped. She slowly turned her head and looked at Nell. "What do you mean, he looked around closely?"

"I mean that he looked round here and there. And I says, 'What's the matter? You think something's gone missing?' And he says, 'I wouldna be surprised if it had. Never knew an Englishman who was true.' And I says, 'How dare you speak of milady in that way? And I'd rather be English than a barbarian Scot.' Then he says, 'Well, thank the saints that you'll never be a Scot, lass, because you don't have the fortitude.' Me! No fortitude! I says to him he's no idea of my fortitude, and perhaps I'm not a beast like him, but I'm *quite* strong."

Margot's eyes widened with alarm. She thought of the knife under the cabinet in Arran's study. "What did he say?"

"Nothing," Nell said with a shrug. "He said not a word more but tramped out of here like a schoolgirl in a snit."

"Did he say what he was looking for?" Margot asked curiously, glancing about. "Has something gone missing?"

"He was not of a mind to tell me," Nell said pertly. "But he ran his hand over every inch of the chest of drawers, then got down on his knees and looked under the bed, and pulled back the bed linens."

Margot's heart felt as if it would burst.

"Then he went into the laird's dressing room and was gone for a time, and then he came back."

Oh God. Margot tried to think. *Dear God.*

"Never knew a man like him, so ill-mannered," Nell said emphatically as she dug in a trunk and produced Margot's boots. And she continued to complain about Jock and his supercilious ways as Margot dressed.

Margot let her natter about it, far more concerned about what Jock might have been looking for. Or rather, if he'd been looking to find what *she'd* been looking for. She hardly had time to think of it now. She was late — but she had at last assembled as close to hunting attire as she might. She hurried down to the bailey, tying the ribbons of her hat beneath her chin as she went.

When she emerged into the sun-dappled bailey, she saw Arran waiting, resplendent in his buckskins and long coat, his hair tied in a queue beneath his hat. He was standing with his arms folded as he watched Sir Worthing and Mr. Pepper and their things loaded into the coach. "You're late," he said

291

to Margot. He gave her a ghost of a smile. "Come on, then." He put his hand on the small of her back and hurried her along, away from the Englishmen and to the horses that had been brought round for the hunting party.

She was pleased to see the Fell pony had been saddled for her. Two men would accompany them, Duncan and Hamish Mackenzie, whom she remembered as the gamekeepers at Balhaire. A pair of Arran's hunting dogs were sniffing about, waiting for a command.

But the one person she'd expected to see was not present. She looked around. "Where is Jock?"

"He had other matters to attend," Arran said simply.

Margot felt queasy. "You needn't say more. I know that he does not care for me."

"Oh, I think that's no' true. He esteems you well enough." Arran turned his head and looked her in the eye and said, "But he doesna trust you. Come, allow Sweeney to put you on your horse."

She did as he bade her.

"He has no reason to distrust me," Margot said as she settled onto the old sidesaddle and Arran swung easily up onto his horse. "Whatever is between us has nothing to do with him."

"Aye, perhaps that is true," Arran agreed. "But he takes great exception to anyone who might want to harm me."

"He thinks I mean to *harm* you?" she asked incredulously. Was he searching for some clue that proved she meant to physically harm her husband?

"A wee bit, aye. Enough of this now. We've work to do."

Did Jock really think she'd been sent here for such nefarious reasons? Did he really think she was the condescending, heartbreaking murderess now?

But it struck Margot that while she was not a murderess, Jock was right in at least one respect — she had been sent here to find something with which to accuse her husband. Was that any less egregious?

Arran signaled and the hunting party moved out.

Everyone but Margot, that was. It took a word from Sweeney and a jerk of the pony's bridle to get Margot's horse to follow the others. The pony broke into a run after the other horses, bouncing Margot around so completely that she almost lost her seat before she'd cleared the castle walls.

CHAPTER FOURTEEN

Margot's horsemanship had not miraculously improved overnight as Arran had futilely hoped. He began to feel a wee bit guilty about her bringing up the rear as she was, her hat having bounced off her head somewhere along the way.

He was also annoyed by the amount of bickering between his two best hunting guides. The brothers were perhaps the best stag stalkers in all of Scotland but could scarcely abide one another. Their discord went back many years and was centered, naturally, on a lass. Arran didn't know what had happened, precisely, or when, but it had become part of the legend of the two men. Now they were known as hunters without parallel, and for their constant strife.

Arran circled his horse around and held it back so that he wouldn't hear the sniping and could walk alongside Margot's pony. His two hunting dogs trotted alongside them, their noses to the ground, their tails high.

Margot smiled cheerfully at him as he pulled in beside her, but her cheeks were stained with the exertion of the effort to hold her seat, and her breath was short.

"I don't know what's wrong with this pony today. I had a much easier time of it yesterday when I rode down to the cove."

There was nothing wrong with the pony. The fault lay completely in the hands of the rider. "The road down to the cove is flat and the distance shorter," he said. "We're moving upglen to Lochbraden on no road at all. It's a harder course."

"Lochbraden! I thought perhaps we were riding all the way to England," she said pertly.

He smiled. "We've no' gone more than three miles, *leannan.* Another mile and we'll come down to hunt. How is it that you've never learned to ride properly, then?"

She looked surprised. "But I am riding properly!"

Her fingers curled around the reins so tightly he wondered if she'd be able to straighten them. "It seems a wee struggle for you."

Margot groaned. "It is more than a wee struggle," she sheepishly admitted. "I was never taught to ride. My father was a very busy man, and my brothers' education took precedence over mine."

That didn't surprise Arran. He supposed the same was true at Balhaire.

"Did your father teach you?" she asked curiously.

"My da was killed when I was a lad," Arran said matter-of-factly. He'd been struck dead instantly when a yard aboard a ship broke free and hit him in the head.

"Oh, yes, of course," Margot said, remembering that detail of his life. "You were fourteen years of age, were you not?"

"Twelve," Arran said. "My ma dead no' a year later."

"I had forgotten how young you were," she said. "I can't imagine how you must have suffered those deaths." She looked out over the landscape, her expression thoughtful. "You were raised by Jock's parents, weren't you?"

"Aye, Uncle Ivor and Aunt Lilleas raised me up to be laird of Balhaire, as was my birthright, alongside Jock and Griselda."

"No wonder you and Jock are completely inseparable now," she mused, and smiled wryly at him.

Arran smiled at that. "We're no' inseparable. You did no' see him in our bed last night, did you?"

Margot snorted. "He would have been there had you allowed it. You may trust that is so."

Arran laughed roundly at that. It wasn't far from true — Jock was intensely loyal and protective of him.

"Your people do love you so, Arran. How I envy you that."

"They are *our* people," he corrected her. "And you were loved in England, as well."

"Me?" She shook her head.

"*Ach,* I have it on excellent authority that you are well admired by the gentlemen, Margot. And that you're particularly proficient at the gaming tables."

She laughed. "I suppose I was admired by some. And I am *more* than proficient at the gaming tables. I am really rather good at it. I scarcely ever dance, so what else might I do?"

Arran chuckled. "In this, I believe you — you are indeed a bloody awful dancer."

"Thank you!" she said with delight. "At last, someone has admitted what I know very well to be true. Someone is forever assuring me I am not as bad as I fear. Nevertheless, I accepted any invitation into society after I returned to England. I made the best of my situation, just as I'm certain you did here."

Arran shrugged. She would never know that for days after she'd left, he'd stumbled about, his thoughts on her, on the things he'd regretted saying, on the things he wished he'd said. He'd felt almost drunk, so much regret and pain slushing around in him.

"You did," she insisted lightly, taking his silence for argument. "You expanded your trade with France after all."

"Aye, I did."

"And you were surrounded by people every day. Your society was here, where you are. You didn't have to seek it."

"It was here for you, as well."

"Perhaps," she said. "But what I saw was an audience to a marriage I did not want and at which I was awful. Even now, it's as if all the Mackenzies are witnessing the reconciliation of the laird and his wife."

"*Reconciliation* is a very strong word," he said. "I've no' agreed that is what we are about."

She blinked those wide green eyes at him. "Haven't you?"

"No."

She pondered that a moment as she studied him. "When will you agree that it is?"

298

"When I am confident you are being completely honest with me."

Her smile faded. "Well . . ." She glanced away, and it seemed to him she was considering how best to respond. But if she meant to speak, he wouldn't know — at that moment, Duncan called to Arran. The grouse had been found.

The party came to a halt on the hills above a tiny loch that drained into the sea. Arran dismounted and helped Margot down, and they walked to where Duncan and Hamish were squatting, looking down a long hill.

"There, in the tall grass, laird," Hamish said, pointing. "We'll go round the far end —"

"The far end!" Duncan snapped. "Ye'll as good as flush them out if you go round the far end."

"Aye, so what would ye have us do, shoot from here, where we can scarcely sight the loch, much less the fowl? What bloody nonsense."

"All right, that's enough of it," Arran said, vexed now. But the two brothers didn't hear him — their bickering had reached a crisis, and they came to their feet, squaring off with each other and exciting the dogs, one of whom began to bark. Behind the two men, the grouse took wing, flying across the loch and deep into a ravine.

"For the love of Christ," Arran said irritably.

"I've 'ad enough of ye and yer fool mouth, I 'ave," said Duncan. "I ought to take yer bloody noggin off with me bare hands."

"Do you think ye're man enough for it, lad?" Hamish shot back, and shoved his brother in the chest.

"Stop this," Arran said angrily. "You're grown men!"

But the wound between Duncan and Hamish flared up like specter between them, and the two men were suddenly grabbing at each other, cursing in their native tongue — each trying to land a fist as the dogs barked wildly.

Arran reached for his gun.

"What are you doing?" Margot cried.

"I mean to shoot the both of them," Arran growled. He meant to shoot above their heads, but he was sorely tempted to shoot them for being so bloody obstinate and losing an entire pack of grouse.

He brought the gun to his shoulder but was startled as Margot suddenly threw herself into the melee between the two men.

"Margot!" Arran shouted.

Hamish and Duncan suddenly stopped fighting. Because Margot stood between them, holding them each at arm's length. They could not swing a fist without striking her.

"What is the matter with you?" she demanded breathlessly. "You ought to be ashamed of such childish behavior!"

"It's him, mu'um," Duncan said just as breathlessly, and tried to reach around and over Margot for his brother. "He's been a thorn in me side for all me life."

"Your whole life!" Margot said incredulously as she pushed Duncan back a step. "I think that is not true or you wouldn't continue to hunt with him," she said, dropping her hands. "Now, what is this all about?"

"He knows what he did, aye?" Hamish said, glaring at Duncan. "He knows."

"I didna do a bloody *thing* —" Duncan shouted and tried to lunge for Hamish again.

"Enough!" Margot shouted.

The two men — and Arran and the dogs for that matter — grew silent. Duncan and Hamish glowered at each other, but thank all that was holy, they were silent for once.

"It is inconceivable to me that two grown brothers could be at such odds with each other."

Both men opened their mouths to speak

at the same moment, but Margot threw up her hands. "I don't want to know," she said. "But I am asking you to think clearly about whatever it was that happened between you. Should it not be forgiven and forgotten? You, sir — who will be there to bury you when you die? An undertaker? Is that what you want?" she demanded of Hamish.

He looked sheepishly at the ground.

"And who, sir, will be there to care for you when you are old and ill?" she asked, swinging around to Duncan.

"Dunno," Duncan muttered, refusing to look at Hamish.

"I think you *do* know. You really must consider what being brothers means. I can't believe that two men would squander all familial ties and the rest of your lives over some old tiff. What does it matter, really, when compared to family? Is it really worth such acrimony?"

Arran was not only astonished by her acumen but also proud of it. He had never seen this side of her, had never imagined this side existed.

"I don't expect you to resolve all your hard feelings overnight. But I want your solemn promise that you'll at least try. Will you promise?"

The two men eyed each other. "Aye,

milady," muttered Hamish.

"Aye, milady," Duncan echoed.

"*Thank* you." She dusted her hands together. "Might we now hunt this grouse? The laird has said my supper will be wanting if we don't."

"You heard your lady, then," Arran said.

The two men gathered up the dogs and their horses and set off to find the grouse. Arran watched them ride on, then looked down at Margot. "Fine work, Lady Mackenzie. You have tread where mere mortals have refused to go."

She rolled her eyes. "The peace won't last. But I should hope it will hold until they at least have bagged my supper."

He laughed, drew her into his arms and kissed the top of her head.

He helped her onto her horse and they followed the brothers around the loch until they sighted the grouse again, as the birds were too fat and too heavy to fly far. As a result, the three men were able to snare a half dozen of them. When the dogs had brought the birds back to them, and Hamish had bagged them all, Arran sent the men and the dogs to Balhaire. "Lady Mackenzie and I will be along," he said. And to Margot he said, "Come," and took her hand, walking down the grassy slope, then pulling her down onto her belly in the grass with him.

"What are you doing?" she asked.

"I mean to make a hunter of you yet, aye? I'll at least have you know how food is put on your table at Balhaire." He put the gun up against her shoulder and showed her how to hold it. He instructed her how to sight the birds. He had no hope that she could bring down a grouse, but he wanted her at least to try.

"They're wandering about," she said as she peered through the sight.

"Have you one in your sight?" he asked.

"Yes."

"Aye, then, on the count of three, pull the trigger. One. Two —"

Margot fired before he said three. And with her eyes closed. The barrel of the gun bucked into her shoulder, and her shot was so wildly awful that he couldn't help himself — he fell over onto his back and howled with laughter.

"That's so unkind!" Margot cried, laughing, too.

"*Diah,* but that was the worst shot I've ever seen," he said, convulsing with laughter.

"Because you're a terrible teacher!" she said, shoving playfully against his shoulder.

Arran grabbed her and pulled her on top of him, rolling with her in the grass. "It's impossible to teach a woman who closes her eyes when she shoots."

"You made me anxious," she said. She was smiling up at him, relaxed. Happy. "I could have done it without you!"

"I donna believe it," he said, pressing his palm to the side of her face. "And you couldna have ridden your pony here without me," he said, and took her head in his hands and kissed her.

He forgot Duncan and Hamish. He forgot the dogs. He forgot how much mistrust he harbored, and everything else in that tall grass. The only thing Arran was aware of was the feel of his wife against him, the soft press of her lips. He rolled them again, putting Margot on her back, and kissed her as a well of tender emotion rose up in him, pushing aside his doubts about her. He wanted this. He wanted his wife, this life. Was it insanity to think he might have it? Was it fantasy that filled his heart?

He lifted his head, removed a bit of weed from her cheek, kissed her forehead and bound to his feet, reaching down to help her up. She brushed off her skirts and fussed with her hair a moment, removing blades of grass, then slipped her hand into his. "Have I earned my supper?"

"Aye," he said, squeezing her hand.

He helped Margot onto her horse, and they trailed behind his men and dogs. Their path took them down to a cliff that overlooked the sea.

"Where are your ships?" Margot asked, looking toward the cove.

"Moored."

"When will you go to France again?" she asked.

Her tone was light. Too light. He glanced back over his shoulder. "Who has said I will sail to France?"

In her green eyes, he could all but see the rapid click of her thoughts. She was suddenly at a loss for words. She looked anxiously out to the sea again and said, "I'm certain you've said it."

"I'm certain I've no'."

"Then I must have supposed it. Mrs. Gowan said you'd given her china to sell — oh look, there's Jock," she said suddenly, pointing ahead.

Arran moved his attention from the sudden flush in Margot's neck to where she pointed. Jock was galloping toward him.

"Jock?" Arran asked when his cousin reached him.

"You are wanted, laird."

Arran studied Jock closely, but his cousin

refused to say more. "Have the English gone?"

"Aye."

Arran nodded. "I'll be along shortly."

Jock wheeled about and sent his horse in a gallop in the direction of the cove.

"I'll see you to the bailey," he said to Margot.

She said very little as they rode back, but her brow furrowed as if she were confused about something.

When they reached the bailey, he helped her down from the pony and gestured for one of the men to take it.

But before he could put himself on his horse again, she put her hand on his arm. "Where are you going?" Her gaze was filled with an anxiety that seemed misplaced.

"You heard Jock," Arran said.

"But . . . where will you meet him?"

He tried to understand what concerned her, what she thought he might be about to do. "Why do you ask?"

Margot's eyes seemed to seek something in him. He didn't understand what it was she sought, what it was she needed from him. "When will you return?" she asked, her voice small, sounding, strangely, almost guilty.

He frowned down at her, trying to work

out this sudden change in her at the same time he worried what Jock had to tell him or show him. "I donna know, Margot. An hour. Perhaps longer. But I must go."

She drew a breath as if to ask more, but Arran didn't want to hear more questions that would make his suspicions about her blossom any more than they'd already begun to do. So he suddenly reached for her, kissed her temple and said, "When I come back, you may ask what you want, aye? But now, I must go."

He mounted his horse and rode away, leaving her and his growing suspicions in the bailey.

CHAPTER FIFTEEN

This was the only chance she would have, Margot knew. She was beginning to feel things for Arran she'd never felt before, had never even believed were possible . . . so if she was going to eliminate all doubts, she had to take this opportunity.

She had to know what was locked in that cabinet.

Margot watched Arran until he'd left the bailey. Her confidence in her emerging beliefs about him had been tested by Jock's arrival and her sense that this meeting was a serious matter. When he'd disappeared through the gates, she walked as casually as she might into the castle, smiling at Fergus, responding politely that, no, she did not require anything and, yes, she meant to retire to her rooms. She moved up the curving staircase as any lady might having just come back from a long ride, as if there were no urgency about her day.

She stuck her head into her sitting room — Nell was nowhere to be seen. For once, Margot was grateful for Nell's penchant for wandering about and gossiping.

Margot slipped into her rooms and quietly shut the door behind her. She paused at the small dressing table and ran her hands over the various items until she found precisely what she was looking for — a hat pin. She stuck it into the fold of her skirt and went through a door to the master's chambers.

There was no one about, and moreover, with Mrs. Abernathy away, it looked as if no one had come in since Margot had left the room this morning. The hearth was cold, the water at the basin unemptied from this morning's toilette.

What if someone came? What would stop anyone from finding her in his study? Margot tossed her hat onto a chair, plainly visible from the door, then removed her coat and laid it across the foot of the bed. People who entered this room would see her things and hopefully assume she was within and seek Nell. Margot didn't know what she'd do if Nell should come looking for her — she had to make haste.

She moved as silently as she might to Arran's dressing room, wincing when the door squeaked as she opened it. She squeezed in through the partially opened door and quickly shut it behind her, then ran to the other end and carefully opened the door to the study.

Empty.

Her hands were shaking now, but she bolted to the small cabinet and fell onto her knees. She retrieved the knife she had dropped and kicked beneath it in her terror yesterday, then jammed the hat pin into the lock and jiggled, trying to find the catch that would turn it. The latch would not spring. She tried again, but no matter what she did, she couldn't get the hat pin to catch the lock. Margot began to panic — surely everyone could hear her trying to open the locked door. Surely men would fall on her at any moment and drag her away to stand before the laird and confess her crime. Surely Jock was watching her now, his eyes gleaming with the satisfaction that he'd finally caught her in an act of perfidy.

This wasn't going to work. The door would not come open, and just as Margot was giving up, it suddenly sprang free and swung open.

She gasped with surprise and jerked around to look behind her for reassurance that no one had come. Hearing nothing, she reached inside the dark interior, groping about for whatever secrets it held. Her fingers brushed against what felt like paper, tied together with a bit of twine. She withdrew the bundle and stared at the stack of neatly folded vellums. The one on top had the unbroken wax seal of the Mackenzie signet ring. What were these, letters? Correspondence with the French? With Jacobites? Had Arran written them? If he'd written them, why hadn't they been delivered? And why was her heart sinking like a stone? She could almost feel his guilt burning through the thick parchment.

Her hands shaking, she untied the twine and turned the folded missives over.

"Lady Mackenzie, Norwood Park" was scrawled in Arran's familiar handwriting across the front. Margot gasped, shocked to see her name, and fumbled with the stack. This was a letter to *her*? Why hadn't he sent it? Perhaps this was his last will and testament, not to be sent unless in the event of his death.

She turned another letter over. It was also addressed to her. So was the next. And the next. She was scarcely breathing as she turned over nine folded vellums, all of them addressed to her. All of them sealed. All of them unsent.

She slowly slid off her knees and onto her

bottom, the letters in her lap. What could they possibly say? She couldn't break the seal! What an obscene violation of trust! It was the very thing he suspected of her.

If he'd meant her to see these letters, he would have sent them. She couldn't stoop so low as to trample on this bit of faith between them. She couldn't steal them out of a locked cabinet that she'd broken into and read them now.

But neither could she leave them untouched. She glanced at the mantel clock — she guessed she had a half hour before someone arrived to light candles and hearths. She looked again at the letters.

No. *No, no, don't do it. Better you admit you intruded on his privacy than break the seal.* Margot tied the twine around the bundle and returned the stack to the cabinet. She shut the door, reinserted the hat pin to turn the lock . . . but then suddenly changed her mind and opened the door once more. Her curiosity was too strong.

"Just one," she whispered. She took the first one from the stack, broke the seal and unfolded it. It was dated more than a year ago, in the winter.

It has been six months since last I wrote you, and the winter winds and ice have come to Balhaire. The storm came on us so quickly that we lost a few sheep in the glen, found them frozen together, their wool not thick enough to save them from the worst cold. I would that you were here to warm my bed. I despise myself for wanting it. I wish I'd never heard your name.

She stared at the letter, the words seeming to move on the page in her trembling hand. What had compelled him to write this nearly two years after she'd left him? Why hadn't he sent it?

There was no going back now — Margot took another one and broke the seal. This one was written a month after she'd fled Balhaire, and she cringed, certain she would read a diatribe against her.

I've tried to understand why you left. We had our differences, but none that I would have guessed would lead to your flight. Had I not been so befuddled by your continued unhappiness, perhaps I might have put it to rights. I would that I knew what I did to harm you so, Margot . . .

He catalogued events — many she'd forgotten — that had led to her tears.

You can be the worst sort of woman, tearful and shrew, secretive and fragile. And yet I miss you here.

Another letter, written a year after she'd left.

Mary Grady was delivered of a son this morning. A happier man than John Grady you've not seen. The boy is healthy and has a full cry, and he took to suckling straightaway. The midwife says he will be a healthy lad. I am pleased for Grady, but may I confess to you that my heart is leaden. My hope for my own son is now in England . . .

There were nine letters in all to her, written in dates spread over the course of her absence. He'd written more frequently at the beginning, expelling his frustration and hurt with her in heavy strokes on the page. But in the last year or so, months had passed between letters. Two or three of them were quite sentimental, telling her of this birth or that death, of people she wasn't sure she'd ever met, much less remembered. One or two of them were written more formally, the words cold, his anger simmering between the lines.

But every single one of them expressed how he missed her.

And then there was the last one, written seven months ago. It was shorter than the others. He began,

This is the last letter I shall ever write to you. I have resigned myself to the fact that I made a mistake in marrying you. But it is done and it cannot be undone. From the moment I swore to God and the queen that you were my wife, you became the beginning of my world and the end of it, and this is as it shall always be. It is my failing that I never imagined the end could be like this, my burden to bear for the rest of my life. But I release you, Margot.

Tears were clouding Margot's eyes as she carefully folded and stacked the letters. She'd never known he felt like this. She'd wondered many times why he didn't come for her, at least send a letter, and had assumed he was glad to be rid of her.

She held the letters in her arms and bent over them, her eyes squeezed shut, her heart pounding painfully. If she'd known . . . if she'd understood that he esteemed her somehow, would it have made a difference to her? Would she have ever left? Would she have spent the last three years dining with friends and laughing around the gaming tables and sending for gowns from London and feeling so empty, so bereft, so despairing of her future?

She tucked the last letter in between her stays and her stomacher, tied the bundle together again, then returned the rest of the letters to their dark hiding place and shut the cabinet door. She used her hat pin to lock it, picked up the knife and slowly gained her feet.

She didn't know if it was possible to repair the damage she'd wrought in his life, and frankly, she didn't know how she would face the damage he might have wrought in hers if he were committing treason. But no matter what else, she couldn't pretend another moment — she had to tell him the truth as to why she'd come back. She had to tell him the truth about her feelings. She owed him these truths.

Margot fully expected to be removed from Balhaire straightaway, and she deserved no less. But it was well nigh time for her to be the woman he'd clearly hoped he'd married.

She returned to her rooms, her presence noticed by no one. She pulled the bell and waited at the window, her arms crossed over her abdomen, staring morosely out at the landscape and a graying day, thinking of a man closeted in his study, writing letter after letter to his runaway wife and locking them away. The image was heartbreaking. He'd had no more idea how to go about their fracture than had she.

She was still standing at the window when Nell hurried into her rooms. "A ship has come," she said excitedly. "And Miss Griselda Mackenzie was on it."

So that was the urgent meeting — Griselda returning from somewhere, probably with news. "Has anyone asked for me?" Margot asked curiously.

"No, milady."

Margot stood up and walked to the window, looking out at the hills. How did one dress to tell her husband she had betrayed him? "I'll have the scarlet brocade, Nell."

"Yes, milady." Nell went into the adjoining dressing room to fetch the gown.

No one came for Margot, but she could hear a lot of running about beyond her door. Servants, she assumed, lighting candles and hearths. She finally left her room and went in search of Arran.

He was not in the great hall. Nor was he in the dining room. It wasn't until she saw Sweeney stationed outside the library, as if he was standing guard, that she guessed where he was.

"Ah, Sweeney," she said, smiling with relief that it was him. "Is the laird within?"

Sweeney's eyes widened. "N-no, m-m-milady," he said, his eyes darting nervously to a point over her shoulder. His lips moved, as if he tried to say something else, but no words came. A thin sheen of perspiration suddenly appeared on his brow.

"What is it, Sweeney?" she asked.

Sweeney's lips curved, but his teeth clamped firmly shut as he tried to say the words he was seeking.

"Never mind," Margot said soothingly, and put her hand on his arm. She stepped around him.

"N-n-no, m-m-milady," he said, but Margot had already knocked on the door.

"It's all right," she said, and knocked again before she lost her nerve. She heard muffled voices inside, and before she could exhale, the door swung open, and Margot's heart seized. *Griselda.*

She stood in the doorway, tall and fit. Her smirk made Margot's blood run cold. There had never been any warmth between them, but Griselda was looking at her as if she had caught Margot in a criminal act and relished it. She was wearing a long plaid skirt and a velvet jacket fitted tightly to her.

"Aye, so it is true, is it? You've come crawling back to Balhaire," she said coolly to Margot.

"Actually, I came by chaise. Good evening, Zelda."

"Mmm," Griselda said. She gestured for Margot to enter.

The room was lit only by a fire at the hearth, but in the shadows, behind Griselda, Margot could see Arran and Jock. Arran was at the window, one arm braced against the frame, the other on his waist, staring out. Jock was standing beside him, his arms folded over his chest. His expression was inscrutable, but he looked as if he were prepared to tackle Margot should she reach her husband.

Margot didn't know where to go — Arran had yet to turn around and acknowledge her — so she stood awkwardly in the middle of the room as Griselda circled her like a hawk lazily circling its prey from above. "Arran?"

He slowly turned. His ice-blue eyes startled her — they were so deeply wounded and full of fury that she was confused. She hadn't told him anything yet.

"Has something happened?"

Griselda snorted from somewhere behind Arran now.

Arran's gaze didn't waver. He stared at Margot, his jaw clenched so tightly shut that the muscles bulged slightly beneath a shadow of his beard. He folded his arms across his chest. "Aye. Word has reached us that there is a spy among us," he said calmly.

Margot's heart began to race. "Oh, I . . . A what?" she said, shaking her head, as if she hadn't heard him or understood him. As if she didn't know what the dreadful word *spy* meant.

"A spy, Margot. Someone who would see me hanged. And then Jock found this in my study," he said, and held out his hand and opened his palm. He was holding the figurine the man in the cove had given her.

She'd put it in her pocket, had quite forgotten it. She stared at it now.

"Is it yours?"

Her heart was pounding so hard she was certain Arran could hear it. Her stomach roiled with dread, and she couldn't form any truly coherent thought. She could not tear her gaze away from Arran's — his eyes reflected such pain.

"Yes," she said, her voice barely audible to anyone but him.

Arran's shoulders sagged. He let the figurine drop from his hand to the floor and turned away.

"I . . ." Words utterly failed her right now. Nothing could convey the depth of her betrayal or her sorrow. Nothing she could ever say that would convince him that her intentions were to save her father. She was certain of that. She saw very clearly how this would all seem to him, and the fear of hurting him even more than she already had made her practically mute. "I can explain," she forced herself to say. "In fact, I came here to explain." Her small voice sounded almost disembodied to her, as if it had come from somewhere above her.

Arran's expression melted into stone, and behind him, she heard Griselda mutter something in Gaelic. "Did you come to *spy* on me?" he suddenly roared to the ceiling, his face ravaged with raw torment, terrifying her. "All the promises you made to me, all the excuses you gave me? Were they lies so that you might *spy* on me?"

"Yes," she said, breathless. She gripped her hands together and held them at her waist, needing something to hold on to. She closed her eyes, swaying a moment before forging ahead with the unvarnished truth. "That is, at first. They were lies, all of them lies in the beginning."

Arran said something in his native tongue that sounded as if it would burn her if he said it in English. And Jock, loyal Jock, put his hand on Arran's shoulder.

Margot tried again. "Arran, please listen to —"

"Get out," Arran spat. "*Now!* Go at once, Margot. I donna care where you go, I donna care what you do, but get out of my sight. I never want to lay eyes on you again."

His words, spoken so acidly, scorched her. She had known this would happen.

"Jock — remove her from my sight," Arran spat.

Miraculously, Jock did not move instantly to do what Arran bid him.

Arran swung around to stare at him with fury.

Jock spoke quickly but softly in Gaelic. Whatever he said made Griselda snort with derision, and Arran tried to move away from him, but Jock clasped his shoulder and forced him to hold still and listen to him. He spoke earnestly, and as he did, Arran's gaze drifted to Margot, then quickly away again, as if he could not bear the sight of her.

And then the three Mackenzies looked at her at once, their gazes blistering. Arran folded his arms and said stiffly, "My cousin believes we must first hear what it is you know before I turn you out."

"Oh God," Margot whispered. Her mind was whirling, her thoughts going back to the meeting in her father's study. She shifted slightly to her left and grabbed the back of a chair to steady herself. Her legs felt like river reeds beneath her, swaying unsteadily in the current of her fear.

"*Speak,* woman," Arran harshly commanded her.

"I don't know anything, really," she started, and Griselda muttered beneath her breath. "But I vow to tell you all that I do know, my lord."

"I'm waiting!" he shouted at her.

Words began to rush out of her. Unpracticed, jumbled, but truthful words. "My father bade me come. He said that there were rumors in London that you meant to bring in French troops —"

More snorting and muttering from Griselda.

"— and combine them with your men. He said you meant to put James Stuart on the throne."

"Why would he say it? What would that give me?"

"Favor with a new king?" she answered uncertainly.

"Aye, and what then?" Jock prodded her, his voice gentler than Arran's.

"He said that as he had brought you into the union of England and Scotland, and had vouched for you, and had given his daughter in marriage to you, that the suspicion of treason would likewise be cast on him, and that he would hang for it."

"The coward sent his daughter to do his bloody deeds, is that it?" Arran spat.

"He said I was the only one who could discover it. That no one would suspect me, that I could discover what you were about, and that it was imperative I do so before anyone else."

"And what did you discover, Margot?" Arran asked, his voice deadly soft. "What have you found that you will scurry back to tell your lord father, then?"

She shook her head. "Nothing. Just . . ." She swallowed. She could scarcely see him now, her vision blurred by tears she would not allow to fall. She couldn't be that woman anymore. If she was going to salvage this, she had to be as strong as he was. "All I have discovered is that you trade with France in goods. Not arms or men."

"Anything else?" he snapped.

Margot looked at the figurine on the floor. "Yes," she said slowly, and looked up at him. "I discovered some letters you wrote."

At the mention of the letters, Arran froze,

his gaze so hard she thought it might cleave her in half. Now he approached her slowly, as if he were stalking her, intending to drive a spear through her and finish her off. "Do you mean to say, then, that you have opened my private mail?"

Margot couldn't find her voice. She could only nod.

"You," he said, his voice a verbal sneer, his expression one of pure contempt, "have crossed an indelible line, madam." He looked for a moment as if he would strike her, but then suddenly jerked about and, with his arm, swiped glasses off a sideboard so roughly that even Griselda jumped when they crashed on the floor. "You have jeopardized everything I have worked so bloody hard to build here! And you have crushed *all* trust between us," he said, thrusting his hand out and curling his fingers tightly over his palm. "And now? Do you think I am a *goddamn traitor* now?"

"No," she said, her voice shaking quietly. "I have never thought so."

Arran pivoted on his heel and stalked away from her. "Get her out of my sight, Jock. Take her ere I do something I will regret all my days, what few I may have left."

Jock moved forward, his massive body shielding her from Arran. But once again, he didn't do as Arran bid him. "Do you know, then, milady, who has suggested this lie to Norwood?" he asked calmly. "Who came from London to say it?"

Margot wanted desperately to answer, but it was impossible to drag air into her lungs at the moment. She tried to see around Jock's body to Arran, but Jock wouldn't allow it.

"Speak, then, lass. Tell me how I might help the laird," he urged her.

Yes, *help* him! Margot latched onto that notion. She stared up at Jock's fleshy face. "I don't know who has said it. I know only that men have come from London. Lord Whitcomb. Sir Worthing and Captain Laurel. Oh, and Thomas Dunn."

Jock's brows dipped. "Are you certain?"

Margot nodded.

Jock turned to Arran. Griselda was suddenly alert, too, staring at Margot, then at Arran.

"Tom Dunn," Arran repeated. He pushed past Jock to reach Margot again. "What do you know of Tom Dunn?"

"Are you acquainted?" she asked, surprised.

He didn't answer her question. "What do you know of him?"

"Very little!" She struggled to think of

Thomas Dunn, a tall, wiry gentleman with a soft brogue, a pointed chin and dark, wide-set eyes. He'd never said more to her than a proper greeting. "He arrived at Norwood Park in June," she said, thinking back. "I don't recall much about him, quite honestly — he kept the company of my father, and I saw him only occasionally."

"Did you no' take a meal with him?" Jock asked. "Did you no' see him at any gatherings?"

She tried to conjure up something that would help. She thought back to the ball they'd held at Norwood Park to mark the start of the long summer months. She didn't recall seeing him there, but then again, the Norwood Park balls were so well attended, the dance floor so crowded, she saw only those gentlemen who sought her out. She began to shake her head, but then a memory suddenly came to her — she remembered she'd gone looking for Knox one evening and had found him in the gaming room with Mr. Dunn. "Yes, I saw him once," she said. "At Norwood Park in the gaming room with my brother. They were playing Commerce, I think. I recall only because Knox was quite happy he'd won. He had markers stacked before him, and the other three gentlemen had only one or two."

"That's in keeping with the debts we've heard of," Griselda said.

"What debts?" Margot asked.

Arran studied Margot. The fury had left him, and in its place was a look of resigned disgust that cut through her like a scythe. He despised her now. The emotion in the letters she'd read had been drowned and washed away by her deceit.

She had to look away from the condemnation in his eyes. "Why does it matter if he has debts?" she asked.

"It matters to *everything,*" Griselda said impatiently.

Jock said, "This man, Tom Dunn, has insinuated to some of the chieftains round us that our laird conspires with the English to betray them."

"Betray them in what?" Margot asked, confused.

"*Ach,* she knows nothing," Jock said impatiently. "Men and women who live in these hills would see James Stuart on the throne, aye? Now they've accused our laird of betraying them. Griselda has come from Portree, where she has heard the accusation said against him. And in England, they say he plots with the French."

"Someone has put him in the middle of a deadly game, and Tom Dunn is the common thread," Griselda said.

Margot looked among the three of them, confused. "But why would Dunn say that of Arran Mackenzie?"

"Because of his debts," Jock said impatiently. "The man changes coats depending on who will pay for his news. He's a gambler, aye? He's more debts than he has friends. He eyes our trade, our lands. He is wagering on who will strike first, aye? And if the laird is found guilty of treason against the queen, our lands will be forfeited — likely to your father."

Margot felt sick. "No," she said, shaking her head. "My father wouldn't take his lands."

"Would he no', then?" Jock sneered. "Aye, he would. And Tom Dunn would get his due for exposing the rebellion. Land, money, what have you. Likewise, if the chieftains suspect our laird of betraying them to the crown, they will seize our holdings by force, and again, something will land in Tom Dunn's hands for having alerted them."

Arran shrugged as if it were a foregone conclusion.

Margot was appalled. How devious was that plan, how treacherous! A man with no loyalty to anyone but his own sorry hide. "What grievance does Thomas Dunn have against you, my lord? There are many other men in Scotland with lands and trade, are there not?"

"*Diah,* because I am married to *you,* Margot," Arran said angrily. "An Englishwoman! We were estranged, and now suddenly united. The speculation for our reunion becomes tales that are easily believed by either side, aye?"

She could see it. Margot could understand how things would be misconstrued by Scottish and English lords alike, depending on who was spinning the tale. How easy would it be to suspect a man with ties to England, especially if one was looking for a scapegoat? This marriage was to have brought him wealth and prosperity — but it was bringing him nothing but heartache and doom.

"All right, then, we can guess it is Tom Dunn who has done this to us, aye? What do we do now?" Griselda asked. "How do we stop it, right it, take it away?" she exclaimed, casting her arms wide.

For the first time since she'd known Griselda, Margot could see fear in her.

"Tom Dunn must admit it," Jock said slowly. "He must admit it before he hides away in England."

"We canna force him to confess," Arran scoffed.

"An authority must hear it," Griselda said. "Someone with the power to stop him, Arran. There are still those who believe in you and put their lot behind you, aye? But Harley MacInernay said Dunn's already gone from the Highlands."

"We must speak to MacInernay and Lindsey at once, aye?" Jock said. "They'll want to know what we've found. They'll advise us."

"Who are they?" Margot asked.

"Men who have invested in our trade. Now we must convince them our laird is no' a liar."

"But how?" Griselda asked. " 'Tis Arran's word only. We need proof, Jock."

"I'm proof," Margot said.

The three Mackenzies eyed her suspiciously.

"They will surely believe it if I tell them what I've done, what I know."

Arran turned partially away from her and ran his hand over his head, as if the idea was disagreeable to him.

"And then we must go to my father and tell him that Thomas Dunn has set you against each other. My father and brother can see that he is brought to justice. My father is an earl! He's a powerful man."

Arran began to shake his head, but Jock

spoke quickly to him in Gaelic. Arran responded simply, in one word or two, sounding cold and firm.

Griselda must have echoed what her brother said, because Arran looked at her with impatience and said, *"No!"*

"What is it, what are you saying?" Margot pleaded.

The Mackenzies stopped talking and looked at her. She could feel their disgust. But she could also feel their need. They needed her.

Arran sighed. "Aye, Margot. You will speak to MacInernay and Lindsey."

CHAPTER SIXTEEN

Uncle Ivor had once told Arran that there was nothing more dangerous to man than a woman. "No beast, no plague, no pestilence," he'd said jovially from his perch on a rock as they'd stalked red deer. "Men live and die for them, lad. You'll see what I mean when you've come of age, aye? The trick is to find a steady one and keep her close."

Arran wished he had heeded his uncle's advice. He was still reeling, his head spinning with rage and the unsatisfying vindication that he'd known all along Margot couldn't be trusted. But that did not make the pain of it any less.

And here was his wife now, as bonny as a Scottish glen in springtime, explaining to two men who'd put their faith in him that she'd set these wheels in motion. That Thomas Dunn had been at Norwood Park.

It was difficult for her to say it all aloud, and it was difficult for Arran to hear it all again. As she spoke, he kept thinking of the letters he'd written her, his own private thoughts scratched out on vellum to help ease the pain he'd suffered when she'd left. She had deliberately broken into a locked cabinet and read them. She had broken the seals of his private torment and given those wounds air. She had violated him in the cruelest way possible, prying his thoughts from his heart.

Lindsey and MacInernay said nothing as Margot spoke. Her voice was clear, although it trembled from time to time. She kept her head up as she told them of the rumors that had been brought to her father. Of being dispatched to Balhaire to determine Arran's guilt. She told them how she believed her father knew nothing of Tom Dunn's scheme, and was as concerned for Arran's head as he was his own.

When she had finished, she looked hopefully to Arran. As if that would appease him. As if she'd done something so right as to erase all the wrong.

Lindsey spoke first, in Gaelic, asking that Margot be sent from the room.

Arran didn't hesitate. "Thank you, Margot. You may take your leave, then."

"But . . . if there are questions, if I can help —"

"Go now," he said, his tone firmer.

She bowed her head. She stood up from her perch on the chair, and he realized how small she looked in this room full of men. He had a fleeting image of her in the vast library at Norwood Park, a small figure in another room full of men as they sent her to do their loathsome deeds.

Margot curtsied, said good-night and went out without looking at him or Jock.

They had scarcely closed the door behind her when Lindsey said, "Norwood is behind it, I'd wager me life on it," gesturing to the door Margot had just gone through. "He means to have Balhaire, aye? And Tom Dunn will profit from it, the dirty bastard."

"*No,*" MacInernay said, disbelieving. "What sort of man would use his daughter so ill? Tom Dunn is an artful liar — he must be exposed, aye?"

"And how the bloody hell will we do that?" Lindsey demanded, tossing back a tot of whisky so violently that Arran was mildly surprised the small glass did not follow the liquid down his gullet. "The bounder is gone from Scotland, back to England, to the lords who trade their daughters only to betray them."

"*You* should go," Lindsay said, looking at Arran.

"And deliver my head to the queen?" Arran scoffed.

"If you stay behind at Balhaire, the Jacobites will hang you, aye? Tom Dunn has made his deal with the devil on both sides of the border. But if there is a chance Lady Mackenzie speaks true, and her father does no' conspire with him — if he is as harmed by this as you — then he may be the only one who can save you now."

"And if she's wrong?" Jock asked.

Lindsay's face darkened. "Then he'll hang."

A silence fell over the men. MacInernay drummed his fingers on the table. "Aye, ye've no choice, laird," he agreed. "It will be worse for you and yours here if you donna clear your name."

"But if you choose to go, Jock must stay behind," Lindsey added.

"I willna —" Jock began to huff, but Lindsey wouldn't hear it.

"Aye, Jock, ye must. There's no one here to man the helm if the laird doesna come back," Lindsey argued. "You're the only one who can. Send an army with him if you must, but ye canna go."

Jock's face began to mottle. He considered it his God-given responsibility to keep his laird safe.

"He's right," Arran said before Jock could argue. "If I go, he's right, for God's sake, Jock." Arran obviously did not relish going to England — visions of being accosted by English troops and sent to London for trial spun sickeningly in his belly. But the prospect of clan warfare churned just as bitterly.

When Arran finally quit the room, it was well past midnight. He felt exhaustion beyond his years — it seemed impossible to believe that only a week ago, he'd felt confident in his life and the things he'd built here, confident in the long-term prosperity of Balhaire.

Now he felt wildly vulnerable, his flanks open to attack from all sides. He was anxious and devastated, with so many conflicting ideas building in his chest, pounding away at his ribs and his heart, beating him down.

God help him, he should never have married her. He should have heeded Jock's warning from the beginning — what good could come from aligning with the English? It had been a doomed union from the start, but Arran had been too blind to see it. And yet . . . he still loved Margot. In some misshapen, ill-begotten way, he still loved her. He despised her for what she'd done, of course, and was gravely disappointed that she had. But Margot had not conceived this deceit. She was simply a fool.

Damn him if he would ever trust her. And without trust, what was left to them?

It was with trepidation that he walked into the master's chambers. As he knew she would be, Margot was there. She was wearing a chemise, and a wrap around her shoulders. She'd brushed her hair from its coif, silken waves of auburn shimmering in the light of his hearth. Her eyes were wide and fixed warily on him, like those of a baby owl. Did she mean to seduce him now?

Arran didn't know what to say or where to begin. He closed the door and stood there, simply looking at her, the beautiful face that had haunted his thoughts for years. Such a treacherous beauty, splitting him in two with equal parts desire and disgust.

"How you must hate me," she said softly, morosely.

His disappointment was strangling him, but he didn't hate her.

"You can't possibly hate me as I hate myself," she said.

"Why?" he asked plaintively. "Why did you open the cabinet — *how* did you open it?"

"A hat pin. My brother taught me when we were children. I opened the cabinet because I had to know, Arran."

"You thought that I would risk all that I've built here to betray the queen and my own countrymen?"

Her cheeks colored with her guilt. "I never believed it. I swear I didn't. But I had to remove all doubt. You've been gone every day, and then there was the urgent meeting . . ." she said, sounding helpless.

He'd gone, all right. To avoid her. To defend her. To learn the truth about her.

"My father said he would hang if you conspired against the queen. He said he was in terrible jeopardy and I was his only hope. Arran, please believe me — everything I told you was the truth."

"How can I believe it?" he asked. "You ask the impossible, Margot. You might have told me straightaway, aye? You might have given me the chance to help you. But what you did has made it far worse."

"I wanted to tell you," she said earnestly. "But I couldn't imagine you would admit the truth if you were . . . that is, if you . . ." She shrugged and looked down, unable to say it aloud yet.

He paused and looked to the ceiling, trying to calm his thickening anger. "Did you think I would *lie* to you?" he asked, his voice low with fury. "Have I *ever* lied to you?

Have I dissembled in any way, then?"

She shook her head. She was fighting tears. Always the bloody tears!

"If you had asked me, instead of skulking around as you did, I would have told you the truth, Margot. No matter what the truth is, aye? I would have told you the truth because I *vowed,*" he said, clapping his hand to his heart, "to honor you above all others. I gave you no reason to distrust that vow."

"No. You're right, of course you're right," she said, nodding, swallowing down her unshed tears. "But on my life, I didn't know what else to do."

"So you opened my private letters," he said sharply.

She tried to speak again, but with a shake of his head he turned away from her. "Save your breath." He was bone-weary now, and he didn't care to hear her excuses. He stalked across the room and sat on the edge of his bed to remove his boots. "We'll leave in two days," he said.

"For England?"

"Aye, for England. I've no choice." It was his only hope. To remain here and do nothing was to invite a raid. "We'll sail for Heysham and ride from there. A chaise will take too long. Griselda will teach you to ride astride. Do as she says, aye?"

Margot wisely did not argue; she pressed her lips together and nodded.

Arran turned back to the task of removing his boots. He felt her weight on the bed, felt her moving toward him, felt her hands on his shoulder. She began to knead the knots away. He tried to shrug free of her touch, but she would not allow it.

"I'll do whatever you ask me to do, Arran. I swear to you."

"Then take yourself from my sight. That is what I ask."

"Oh God," she said behind him. "Please don't —"

He jerked around, forcing her hands off him. "What did you possibly think would come of your betrayal, Margot?"

She was on her knees in the middle of his bed, the wrap slipping from her shoulders. "I'm so very sorry, Arran. For everything. For leaving you. For —"

"Why did you read them?" he suddenly roared, his frustration with her exploding around them.

Margot anxiously rubbed the palms of her hands against her knees. "Why didn't you send them? Why didn't you say those things to me?"

He snorted. "Would it have made a bloody

bit of difference?"

"I don't know," she said. "I honestly don't know. But it makes a difference now. I realize what a horrible, wretched mistake I made then."

"Aye, that you did," he said flatly.

"I want to make it up to you," she said, reaching for him. Arran suddenly stood, moving away from her touch, and her hand fell to the bed. "I will do whatever it takes — I will beg your forgiveness."

Arran laughed ruefully. *"Forgive* you? I can scarcely stand the sight of you, *leannan."*

Margot scrambled off the bed and walked to where he stood. He tried to avoid her, but she matched his step, put her hands on his chest. "Maybe you will never forgive me. I understand. But I will die trying to set it to rights, Arran."

He tried to turn away, but she caught his head in her hands. "Don't give up on me!" she begged him. "You've kept your hope all this time. Please don't let go of it now." She rose up on her toes and kissed him.

Her touch, her kiss, was his undoing. It was always his undoing. He was burning inside with all the anger and disappointment he felt. He wanted for this all to be a bad dream, but the burn in him wouldn't let him believe it. There were flames licking at his head and his heart, angry lustful flames.

He yanked the plaid from her shoulders and filled one hand with her breast. That didn't satisfy him — he grabbed fistfuls of chemise, dragging it up until he held the flesh of her hip in his hand, squeezing it, kneading it. He pushed her back, kept pushing until she was against the bed, and then pushed her down. She landed on her back, her gaze devouring him. She was aroused by his frustration with her.

So was he.

The fire in him began to rage out of control; monstrous desire had erupted and there was no turning back. Arran yanked at his clothes, removing them, then pulling her free of the cotton chemise so that his hands could feel her warm, scented flesh, his mouth could taste her, his eyes could consume the curves and lines of the powerful potion that was the woman's body.

His hands and mouth moved on her, sucking here, nipping there, his thoughts drinking from the well of lust. Margot groaned with pleasure, fanning the flames burning through him. He felt her heartbeat in the hollow of her throat, the heat of arousal, the wet slide of her body as he moved between her legs. She was panting, her legs open to him now, her hands moving so deftly over him, swirling around his thickness, cupping him, urging him to enter her.

He was lost, he was beyond hope, and he surged into her. She closed her legs around him and wildly sought his mouth as he moved in her, their tongues matching the rhythm of their bodies. Her hands flitted across his temples, his shoulders, his neck.

Arran never wanted to stop, never wanted this moment to end. He was almost delirious with the fever in him now, moving hard and long, striving to free himself from his tattered confidence, his waning faith, his fear of what was coming.

When at last his fury exploded into a rain of sparks, and Margot cried out with the ecstasy of it, Arran felt himself fading back to his windless self, the storm in him settling into smoother waters. He slowly removed his body from hers and rolled onto his back. "God help me," he said breathlessly.

Margot draped her arm over his middle, kissed his back. "Can you ever forgive me?"

Arran had to think about that. He covered her arm with his own, felt the comfort of having her there beside him nudging in beside the unease. "Forgive you? I donna know. But I will never trust you."

He heard her small sigh. She rolled away onto her side, her back to him.

The warmth of her body quickly dissipated in the coolness of the night, and Arran rolled onto his side, too, and shrouded himself in his mistrust of her.

CHAPTER SEVENTEEN

Griselda sent word to Margot at noon the next day that she was prepared to begin her riding lessons. The word arrived with a bundle of clothing that consisted of a pair of brown trews, a woolen coat and a lawn shirt that she was instructed to don.

"I can't wear this!" Margot said, horrified at the pieces as Nell held them up.

"Must you go at all, milady?" Nell asked.

"Unfortunately, yes, I must," Margot said, annoyed with Griselda for the clothing. She meant to humiliate her, surely. It would take more than this — Margot had been brought too low in the last twenty-four hours. "I shan't be gone long," she said, studying the trews.

"Must you go to England, that is, milady."

"Pardon?" Margot shifted her gaze to Nell. She was wringing the kid gloves Knox had given Margot for riding. Margot reached for them, gently removing them from Nell's grip.

"That man says you're to go to England with the laird, that you'll be gone and I'd best keep out of his way, and keep your things as they ought to be. And I says to him, 'I know what I'm to do, I don't need you to tell me, but her ladyship's not said a word of it, and I don't believe you.' And he says, 'Well, she is, and you can pout that she didn't tell you before I did, or you can help her, but whatever you choose, stay well out of my sight.' "

"It's true, Nell," Margot said wearily.

"No, milady, please don't say you mean to leave me here!"

"I'm not leaving you. But I can't take you with me, not this time. You must stay here and do as Jock tells you."

Nell gaped at her. "Here! With *no* one —"

"Yes, Nell." Margot stood up and grabbed her maid's hands. "You must. And you mustn't complain, God please, don't you complain. Stay out of Jock's path and do as they say. Please, Nell, it's quite important. *Please.* "

Nell looked terrified. She glanced around the dressing room, at the door that led to the smaller chamber where she slept at night.

"Think of it — you'll be quite all right.

You'll be safe, you'll be fed, and you need only keep my things and these rooms while I'm away. You might take your leisure every day." Margot glanced at the clock on the mantel. She was going to be late. "I have to go, Nell. Help me don these . . . things. You mustn't fret! You have my word that all will be well." She mustered a smile that she hoped looked as if she meant what she said, and handed the clothing to Nell. "Help me out of this gown," she begged.

A quarter of an hour later, Margot hurried down the curving staircase.

At the bottom of the stairs, Griselda was pacing the floor, and surprisingly, at least to Margot, she was dressed in the same strange clothing. Except that Griselda had braided her hair and had wound it into a knot at her nape.

Margot took her in from head to toe as Griselda tapped a crop against her leg. She looked almost natural in these clothes, but on Margot, the trews fit tightly across her bottom and did not reach her boots, and the coat overwhelmed her. "Why are we dressed like this?"

"Because you canna ride to England in a fancy ball gown, aye?"

Margot snorted. "I don't ride in fancy ball gowns, Zelda. But this is indecent!"

"Aye, you'll thank me after a day or two," Griselda said. She walked to a chair, picked up a tricorn hat and thrust it at Margot. "Learn to wear it. Come on, then. I've only a day to teach you to ride astride and shoot."

"Shoot!"

"*Ach,* you natter on, do you no'? Come on, then. I'd no' be the least surprised if the pony had gone back to the stables for his supper by now."

Margot would have no such luck — the pony was standing in the middle of the bailey when they walked outside. She was acutely aware of the eyes on her — or rather, her legs, the shape of them so indiscriminately displayed in the tight trews. As Margot looked on with surprise, Griselda hoisted herself onto a bay's back.

Margot required help. The young man vaulted her up, and she landed so hard on the saddle she feared the trews had split their seams.

"Do you know how to rein?" Griselda asked.

"Of course I know how to rein," Margot said irritably. "It's not as if I've never sat a horse."

"Hmm," Griselda said darkly. She expertly pulled her horse around and, with a kick to her bay's flank, set the horse to a trot.

Margot tried to do the same, but as usual, the pony was not very attentive. The man who had helped her up reached for the bridle. "Ye must tug like this, aye?" he said and, using the slack of her rein, yanked the pony's head so hard Margot thought the equine might take exception. But in the next moment, she was bouncing uncomfortably on the back of the pony as it trotted out behind the bay.

They rode along for what seemed an interminable amount of time, with Griselda two lengths ahead. Margot could imagine that Griselda was intent on getting as far from the castle as she possibly might. She could imagine her pushing her off a cliff and dusting her hands of the bother that was her cousin's wife. But they at long last reached a small meadow, and Griselda reined to a stop.

She squinted back as Margot and the pony plodded forward, the both of them already exhausted.

"Have we reached England?" Margot drawled. "Surely we are not far from it now."

"On my word, if I could deliver you to England, I would," Griselda shot back.

Margot rolled her eyes. "As you can see, I can ride. Are we done here?"

"You donna ride, Lady Mackenzie. You

cling to the horse. Your arse must feel like fire, aye?"

Margot made a sound of indignation — even though it was true.

"Bring your horse to a canter, aye? It's a smoother gait for riding. Watch me."

She spurred her horse to canter across the meadow, looking quite comfortable on the bay's back as she moved up and down in rhythm with the horse's gait. She circled back around and trotted back to where Margot sat woodenly on the back of the pony.

"Now you."

Margot spurred the pony, but he wouldn't budge. All of Scotland was against her, including this beast.

"Use your crop!" Griselda said impatiently.

"I haven't got a crop!" Margot said just as impatiently.

"For God's sake." Griselda moved closer, reached across the space between them and handed Margot her crop. "Spur and crop, all at once, then lower yourself over his neck so he knows you donna mean to amble along."

There were a million things Margot wanted to shout at Griselda in that moment, but, in the interest of ending this wretched lesson, she did as Griselda instructed. The pony lurched forward a step or two.

"Do it again! Donna tap him, *crop* him!"

This time, Margot did what Griselda suggested with vigor, and the pony took off in a gallop so unexpectedly that Margot was almost unseated by it. With a shriek, she clung to the horse and lowered herself over its neck, gripping with her legs as hard as she possibly could . . . until the pony realized she didn't mean to run at all and slowed its gait to a trot, turning back without her prompt.

When she arrived back to a very smug Griselda, Margot was breathless. "As I said, you've no notion how to ride," Griselda said with great eminence.

"All right, all right, you win, Zelda! I am a poor rider, a worse dancer, a wretched wife! Let's go again."

The two women spent the afternoon practicing the art of riding astride. Griselda taught Margot how to slow a horse, how to accelerate its speed. She learned how to signal the pony to walk, to trot, to canter, to gallop and then do it all again. Margot was exhausted, her legs and abdomen ached with the exertion of it, and at long last, Griselda took pity on her. They came down off their mounts — Griselda with ease, naturally, and Margot practically falling — to eat some bread and cheese Griselda had brought.

They sat with their backs against a rock, their legs stretched in front of them, eating in silence. Until Griselda giggled.

Margot glared at her. "What is so amusing?"

"You," Griselda said. "You look as if you've been tossed and turned upside down." She lifted a tress of Margot's hair that Margot hadn't realized had come undone. "You must learn to pin it up without the help of a *ladies' maid,*" she said with a prim English accent.

"I know how to pin my hair," Margot said, frowning at her.

Griselda snorted.

"For the love of — All right, Zelda, you can stop. I know you don't care for me and wish I'd never come to Balhaire. You needn't press the point home at every opportunity. But I'm here! I was bartered off to Arran like a hold of fish. I was meant for London ballrooms, not old castles in Scotland."

Griselda clucked her tongue at Margot. "I liked you well enough until you wounded Arran."

"Well, *that* is hardly true. Need I remind

you of the time you put pepper in my bowl of soup? It's a wonder I've stopped sneezing yet."

Griselda's face broke into a wreath of a smile. "No need to remind me — I recall it with fondness." She laughed.

Margot couldn't help it — the memory of her fleeing the great hall, sneezing over and over again, made her laugh, too. The two of them looked at each other and giggled like girls over it.

"All right," Margot said, wheezing between laughs, "We are two grown women. We'll likely never be close friends, but surely we can agree to coexist at Balhaire when Arran and I return?"

Griselda's smile faded. "When you return?" She suddenly tossed the rest of her bread into a bag. "You're a fool yet, Margot Mackenzie. You'll no' come back."

"I will," Margot said. It was the first time she'd said it; the first time she'd allowed herself to think that far ahead. It surprised her how easily the words came. Was it her true desire? In the maelstrom of the last few days, she hadn't thought of the future.

"You honestly think that either of you will come back to Balhaire?" Griselda thundered. She suddenly scrambled to her feet and strode away.

Margot groaned. "What have I said now?" she shouted after Griselda.

Griselda stopped and whirled about. "Are you really so daft?" she asked, jabbing at her own head.

"I beg your pardon!"

Griselda began marching back to where Margot sat. Margot hopped up, uncertain if she'd have to fight this woman. "You'll no' come back, and neither will Arran. How can you no' understand that is so?"

"Why would we not?" Margot demanded.

Griselda gaped at her. "They will *arrest* Arran! The English will say he is a traitor and they will take him!"

"No, they won't," Margot said hotly. "That's precisely why we are to England, Zelda. My father is an influential man. He would never allow it to happen."

"He's already allowed it to happen, aye?" Griselda said just as hotly. "*He* has cast all aspersions at Arran. He has said to you, and to anyone else who asks, that Arran is a traitor —"

"He would never!" Margot cried.

"— and he will make doubly sure Arran is arrested so no blame falls on his fair head, aye? And if, by some miracle, Arran might escape England, he could very well be murdered as he sleeps at Balhaire for all that they say of him now. The Highlanders call him traitor, too."

Margot stared at Griselda, her thoughts churning, her heart sinking. "You're wrong," she said, her voice shaking. "You're hysterical —"

"And you are bloody naive, Margot. Arran is suddenly the most wanted man in England and Scotland, and *you*! You fret over what you will wear and if we can be friends! You donna know *anything.*"

Margot felt sick. She couldn't move. She could only stare at Griselda as the truth began to seep into her brain.

Griselda's shoulders sagged. "Come on, then," she said, her voice gone dull. She brushed past Margot to collect the food. "I must teach you to mount a horse by yourself. We'll save the shooting for the morrow."

The sun was sliding toward the west when Griselda and Margot returned to Balhaire. Margot could scarcely walk, but she somehow managed to march through the bailey and into the foyer. "Where is the laird?" she asked Fergus.

"His study, milady," Fergus said, his gaze and tone cool.

Margot determinedly made her way to Arran's study.

She knocked once, twice on the door,

heard his muffled voice and entered the room.

Arran immediately stood up. His gaze raked over her, a frown forming in his brow as he took in her trews, her boots and coat.

"Is it true?" Margot demanded.

"What?"

"Do you honestly believe you will be arrested? That my father would turn on you, and by doing so, turn on *me*? Is it true you could be murdered in your sleep here at Balhaire?"

Arran sighed and rubbed his eye. "Zelda's nattering, is she?" He settled one hip against his desk, folding his arms across his chest.

"Is it true?" Margot asked again, her voice now weakened with her despair.

"I donna know. Possibly." He shrugged. "Probably. I am the name on everyone's lips, aye? I need to put Tom Dunn's name there, and I hope to God your father will help me. But it may verra well be too late."

The weight of his admission collapsed Margot. She staggered a step forward and fell into a chair. She could not imagine that her father would be involved in something as horrible as this. "You're wrong, Arran. You're *all* wrong. My father will protect you, of course he will. You are my *husband*! How could he possibly do less?"

Arran smiled, and she bristled at how patronizing his smile seemed to be. As if he thought she was a precocious child insisting that faeries were real.

"All right, you don't believe me. But I am certain of it," Margot snapped. "I have done an awful thing, coming here as I did under false pretense. But that doesn't mean my family is corrupt. It means only that my father is frightened."

He didn't speak.

She came to her feet. "Everyone around you is so convinced of it, aren't they? But perhaps they forget that when something so horrible is said of you, it is also said of *me*. And I am the earl of Norwood's daughter! I know my father, and he will not stand for such slander. He will protect us with all that he has."

Arran steadily held her gaze.

"You'll see soon enough," she said, and stalked angrily from his study to her own rooms.

Margot wished she felt as confident as she presented herself to Arran. She believed what she said . . . but nonetheless, the next morning, she took her lessons in earnest.

CHAPTER EIGHTEEN

A quick departure from Balhaire required a monumental effort, especially with the possibility of no return looming over Arran like a dark cloud. There were so many things to do, so many people to see and things that must be said.

And yet, in spite of the gloom that surrounded him, the speed with which he was forced to muster was also a blessing — he had very little time to ponder the many what-ifs running through his thoughts.

He and Margot hardly spoke at all, both of them preoccupied with the imminent departure. When Arran arrived at his chamber well after midnight, he would find her curled into a ball in a fast sleep. He was thankful for that, too — with the exception of the night he'd learned the depth of her betrayal, his mind could not be persuaded to amorous events.

But when he gazed down at her, her face

awash in the innocence of a mind quieted by sleep, he wondered . . . could she be leading him to his doom? Had this been the plan all along? Could he be so blind that he didn't see the truth?

Arran was not alone in his suspicions — Jock had them, too. Late Wednesday, a messenger sent by MacLeary arrived from Mallaig with the news that there was more talk of a traitor in their midst, a cancer to the ideals and spirit of the Highlands.

"Aye, this news I know," Arran said impatiently. "What else?"

"The laird bids me tell you that there are those to the north who believe the cancer must be struck out before it corrodes their plans for the future of Scotland."

"Is that all there is?" Jock growled at the man.

The messenger nodded.

"Go on with you, then. Fergus will take you to the kitchens to fill your belly, aye?" Jock said, and handed the man a few coins before ushering him out.

Having delivered him into Fergus's hands, Jock shut the door, walked to the sideboard, poured two drams of whisky and handed one to Arran.

"Well, then," Arran said. "Either I might draw the cancer out myself or become the cancer, aye?" He downed his whisky.

"Assuming the Lady Mackenzie has no' begun to cut already," Jock muttered.

Arran understood his cousin's grave doubts — God knew he had them, as well. But he didn't know what else he might do. To stay at Balhaire with the Jacobite rumors swirling around him made him nervous. To go to England was to face arrest and execution. The only hope he had was to expose Tom Dunn before anything might happen.

At four o'clock Thursday morning, he roused Margot out of a deep sleep and told her to ready herself. It was time to go.

He stood in the foyer of Balhaire and looked around him. These familiar stone walls, the place of his youth, of his manhood. He spoke softly to Jock — and tried to ignore that the big man fought back tears. He squatted down and rubbed Old Roy behind the ears and received a *thump thump thump* of his tail against the floor in gratitude. Roy likely would be gone by the time Arran returned — if he returned. And looking into Roy's brown eyes, he felt his own mortality.

He stood and walked out of Balhaire without looking back, lest his grief bring him to his knees.

They set sail with the morning tide. Two

days later, they landed at Heysham on England's shores and began the ride to Norwood Park. At least Margot's riding had improved. She kept pace and seemed more at ease on a horse than before.

They were guests at the modest home of Mr. Richard Burns near Carlisle their first night in England. Mr. Burns was a Scot and his wife's cousin a Mackenzie. Burns generally was happy to welcome Scots entering England, but he looked quite unhappy to see Arran. He allowed Arran and Margot to enter his home but sent the four men who accompanied them to sleep with the horses. And even so, he glanced nervously about in the gloaming, as if expecting an army to emerge from the bushes and attack them.

Inside the small foyer of the house, Margot removed the heavy woolen coat, revealing her trews. Mrs. Burns stared at her so intently, her gaze wandering over Margot's frame, that Arran could see Margot's cheeks blooming in shame.

"You'll forgive my wife," he said to his hosts. "She takes no pleasure in these clothes, but it is a necessity for riding long hours over the course of two days."

"You'll want some supper," Mrs. Burns said stiffly, and gestured for them to follow her down a narrow hall and into a dining room.

Mrs. Burns set the rough-hewn table with two tallow candles and pieces of tarnished silver and bowls. She poured ale from a ewer. A small lass, no more than ten years, appeared with a pot she could scarcely carry. Arran took it from her and ladled hare stew into his bowl, and then Margot's, before giving the pot back to the girl to carry to the other side of the table.

There was very little discussion over supper. Mrs. Burns asked after Balhaire and her cousin Mary.

"She is well," Arran said.

"God keep her," Mrs. Burns muttered.

Mr. Burns ate quickly and stood when he'd finished his meal, apparently wanting to be gone from them as quickly as possible. Arran had been a guest in this house more than once, and Burns had never been anything but welcoming. He could only assume that word of treason had reached this man's ears.

When the meal was finished, Mrs. Burns led Arran and Margot by the light of a single tallow candle up to a room at the far end of the hall.

"It's lovely. You are very kind to offer us a bed," Margot said.

Mrs. Burns grunted some response and went out, closing the door firmly behind her.

Arran locked the door. He walked around the small room, moving the drapes so he could see what was out the window in the unlikely event they should be forced to exit from here. He wouldn't rule anything out — he did not feel entirely safe.

When he was convinced there was no one lurking to slay them in their sleep, no poisonous asps, no deadly spiders, he turned around. Margot was standing in the middle of the room, her shirttails pulled free of her trews. Her hair was sticking up in strange places, and her coat was dirty, as if she'd brushed up against a tree covered in lichen. Dark circles were beginning to shadow her eyes.

"You are weary," he said. He took the coat from her and laid it on a chair. "Sit," he commanded, gesturing to a bed so small he couldn't imagine how it would hold both of them.

Margot sat and watched impassively as he knelt down on one knee to remove her boots.

When he'd pulled them off her feet, he glanced up. Her face was ashen. "What's wrong?"

"Don't do that," she said, looking at her feet. "Don't be kind to me. I don't deserve your kindness —"

"Margot —"

"I don't!" she exclaimed, and covered her face with her hands. "I've been so *cake-headed*. You're all right, I've been the biggest fool — how could I have been so stupid?"

Arran waited for tears. Three years ago, she would have disintegrated with them. But when she lifted her face from her hands, Arran didn't see tears. He saw the fire of anger in her eyes. "I am *filled* with fury," she said low, her hands curling into fists.

"You canna blame yourself for believing those who are duty-bound to protect you."

She seemed not to have heard him. "It will be all right, Arran. I know you don't believe me, but I swear it on my life."

"I'd rather you no' swear so zealously in the event —"

"I mean it. I will never be so naive again."

Arran couldn't help a wry smile. He cupped her face with his hand. "Donna promise what's impossible, *leannan.*"

She ignored his teasing and wrapped her fingers around his wrist. "Are you still angry with me?"

"*Ach,* no," he admitted. He understood

366

the untenable situation in which she'd been placed. "But I am disheartened."

Margot groaned and bowed her head. She dropped her hand from his wrist. "I think that is far worse."

Arran heaved himself up, falling onto that lumpy bed. Margot curled up against him. He felt some small comfort in her soft shape against his and slipped his arm beneath her, holding her firmly against him.

At dawn the next morning, they rode out. Their travel was long and grueling, and Arran expected Margot to crumple the closer they drew to Norwood Park. He expected tears and complaints. But she surprised him — she stoically bore the hardship, and to his greater surprise, she even took responsibility for her horse. She fed the pony and brushed him. She led him to drink and delighted when she found brambles to feed him. This woman, with the tangled auburn hair and filthy clothes, was so far removed from the lass in the ball gown he'd first seen on the balcony at Norwood Park that Arran scarcely recognized her.

He loved the woman she was now. She was slowly becoming the sort of woman he'd always imagined he would marry. Seductive and elegant, yet battle-tested and strong. And as he looked at her on the back of the pony, he couldn't help but wonder if this would be the end of their story.

The story seemed unfinished.

Perhaps that was his wishful thinking.

They were only hours from Norwood Park when they stopped at a proper inn for the night to rest and prepare for meeting her family. Arran sent for a bath — it cost him a proper fortune, but he didn't care. Margot was delighted; when the lads had filled the tub, she quickly stripped down and sank into the steaming water. "Oh my," she said, and closed her eyes and leaned her head back against the edge of the tub. "It's heaven, Arran. A white fluffy piece of heaven."

"I'll wash your hair, shall I?"

"Oh, please."

He used a pitcher from the water basin and poured water over her tresses.

She'd closed her eyes, and dark lashes fanned out against skin that had turned pink and freckled in the sun during this journey.

"Do you think Roger has enough to eat?" she asked as she idly trailed her fingers across the surface of the water.

"Roger?"

"My pony," she clarified.

"You've named him, have you?"

"Of course! I've been so intimate with only one other being in my life, so it seemed proper that I at least know his name." She opened one eye and smiled up at him.

Arran began to lather her hair. "And what, then, does Roger call you?"

"Heavy." She laughed at her jest. "Do you know what I wish, Arran? I wish I had learned to ride astride before now. There is something quite freeing about it, riding without a lot of rules and expectations about how one should sit, or how long one should ride, or what one should wear. I've never had that sort of freedom in England. But in Scotland, it seems as if no one is the least bit scandalized by a woman doing as she pleases. All that coming and going from Balhaire — do you know that no one ever tried to stop me? I thought it was because they reviled me and didn't care if I was set upon by thieves. But now I think it is that everyone is . . . *free.*"

Arran pondered that. "They might have reviled you a wee bit."

Margot laughed and playfully splashed water on him.

"Sit up now."

Margot did as he asked, hugging her knees to her chest as he poured warm water over her head, rinsing the last bit of soap from her hair.

"Now you," she said. "I'll shave you if you like."

Arran was happy to join her. He arranged the razor and strop next to the tub, then stripped off his clothes and crowded into the tub with her, splashing water over the sides as he tried to fit his much larger frame in the small bath with her. Margot had to settle on top of him to allow room; he held her hips in his hands.

She hummed as she lathered his face, and then leaned in to scrape the beard from his face. "Do you remember when I first tried to help you shave your whiskers?" she asked.

"How could I forget it, then? You came quite close to slitting my throat."

"You fidgeted so! You'd not sit still for a moment."

"That's because you were so timid, Margot. You'd no' employ the razor as it needed." He mimicked her technique.

Margot giggled, and when she did, the razor slipped a little. "That was an accident," she said solemnly, then giggled again.

He watched his wife, with her lips pursed and her brow furrowed in concentration, shave the beard from his face.

She glanced sidelong at him. "What do

you think would have happened had I remained at Balhaire? Would we have found our way, do you think?"

"I'd like to think we would have overcome our differences, aye."

"You mean I might have overcome my differences."

He smiled.

"And what of you, Laird Mackenzie? You were not so pleased with me, if you've forgotten."

"I wanted to turn you over my bloody knee," he agreed.

She giggled again and pushed wet hair from his face. She was so bloody bonny when she smiled. Eyes sparkling with mirth, a smile that seemed to reach from ear to ear.

"Aye, but I was smitten," he grumbled as she sank down onto his chest. "The mistake I made was thinking you might be a wee bit smitten, too."

"Some fall hard into affection, while others land softly. I was intrigued by you, but I was so fearful. I'd scarcely been away from Norwood Park in all my life."

"No matter — look at you now, *leannan*. No' a trembling bone in your body, aye?"

Margot leaned forward and kissed him.

"What a journey we've had, my lord husband."

Aye, what a journey they'd had. He lived with a constant sense of unease, what with the lack of trust between them and the uncertainty of what would happen at Norwood Park. If by some miracle he was able to survive this, he wondered whether she would return to Balhaire with him. Or would she remain in England with her balls and gaming tables and gentleman admirers?

What if she returned to Balhaire? Would he ever learn to trust her again? He wanted children and laughter and to grow old with his spouse, to watch her hair turn to silver. He did not want to live his life wondering if she would leave him again, if she was conspiring against him again.

"What are you thinking?" she asked.

"That when your father first came to me with his proposition, I was a young man with many dreams," he said. "I was finding ways that Balhaire might prosper and I might sustain it for my clan. Marriage, an heir — I couldna accomplish all that I desired without them, aye? It seemed a perfect union — it gave me lands in England, a woman to give me sons."

"That is what marriage is generally about," she said absently as she combed her fingers through his wet hair.

"Aye . . . but then I saw you, Margot," he said, brushing his hand roughly against her face. "I saw you on the balcony at Norwood Park, and from that moment on, my life could never be the same."

"Oh, Arran." She sighed.

And then he was kissing her, and then he was standing, lifting them both out of the bath, and carrying her to an old, squeaky bed. He did not want to think now. He did not want to know what would happen tomorrow when they stepped into Norwood Park, into all that glistening opulence.

But he was also aware, as he covered her damp body with his mouth and his hands, his tongue tracing a long, tantalizing line down her belly and between her legs, that no matter what happened between them, there would never be another for him.

CHAPTER NINETEEN

Margot awoke before Arran the next morning, when it was still quite dark. She sat on the edge of the bed, drew her legs to her chest. She hadn't slept well at all, her thoughts tossing wildly about in and out of her dreams. In one dream, her father raged at her for bringing Arran to Norwood. In another, she and Arran, her father and brothers, all ran from some unseen and menacingly dark force.

The dreams were unsettling and had left her feeling a bit queasy. But as the fog cleared from her mind, Margot had no doubt her father would help them. He had given her life and brought her into this world, had provided a life of privilege, and he would not forsake her.

Margot began to rummage through her portmanteau, into which she'd put a proper gown.

"What are you about?" Arran asked sleepily, awakened by her movements.

She smiled at him over her shoulder. "Today we reach Norwood Park, and I must dress properly for it."

When she was dressed and had pinned up her hair as best she could without help, she turned to him. "Well, then, do I look convincing as a laird's wife?"

Arran — dressed now, too, in pantaloons and an inky black coat — allowed his gaze to travel slowly over her. As if he was memorizing her. "Aye, quite convincing."

She pressed her hand to his chest and rose up to kiss him. She could see etches of concern around his eyes. "You mustn't fear, Arran. I know my father."

Arran turned away. "It's no' your father who concerns me at the moment."

Margot didn't know what he meant by that. And she didn't ask.

The last bit of road to Norwood Park was much more tedious now that Margot was wearing a gown, because she had to sit with her legs draped to one side over Roger's back, and it was difficult to maintain her balance. But at last they began to pass through woods that were familiar to her. Past crofter cottages with the smoke of the morning fire rising from their chimneys.

Past cattle grazing in the fields, and then sheep. There was the church spire in the distance, and down in the valley, through the trees, she could just make out the dozen chimneys of Norwood Park.

As they approached the gates, Arran slowed. He spoke low to his men in their native tongue. Whatever he said was met with some resistance. One of them in particular — Ben Mackenzie — seemed to argue with him. And then three of them turned their mounts about, and one of them led the way through the gates.

"Where are they going?" Margot asked as the three men rode away.

"They will remain behind for the time being. If necessary, they will carry a message to Balhaire."

Margot clucked her tongue. "You are too cautious. You'll see — we'll be inviting them to dine." She spurred her horse to canter so that Arran would not see just how her heart pounded with the anxiety from the tiny tendrils of doubt that were wrapping around her. *What if I am wrong?*

They trotted beneath the branches of the towering sycamores that lined the long drive and along the trimmed hedgerow and gardens bursting with summer flowers. They rounded the large fountain in the middle of the drive, and as they came around to the front of it, the door opened and two liveried footmen hurried out to help them dismount. One of them produced a block so that Margot could step down. "Welcome home, milady," he said.

"Thank you, John." Margot felt suddenly exhilarated. She looked around for Arran. He'd swung off his horse, had handed his crop to the footman and now held his arm out to her so that he could formally escort her into Norwood Park.

"Lady Mackenzie, you are most welcome," said Quint, the family butler, coming out to greet them. "We were not expecting you."

Margot was so happy to see the old man she almost hugged him. "Thank you, Quint."

"Welcome, my lord," Quint said to Arran. Arran nodded.

"Shall I have your luggage taken up?"

"Please," Margot said. "To the green suite, if you please. I've always admired the view from there."

"Yes, madam." Quint stood back so that they could enter the foyer. Margot was first inside, and she paused in the middle of the grand entrance, looking around at the marble tile floors and the high painted ceiling. At the staircase bannister polished to a gleam. And above her, a massive crystal chandelier. It was an entirely different world from Balhaire, one of finery and sophistication. "Is my father at home?" she asked Quint as she removed her grimy riding gloves and handed them to the butler.

Quint glanced at her gloves a second longer than necessary, no doubt wondering why she'd not had them properly cleaned. "His lordship and Master Bryce have called on Mrs. Sumpter, who has taken quite ill. I'll send a messenger with the news of your arrival."

"Thank you," Margot said. "And Knox? Is he at home today?"

"I beg your pardon, madam. I cannot say. I have not myself seen him since yesterday morning. Shall I ring for tea?"

"Please."

Quint bowed his head and moved toward a corridor, presumably to order tea.

"Pardon," Arran said.

Quint halted and turned back. "My lord?"

"Can you tell me where I might find my man Dermid Mackenzie? He was a frequent guest here for a time, aye?"

Quint looked at Arran strangely, as if he thought Arran should know where Dermid was. "I couldn't say where, my lord, no."

"But you can give him a message, can't

you?" Margot asked. "When he comes in
—"

"He has gone from Norwood Park,
madam," Quint said.

Chasing after her, Margot assumed.

But Arran seemed concerned. "Did he say
where he might have gone?"

"Not to me, my lord. I had supposed he
returned to Scotland. He's been gone quite
some time."

"We'll inquire of Pappa when he comes.
Thank you, Quint."

He nodded and set off again.

Arran watched the butler go, his jaw working as he clenched it.

"Don't fret, Arran," she said. "Dermid
Mackenzie has gone in search of me, that's
all. There is nothing troublesome about it.
Come," she said, and took his hand. "There
is something I want to show you."

She led him through the grand house to
the back terrace and the vast sweeping lawn
behind it, down a flight of flagstone steps
and into the garden. Margot turned right at
the large fountain and led him down a path
between rosebushes that were taller than
she. When she reached an ivy-covered stone
wall, she dropped his hand.

"What is it?" Arran asked.

Margot found the small latch she was

looking for. It was rusted, and she had to jiggle it into life, but she managed to lift it up and shoved the hidden gate open. It creaked loudly as she pulled vines away with her hands so she could push it a little wider.

Arran peered curiously into the gap.

"Come," Margot said, and slipped through the gate, into a secret garden her father had built for her many years ago. It was wildly overgrown now; roses climbed the wall untrimmed and untended. A birdbath had been overturned. Vines as thick as her finger spread along the raised beds. But the swing still hung from a tree, and the child's table and chairs were still in the middle of the garden. Just beneath the table was the little carriage that she would hitch to her spaniel and laugh with delight as he pulled it down the path.

Arran fit himself through the opening. "What is this, then?"

"My secret garden." She smiled at the memories she had of this garden. Of playing here with Knox for endless afternoons while their governess nodded off in the corner. "Pappa built it for me when I was a small girl. Isn't it delightful?"

"Aye," he said. He squatted down and picked something up off the ground. He examined it, then held it out to Margot. It was a toy soldier, no bigger than a large acorn. "That belonged to Knox!" she said, and took it from his hand.

"Aye, it's lovely, Margot. Now that you've seen it, we ought to return —"

"I wanted to show you this so you'd understand," she interjected.

"Understand what?"

"That a father who cared so much for his daughter he would create this special place for her would not one day betray her. It's impossible."

Arran looked around them before his gaze settled on her. He reached for her hand. "We must go back now, aye?"

He didn't believe her yet.

In the house once more, they settled in as if they had come back from a grand tour and meant to stay for a time. They had just sat down to afternoon tea — or rather, Margot to tea, and Arran at the window — when her father came bustling into the room with his arms open. "Margot, my love!" he exclaimed warmly, and wrapped her in a tight embrace, kissing her cheeks, then holding her back to look at her before hugging her again. "I cannot believe my good fortune! I assumed it would be quite a long time before I saw my darling girl again."

Margot laughed. Bryce had come in, too. He looked decidedly less pleased by her appearance. "It's so good to see you, Pappa! And you, Bryce." She lifted her cheek to be kissed.

"Ah, our favorite Scot," her father said, and embraced Arran as if he were his own son.

Margot was terribly relieved. The small part of her that had doubted her father disappeared. She was right — he was not conspiring against Arran.

"This is such a pleasant surprise," her father said. "There is so much we must catch up on, isn't there? But first, let us prepare for dinner, shall we? When I heard you'd returned, Margot, I sent a messenger straightaway to Lynetta and invited her family to join us this evening."

"Oh." She wasn't prepared for guests. They had only just arrived — it seemed too soon. "And Knox?"

"Knox? Regrettably, he is away just now," her father said with a wince. "Now, go, have a rest and dress for dinner. I'll have a word with your husband."

Margot looked at Arran. "But should I not stay —"

"Not unless you want to hear a lot of tiresome talk about land and such. I'll send him up to you directly," her father said, and gave her a squeeze of her shoulders before opening the door for her.

Still, Margot hesitated.

"There's my girl," her father said with a pointed gaze.

She had been dismissed. She glanced at Arran, and he gave her an almost imperceptible nod, so she went out.

No sooner had she stepped out than the door was shut at her back.

The minutes dragged by as Margot waited for Arran to join her in their guest suite. She felt as if she'd been pacing for an hour when at last he did come, and she was surprised by the enormous wave of relief that swept through her when he walked into the room. She threw her arms around him, almost to reassure herself that he was actually there.

"Easy, Margot, aye? It's all right," he said, his hands steadying her at the waist.

"What happened? What did he want?"

Arran shrugged as he set her back. "He asked after Balhaire. The strength of trade, how many Mackenzies take their livelihood from the estate. He talked about Norwood Park and the plans he has for the acreage I own."

"Did you tell him about Thomas Dunn?"

Arran shook his head. "I should like to speak to him alone about it, aye? Your brother . . . he doesna care for me, it's plain. I think it best I have the discussion with his lordship alone."

"Bryce doesn't care for anyone but himself, I think," Margot said absently.

Arran shrugged out of his coat. "People are beginning to arrive. You'd best go down and greet them."

"Not without you," she said.

She waited for Arran to prepare himself for the evening, and they went down together. But the moment she saw Lynetta Beauly, she quite forgot her husband and grabbed her friend in a tight embrace.

It was a happy reunion, and Margot sat between Lynetta and Arran at supper. The wine flowed quite freely around the table as everyone talked over each other. There was laughter, and many toasts were made. Even Arran seemed to relax, if only a bit, when Mr. Beauly engaged him in conversation.

Lynetta nattered on about her upcoming nuptials, and when she had exhausted that, she began to give Margot all the gossip from around Norwood Park. Mr. Franklin Carvey now held Miss Viola Darfield in great esteem, but Mr. *James* Carvey could not pay his debts, and his father was seeking a military commission for him.

"It's a wonder it's taken this long to note his debts," Margot muttered, leaning to her right as Quint poured more wine.

Lynetta laughed at the memory. "Do you remember winning ten pounds from him? I was quite pleased you were the victor that night. He seemed rather pompous to me, so very sure of his abilities. Oh, Margot, how diverting it was! And you, always teasing the poor man. How I miss you."

Margot smiled thinly. It all seemed so frivolous to her now — all that flirting and gambling. She'd been more concerned with her insular society than anything else. What a shallow existence she'd had.

She stole a look at Arran, who was listening politely to Mr. Beauly. She thought of how he presided over Balhaire and his clan. Of the many needs and responsibilities of overseeing all those Mackenzies and their prosperity. How did he abide her? How had she preferred this — this trifling existence? She felt oddly ashamed.

"You can't tear your eyes from him!" Lynetta said, nudging Margot. "I scarcely blame you. He's quite . . . robust." She giggled. "Why is it that the gentlemen in the north of England are lacking in such health and vigor? I've never seen a gentleman as virile as *your* husband. Not even can I say it of my own fiancé, Mr. Fitzgerald."

"As I recall, you seemed to think Mr. Dermid Mackenzie was . . . *virile,*" Margot teased her.

"Why on earth would you bring *him* to mind?" Lynetta said, sounding quite appalled. "He's a thief!"

Something twitched deep in Margot. "I beg your pardon?"

"Have you not heard?" Lynetta whispered. "Shortly after you left, they arrested him. They said he stole from Lord Norwood."

Now Margot's gut twisted uncomfortably. "That can't possibly be true," she said. "I'm certain I would have heard of it." She had never paid Dermid Mackenzie much heed, particularly since he'd been sent to keep watch over her — but he'd never been anything but polite and respectful. Margot didn't believe he'd stolen a thing — Arran's men did not *steal.* "Who accused him?"

Lynetta shrugged. "I don't know. They say he took something of great value and he was taken away in shackles."

Margot began to feel queasy, the wine mixing with a sickening, anxious feeling.

"What is it?" Lynetta asked. "You look ill."

"Nothing. The partridge, I think," Margot said, and pressed a hand to her belly. "Where did they take him?"

"Oh, I've not the slightest idea," Lynetta said breezily.

"But —"

"Ladies," her father said, interrupting them. "Shall we all repair to the salon? Margot, darling, I'm afraid I've boasted quite relentlessly of your talent on the pianoforte. Would you grace us with a song? Perhaps Miss Beauly will accompany you with her angelic voice."

Margot looked at Arran. He smiled. He did not know about Dermid.

In the salon, Margot did as her father asked. But her play was wooden, and Lynetta kept shooting her looks. Margot could hardly help it — she was nauseated with anxiety. Dermid Mackenzie being accused of thievery was wrong. And why hadn't Quint said so when they asked? Had he kept quiet to spare Arran's feelings? Did he think perhaps they should hear it from her father? And when, exactly, did her father intend to tell Arran what had happened to his man?

Her father seemed perfectly jovial and at ease this evening. He laughed and teased, applauded and poured wine for everyone. He did not seem like a man who had any unpleasant news to share. He looked happy to have his daughter home.

Maybe Lynetta was wrong.

And yet Margot couldn't shake the feeling that something else was very wrong.

When the song came to an end, Mrs. Beauly and Mr. Beauly stood up to perform, and Margot was thankfully relieved of her duty. She resumed her seat next to Lynetta, Arran standing behind her. His presence was comforting to her. But his expression was unreadable. She suspected he found the evening quite tedious, and honestly, Margot kept nodding off as the Beaulys sang. She'd more wine than was her custom, and her thoughts kept drifting to nights at Balhaire, to those occasions of lively music and chaotic dancing. Just in the last fortnight, she'd been far more entertained at Balhaire than by the very prim performances in this drawing room. She suddenly wished that they could all come out of their seats and dance. She imagined Bryce hopping about in a Scottish reel and couldn't suppress a smile. Oh, how he would *loathe* it.

She often felt as if he despised her.

But why would he? She was being overly suspicious now. The journey to England, her nerves, her doubts and the anticipation of what was to come — all of it began to weigh on Margot. She could scarcely keep her eyes open.

It was half past one in the morning when the Beaulys took their leave, and in the foyer of her home, she held Lynetta tightly to her. "You are always welcome, no matter where I am, Lynetta."

Her friend giggled at her. "I *know*, Margot. How silly you are! You look completely exhausted, darling — you really must go to bed."

The two young women said their good-byes, and Margot stood on the steps of Norwood Park as she had a thousand times before, waving to their guests. Arran stood beside Margot, his hand on the small of her back. Her father and her brother stood below them, speaking low to each other.

Margot took Arran's hand. "I'm so weary I can scarcely walk. Shall we retire?"

"You go, *leannan,*" he said, and pulled her into his side and kissed her temple. "I'll have a word with your father."

"But I've so much to tell you. And it's so late!" she complained.

"Aye, that it is. Go on, find your bed. I'll wake you when I come."

Margot was too weary to argue. She said good-night and trudged up the stairs to the green suite of rooms with the view of the lake and rolling hills of northern England.

She undressed, brushed her hair and crawled into the four-poster bed, sighing as she sank into the down mattress and pillows. Her lids were heavy, but she was determined to wait up for Arran. She would tell him, "There, do you see? No one here wants to harm you." And he would say, "You were right all along, *mo gradh.*" She would say, "Dermid has been arrested!" and he would say, "Aye, your father told me, but I didna care to distress you."

She could almost hear his deep brogue saying those words to her now, could almost feel him crawling into bed beside her to keep her warm. *Tomorrow,* she thought. *Tomorrow, tomorrow* they would decide what to do next.

It was a lovely little dream. But it was nothing more than the dream of a naive young woman.

Because Arran never came to bed.

CHAPTER TWENTY

Margot's sleep was a dead one, the sort from which it's hard to wake. As sunlight began to filter into her consciousness, she startled awake and sat up. Sunlight meant it was well past dawn. She hadn't meant to sleep so long.

She looked around the room, saw no sign of her husband. She thought perhaps he'd been lost in a dark house last night and had found another room.

She rose and hurried through her toilette. There was no maid to help her, so she dug through a trunk of her things she'd left behind until she found a serviceable day gown and donned it. She left her hair undressed and went down to breakfast.

Quint and a footman were clearing dishes from the sideboard. Margot looked at the mantel clock — it was half past ten! "Where is everyone?" she asked.

"The gentlemen have gone to Fonteneau,

madam," he said.

"Fonteneau," she repeated, her brow wrinkling in her confusion. Fonteneau was an old fortress abbey, a place she had frequented as a child. She remembered it had gardens and steeples built so very high, and birds nested at the tops of the spires. It had been a gloomy destination as a child, but since the ancient viscount of Fonteneau, Lord Granbury, had fallen ill, the place had fallen into deeper disrepair. Granbury had a son, Lord Putnam — but the last Margot had heard of him, he'd lost a fortune in London. "Why Fonteneau?"

"His lordship did not say," Quint said.

"My husband, too? And his man?"

"Yes, madam."

When had they gone? This morning? In the night? Why hadn't Arran awoken her to inform her? "They left with no note for me? No explanation?"

"His lordship did not leave a note that I am aware," Quint said. "Shall I prepare hot chocolate for you?"

"No, thank you," she said absently. Was it her imagination, or did Quint hasten out the service door?

With each passing hour, Margot's heart deflated a little more. She spent the day at the window, looking for any sign of her husband, her father or a messenger who would tell her when her husband and father would return. She tried to recall how long the journey to Fonteneau might take. Five hours? Long enough that they would stay overnight in that dreadful old abbey fortress with its thick stone walls and drafty windows? What business could Arran and her father possibly have there? It simply made no sense.

When no one had returned by nightfall, Margot was ill with worry. She went in search of Quint again. "I want a messenger," she said when she found him in the dining room, setting the table.

"Straightaway, madam," he said. "Shall I send him to the drawing room?"

"Yes." She marched to the drawing room to wait.

Moments later, a young footman appeared in the drawing room. "Stand there," Margot warned him, afraid that he, too, would disappear. "Don't move as much as a muscle until I've written this note." She had found pen and paper, and dashed off only a few words: "The laird has been taken to Fonteneau." She didn't sign it; it wasn't necessary. She only hoped that the men who received it could read English. She waved the paper in the air to dry the ink, then carefully folded it.

"Take this to the village," she said, speaking low. She glanced around her, uncertain if someone was listening. Fear was creeping up her neck, sinking into her veins. Something dreadful had happened today, and she didn't trust anyone. "There are three men there, from Balhaire."

The footman looked confused. He was a few years younger than she, his cheeks still pink with his youth. "They are Scots," she said. "Give this to one of them. It hardly matters which. Just give it to one."

"Yes, milady." He tucked the note into his pocket, bowed and turned to go.

Margot caught his arm. "What is your name?"

"Stephen, mu'um. Stephen Jones."

"You mustn't return until you deliver this note, do you understand, Stephen?" she asked, squeezing his arm. "If you are forced to wait all night, then wait all night. Don't you dare leave until you hand this note to one of those men."

"Yes, milady," he said, his eyes widening slightly at her desperate tone.

"I'm trusting you, Stephen." She had the anguished thought that this young man was her only hope, and to her horror, her eyes suddenly welled with tears.

Stephen Jones looked quite mortified. He leaned away from her as if he feared her tears were contagious.

"Just . . . please do as I ask," she said, and removed her hand from his arm.

"You may depend on it, milady."

"Thank you," she said gratefully. "Now go, go — there is no time to waste."

Stephen gave her a curt nod and hurried from the room.

Margot resumed her pacing. Her thoughts were in such turmoil that her head ached, and her stomach in such knots it fared no better. She realized how inept she was — she had no notion what to do. She was as she had always been — entirely dependent on men.

Dark descended with a vengeance, and with it, rain, and still, no one came. She imagined any number of scenarios: highwaymen had captured them. Or Arran had kidnapped her father and brother to draw Thomas Dunn out of hiding. Perhaps her father had kidnapped Arran. But why had they gone to *Fonteneau*?

Quint found her after nine o'clock and urged her to eat something.

"I couldn't possibly," she said, waving him off. "Is there any word?"

"No, madam," he said, and gave her a

piteous smile that made her loathe him in that moment.

"Where is Knox?" she demanded.

Quint hesitated. The top of his balding head seemed to shine more than usual. He said, rather carefully, "I cannot say with all certainty, but I believe your brother might have taken rooms in the village."

"Rooms?" Margot repeated. "Why? Has he had a falling-out with Bryce?" It wouldn't be the first time.

But Quint colored and said, "I would presume, madam, so that he might be closer to the object of his esteem." One of his thin brows drifted upward.

"His what?"

Quint pressed his lips together and refused to say more.

Margot thought a moment. "*Oh.* I see. If there is any word, come at once, will you?"

"Of course."

Quint didn't come to her again.

Nor did her father or Arran return to Norwood Park. At one o'clock in the morning, exhaustion drove her to her bed, but her sleep was tormented.

Arran would never leave her like this, without a word, without a proper explanation. But that was precisely what she'd done to him. She despised the girl she'd been then. Shame nudged in beside her worry to make her feel even more ill — she would be devastated if she never had the opportunity to make amends. She pulled the letter he'd written her from her pocket and read it again. *"The beginning of my world and the end of it . . ."*

She asked herself for the thousandth time, why Fonteneau?

The next morning, Margot tried to eat a bit of toast. She could scarcely make herself chew it; her stomach was roiling with anxiety, but she needed to keep her strength. She would be of no use to Arran if she fainted with hunger.

Stephen found her in the dining room. He was smiling. "I beg your pardon, madam, but I was indeed able to deliver your letter."

Margot gasped. "What did he say?" she asked eagerly.

Stephen blinked. "Was I to bring a reply?"

Margot sighed. "No, Stephen. Thank you," she said, and patted his shoulder as if she were his grandmother.

By early afternoon, Margot was in such a state of despair she began to fear she was losing her mind. It was as if she was walking through a nightmare from which she could not wake. She'd managed to get a few bites down and had resumed her pacing.

Then she saw through the window horse-men approaching Norwood Park.

Her father.

Margot raced to the foyer, arriving at the same moment her father entered, bellowing for Quint.

With a cry of relief, Margot ran to him, hugging him tightly. "You've had me sick with worry, Pappa. Why did you go to Fonteneau?" she asked, and looked around him, to the door. "Where is Mackenzie?"

"He has remained at Fonteneau," her father said. "Move aside, Margot. I can't give Quint my gloves with you standing there," he said, and shunted her aside.

"Why did Arran stay at Fonteneau?" she asked, panic filling her. "There was no note, no explanation —"

"Margot, please. I'm quite exhausted," her father said dismissively. "I need to sit and think before you begin to bombard me with questions. We'll speak later." He brushed past her, striding in the direction of his study with Quint on his heels.

Margot was so stunned she was rooted to the marble tiles of the foyer, capable only of gaping after her father. So stunned that she scarcely noticed Bryce until he walked past her with a passing glance, following her father.

This cannot be happening. They had left with her husband and had returned without him, and now treated her as if she were a piece of furniture to be stepped around. A rising tide of anger began to push aside Margot's astonishment. Fury began to beat down her exhaustion and fear and anxiety.

She refused to be treated like this.

She abruptly marched to her father's study. She did not pause at the closed door, oh no — she shoved it open with all her might and strode through the door.

"Margot, for heaven's sake!" her father snapped, startled by her entrance.

"Where is my husband, Pappa?" she demanded. "Why did he leave Norwood Park, and why hasn't he come back?"

Her father's face darkened. "You will not speak to me in that manner —"

"Tell me where he is!" she said sharply.

Her father's expression turned stormy. "I'll tell you where he is — in chains, as well he ought to be."

For a sliver of a moment, Margot was certain she misheard. But the look of raw detachment on her father's face slapped her awake to the truth. She grabbed the back of a chair, the news a physical blow to her. "Wh-what have you done, Pappa?" she stammered, her voice shaking. "We came to

399

you for help. We came to tell you that
Thomas Dunn —"

"I know all about Thomas Dunn!" he
snapped. "Foolish girl! You thought I would
help you? Thomas Dunn is a drowning man.
Don't you know what to do with a drowning man? Kick him away so that he doesn't
drag you beneath the surface with him."

Margot gasped. It was impossible to
comprehend that the man saying such a vile
thing was her *father*. "So you allow him to
drag Arran down with him?" she asked,
incredulous. "When the two of you, together, could bring a traitor to justice?"

Her father snorted and flicked his wrist at
her. "Thomas Dunn is a nobleman and has
favor with the queen. Do you think anyone
in England will believe a backwater Scotsman over him? He may say what he likes of
Arran Mackenzie precisely because he's
made sure that no one will stand up for
him."

"But *we* can stand for him!" she cried.
"You, Pappa!"

He snorted.

"He is my *husband*," she said, her voice
shaking with fury.

"In name only."

"No! He is my *husband*, Pappa!"

"What, have you suddenly developed

400

tender feelings for him, Margot?" her father snarled. "*You?* You have despised him from the moment I told you what your duty must be. You *fled* him. You wailed like a child when I told you that you must go back to Scotland for the good of your family. And now you would have us believe he is your dear husband?" He snorted disdainfully. "You did what I needed you to do. Now go and host a ball or a soiree. Gamble if you like. Go to London, order gowns for the Season — I don't care what you do. But leave me be — I'm tired."

Her breath was being squeezed from her lungs and the rush of blood in her head was deafening. At any moment, she would either faint or strike her father. "You have used me ill, my lord," she said, her voice shaking as she clung to the chair with impotent rage.

"For God's sake," he said impatiently.

"*You* convinced me to marry him. You gave me no choice! *You* convinced me to return to him — to save this family, you said! I did as you asked. I tried as best I could to forge a marriage with him. And now that I have, you've thrown him away like so much rubbish and with no regard for me, your only daughter."

Her father sighed. He looked impatiently at her as if she were a naughty child. "Of course I have regard for you, Margot. But sometimes we must do things we don't want to do for the good of the family."

"Oh? And what have *you* done? Or Bryce? What has anyone here done for the good of this family? I'm nothing but a pawn to you!"

Her father's gaze turned as cold as winter ice, and for once, Margot saw the sort of man he truly was, and it was devastating. Everything she thought she knew, everything she thought she was, now seemed a lie. Because *he* was a lie.

"If you say so," he said deliberately.

"Margot," Bryce said. She had forgotten he was here at all, but now his hand was on her back. "Come away," he said, and put his hand on her arm, forcing her from the room. Margot allowed him — she was so stunned, so shattered that she couldn't think for herself in those few moments. Neither could she bear to look at her father, a man she had once respected. Had *believed.*

But once outside the study, she jerked away from her brother.

"Don't make trouble," he said quietly.

"What sort of man are *you* to allow this to happen?" she asked acidly.

"What do you want?" Bryce asked, his voice calm. "Do you want us all to lose our heads? Our lands? Everything of value? Or

402

would you have us protect a Scot with nothing to recommend him?"

"Nothing to recommend him? He has more honor in his finger than any man in this house," she snapped. "If we could expose Thomas Dunn —"

"We *can't*," he said emphatically. "We risk too much. Dunn has connections in London. He is an intimate of the *queen*. It's impossible —"

Margot whirled around, intending to storm away from him, but Bryce caught her arm and held her tightly. "Heed me, Margot — don't make trouble. It will not go well for you if you do."

She glared at him. "Are you *threatening* me?"

Bryce smirked as he let go of her arm. "Do you want to marry again? Of your own choosing? I suggest you do as we tell you."

What fragments were left of her heart disintegrated. What had happened to her family? When had they become these men? Had she been so caught up in her own society that she hadn't seen them for the evil men they were? Or had something happened to turn them to curs?

Still, as shocked and sickened as Margot was, she instinctively knew that she had to pretend to accept what he was saying.

"Fine," she said curtly, and flounced away from him, running when she turned the corner, fleeing to the privacy of a suite where she could wail and cower and scream into a pillow.

Margot did precisely that. Every emotion that had built in her in the last twenty-four hours came crashing out of her on a tidal wave of enormous frustration. But when the screams were done, she knew what she had to do. She didn't know what had happened to her family, couldn't begin to guess when everything had gone so wrong. But there was one man on this earth whom she needed above all others, and that was Arran Mackenzie.

And to reach him, she needed Knox. God help her if Knox was against her, too.

CHAPTER TWENTY-ONE

Another night tortured with dreams and the dull ache of hunger woke Margot well before dawn. She dressed in a drab day gown of brown muslin and sat in a chair facing the window, waiting for the sun to come up.

She tried not to despair, but it was increasingly difficult. Her thoughts wandered through her memories of Arran. Of the way he had looked on their wedding day, so tall and handsome and pleased. Of the way he'd held her the first night they'd lain together as man and wife, as if she might break in two. Of the things he would say that made her laugh. Of the letters he'd written her and the night he'd told her he had loved her since the moment he saw her.

She reread the letter. *"The beginning of my world and the end of it . . ."*

His end.

She calmly folded the vellum. It was grimy

and worn now, the vellum as limp as cotton. She put it in her pocket. She'd been his burden for too long. No more.

When the sun peeked out over the tree-tops, Margot went down to the dining room, pausing just outside the door to arrange a smile on her face. When she was hopeful she had it, she entered the room.

Her father was seated at the table, buttering his toast. "Good morning," she said brightly. But she did not kiss him. She went directly to the sideboard.

"Good morning," he said, his voice full of question. "What has roused you at such an early hour?"

"Is it early?" she asked lightly. "I hadn't noticed. I thought I'd go to the village and pay a call to Mrs. Munroe. I left my best gowns in Scotland and will need to replace them. You don't mind, do you, Pappa? Oh, and I should like to send for Nell, if you please. I'm quite lost without her."

Her father didn't respond right away, so Margot glanced at him over her shoulder, still smiling. His gaze flicked over her, assessing. "As you wish."

"Thank you." She picked up a piece of toast and started for the door.

"Margot?"

She closed her eyes, took a breath, then

turned back with her false smile. "Yes?"

"Have a footman accompany you to the village."

His concern was maddening, given what he'd done to her. He certainly hadn't cared about her when he'd discarded her husband. Margot very much would have liked to have said as much, too, but her soaring indignation was child's play compared to what he'd done to Arran, and she had to keep her calm if she had any hope of helping him. "Of course. Good day, my lord." She gave him a cheery wave and went out.

The footman Stephen was sent to accompany her. Margot brooded as he handled the team, slouching in her seat, her gaze fixed blindly on the passing countryside. When they reached the village, she sat up and composed herself. She turned to Stephen and said, "I mean to call on Mrs. Munroe."

"Yes, milady."

"And in the meantime, I should like you to give over the reins to one of the boys there," she said, nodding at the boys from the mews. "Have them mind the team, and then you may go around to the butcher and buy a ham. I am of a mind for ham."

Stephen looked up the high street. "We've

ham at Norwood Park. They were butchering —"

"I want *this* ham," she said a bit curtly to ward off any further arguing the footman thought he ought to do on behalf of the Norwood Park hogs. She reached into her reticule and retrieved two shillings. "For the boy," she said, and hopped down from the carriage before Stephen could come round to help her. "Very well, Stephen, go now and see about that ham."

"Yes, milady," he said uncertainly. But he started up High Street all the same.

Good man, she thought. Obedient. Just as she'd been all her life. A mouse of a thing, always doing as her father and brothers instructed. Oh, but that girl was dead now, never to be resurrected.

Margot strolled along until she was certain Stephen couldn't see her, then reversed course and hurried down High Street toward the Ramshorn Inn at the bottom of the road.

The innkeeper came bustling out from behind the counter the moment she stepped inside, wiping his hands on the bottom of his stained apron. "Madam," he said, his eyes darting around the common room, as if he feared he'd left it cluttered.

"Good morning, Mr. . . . ?"

"Collins, milady. Willie Collins." He yanked a dirtied rag from his pocket and made a show of dusting a chair for her.

"Thank you, but I won't stay. I've come only to have a quick word with my brother Mr. Knox Armstrong. I understand he has taken rooms here?"

The man blinked. "Yes, milady. A pair of them."

Whoever the bird was, she must have been quite something for Knox to take a pair of rooms. "Would you please send someone up to him and tell him I have come?"

"Eddie!" Mr. Collins shouted.

A dusty little boy appeared from the back of the inn. Mr. Collins took him aside and leaned over him. He glanced back to Margot as he spoke to the boy.

The boy sprinted up the stairs, tripping over one in his haste. Margot could hear his ungainly clomp as he ran down a hall above her head. She and Mr. Collins looked up, as if both of them expected joists would begin to rain down on their heads. The boy's heavy footfall was followed by the sound of a door slamming, and then another, and then the boy was running again, down the hall and stairs.

"I've done it, Papa!" he called as he skipped across the inn into the back room once more.

Mr. Collins smiled anxiously when they next heard the footfall of a man striding down the hall above.

Knox appeared, taking the steps two at a time. "Thank you, Collins," he said briskly as he leaped to the floor. The innkeeper scurried to the back room as if escaping a melee.

The melee was Margot's brother. Knox looked a mess. He did not wear a wig, his blond hair was uncombed and his shirt hastily donned and opened at the collar. He sported a scraggly beard as if he'd gone unshaven for several days. "Margot!" he said, casting his arms wide. "What are you doing here?" he asked jovially as he embraced her and hugged her tightly.

Her brother smelled of sweat and a woman's perfume. "A better question is, what are *you* doing here?" she asked, stepping back.

"Enjoying my life," he said with a wink, and took her by the elbow. "Collins! Send tea up for the lady!" he bellowed over his shoulder.

He led her up the stairs as he chatted about how happy he was to see her, wondering aloud how long it had been, and how he hoped that she'd come home for an extended stay. They reached a door that he pushed open. He stood aside so she could enter ahead of him.

Lord, but the room reeked of sex. Margot was uncomfortably aware that she'd interrupted her brother in coitus.

"It looks a fright," he conceded. "But I was not expecting company."

"At least, not *my* company," she said, glancing at his disheveled bed.

"All right, so you've caught me," he said with a chuckle. "Will you scold me now?"

"No. I hardly care — I came because I need you, Knox. Quite desperately, as it happens."

Knox's smiled faded. "Why? What's happened?"

"Everything! Pappa and Bryce have done the most extraordinary and wretched thing," she said, and felt tears welling. She clenched her fists to keep them from falling. Tears solved *nothing.*

"Margot, God in heaven! What is wrong?"

She told him everything. About Scotland, and Arran, and how she had come to see that wild, wicked Scot in a different light. She told him that Arran wasn't dealing with the French at all, and that Thomas Dunn had spread scurrilous rumors about him in England and in Scotland and had turned

411

him into a reviled man. How the rumors, presented in a certain light — such as an estranged marriage with an English heiress — made them seem true. And how they had come to Norwood Park for help, but her father had handed him over to England.

Knox's frown deepened as she spoke. He shook his head. "That doesn't make sense —"

A knock at the door signaling the arrival of the tea interrupted Knox. He opened the door, and when Mr. Collins had deposited the tea service and quit the room, Knox poured tea for her. "It doesn't make sense that Thomas Dunn would say things about your husband for no reason."

"Dunn is in debt. He wants Arran's lands and trade," Margot said.

"No," Knox said. "I suspect Father knows something he's not telling you."

"Oh, I think he's told me all, Knox. He certainly told me that it was either Arran or him," she said bitterly. "He somehow took him to Fonteneau —"

"Fonteneau!" Her brother looked stricken.

"Why do you look like that?"

"That's where they took the other Scot."

That dull twist in Margot's gut took another painful turn. "*Dermid?* Why?"

"Fonteneau is an old abbey fort. It has

dungeons." He frowned down into his tea. "Lord Putnam has fallen on desperate times and has turned the abbey into a jail of a sort. It's where they keep men bound for trial in London. Until the proper authorities can come for them."

Margot jerked involuntarily and sent her teacup flying. She suddenly couldn't draw a breath — it was as if her throat had closed. She began to wheeze.

Knox calmly stepped in front of her and pushed her head down, between her knees. "Breathe."

"I have to go," she said hoarsely when she at last managed to catch her breath.

"Where?"

"Fonteneau!"

"Margot — how will you go?" he asked. "Think of what you're saying."

"I'll ride," she said, and pushed his hand from her head so she could sit up.

Knox snorted at that. "You can't *ride* —"

"Yes, I can! I have learned to ride at Balhaire."

Knox chuckled. Margot roared with despair and frustration as she shot up from her seat and shoved against his chest with all her might. "I'm going, Knox! I am going to find a way to free him! This is all so very wrong and it's *my* fault. You can help me, or you can wallow in your bed!" She tried to push past him, but Knox caught her arms.

"All right, all right, darling. Calm down —"

"Don't tell me to calm down!"

"Margot!" he said loudly, taking her hands in his and pushing them down. "But let us speak rationally. You don't know Fonteneau as it is today. The old man is doddering and decrepit and keeps to his bed, and Putnam has given his life up to drink and debt."

"He likes to game," Margot said. "Take me to Fonteneau. I can occupy Putnam while you free Arran."

"That's madness," Knox said. "Do you know what will happen if you are caught trying to free an accused traitor?"

"No, I don't. I don't *want* to know. Can you not understand, Knox? I am his only hope. Do you see? I am his *only hope.*" And there they were. The tears she'd been fighting for days began to fall, silently streaming down her cheeks. She bowed her head, ashamed of them.

"Good God. Margot . . . do you *love* him?" Knox asked, his voice full of surprise.

She did, didn't she? She *loved* him. She nodded, swiped her fingers beneath her eyes. "I suppose that I do."

"Bloody hell." Knox sighed and gathered her in his embrace, resting his chin on the top of her head. "Then I suppose we must go, mustn't we?"

Margot lifted her head. "You'll help me?"

"I'll help you. Against my better judgment, I'll help you, love. Now listen to me and take heed — be ready to ride at two o'clock. Bribe one of the grooms there if you must, and tell everyone far and near that you mean to call on your friend Lynetta Beauly in my company. Then slip out of Norwood Park like a wraith so that no one can say precisely when you left to call on her. Can you do that?"

She nodded.

Knox caught her chin, forcing her to look at him. "Margot — can you do that? Because if you can't, and we are caught, that will be the end of it. Of you and your Scot."

For once in her life, Margot was confident in the decision she was making. For once in her life, she was entirely confident she could do what she was being asked to do, without equivocation. Whatever it took to free Arran, she would do, without complaint.

She peeled his hand from her chin and stood up. "I can do it."

Chapter Twenty-Two

Fury was an inadequate word to describe what Arran felt. He assumed they'd put laudanum or some witch's brew into his brandy, for nothing else explained how he'd become so leaden and incapable of defending himself. It had taken a full day to rouse himself from that fog — at least, he thought it was day — only to find himself in a dank hole. He was not alone; two of his men were nearby. Ben, whom the Armstrongs had rounded up when they'd drugged Arran. And Dermid, who, near as Arran could tell, had been in this hellhole for a month. He couldn't see them, could only hear them. He couldn't see anything, quite literally, as there was scarcely any light at all.

But the English were arrogant, stupid pricks. Not only had they failed to divest him thoroughly of plausible weapons — he had an eating knife tucked away into his boot — but also they'd left the three Scotsmen unattended for the most part, appearing only occasionally to push food through narrow slots in the doors. Arran and his men shouted to hear each other, but no one seemed to care that they did. Their voices brought no one.

At the top of the wall in Arran's cell was a narrow window that allowed a bit of light. The opening was too small for a man to fit through. There was a hole in the window, big enough to allow bitterly cold air to filter into his cell at night and to carry the sounds of people and beasts moving about during the day. He had gathered, given the stench and the sounds, that they were somewhere near the stables.

He'd also determined that whoever brought food to them each day trudged across flagstones that passed near his window. He heard the heavy steps, then heard a door open. Then heard the clang of it as he drew it closed, somewhere inside this building.

Arran had a plan. He would feign illness and refuse to touch the food the man brought. Eventually, someone would have to open the door to see if he was dead. When that happened, he would overpower the bastard, kill him if necessary and take the man's keys. He'd have to be precise about it — his knife was too small to inflict deep damage. He'd have to slice across a throat. He reasoned he had one chance — it was either kill or be killed.

Well. It was kill.

Then he would free his men, and they would fight their way out or die.

Arran wondered how long before his keepers realized he was not eating and opened the goddamn door.

In the meantime, he had ample opportunity to brood about that night in the Armstrong study. He'd been bloody stupid for having trusted Norwood.

In the study that evening, he'd watched Norwood pour three brandies, had accepted one and had drunk deeply before he broached the subject of Thomas Dunn. Norwood had seemed neither surprised nor particularly knowledgeable about Dunn. He'd merely smiled at Arran, put his hand on his shoulder and said, "You will understand, sir, when I say that in this regard, it's either you . . . or me."

And then a deep Highland mist had sunk down on Arran's brain. He had been helpless, unable to lift his arms, as Bryce and another man overpowered him. He vaguely remembered being tossed into a carriage, and that his head kept bouncing off the squabs as they'd moved down the road. He recalled nothing more until he'd woken up in here. He had a straw mat, a bucket for waste and one filled with water.

He'd roared his frustration when he at last came to, which was how he'd found his men.

And then he'd continued to roar with frustration. For allowing himself to latch onto the slender ray of hope Margot's assurances had given him.

Did she know he was here? His instincts told him she was as much a victim in this as he, but there was another, albeit smaller, part of him that wondered if she hadn't known this would happen. She'd seemed in her cups that night, a condition he'd never known her to be in. Was it possible she'd been poisoned, too? Or had she drunk so that she wouldn't have to face what was coming?

Arran had lost track of time when he heard the familiar footsteps outside the cell, trudging toward a door somewhere, and the sound of slop in a bucket knocking against a leg. He lay down on the straw mat and rolled on his side, facing the wall. He heard the sound of the jailer sliding food in to his men, then making his way down the hall to Arran's cell.

He repeated the same thing here — he opened the door to the shelf, slid a cup of what smelled like cabbage soup and bread onto it, and then shut the door and turned the lock.

As unappetizing as the soup smelled, Arran's belly rumbled. But he left it there, untouched. Tomorrow the man would return. He would see that Arran hadn't eaten. He would wonder. He might go another day, or even two. But eventually, he would open the damn door.

Arran slowly sat up and leaned his head against the wall. He closed his eyes and listened to the jingle of bridles and squeak of leather saddles as riders passed by. Arran's thoughts filled with images of Margot, dressed in trews, her cheeks appealingly flushed by the exertion of the ride. The image was a peculiar draw in his belly, a sadness mixed with regret and the misery of knowing he'd likely never see her again. *"Margot,"* he whispered.

He heard her laugh, a sound like a sweet confection.

As if his predicament could be any worse, now he was hearing things.

And then he heard the laugh again. He opened his eyes. That was definitely feminine laughter. He didn't hear the clop of horses hooves, which said to him the riders had stopped. Arran vaulted up and lunged for that window, leaping as high as he could, his fingers seeking a hold on the grainy sill. But he couldn't hold it and slid down the rough stone wall. He backed up and tried again, this time bracing his foot against the wall to vault himself higher.

He failed to reach it. *"Margot!"* he shouted.

The sound of horses again — the riders were moving away. *Diah,* had he imagined it? Was he losing his mind? Arran stared up at the window. He'd lost track of time; the light that came in through the windows was gray and dirty, hiding the sun or the moon. He couldn't say if it was morning or afternoon.

He tried to think through all the reasons Margot would be close by. Was something to happen? Was the trial to be held here? Had she come to see him hang? He stood in the middle of the cell, staring at the window, trying desperately to think.

"Remember, we were riding to Keswick to call on the Daltons when we were diverted because the road had fallen into great disrepair," Knox said low as they gazed up at an abbey door in need of a coat of paint. The entire abbey looked ramshackle.

"I remember," Margot said.

"Listen to me, Margot," Knox said, catching her hand.

She made herself turn her attention away from the derelict abbey.

"He will know if we dissemble. You must make it seem quite sincere, do you understand? You were scarcely able to hobble along, and so forth."

"Knox . . . I understand," she said calmly. She looked back at the abbey facade. "It almost seems abandoned."

"Not yet. But let this be a lesson to us all — this is what happens when one amasses gambling debts. All right, then, shall we?" Knox said, and together, they walked up the steps to the door.

Knox lifted the brass knocker on the door and let it fall once, then twice more. Eventually a man opened the door. He was wearing an old-fashioned powdered wig, and his well-worn pantaloons were sagging at the knees. He peered curiously at them.

"How do you do?" Knox said. "I am Mr. Knox Armstrong. My apologies for arriving quite unannounced, but my sister, Lady Mackenzie, was taken ill on the ride to Keswick. Is Putnam about?"

The butler squinted. "Unfortunately, his lordship was just set to leave. He has been

422

invited to dine at Chessingham Hall."

"Perhaps you could tell him that Margot Armstrong has come?" Knox asked.

The man frowned.

"Please," Margot added. "We are old, dear friends, Putnam and I. I know he will take pity on me. I am really rather ill."

Knox touched her elbow, warning her. But Margot ignored him. She needed only to convince the butler of their friendship. She moved up one step, smiling as seductively as she knew how to smile. "It was my suggestion, in truth. When I fell ill on the road to Keswick, my brother urged me to ride on, but I told him I knew who would offer me comfort straightaway."

The butler glanced uncertainly behind him, and Margot saw her opportunity. She brushed past the unsuspecting man into the foyer and began to remove her gloves. "I think his lordship would be *very* displeased if he knew I'd been turned away."

The butler glowered at her. "Wait here," he said curtly. "I'll tell his lordship you've come." He walked off, his shoes echoing on the stone floors.

"Wherever did you learn to be so bold?" Knox muttered as he removed his gloves.

"What do you think I've been doing the last few weeks?" she whispered as she removed her cloak and hat.

They heard the sound of a door being soundly shut, then footsteps scurrying away from them. Another few minutes passed, and they heard the footfall of someone striding in their direction. Quickly.

Putnam suddenly appeared before them, bleary-eyed, his face a mask of confusion as he peered at them. His shirt was only partially tucked into his pantaloons. His waistcoat and coat were unbuttoned, and his wig looked as if he'd slapped it onto his head without benefit of a looking glass. "Miss Armstrong?" he asked uncertainly.

"My lord," Margot said, sweeping toward him. "Actually, it's Lady Mackenzie now."

"Ah, yes . . . Yes, I recall," he said uncertainly, as if he didn't really recall at all.

She curtsied deeply. When he didn't move to help her up — he seemed paralyzed in some way — Knox stepped forward and did it for him.

"Putnam," Knox said. "Our sincere thanks for allowing us to intrude on you in this manner."

"No, no," he said. "I'm . . . surprised." His gaze was still on Margot. "Come in."

He led them into the drawing room that Margot remembered from her childhood. The last time she'd been here, it had been furnished with Aubusson carpets and crystal chandeliers. The carpets were gone, and elegant chandeliers had been replaced by wooden wheels sporting cheap tallow candles. Moreover, the room had not been cleaned — the floors were unswept, and evidence of dogs and rodents apparent along the baseboards. Papers and books were strewn across the writing desk and spilled onto the floor. And the hearth was burning peat.

"May I offer you some wine?" Putnam asked.

"Thank you. You'd not believe the journey we've had!" Margot said. "It was impossible for us to avoid calling on you so unexpectedly, my lord. But the road to Keswick has fallen into severe disrepair since last I was in England, and I began to feel quite ill, what with all the bouncing. Knox insisted that we must keep on, that it would be quite untoward to call on someone without invitation. But I assured him that you would welcome us for a night."

"Yes, the roads are quite unbearable," Putnam said, and downed the glass of wine his butler had given him, then thrust it back at him for more before the butler had even poured for Margot and Knox.

When the butler served the wine, Margot

found it to be sour and unfermented. It was the sort of wine that was made in kitchens. Knox took his and wandered around the room.

Margot fixed her smile on Putnam and moved closer. "How does your father fare?"

"Oh, he . . . well, he's unwell."

"I'm so very sorry," she said softly. "You must give him my regards and wishes for good health."

"Of course." Putnam was watching her warily.

Margot moved closer. "I am very happy to find you home, my lord. Do you recall that night we played Commerce? There were ten of us in all, were there not? I recall those days of our youth with great fondness."

He scratched at his head. "I think I lost quite a lot of money that night."

She laughed. "We were only learning the game."

"Yes," he said vaguely. He looked around him almost helplessly, as if he didn't know what to do with her, or the room, or even himself. He seemed quite ill at ease and suddenly downed the wine and handed his glass to the butler for more.

Margot considered the options she and Knox had discussed. Knox had some idea of where the old dungeons were. His plan was to find the opportunity to have a look while Margot kept Putnam engaged with a game. Judging by the look of the place, she decided he would be very interested in Arran's purse she had beneath her skirts. Margot smiled and lifted her glass in a mock toast to Putnam.

She shifted even closer as Knox moved to the far end of the room and made some remark about the ceilings, as if he were admiring them. Margot shot a sidelong look at Knox's back and then smiled at Putnam. "Is it obvious that he's my keeper?"

Putnam blinked. He looked at Knox, too.

"Quite honestly, I wish he were somewhere else," she said with a sigh. "Would it not be diverting if we were to have a game?"

Putnam slanted her a look. "A game."

She arched a brow and shrugged lightly as she lifted her glass to her lips.

"What do you want?" Putnam suddenly demanded.

"Whatever do you mean? As I said — travel to Keswick on those wretched roads has made me ill. And to think, all that trouble to call on the Daltons. You remember William Dalton, don't you? Can you imagine a more tedious evening?" she asked, and slyly touched Putnam's hand.

427

She might as well have singed him; Putnam jerked his hand back quickly.

"What are — Need I remind you that you're *married*, madam," he hissed. "Is it not your husband that languishes in our dungeon?"

Margot's heart seized. She'd expected it, but nonetheless, it was a miracle that she managed to keep her countenance. "Oh dear, my lord, you haven't heard, have you? He is my husband, yes, but in name only. He's a Highland savage and truly belongs in a cage."

"I've nothing to do with it," he said quickly. "I merely hire the space out to whomever needs it."

"No, of course not!" she said brightly. "It is all my father's doing. He was right to do it, too. Do you know what that savage left me besides an unspeakable reputation?"

Putnam shook his head.

She leaned in. *"A fat purse,"* she whispered. "So fat that I might amuse us both with a bit of gaming before I am pressed by my brother to carry on to the bloody Daltons." She rolled her eyes. "I'm finally free of that beast and the Daltons are my only diversion?" She glanced over her shoulder at Knox, playing the part. "I told him I wanted *amusement.* Not tedium."

She had Putnam's undivided attention now. "What sort of gaming?"

"Commerce?" she suggested. "For the sake of old times?"

"What are you saying?" Knox asked. "Margot, we should carry on and leave his lordship to his evening."

Knox was the perfect partner. "Knox, really!" she complained. "We can't possibly reach Keswick by nightfall."

"Nevertheless, we will not impose on Putnam another moment —"

"No, it's quite all right," Putnam said, waving a limp hand at Knox. "Lady Mackenzie has invited me to game until her health is improved."

"You don't mind, do you, Knox?" Margot asked sweetly.

"I think that —"

"Have you an interest in architecture, Mr. Armstrong?" Putnam said, turning his attention to Knox.

Knox paused. His gaze flicked over Margot. "Why do you ask?"

"No reason, sir. Except that Fonteneau boasts some of the finest medieval architecture in all of England. If you'd like, my estate agent might show you about."

Putnam poured more wine down his throat. He was perspiring now.

"I think we should go," Knox said.

"Please, Knox?" Margot asked sweetly. "We'll go, I promise we will, but allow me a bit of a laugh and a game with Lord Putnam first."

"Joseph, show Mr. Armstrong to Mr. Cavanaugh's office, will you?" Lord Putnam said. "Mr. Cavanaugh will be more than happy to show you about the abbey."

"Well," Knox said, feigning uncertainty. "I suppose I might have a quick look. And then, darling, we really must be on our way and leave Putnam to his work."

"We will," she agreed sweetly.

Margot watched the butler escort Knox out of the room, then turned her most winsome smile to Putnam. "At *last,*" she said, relieved. "My brothers are like vultures, watching every move I make. And they certainly don't care for me to wager on card games, so thank you for that."

"No?" Putnam asked, assessing her.

"Oh no," she said with a gay laugh. "They claim I've already lost too much of the family fortune."

Putnam smiled slowly. He poured more wine, then gestured to a table in the middle of the room. "Allow me to help you lose a bit more, Lady Mackenzie."

He pushed the papers and books off the

table and let them fall to the ground. As they sat down to play, Margot really had no plan other than to allow Putnam to win by making some poorly placed bets. She reasoned that he would gain confidence so that when the time was right, she might make a very large wager. One that freed Arran. Her deal with the devil, so to speak. Admittedly, her only real hope of winning that wager was if he drank himself into unconsciousness.

But surprisingly, it proved very difficult to lose to Putnam. He was so fearful of losing that he seemed to agonize over every decision. He drank through one bottle of wine, then another, and sank deeper and deeper into his cups, moaning at each loss as if he were physically ill.

Margot began to take pity on him, especially when he insisted they go again every time he lost. Lord Putnam was a galleon, sailing straight into the rocks. And when that ship wrecked, she would have her husband back.

It had been an hour or so since Arran heard voices. But this time, the voices belonged to men, their low conversation punctuated by their strolling footfalls. Arran had paused in his pacing and stood as still as he could to listen. He'd determined they were walking away from him, and one of them was thanking the other for the tour. *Tour of what?*

Moreover, that Englishman's voice had sounded vaguely familiar. But then again, Arran wasn't certain he wasn't hearing things now. Surely he'd imagined Margot's laugh.

He was trying to will himself to face another night when he heard footsteps coming back toward him. But these weren't the footsteps of the jailer. These were quick and light. He heard the clang of the door, and the footsteps were now inside. Someone was moving down the hall, jangling the doors, trying to open them.

The doors opened, and he heard Ben shout; then a male voice shouted back. "Mackenzie!"

Arran froze. Was this it? Had they come to take him for the mockery that would be his trial? But wouldn't there be more than one of them to take him?

"Aye, here!" Ben shouted. Arran realized at once what Ben was doing — his men would do anything to protect him, including pretending to be him now. He suddenly shoved aside the soup from the shelf and shouted. "Here! The laird is here!"

The footsteps hurried toward him. He

heard a fumbling of keys, first one in the lock, then another. Then a third. A moment later, the door swung open, almost hitting Arran. He blinked against the candlelight, still unable to make out who was there.

"For God's sake, come on," the man said. "The jailer will return at any moment."

"Who —"

"Are you blind? Knox Armstrong."

Arran couldn't gather his wits. He didn't know why Knox was here, and he could only assume that like all of the Armstrongs, Knox was against him. But Knox's arm appeared through the candlelight, and he grabbed Arran's forearm. *Come,*" he demanded. "You'll have us all killed."

"My men," Arran said.

"We've no time —"

"My *men,*" he said again.

Knox threw the keys at him. "I'll keep watch. Make haste, make haste," he urged him, and hurried down the corridor.

"Here, milord!" Ben said, his hand showing in the slit of his door.

Arran fumbled with the keys, found the one that worked and opened the door. Ben burst through and grabbed the keys from Arran. "Go, laird, donna wait for us. Dermid is ill, aye?"

Ben lunged for a door across from his. He

opened the door and disappeared inside. He reappeared only moments later with Dermid half-draped over his shoulder.

"*Diah*," Arran exclaimed. The man was emaciated, his hair matted against his skull.

"Go milord," Ben urged him. "The clan can survive without me or Dermid, but they canna go on without you. Save yourself."

"The hell I will," Arran said. He took part of Dermid's weight from Ben, and together they dragged the ailing man from the jail.

Just outside the door, Knox was waiting. "The keys, the keys," he said, gesturing for them. "We've not a moment to waste."

Ben handed him the keys.

"Just at the bottom of the hill are the stables," Knox said, speaking quickly and quietly. "They are unmanned tonight — I've just come from there. Saddle your horses. Be prepared to ride."

"And you?" Arran asked.

"I'll lead you out of here," Knox said. He turned and began to stride away, the candle-light bobbing with his near sprint.

Arran didn't pause to question Knox's intent. At least they were out of the cells. At least now they had a fighting chance. "Aye, let's go, then," he muttered to Ben, and together, they carried Dermid down the road.

Margot was beginning to panic. Putnam was frightening her. She had two of his markers on the table before her, and he was perspiring heavily, alternating between tears and anger. *Where was Knox?*

She forced herself to draw a steadying breath and mentally ran through her options: she could scream, which would surely bring someone . . . if there was anyone lurking about this old abbey besides the butler. She could pretend that she needed a retiring room and flee. But if Knox hadn't found Arran, where would she go? And how would she come back for him?

As she was debating what to do, Putnam picked up the deck. "Again," he said.

"My lord, you are distressed —"

"I am *not* distressed! I've been divested of my money by a woman who has come here on disagreeable business! Do you think me ignorant, Lady Mackenzie? I know what you're about," he snarled.

Good God, where *was* Knox?

"You want that bloody Scot, do you? That traitor to your queen?"

She resisted the urge to argue with his slander. She had to be calm, quite calm, and slowly began to gather the coins and markers before her. His eyes seemed almost to bulge now as he watched her. "I don't know what you are implying, my lord. I meant only to enjoy a bit of sport, as I said. My father has freed me from an unbearable marriage and I assure you . . . ." She lifted her gaze, looked him directly in the eye and said gravely, "*I don't want him back.* Perhaps a better question is, what do *you* want?"

Putnam slowly licked his bottom lip, as if seeking the last drop of wine.

"I think I know what you want," she said calmly. "I think you want my money. Quite desperately."

Putnam's face mottled, and for a moment, she thought he would explode with anger. He looked as if he might lunge across the table for her throat at any moment, wrap his fingers around her gullet and squeeze. But then, inexplicably, he lowered his head and dissolved into tears. "I've lost everything," he sobbed.

"I beg your pardon?"

"Everything, all of it!" he cried, sweeping his arm across the table and sending markers and cards and his empty glass sailing and breaking on the stone floor. "I've nothing! Nothing at all!" He tore the wig from his head and threw it on the ground, then stood and staggered across the room.

"My lord!" Margot exclaimed. She could feel his despair coming off him in great lapping waves. Worse, she understood it. She'd felt that sort of bone-deep despair three times in her life: when she was told she would be married. When she was told she would return to her husband. And in these last two days, when she thought she'd lost him.

Margot stood up and gathered the coins and markers and went to him before he could pour more wine. "Lord Putnam," she said, catching his arm as he reached for the decanter. He tried to shake her off. *"Richard,"* she said, her voice quiet and soothing. "Here — this is for you. And . . . and this," she said, and reached into the pocket of her gown for Arran's purse.

He looked down at the bounty she forced into his hands, then up at her again. "No," he said. "I won't take charity —"

"It's not charity," she said, and folded his hands over the money. "It's a loan. You'll repay me when you can."

"But I can't —"

"You will," she said. "Oh, my lord, you *will*," she said earnestly. "I have every faith in you."

Putnam began to sob, his body racked

with them. He clutched the money to his chest as he slipped down and landed on his rump beside the sideboard.

Margot had never seen a man lose his composure so completely, and she was overcome with a strange mix of empathy and revulsion.

"Margot."

She startled, whipping around to Knox. He, too, was staring at Putnam. "Come away," he said, taking her by the elbow. "Come now."

Her brother pulled her from the room, as she was unable to tear her gaze away from the broken man who took in prisoners for money.

Once outside, Knox moved her along much more quickly, and she struggled to keep up with him. He paused at a closed door near the entry and pushed it open. "Your master needs help. He needs to be carried up to his bed," he said to the startled butler. "Lady Mackenzie and I will take our leave now." He did not wait for an answer, but he pushed Margot out the door, pausing only long enough to pick up her cloak and gloves.

Outside, the night was so dark that she could scarcely see in front of her.

"Knox, wait, *wait,*" she said, using both

hands to slow his step.

"There is no time, Margot," he said, and put his arm around her waist as he hurried her down the road.

"But did you — Have you found him?"

Knox grunted and pushed her around the corner.

Her answer was standing there in the shadows. Margot would have known his figure anywhere. She didn't think; she broke away from Knox and ran, her feet scarcely touching the ground. She vaulted her body at him, flinging her arms around him, desperate to feel him safe in her arms, and just as desperate not to lose him. "Arran, Arran . . . I thought you were lost to me," she said. "I thought you were *lost*."

"Come now, Margot." He peeled her arms from him. "Come now, aye? We must make haste. Go and help your brother bring horses," he said, and set her back, pushing her lightly into a paddock, where their mounts were grazing, still saddled.

Everything happened so quickly — Margot couldn't say how, exactly, but she was in the saddle, and they were riding. Four horses, riding into the inky black of a moonless night. No one spoke. They just rode as quickly as they could with only the light from an anemic night sky to guide them, the only sound the horses laboring and their staccato cantering.

It seemed like hours to Margot before Knox drew up, bringing the party to a halt. They had come out of the forest and were riding alongside the sea now. The clouds had cleared, and the moon provided enough light to see the road.

"How did it come to this?" Knox asked Arran.

"You might ask your da that, aye? He drugged me so that I couldna resist him, then threw me into a hole."

Even in the moonlight, Margot could see a fury on her brother's face she'd never seen in him before.

"Stay to this road," Knox said. "You might reach Scotland sometime tomorrow."

"But you're coming with us," Margot said. "You *must* come with us! Pappa will take his anger out on you —"

"I can't," Knox said flatly. He caught her horse's bridle and pulled her aside, off the road.

"Don't go back, Knox," she begged him. "Come with us! Balhaire is not so very awful. You'll see. I know I've said that it is, but I've been unfair —"

"Hush now," Knox said quietly. "Listen to me, darling. Someone must stay behind. If

Mackenzie is innocent, someone must discover what Thomas Dunn is about. Someone must be here who will speak for him and for you, and you know there is no one here who will speak on your behalf save me. Something is amiss — there is no reason that Thomas Dunn would randomly choose Mackenzie to torment. Something is rotten and I intend to determine what it is."

The stress of the last few days began to feel like a crushing weight on Margot's chest. Was there no right way to turn? Was every decision steeped in loss? "You'll be lost to me," she said weakly.

"What I must know — Margot, look at me. What I must know, and know now, is if this is what you truly want," Knox said, gesturing toward Arran and his men. "Because if you choose him now, if you do not turn back with me now, likely you will be in Scotland for the rest of your life. You'll not come back to England, not with the cloud of suspicion surrounding him. Do you understand me? You can't come back, not for a very long time, or you'll risk too much."

The night air felt thick; she was having trouble catching her breath again.

"Are you all right?" Knox asked, reaching for her hand.

How could she be all right? She was on a road in the middle of the night, faced with an untenable choice. Margot shook her head.

"Ah, love, I understand. But I must press you for your answer. These men need to be as close to Scotland as possible when day breaks. What do you want, Margot?"

What did she want? She wanted things to go back to the way they were three years ago. She wanted to do it all again, to say the right things, to stand up for herself and her desires. She wanted a completely different history than the one she'd been thrust into. "I don't know," she said, her voice shaking.

She heard a horse move toward them, heard Arran's low voice as thoughts roared in her head. She heard Knox wheel his horse about and move up to the road.

"You're shaking like a leaf, lass," Arran said. His hand closed around hers, his fingers squeezing hers. "You need only say it, aye? Whatever you want, *leannan.* Say you want to end it, and it is done."

"That's not — I wasn't thinking that at all," she said desperately.

"Aye, of course you are. How could you no'? It's a bloody bad decision for you, that it is." He suddenly leaned over her, his hand going to her nape, drawing her forehead to his. "You saved my life, Margot. I willna keep you tied to me if you wish to remain in England. But I *canna* remain here, and with every moment that passes, I put my men and myself closer to danger. As cruel as it is, you must decide now. But know this — if you come with me now, I will give you all that I have. I will honor you and cherish you for as long as I live, with or without you. The decision is yours."

He seemed almost preternaturally illuminated in the moonlight. Margot pushed aside her cloak and reached into the pocket of her gown. Her fingers closed around the letter he'd written her and never sent. "I'm coming."

"Donna say it if you're no' certain —"

"I'm not certain. I can't possibly be certain! But I must make a decision here and now, and, Arran, I choose you."

His gaze moved over her face. He suddenly pulled her forward and kissed her hard on the lips. "I will spend every day of my life making sure you donna regret it." He let her go. "We move now."

Margot twisted about. "Knox!"

Her brother was there in a moment. "I will do what I can to clear the Mackenzie name," he assured her. "You have my word. Now let me have your word that you will write often."

She couldn't bear the thought of not seeing Knox again. She loved him so much, and to leave him behind, perhaps forever, was the cruelest pain.

Knox sensed it. He grabbed her, hugged her as tightly as he could across the horses. His heart was beating wildly, too; she could feel it through his coat. "Nothing is forever, Margot. Have faith." He kissed her cheek and let her go, then turned his horse about and rode away.

"Come, *mo gradh,*" Arran said. He reached for her bridle and urged her horse forward. On they rode, into darkness.

CHAPTER TWENTY-THREE

It took days before they were deep enough into Scotland that Arran felt safe. It was hard traveling — with no money, they were forced to make mean camps and hunt for food.

Margot had explained to him that she'd given his entire purse to the man who had held him captive. Arran had privately winced — it was quite a lot of money. But he would never say so to her, because Margot had saved his fool life.

She tried to force the emerald he'd given her on the occasion of their wedding into his hand. "Sell it!" she urged him. "Feed these men, these horses."

"Aye, if it comes to that," he said, pressing it back into her hand. "But we lads know a wee bit about surviving."

It was Margot he fretted about. She'd thought to don the trews beneath her gown so that she could ride with some ease. But she was quite evidently exhausted, completely spent by what they'd endured. Even more alarming, she seemed devoid of any emotion. Each day that passed, her spirit became flatter, her words fewer. Arran was not a man who understood women well . . . but what he knew told him that when a woman didn't speak, something was very wrong.

The return to Scotland was made interminably long by the fact they were riding as opposed to sailing, across heather and hills rarely traveled by man. The only bright spot was that Dermid began to improve. With a bit of rabbit meat in his belly, he slowly began to find some strength.

By the seventh day, Margot rode with Arran so that Dermid might have his own mount. It made the travel a little quicker, for as hearty as his wife had proven to be, she was slower than the three men.

On the twelfth day, they reached the farm of Ben Mackenzie's uncle . . . but they were not welcome. Mr. Mackenzie spoke in Gaelic. "You must go," he said. "They're looking for you."

"Who?" Arran asked.

"The Gordons," he said, looking nervously about, as if he expected them to leap from the trees and attack. "Word has gone round that you escaped to England and now they wait for you to return. You can't stay here, laird. I don't want trouble."

Arran frowned. This news meant he couldn't go to Balhaire without risking confrontation. "Give us bread, some meat and cheese," he said. "Ale if you can spare it."

"Why aren't we dismounting?" Margot moaned, leaning back against him as they waited for Ben's uncle to bring them food.

"We willna stay," Arran said. He looked across at Ben and, again, spoke in Gaelic so that he'd not unduly alarm Margot. "Take Dermid to Balhaire. We'll carry on to Kishorn. Ride as hard as you can, lad. Tell Jock that no one must come to us. *No* one, not until it's safe. There will be eyes everywhere, aye?"

"Aye," Ben said.

Mr. Mackenzie appeared again with a large bundle of food for them. Arran nodded at Ben; he took the bundle and divided the food inside. He gave half to Arran and said, "Godspeed," and he and Dermid turned toward home.

Arran headed north.

"Where are we going?" Margot cried, and tried to sit up.

"Uist," he said, pulling her back into his

chest. "It willna be much longer now."

"But . . ."

That was all she said — the woman was too beaten to argue.

They reached Kishorn just before nightfall. Thank God for it — Arran knew that neither his horse nor Margot could endure another step. Margot slid off the horse before him, and her legs collapsed under her. He was instantly beside her, helping her up.

"I didn't realize . . ." She shook her head. "Where are we?"

Arran looked up at the old hunting lodge that had been in his family for centuries. He slipped one arm under Margot's knees, the other behind her back, and picked her up.

"I can walk," she protested weakly.

"You're exhausted." He walked to the entrance, put her down and opened the door, pushing it wide. Just inside the entrance he found candles and a tinderbox. He lit a candle and held it aloft, fit it into a candelabra, then lit two more.

Margot had stepped inside behind him and was looking around at the beamed ceiling, the stone walls. "What is this place?"

"A hunting lodge," he said. "One that has belonged to a Mackenzie for two centuries.

It was abandoned, but Griselda has decided it will be used again. She's done a bit of work."

At one end of the room was a long table with a pair of benches for sitting beside a small stone hearth. At the other end was a larger hearth and chairs gathered before it. Directly across from the entrance was a corridor that led to sleeping rooms, and beyond that, kitchens, a small terrace and a barn. Griselda was to be commended — the floors were swept and scrubbed, the walls scraped clean of smoke and tar. Mackenzie plaids now hung on the walls to warm the room.

Margot walked unsteadily to a wooden settee and sank onto it, then down, until she was lying on her side. Arran squatted beside her and caressed her dirtied face. "I'll tend to the horse and make a fire, aye? You rest."

"Mmm," she said. Her eyes were already closed.

Arran stabled the horse before it was completely dark, brushed him and fed him oats, which, thank God and Griselda, there seemed to be quite a lot of in two large urns. When he was satisfied his horse could rest for the night, he grabbed the food Mackenzie had given them and returned to the lodge.

Margot was still asleep on the settee when he returned. He built a fire in the great room, then went into the kitchen and built another. With that fire burning, Arran went in search of a bucket. He found one and took it out the back door to the well. After a few strong-armed pumps to force the rusted lever, he filled the bucket, returned it to the kitchen and put it over the fire to heat. It was the best he could do for bathing.

When he had water warm enough for his wife to wash, Arran returned to Margot's side. She was curled on the settee, one arm bent to pillow her head. He nudged her with his hand.

"No," she murmured.

"I've hot water if you'd like to bathe."

She slowly opened her eyes and turned her head. "Truly?"

Arran caressed her arm. "I'd no' tease you about something so important, would I?"

She slowly pushed herself up. "For your sake, I hope not."

He chuckled low and helped her to her feet. Then, with an arm around her waist, he led her to the kitchen. Margot peeled off a layer of filthy clothes, down to a filthier chemise, and plunged her hands into the water. She sighed with contentment, then bent over it and began to scrub her face.

Arran found a cloth for her and watched in mute fascination as she scrubbed herself clean with the hot water. When she had finished and had wrung her auburn hair as dry as she might, she said, "I haven't anything to wear."

"I'll have a look about, aye?" He handed her a plaid that she wrapped tightly around herself.

He found some buckskins, a moth-eaten woolen coat, a yellowed lawn shirt and a plain brown skirt, the sort a crofter might wear. He returned with his finds to the kitchen. Margot was in a chair near the fire, her knees up under her chin, her hair long and tangled.

She looked at the clothes with blank eyes. "Why are we here? And for how long?" she asked. "And why did your men go another way?"

He laid the clothes on the table. "Someone is looking for me yet. It wasna safe to return to Balhaire."

Her brows sank into a dark frown. "Scotsmen? Or English?"

"Scotsmen. Probably English, too, then."

"What are we to do?" she asked softly.

"I donna know," he responded truthfully.

451

He was too weary to think clearly. "For now, we hide."

"Without food or clothing?"

He shrugged. "We'll manage, we will." He didn't say that he feared it would be a very long time before they could leave here. That they would have to manage or starve.

She turned her gaze back to the fire. "Are we safe here?"

"Aye, for the time being."

"But not forever." She glanced back at him. "We can't run forever, can we?"

It was not a question, really, but a remark. Arran couldn't offer her the reassurances she wanted, and he didn't want to try.

He turned away from her and used the water to bathe himself as best he could. He had close to a full beard now. His hair had come out of its queue at some point. He wet his hair and pushed it behind his ears. When he was done, he pulled on one of the lawn shirts and the buckskins and joined a contemplative Margot at the fire.

"What are you thinking?" he asked.

"That you haven't said you were right," she said, and rested her chin on her knees.

"About what?"

"About my father. You haven't reminded me that you didn't trust him all along. Or that I so foolishly did."

"I didna think you needed reminding, *leannan.* You discovered it on your own, aye?"

"Do you know what I've discovered? That I am nothing more than a pawn in this world. To be bartered and traded and cast aside when I am no longer useful."

She sounded bitter, but Arran couldn't disagree with her. That's what daughters were to many families — bargaining power. Very few had managed to forge their own paths and do as they pleased. Griselda had, only because Uncle Ivor adored her so. He'd allowed her to refuse suitors and live freely, without a husband.

"I will never be a pawn in someone's scheme again," Margot murmured. "I should sooner live in poverty, all alone, than live with others in opulence for no better reason than my name and the connections I can bring to them."

"You are no' only a name to me," he said.

Margot didn't seem to have heard him — she was suddenly looking around her. "I don't know how to live like this," she said plaintively. "I am so useless to you that I can't as much as bake a loaf of bread."

"It doesna matter —"

"It *does* matter, Arran! I've lived like a privileged blind woman. I despise myself for

453

it — but I will never make that mistake again," she said. She sighed. "I'm tired. Can we go to bed?"

They found one room with a bed large enough for the two of them. They both fell into it, exhausted beyond measure. Margot rolled into his side, nesting there. "I don't know how to exist like this," she said again.

Then there were two of them, because neither did Arran. He could hunt and fish and keep them alive, but he didn't know how to exist like this. Without a clan. Without his family. Alone, with a wife who, in spite of the events the last several days, he still didn't know if he could fully trust.

He fell into a deep sleep, the first real sleep he'd had in weeks. So deep, in fact, that he never heard Margot leave him early the next morning. But when he awoke, she was gone. Arran panicked; he pulled on his buckskins and went in search of her, looking in every room until he'd made his way to the kitchen, fearing she'd taken the horse and tried to leave like a madwoman.

But Margot hadn't left him. She was in the kitchen, her back to him, dressed in the old skirt he'd found. It was far too big for her and dragged the floor. She had tied the lawn shirt in a knot at her waist and had tied her hair into a knot at her nape. She was working at something on the counter that he couldn't see.

He walked deeper into the kitchen. She looked up with surprise, and her face lit with pleasure. "Look!" she said excitedly. "I found a potato!" She held it up to him. "There were turnips, too. And leeks, I think."

Arran was, he realized, bowled over on a wave of relief. He'd had that awful thought that she'd left him again. Improbable, impossible, and yet that was the fear that had crept in around his heart when she wasn't in bed this morning.

As she bubbled on about the garden she'd found, and how she did once accompany her grandmother to pick brambles from the bramble bush and could certainly do that again, Arran knew he would have lost his mind if she'd gone.

Her words filled the space around them, swelling up and surrounding him while a river of love for the woman burned through him.

It burned bright.

CHAPTER TWENTY-FOUR

It had all seemed like a dream to Margot. From the moment Knox had ridden away from her, and every moment that passed as they moved farther north, she had grown more and more uncertain about her choice. The thought that she would never see England again, or Norwood Park, or Knox and Lynetta, began to weigh heavily in her heart.

And then to arrive at this deserted lodge at the end of a deeply remote loch to fend for her life? It was all too much to bear. She was unprepared for this. She didn't have the slightest idea what to do in a kitchen, had scarcely been in them at all, save those few times she went in search of an apple or orange. And that was only the beginning of her ineptitude.

As a result, she and Arran stumbled through the first few days at the lodge. Of course he was more adept at making do than she was, but he was no more accustomed to keeping a house than she was, really. They had quite a row when he proudly presented her with a duck to pluck.

"Pluck?" she echoed, looking at the bird in horror.

"Aye, the feathers." He held it out to her.

"But . . . *how?"*

Arran looked at her strangely. "You remove them. *Pluck."* He jerked a feather free of the bird.

Margot recoiled.

He frowned. "Do it, Margot. I canna do everything."

"I am aware!" she snapped. She took the bird and, wincing, began to pluck. It was a horrible, wretched mess. She fought tears for the damn bird — such indignity in his death! Or was she fighting tears for the loss of her dignity? But she plucked it clean, and when she presented the battered carcass to Arran, he was not impressed by her effort. "Aye, I see. And now you must clean it."

"I will not!" she cried, and fled the kitchen when Arran seemed determined to force her.

Later, after Arran had cleaned it and cooked it, Margot had to admit the duck made for an excellent meal.

When Arran gave her a duck a few days

later, Margot could pluck it well enough and without complaint.

But she felt entirely useless to Arran and began to forage for food, picking brambles and gooseberries and holding them in the tail of her shirt. She dug around the old garden for leeks and potatoes, not giving up until she found a few. Granted, the potatoes were rock-hard and the leeks spindly. But she found them. She took their clothes down to the river to wash as she'd seen women doing on the way to the village at Norwood Park. But she was too earnest in her attempts and rubbed a hole in her gown. Neither did she hang the clothes properly to dry, so they were misshapen.

Arran, bless him, said not a word.

They did not talk about the past or future in those days. They were too engaged with the business of surviving to address old wounds. They talked about silly things when they came together for meals. Margot liked to tease him, to see the change of color beneath his beard. She told him he was shy in the presence of Lynetta Beauly, to which he took great exception.

"That is no' so. Miss Beauly canna stop talking long enough to draw a breath."

"That is true. But she is quite comely."

Arran snorted and turned away. And he

did not deny it.

He laughed so hard when she cut up potatoes to boil them that tears of laughter rolled down his cheeks. "There is no' a thing any simpler than this, aye? You put the bloody potato in the pot, *leannan.*"

"How was I to know?" she demanded. "Potatoes are generally served to me in pieces."

After a fortnight, the most impossible thing happened — Margot was at ease with the many things she had to do each day. She swept floors and boiled the single cloth they shared for washing. Arran chopped wood and she helped him pile it high near the door, laughing about the siege he was apparently expecting.

Their existence was quite companionable, and when the day was done, and their muscles ached and they could scarcely keep their eyes open, they fell into each other's arms.

Their nights were filled with lovemaking, sometimes so tender that Margot wanted to weep, and sometimes so lusty that they rolled onto their backs laughing when it was done.

They filled each other's bodies and thoughts and senses in every way, as if they were the last two people on earth.

When she was alone, Margot would often pull his letter from her pocket and read it again. *"The beginning of my world and the end of it . . ."* She wondered, was this the end of their world? Would this *be* their world? Margot slowly began to comprehend that she wouldn't mind in the least if it was their world. How curious that she had feared this sort of life, loathed it from afar . . . yet this life had made her feel strong and capable in a way she'd never felt in her life.

Unfortunately, the rest of the world began to creep into theirs.

They were dining on leek soup one evening and were sitting together at the kitchen table, drinking from earthen bowls.

"I saw riders today," Arran said.

Margot gasped and looked up. "Where?"

"Going north. They didna see me."

"Are you sure? What if —"

"No, *leannan,* they didna see me."

She was struck with the cold fear of what would happen if they were discovered here.

"What would you do?" Arran asked.

"If I saw riders?"

He put down his spoon and held her gaze. "If I were captured. What would you do then?"

The thought made her feel sick. She suddenly stood up from the table with her bowl and carried it to the pot. She didn't want to speak of it. "Don't even speak of it."

"Would you return to England?"

"England! I'd likely die right here!"

She heard the scrape of his chair, heard him come up behind her. He slipped his arm around her waist and pulled her into his chest. He took the bowl from her hand and set it aside. "If there comes a time that we might return to Balhaire, what then? Will you stay? Or will you return to England?"

She hadn't thought of England in days, maybe even weeks. She'd concentrated on existing and had not allowed her mind to be cluttered with all the scenarios of what-if. "I don't . . . I don't know," she stammered.

Arran suddenly let go of her. Margot whirled about as he stalked to the door. "Wait. Where are you going?"

"The hell if I know."

"Why are you asking me these questions?" she snapped. "I've not thought of it. I've only thought of us here, and now —"

He grabbed the handle of the back door. "That's the difference between you and me, aye? I think of little else." He barged out, the door banging behind him.

She thought of the two of them, too —

she thought of them all the time. But Margot was a different woman now. She was her *own* woman. But she hadn't figured everything out just yet.

Arran did not come back in until it was pitch-dark. Margot was in bed, lying on her side, her back to the door, when he loudly entered the room. She'd built the fire tonight, and he wordlessly shed his clothes before it, then climbed in beside her. He pulled her to his body, kissing her neck, his hands roaming her flesh, sliding in between her legs.

"Once," she whispered into the hair at the top of his head as he kissed her breast, "I was a silly girl. I thought only of arranged marriages and fortunes, of what I would wear and who esteemed me and what things I might have around me. But I'm different now, Arran. I don't even know myself any longer."

He grunted his response, moved down her body, spread her legs apart and sank between them, as if to say he knew her. And that she was part of him.

The days began to grow shorter and the nights colder. Two hares and a grouse hung in the barn. Late-blooming flowers were growing around the lodge. Margot was in the garden one afternoon, taking cuttings of the flowers, when she heard a sound that didn't quite register. She paused, listening . . . and slowly understood that what she was hearing were riders.

She felt a swoon of apprehension as she slowly lifted her head and looked over her shoulder. There, down the narrow glen, cantering alongside the loch, were four riders. They were coming to the lodge.

Everything seemed to suddenly grow too bright. Margot dropped the flowers and ran around the corner of the lodge to the outbuildings, flinging open the door where Arran was working.

"Christ in his heaven, what is it?" Arran asked when she burst through the door. He caught her with one arm and held her still. "What is it, Margot?"

"Horsemen."

Arran pushed her aside, grabbed his gun from the wooden table and strode outside. Margot looked wildly about for something to defend herself with. She spotted the little knife he often carried in his boot, grabbed it and ran after him. She caught up to him just in front of the lodge. But his gun was pointed at the ground. "Aye, that's Jock," he said. "There is only one man who sits a horse like that."

He strode out to greet his cousin.

But as the riders drew closer, Margot saw someone else that made tears spring to her eyes. Knox was with him. She raced to her brother, leaping up to hug him before he'd had time to come down from his horse.

Knox laughed into her embrace. "You'll break my fool neck, Margot. Come," he said, wrapping his arm around her waist. "There is much to tell you and Mackenzie."

They gathered inside the lodge, and after the party from Balhaire was assured that Margot and Arran were indeed quite well, Jock told them what had happened.

"It was quick-like," he said. "Rory and Bruce Gordon were accused of throwing in with the Jacobites, and the crown come looking for them — English soldiers all, forty of them if there was a one. But do you know, they slipped out under a heavy mist, bound for France."

"This doesna surprise me. I've never put much store by Gordon," Arran said.

"But that wasna the whole of it, laird," Jock said. "Gordon left behind a few things, and one of them was a letter from Tom Dunn, aye? In the letter, he insinuates that he and his partner will share the wealth of Balhaire when you are hanged for treason."

Arran swallowed. "As we suspected," he

muttered darkly.

"But did you suspect his partner was my father?" Knox asked.

"What?" Margot said. "That can't possibly be."

"But it is, darling," Knox said. "Thomas Dunn was steeped in duplicitous dealings. When the authorities came for Father, he finally confessed to me what he and Bryce had known all along — Thomas Dunn was in a great deal of debt. Moreover, he'd fallen out of favor with the queen as talk of uprisings and conspiracy to remove her from the throne kept coming from the very men he'd vowed would keep James Stuart from our shores. He was desperate, and he devised a scheme to cast the blame on someone else and profit from it at the same time. He landed on Mackenzie because of his self-made wealth and his marriage to you."

"Aye, this we'd surmised," Arran said impatiently.

"But how was Pappa involved?" Margot asked.

"Dunn told him that Mackenzie was a traitor. Father panicked and sent you to discover if that was true before Dunn could act. But while you were gone, Margot, Dunn apparently realized that it could all go wrong and he'd be exposed. So he offered our father a deal of sorts — if Father would agree to corroborate his accusations against your husband, he would receive a substantial stake in the Mackenzie holdings once they were forfeited. Dunn assumed the holdings would come to him for exposing the treason."

This news was a knife to her heart. She knew her father was culpable in some way, but this was so despicable it knocked the breath from her. *"No,"* she whispered. "How could he?"

"It was dirty business," Knox said quietly.

"Will he hang?" Arran asked flatly, and Margot's heart squeezed. She was as disillusioned and hurt as she'd ever been in her life, but she did not want to see her father hang.

"No," Knox said with a shrug. "Although he may well wish he had. The queen has stripped his title and bestowed it on me, and has decreed his holdings to be divided between his only daughter and his bastard son." He glanced at Arran. "Begging your pardon, laird, but the queen refused to bestow any of the English holdings on a Scottish laird, not with all the unrest."

Arran shrugged indifferently.

Margot suddenly sat down, the weight of this news too much to hold. "What of

Bryce?" she asked weakly.

Knox smiled thinly. "I suggested he look into the vicarage."

"The Mackenzie name is cleared, then," Arran said.

"I cannot speak for your side of the border, but your name has been exonerated in England," Knox said proudly.

Arran looked at Jock. "*Ach,* you know as I do that Highlanders are a distrustful lot, aye? There are those who still doubt you," Jock said. "But more who donna doubt. It's safe to return to Balhaire."

Arran shifted his gaze to Margot. She could see the same conflict in his eyes that she felt swirling in her. "Well, then," he said. "This is quite a lot of news, is it no', Lady Mackenzie?"

"Quite," she managed. She should have been happy to be freed from this exile, but she felt only an overwhelming sense of melancholy. She was grief-stricken at the loss of her father, devastated that he'd wrought this tragedy in their lives. She felt grief for the loss of the life she'd once had and uncertainty about what came next. But her agony went unnoticed — Jock had brought ale, and the men drank, exchanging tales of what had happened in the last few weeks.

It was decided, given their mean surroundings, that they would leave on the morrow. Leave this place of peace, she thought morosely, where she and Arran had, for the first time, really, lived as a married couple ought. The sense of loss was now overwhelming, and Margot excused herself, retiring to the small room she shared with Arran.

Arran joined her sometime later and wordlessly slipped into bed with her. Margot had not slept; her mind had been racing with the sudden change in their existence. She felt his hand seek hers, lacing his fingers with hers. They lay wordlessly on their backs beneath a woolen plaid, staring up into darkness, each of them, she supposed, trying to take in all the astounding news. After living on the edge of emotion and fear, to have it all suddenly released from them was not as freeing as she might have imagined.

"You must be relieved," Arran said at last.

Was she relieved? She felt sick with sadness. "Do you know that I really rather liked it here."

Arran squeezed her hand. "Aye," he said. But he suddenly let go of her hand and sat up, swinging his legs over the side of the bed and bracing his hands on either side of his knees.

Margot sat up. "What's wrong?"

"The same that's been wrong for far too long — I donna trust you."

Margot blinked, surprised. "Surely now you know I had nothing to do with it."

He shook his head. "You donna understand me. We've existed, you and I, these long weeks, aye? You've done your best, God knows you have, but now, Margot, now you're a rich woman in your own right, are you no'? And I'm a Highlander. You might do as you please and I . . . *Diah,* to this day, I donna know that it pleases you to live as a Highlander's wife."

"But I —"

He stood up and stalked to the window, as if he didn't want to hear what she would say. He opened the window to the night breeze. "I've loved you since the moment I laid eyes on you. You've astonished me, you have. You've become a woman I never thought you'd be, aye? *A Diah,* it only makes me love you more. But you are free now, Margot, and I donna trust you to stay true to me."

Her heart squeezed with trepidation. "Are you . . . Are you sending me back to England?" she asked disbelievingly.

"*England?*" He turned from the window and looked at her over his shoulder. "Do you no' understand me yet?" He suddenly came back to the bed and went down on one knee before her, his hands clasped together on the bed almost as if he was praying. "I'm no' sending you away, Margot, no — I'm on my knee, begging you no' to leave me. Never leave me, do you hear me? No man will ever love you as I do. No man will ever honor you as I will all my days." He groaned and closed his eyes, anguished. "I will always love you, but I'm begging you now to release me as I've released you. If you donna mean to remain in Scotland, then donna torment me. I canna live my life fearing that you will go."

Margot pressed her clasped hands to her mouth. Her heart was racing, and with a silent sob, she leaned over this man and stroked his face. She could see the terror in his eyes — she recognized it because she was feeling the same terror. It had struck her the moment she saw riders approaching — the terror of living a single day without this man. When she had seen them coming, she knew how much she loved him. "I understand," she said, and Arran's eyes welled with tears. "But, Arran, my love, you will never love me as much as I love you."

Arran stared at her, his expression wild with hope. "You've never said it," he said roughly.

"Yes, well, that's another mistake in my very long list of them," she said apologetically. "But in this, you must trust me. Arran, for heaven's sake, you must, at last, *trust* me. I love you, and not because our fortunes were aligned. Because in this little lodge, you taught me what is important. You taught me what it meant to care for someone. I don't care about balls and society. I care about how many potatoes the earth will yield, and how I might mend the hole I put in your shirt, and if you will love your child as much as you love those wretched dogs at Balhaire."

He bowed his head, sighing with relief. "Margot . . . *Diah* —"

She took his face in her hands and made him look up at her. "You became the beginning and the end of my world here, and I choose you. I will always choose you." She kissed him tenderly.

Arran pulled her hands from his face and peered at her, his eyes narrowed. "What do you mean, then, you hope I love my child as much as my dogs?"

Margot smiled. "Just that you are unnaturally attached to those dogs, aren't you? The child will need your attention, too."

Arran's frown deepened. He cupped her

471

face. "*Diah,* Margot, you must speak plainer than this. Do you carry my child?"

Margot laughed. "I think so," she said hopefully. "Yes, I think I am."

Arran lurched forward, reaching for her waist and tumbling back into the bed with her. "Woman, you canna be rid of me now," he said gruffly. "A child!"

He began to kiss her, every inch of her, muttering how happy she'd made him, and Margot thought, as she smiled up at the rough, wood-planked ceiling above them, that this was just the beginning of her new world.

EPILOGUE

Balhaire
1713

The lad was nearing his second birthday, and already the old dogs waddled after him as if he was leading them into battle. Naturally they would think so, because the boy wielded his wooden sword everywhere he went.

They'd named him Cailean after Arran's father. He had the look of the Mackenzies of Balhaire — big for his age, a crop of auburn hair like his mother and the stark blue eyes of his father.

"He'll break hearts across Scotland one day," Margot predicted.

"He'll break noggins," Arran said with gruff pride as they watched him terrorize Fergus with his little sword.

Arran helped ease Margot into a chair — she was heavy with child again, and he could scarcely contain his excitement. The midwives said she would deliver him a girl, and secretly, Arran hoped it was so. He had in mind to give his daughter the sort of life Margot had been given, with balls and ponies and pretty gowns.

"I hear the pipes, Arran," Margot said.

"Aye." He signaled Sweeney to wrangle Cailean. The wedding party was nearing the great hall.

"We didn't have a procession for our wedding," Margot mused as the doors swung open and the first of the revelers entered.

"Would you like a procession, then, *mo gradh*? I'll give you one."

"What I would like is for this child to proceed to be born," she said with a sigh, and rubbed the bottom of her belly. "She's a hellion, always kicking."

"Patience."

"That's quite simple for you to say, isn't it, a man quite at his leisure without a small piglet in his belly?"

He squeezed her hand fondly. "*Uist,* now, the bride and groom are coming."

The bride and groom entered the hall behind the standard bearer, the groom dressed in a plaid and standing very tall, a head taller than anyone, and the bride in a wreath of flowers and a sash of plaid. "I don't believe it!" Margot exclaimed. "She wore the plaid!"

"Did you think she'd no'?" Arran whispered.

"No! Nell is quite opposed to Scottish customs, you know," she said. "She says they are for heathens, and that Jock is the biggest heathen of them all."

"Aye, that he is," Arran agreed. "But a gentle heathen. And she doesna seem unhappy."

"No," Margot said, smiling fondly. "On the contrary, she seems indescribably happy."

It was true — Nell was beaming. And so was Jock. Arran had never seen a smile as wide as the one he wore now.

They reached the dais, and Jock bowed to Arran. Arran stood up to receive the couple and bless their union. He stood aside as the vicar received their vows and proclaimed them husband and wife. He turned them back to the crowd gathered and pronounced them as Mackenzies of the clan, and the round of toasts, as was the clan's custom, began.

Margot touched his leg.

"One moment more — I must give the final toast, aye?"

"You'd best be quick about it," she said.

"I know you're uncomfortable, but we

must let them have their day."

"Of course. But someone else is going to have her day, too."

Confused, Arran glanced down. Margot arched her brow and pointed at her belly.

Vivienne Mackenzie was born twelve hours later, her little wails so loud that the crier was not needed. When Cailean was brought in to see his baby sister for the first time, he said, *"Leamsa."*

Margot didn't understand at first. Arran told her that the word that sounded like *loomsa* meant *mine* in English.

"Oh no, she is not yours, my love," Margot said, catching Cailean's little hand before he could grab the infant's hair.

"Leamsa, leamsa!" he crowed.

For the first year or so of her life, Vivienne was known as Loomsa. Arran and Margot tried everything to convince the boy his sister was not his property. They gave him puppies. Ponies. More wooden swords. But the lad would not be persuaded. Little Vivienne, his Loomsa, belonged to him.

When a third child was born, the name Loomsa was passed to the baby boy, and Vivienne was restored her rightful name.

All of the children that would come after Cailean, four more, were, at some point, called Loomsa. And a few dogs. A bird and at least a pair of ponies.

One night after Vivienne's second birthday, when a gentle snow had begun to fall on Balhaire, Arran drew his wife to his warmth. *"Leamsa,"* he whispered into her hair.

Margot closed her eyes and sighed with contentment. "I am that," she assured him. She was exhausted — she was carrying her third child and had spent the day milling soap with Mrs. Gowan. Her lids began to close.

But Margot was rudely awakened by the sudden weight of a beast. She opened her eyes with a cry, and Cailean giggled as he fell onto her, his little arms around her neck. He was followed by his sister and two dogs, all of them crowding into the bed with her and Arran.

"You heathens will no' sleep here," Arran said gruffly. "No' all night, you willna." But he was covering them with a thick wool blanket as they jostled for position between them, kicking and giggling.

"Quiet now," Margot said. "Your poor mamma needs her sleep." She sighed and clung to the very edge of the bed, aware of the little foot in her back. But she smiled. She was safe in the arms of the beginning and the end of her world.